The Lions and the Wolf

In Hannibal's Shadow

By
Garrett Pearson

Published by Morepork Publishing

Cover Design: More Visual Ltd

Beta Reading: Scott White

ISBN: 13-9780473461485

This Book is for my parents, J&H

Principal Character List

Adharbal Samilcar* Second son of the prestigious Carthaginian family of judges and business people. Brother to Serfina, Carthalo and Sakarbaal.

Aemilia Paulla Daughter of the Roman General, Lucius Aemilius Paullus and betrothed to Cornelius Scipio.

Andulas* Lingone Warlord and eldest son and heir to Gundulas, half-brother to Tuireann.

Armaco Salamar* Professional mercenary soldier with Balaam's company, friend to Baldor.

Balaam* Carthaginian mercenary Captain, veteran of the first Punic war.

Baldor Targa* Young Carthaginian man born into the Targa shipbuilding family and the sole surviving family member.

Clitus* Commander of the Cretan archers and Rhodian slingers under Baldor's command.

Cornelius Publius Scipio Roman Centurion, son of Publius, nephew to Gnaeus.

Gaius Laelius Roman Centurion, friend and mentor to Cornelius.

Gnaeus Scipio Roman General, brother to Publius and uncle to Cornelius.

Gnaeus Servilus Geminus Consul and General of Rome.

Gundulas* Chief of the Lingone tribe, father to Andulas and Tuireann.

Hannibal Barca Carthaginian General, Commander in Chief of the army, brother to Mago and Hasdrubal.

*Harbro** Professional mercenary soldier and second in command with Balaam's company.

Hasdrubal Gisgo Carthaginian General.

Hasdrubal Barca Carthaginian General, brother to Hannibal and Mago.

*Lugobelinos** Chief of the Cenomani tribe, brother to Magalus and ally of Rome.

*Magalus** Cenomani Warlord and brother to Lugobelinos.

Mago Barca Carthaginian General, brother to Hannibal and Hasdrubal.

Maharabal Hannibal's Cavalry General.

*Malo** Professional mercenary soldier with Balaam's company.

*Marko** Professional mercenary soldier with Balaam's company, veteran from the first Punic war.

Publius Cornelius Scipio Consul and General of Rome, father to Cornelius, Brother to Gnaeus.

*Serfina Samilcar** Daughter of the Carthaginian family of judges and business people. Sister to Adharbal, Carthalo and Sakarbaal.

Tiberius Sempronius Longus Consul and General of Rome.

*Tirus** Spanish mercenary in command of the Scutarius and Caetratus infantry contingents under Baldor's command.

*Tuireann** Lingone Captain and half-brother to Andulas.

* Denotes fictional characters

Glossary

Siege Machines

Ballista A dart or stone throwing siege machine. Manufactured in a range of sizes.

Catapult or Mangonel Stone throwing machine, again manufactured in different sizes, also capable of hurling fire pots. (Naphtha)

Vineae Mobile troop shelters mounted on wheels, made of timber and covered in un-tanned animal hides.

Weapons

Caetra Small skirmishing shield or buckler, favoured by the light Spanish troops (Caetratus) from which the warriors take their name.

Falcata Carthaginian short sword, albeit Spanish in origin.

Gladius Roman short sword, with a heavy straight blade, predominantly used as a thrusting weapon.

Hasta Roman fighting spear, 8 – 10 ft. in length.

Naphtha Liquid chemical, probably phosphorus. Water will not quench the flames.

Pike Long spear 16 – 18ft in length used en-masse in phalanx formation by the Carthaginians.

Phalarica Spanish javelin, wooden shafted with soft iron head.

Pilum Roman javelin, wooden shafted with soft iron head.

Scutum Legionary shield, large and oval in shape.

Soliferreum or Saunion Spanish javelin made solely of iron with a small dart shaped head.

Spatha Cavalry sword approximately 30" in length, a straight bladed slashing weapon.

Troop Types

Caetratus Spanish light infantry.

Equites Roman Cavalry, approximately 300 attached to each legion.

Hastati Roman medium/heavy Infantry, the first real line of defence after the light troops or skirmishers, armed with the Pilum. These soldiers were generally younger men.

Princeps Roman medium/heavy infantry, the second line of defence after the Hastati, armed with a fighting spear (Hasta) rather than the missile Pilum. Men in the prime of life, experienced and tough.

Scutarius Spanish heavy infantry.

Triari Roman heavy infantry, the third line of defence after the Princeps. Again armed with the Hasta, these soldiers were the eldest and most experienced of all, used as reserves and as a steadying influence for the front ranks.

Velites Roman light infantry or skirmishing troops, also used as foragers.

Musical Instruments

Carnyx Celtic war horn.

Cornicen Roman war horn.

Country & Place names

Arretium Modern day Arezzo in Italy.

Ariminum Modern day Rimini in Italy.

Carthage Founded by the Phoenician's, now within modern day Tunisia.

Cartagena Nova Modern day Cartagena in southern Spain.

Drepanum Near modern day Trapani in western Sicily.

Gades Modern day Cadiz in Spain.

Gaul France, Belgium, Switzerland etc. Most of Western Europe except Germany and Spain.

Icosium City in the kingdom of Numidia, now modern day Algiers.

Iberia Modern day Northern Spain.

Igilgili City in the kingdom of Numidia, now the modern day city Jijel in Algeria.

Lilybaeum Modern day Marsala in western Sicily.

Massilia Modern day Marseilles in France.

Nubia Modern day southern Egypt and northern Sudan.

Numidia Modern day Algeria.

Placentia Modern day Piacenza in northern Italy.

Rusucurru City in the kingdom of Numidia, now the modern day city, Delles or Dellys in Algeria.

Saguntum Modern day Sagunto in the province of Valencia, eastern Spain.

Salamantica Modern day Salamanca in western Spain.

Saldae City in the kingdom of Numidia, now the modern day city Bejaia in Algeria.

Tarraco Modern day Tarragona in north-eastern Spain,

Tarascon in Provencal, near to the Rhone southern France.

Victumulae Outpost or township somewhere in the Po valley. (The exact location is unknown)

Units of measure

Cubit Ancient unit of measure, 1 Cubit equals 24 Inches or 2 Feet.

Stade Ancient unit of distance, 1 Stade equals approximately 175 meters.

Roman Mile 1,481 meters.

Open Wound

Neither brother by kin or name
Nor a brother by tie of blood
But a man both true and brave
Like any good brother would

I weep for you my brother,
When you died there on Ticinus Field,
You, who loved my like no other,
My friend, my guide, my shield.

A reckoning there must be then,
My vengeance from the Gods I so demand
The Scipios' shall know a blood-red sea
Ere my bones rest beneath this curse-ed land

"When the killing is over and battles won
Speak to me not of great Generals,
Kings and their ilk
Tell me of the ordinary men who have
bled, fought and died to make it so"

Anon

Part 1

Garrett Pearson

Chapter One

The River Ticinus, Cisalpine Gaul (Northern Italy) winter 218 BC

The shadows were falling as the light faded into shades of ever darkening blue, in the west the sun bade farewell to the day as it slipped beneath the distant, snow-capped mountains. In the lee of a small copse, five heavily armed and grim looking Carthaginian warriors worked silently in the gathering gloom, all still encased in blood spattered and sweat damp leather corselets, their hands and faces caked in grey dust and streaks of brown, dried blood. The flames of their pitch torches flickered and danced in the ice-edged breeze that slowly strengthened and blew over the dead still littering the field of Ticinus here on the plains of Po. One of their mounts whickered and stomped nervously, pulling on its tether as it sniffed a spoor on the breeze, the men's hands grasped sword hilts in readiness but looking up and seeing two of their own infantrymen passing close by they returned to their work. Despite their 'first blood' victory that morning, on Roman soil and over the Roman cavalry these horse warriors had neither smiles nor belligerent words of joy to share, in contrast their weary and morose humour spoke of defeat or heartfelt loss.

They collected, carried then stacked branches beneath and around a crude timber dais that stood waist high from the ground. The legs of the structure were fresh cut boughs as thick as a man's arm and hammered into the earth with smaller limbs lashed crossways as braces tying the uprights together making them rigid. Branches, trimmed and tied along the top of the structure made a flat platform for the pyre upon which the body of a large, blonde haired warrior laid. The dead man was still attired in his battle gear; the linen tunic beneath his battered corselet heavily stained with blood at the right shoulder. He though, had been washed and his hair combed then fastened back into a neat ponytail, his muscular arms laid over his chest with his Gallic broad sword tucked beneath them.

"That should suffice Baldor." Armaco said quietly to the youngest of the group as he watched him place another armful of dry wood against the structure.

Baldor however, seemingly oblivious carried on working, adding more timber to the pyre. The other warriors ceased their labours, listening then watching as Armaco hailed Baldor once more, again to no response. Sighing wearily, the one-eyed warrior approached the younger man and gently took the wood from his hands stopping him from his work.

"It's enough Baldor."

Placing his hands on Baldor's shoulders, Armaco turned him slowly towards him. Looking past the rust coloured blood that crusted Baldor's mouth and smashed nose he saw the distraught, broken look of a man who'd lost everything. His face and skin were pale and drawn while his black-ringed eyes had the ghostly, unseeing stare that spoke of horror and heartache verging upon madness.

"I'll fetch some oil and you can say the words eh?" He said quietly while slipping his arm around Baldor's shoulder pulling him close in a show of rough affection. "Lad's! … If you wish to pay your respects?" Armaco looked towards the warriors and nodded to the pyre, leaving the question hanging he turned to fetch the oil.

Marko and Harbro, the two eldest of the small group removed their helmets as they approached the platform. Marko sighed regretfully and shook his head as if in disbelief at what he saw, slipping a silver shekel from his purse he placed it gently over one of the dead warrior's eyes.

"For the ferryman, Gestix. May your Gods keep you and bless you always; I'll remember you in my prayers, farewell old friend."

Marko bowed his head and held his closed fist to his heart in salute.

Harbro whispered his blessing as he added a second coin over Gestix's other eye. "Wait for us on the other side of the Styx, Gestix there'll be more of us along to keep you company ere this war's done." Adding his salute, he and Marko stood back.

Malo came forward next; the tall, slight Nubian almost indistinguishable from the approaching night, so black was his skin. His composite bow of horn and wood still slung across his back along with a quiver of brightly fletched arrows; he carried a large brown hare that he laid carefully at Gestix's feet, adding a small, red leather wineskin alongside. He drew patterns in the air with his hands while speaking quietly in a dialect none of the others understood, the meaning and regret however were as clear as those that had spoken before him. Armaco returned with an earthenware pitcher and walked around the pyre emptying the contents liberally over the kindling then reverently over the body. As he finished he stepped closer placing his left hand on Gestix's chest and his right to his own heart.

"You were a great warrior, Gestix and a good man but above all you were my friend. This shithole of a world and we that remain are the poorer for your passing. You'll not go un-avenged though, not if I have my way." He paused as he felt his voice quiver. "Don't worry about the lad; I'll look out for him as I promised. You rest well and wait for us but … but don't expect us along too soon, we've scores to settle." He managed a sad smile then bowed his head offering his blessings. With the rites done, he picked up a torch and turned back to the waiting men and nodded gently then beckoned Baldor forward to the pyre.

"Come Baldor, you need to say the words and prepare the way to Elysium for him, you knew him best of all." Armaco offered the torch as he spoke.

Baldor just stared trance like, his mind elsewhere. Armaco sighed, rubbing his hand wearily over his cropped hair and down over his face massaging his temples with his fingers then readjusting his eye patch. He stepped alongside Baldor and whispered quietly but firmly.

"Baldor! You need to say the words, don't let him go into the next world unannounced. Baal knows it's hard but he would have suffered it had it been you upon the pyre, he deserves no less! … He loved you! You must be strong for him!" He offered the torch again.

Baldor seemed to return from wherever it was his mind had been and looked around confusedly as if waking from a dream. He lifted the harness straps of the two falcatas he wore crossed on his back easing their weight then took the torch from Armaco. Holding it aloft, he stepped forward to the pyre. He gazed at the warrior laid before him then bowed his head. He maintained his statue like position for a considerable time then just as Armaco was about to prompt him again he raised his head and passed the torch back to him. He pulled at a heavy silver bracelet on his wrist, easing the torque styled ends apart removing it from his arm. He scraped and rubbed the dirt away with his fingernail and looked at the deeply engraved script that read 'For honour and courage.' As the cleaned metal shimmered in the yellow glow of the torchlight he pressed it to his lips then cleared his throat.

"My ... my last gift to you, Gestix son of Teutorix ... f ... for your honour and your ... your courage and for trying to teach me both."

The words tumbled out in a tortured, rasping whisper as he opened the bracelet wider fitting it on the dead man's wrist. Fumbling inside his corselet, he pulled out a tiny bronze figurine of a woman, riding sidesaddle on a horse with a bird resting upon her outstretched arm. He rubbed his fingers gently over the small greening effigy sobbing dryly as he did so, his eyes closed as if in prayer, the tears never the less forcing themselves from beneath the lids and wetting his lashes.

"You're Goddess, she'll ... she'll take care of you now." He said in a husked, broken tone as his voice dried in his throat. His eyes opened again and his tears overflowed, streaming copiously over his bloodied cheeks onto his chin before dripping onto the dead man's body.

He lifted Gestix's hand easing the already stiffened fingers open placing the figurine in them and then gently pushed them shut. Taking the torch back, he held it above his head again, its flames driving the darkness back and illuminating the pyre in a flickering yellow light. He tilted his head back, his eyes looking skyward.

"Epona!" He called but his voice died away, his throat dry with thirst and swollen from stress. He coughed to clear it before beginning again. "Epona ... Epona!" He called as his voice strengthened a little. "Goddess of horses and beloved of cavalrymen,

16

welcome this warrior, Gestix son of Teutorix, son of Catutigernos of the Boii tribe, to Elysium and your side. In life he revered you above all others, I ask that you care for him in death!"

Behind Baldor the bowed, weary heads of his comrades lifted quickly from their chests listening intently as he began to unfold some of the dead Gaul's life. His voice faltered and faded once more as raw emotion rocked him and his unashamed tears fell again, cutting more rivulets through the blood and grime that covered his face. He paused again, attempting to regain his composure, trying to stifle the sobbing that stole his breath and words.

"Brecca! … Lady, your husband comes. As good a man and true as when you saw him last. You also he loved and held above all others. Cadeyrn, Caedmon! Your father comes. Cherish him and love him for I have fallen short in this."

His head fell forward, the terrible sadness and pain of the ordeal heaving his chest in stifled, racking sobs. He staggered slightly as the bone weariness from the battle began to take hold in his body. Armaco stepped alongside and Baldor seemed to draw strength from the closeness then gathering his wits and breathing deeply he continued.

"Asmilcar, Melandara … Father, Mother your good friend comes. Meet him, guide him and love him as he has done for me, for without him I'd be but dust on the wind."

His head spun pausing his liturgy, his balance awry, he staggered and his arm shot out seeking support from the pyre to steady himself. Physical and mental exhaustion was quickly claiming his body as the adrenalin that had fueled him through the morning's battle, Gestix's death and now the funeral finally began slipping away. Armaco, seeing him falter held him. Balancing himself, he gently eased Armaco's arm away, the dry, wracked sobbing and stolen breath however, he couldn't stop, he stepped closer to the body offering his private words.

"I blame myself for this. For your pain and death. For the path that we've followed. If … if I'd listened to you and gone to my family in Spain you'd be alive and I'd not be here mourning your passing. You … you who cared for me when there was no one else and … and then suf … suffered my black temper for your pains, I'm … so … so sorry!" The deep sobbing stretched his words causing him a moment's pause. "You structured your life to suit mine; you risked your life to save mine, never once thinking of yourself." He stifled another sob and seemed to grow a little stronger; he wiped a hand over his face, smudging the dirt and tears before beginning again. This time the words were spoken with oath swearing vehemence.

"I swear I will strive to be the man that you were and that you taught me to be … honourable, truthful and brave … and to live my life fully. And I swear … swear, upon the honour of my house and my life that I will dedicate the rest of it to the destruction of Rome and to the vengeance I will have for their taking you from me … I swear it!" The last words came out coarse and gritty from between clenched teeth as the terrible anger and hate building inside him bubbled over. "I swear it!" He repeated again. He stood quietly for a moment, his body shaking. He leant over the body placing his hand over Gestix's heart and lowering his voice. "I miss you already … my blessings … my love … and my farewell, till we meet again."

Stifling a sob that caused his jaw to shake he placed his right fist over his heart and bowed his head then pushed the torch into the kindling; the air popped as the oil wet wood flared, crackled and began to burn. He walked around the pyre applying the torch and spreading the fire, the flames growing as they took hold, their glow driving the darkness back. Completing his task, he threw the torch amongst the kindling and stood back as the flames roared and flared greedily devouring the timber.

The warriors remained about the pyre with heads respectfully bowed until it was fully ablaze. Only as the flames reached the body and found cloth, skin and hair and grew again in intensity as they consumed the new fuel did they pick up their helmets and turn slowly away, their respects paid they could finally look to themselves. They were exhausted; none had eaten since breakfast that morning nor rested, having come straight from battle to laying out their friend. Cold, hungry and weary with the day they sought food and rest. Armaco looked back to see Baldor still in front of the pyre.

"Come Baldor we need to eat, you need to eat!" He walked back placing a hand gently on Baldor's arm. "You've done right by Gestix; he can be at peace now … come … come!"

"Thank you Armaco but I need just a while longer. You go … I'll be alright." The words dropped to a saddened whisper.

Armaco nodded resignedly, patting Baldor's shoulder comfortingly before following after the others.

****

The warriors were wrapped in furs and heavy cloaks and warming themselves around the camp fire quietly eating supper when Balaam appeared. Despite stiff and aching limbs they began rising to their feet offering tired greetings to their Captain. He quickly gestured them back down while gingerly picking a piece of sizzling meat from the pan and shuffling in amongst them, swapping the hot meat from hand to hand, as he did so.

"Sir, I have the casualty list, do you wish to hear the report and names now?"

"Eat first Harbro, you lads look all in." He bit at the meat sucking in air to help cool it as he ate. "The Romans have retreated across the Ticinus destroying the bridges as they went." He chewed noisily as he spoke, his mouth full. "We think their Consul or General is wounded at least, the bastards fought tooth and nail to force a small mounted unit through us before the last bridge went down and they had a well armoured but crippled looking officer in midst of them."

Armaco's ears pricked up but he continued to eat and listen.

Harbro interjected "That'll be right sir; we gave chase to a group like that. There was what looked like an injured senior officer amongst them. We couldn't catch them though, our horses were blown."

"Pity! The capture of someone like that would've added further luster to our victory. Mind you, the General's well pleased anyway, first blood to us eh! This should bring the local Gallic tribes over to our standard which will help make up for the men we've lost along the way … speaking of which, were our casualties light?"

"Light enough sir, considering, but …"

"But what? … Light's good isn't it?" He said leaning across the fire and carefully picking more meat from the pan.

The warriors all looked at Harbro. Balaam felt the silence and sensing the trepidation looked around the group then back to Harbro, his eating stopped. "Go on …"

The thick set, bull like warrior looked awkward, he huffed and cleared his throat as if seeking the right words. "We have two dead sir, eight wounded and one still missing. Of the wounded though, all should recover."

"Hmmm." Balaam began chewing again. "As you said, light! That's not too bad, unless you're one of them of course … who're the two dead?"

"Jamaal and Gestix."

"What!" Balaam sat upright, spitting a lump of gristle onto the fire his chewing slowed and stopped. "Gestix? … Gestix! Are you sure?"

Harbro looked at the ground and nodded slowly.

"Baal's teeth! … Gestix! … Gestix, gone?" He stared into the fire shaking his head. "Are you sure Harbro?"

"Sure sir." Harbro said regretfully, his head still lowered.

Balaam stared into the fire as if seeking his words. "I've known Gestix for over twenty years. We were just young men when the last war with Rome finished. Warriors and men don't come better than him … I've never seen him bested in a fight either; be it fists or blades." Balaam continued his blank stare, not speaking to anyone in particular; he just talked as if making a statement. A piece of crackling wood seemed to bring him from his apathy and he rose wearily to his feet throwing the meat onto the fire his hunger forgotten.

"Where is he?"

"This way sir" Harbro replied, standing himself. "We've done the right thing; he's on his way to Elysium."

"Does the boy know?"

"Aye sir, he was with him when Armaco found them."

"Do you know what happened?"

"Well, we'd seen that General or officer you mentioned being carried off as we returned to the field so we split our unit, I took most of the men and gave chase till our horses …"

"Yes, yes! You said that." Balaam cut in quickly, clearly agitated. "Come to the point man!"

"No sir, we don't know what happened." Harbro affirmed. "Armaco, Marko and Malo went to see to the lad, he was signaling and calling us to him."

Balaam whipped his head round the group seeking the three warriors Harbro had named; his eyes found Armaco first who still sat quietly eating.

"What happened?"

The one-eyed man looked up from his plate; he swallowed his food then paused considering his words.

"In truth, I don't know either sir. We found them both amongst the dead, the lad was in a bad way and Gestix was dying …"

"What's wrong with the boy?"

"He'll be alright physically sir, nothing that won't come aright, some cuts and bruises, a smashed nose and face but …"

"Where is he?" Balaam snapped, his agitation growing.

"He's still at the pyre sir, he wanted a while longer, I guess to offer more prayers and …"

"Did he say what happened?"

"No sir, he's other than himself, as you'll understand."

Balaam nodded, "Aye … I understand." He said bitterly. "I should go and offer my respects, which way?"

Harbro gestured the direction again. As Balaam turned to go, Armaco reached down to his belt and pulled a bloodied strip of cloth from it. He fingered the cloth hesitantly and chewed his lip as if considering before speaking.

"There is this, Captain."

Balaam stopped and turned back, he saw Armaco's outstretched hand holding the piece of rolled cloth. He looked at the cloth bemused as Armaco gestured him to take it. Balaam unfolded it from his hand; it looked like any other piece of cloth cut long and wide to make a bandage. Still not understanding he felt the texture through his fingers, noticing the dampness but also the softness and richness of the fabric, then seeing the tasseled ends turned back to the firelight holding it up to inspect. Despite the dark, wet staining, the sash still maintained dry patches that showed its rich purple colour.

"Tanith's breath! Do you know what this is?" Balaam sounded incredulous and exited. He used both hands to closely examine the sash. "Tanith, mother of all that's holy! … Tell me … tell me this is Roman Blood, a Roman General's or Consul's blood!" His eyes wide and staring. "Where did you get it?"

"From Baldor, sir! But it's not Roman blood, its Gestix's, I think."

"From the boy? … Gestix's blood? You think? Damn it man, you're not making sense!"

"We found it as we ministered Gestix's injuries. It was pushed into the wound as wadding. I think Baldor must have done it as there were no others alive near …"

"Where did he get it?" Balaam snapped.

Armaco shrugged his shoulders. "I don't know sir."

"Where is he? Get him here now! I need answers!"

"I asked him sir and …"

"Well! What did he say man?"

"Nothing sir, he said nothing. He needs a little time to come to terms with …"

"The General will need to know now! Get him here!"

"No!" Armaco snapped. "Sir" He added more respectfully.

Balaam stared as though he'd been struck, his face darkening to a scowl as his anger came. Before he could reply, Harbro cut in, stepping between the pair as he spoke.

"Armaco means we'd all rather you leave it for now, sir … if you please?" His tone conciliatory. "The lad is all but done in, we don't think you'll get much sense from him tonight anyway, we couldn't. Armaco could try first thing in the morning … sir?"

Balaam looked around at his men, seeing weariness and sadness on their faces but also sensing the aura of protection that came from them all regarding Baldor. His snarl slowly eased away.

"Very well." He nodded. "Very well … we'll leave it till the morning but then I want answers! Do you hear me? … Answers!" He pointed and glared at Armaco. "Now, show me to Gestix so I can pay my respects as a friend should."

Chapter Two

It was late afternoon of the day following the battle at Ticinus when Baldor awoke again, the noises of routine camp life finally pervading his exhausted sleep. His body ached wherever he moved or turned and his blackened, swollen eyes felt as if there was fine, grainy sand lodged in the back of them. His head throbbed and the thump, thump of his heartbeat pounded drum like in his ears, his broken face felt fragile and hollow as if it would collapse if he moved. His nose had swollen to twice its normal size and his nostrils crusted inside with flakes of old blood where it had dried, bled and dried again whilst he slept. Thus, he lay still and quiet trying to ignore the pain and collect his wits while struggling to fathom the time of day or even what day it was.

Balaam had been to visit him that morning or at least he thought it was the same morning? He'd pressed him with questions regarding Gestix's death, the Roman Consul and the bloodied sash. After wringing the information from him, Balaam had then to calm him from his hot and bitter threats of bloody retribution for Gestix's slaying as his temper flared to vengeance in the telling.

He closed his eyes again seeking a return to peace and hopefully more sleep; he sighed despairingly as his mind instead moved to full wakefulness raking over the traumatic events of yesterday. Like a hammer blow striking both his heart and head, the awful realisation hit him that Gestix was gone, gone from this life and from his world. No more would the big man be there to guide and help, to impart his wisdom and skill and to love him like a brother. His anger flared again but this time directed at himself as he saw his selfishness surface, the same self-centeredness he believed had brought about his friends death. The disbelief and frightening reality of the loss hit him harder than any physical blow and hurt far more deeply than any injury he'd ever suffered, even the heartbreaking pain of Aiticia's death seemed to pale against this new and terrible grief.

As weary as his body was and as still as he laid, wishing and begging for sleep it wouldn't come, his battered body cried out for it wanting time to rest and heal, his mind needing it to take the mental pain away, for a while anyway. Nevertheless, the hole in his chest where his heart used to be ached like a poisoned wound and his mind would not stop. It went over and over the regret and blame he felt for his friend's death torturing him with memories. It brought remembrance of the harsh words uttered over the years and the precious time lost in anger when he'd not spoken either out of petulance or for an imagined slight at his damnable, foolish pride. All his failings, from earliest childhood to the present visited him, tormenting and eating at him, consuming him like a sickness, ensuring neither peace nor sleep would come. Weary and frustrated he sat upright on the small camp bed pulling his cloak about his shoulders with his mind troubled, his heart broken and he now wide awake.

He groaned as his body sent pain wracked objections to the sudden movement, forcing him to rest his brow gently on his upraised knees in an attempt to ease it. Lifting his hand to his throat, he fingered the beautifully coloured marble that hung there encapsulated in its gold wire net. The sphere was a striking blue shade of the summer sky against which slanting, crimson-tailed flecks fell like a rainstorm of fire, as he caressed the bauble his mind raked over the begetting of it and that traumatic event of his childhood so long ago. He thought of the explanation he'd given his Captain and its linked pertinence to the questions concerning the Roman Consul and the events of the last two, terrible days. The Gods appeared to be conspiring once more and playing fickle with his life, and these Romans … these Romans who appeared like storm-crows before a catastrophe, seemed to be harbingers of trouble and woe.

His fingers fished around his neck again, this time finding and pulling a leather cord upon which hung a small, oval shaped, silver cameo. He traced his fingertips slowly and lovingly over the finely etched lines of the embossed image, the likeness of which showed the head and shoulders of a beautiful young woman, his wife, his beloved Aiticia. Seeing her likeness awakened more memories and his eyes misted with tears, he bit his lip in an attempt to choke off the hurt he felt welling inside.

"First you my love and now … now, Gestix." He raised the cameo to his lips kissing it gently, tasting his tears on his lips. He stifled a sob that made his chest heave as he closed his hand around the silver holding it tightly like a drowning man gripping a lifeline. "Oh my love, my love! What am I to do? If I could only turn back time, if only I had died at the hand of Carthalo it would have saved all your deaths and spared me this heartbreak." He whispered his dread thoughts into the cavernous gloom of the tent, crying softly.

Armaco ducking through the tent doorway interrupted his grief. As he turned to fasten the flap against the wind, Baldor pushed the cameo back into his shirt and wiped a hand quickly across his eyes before looking towards his visitor.

"How are you feeling?" Armaco asked tentatively while trying to sound and look a little cheerful, his demeanor much at odds with his normal brusque manner.

Baldor just nodded gently not trusting himself to speak.

"You're in the best place." He nodded to the bed. "It's as cold and hard as an unpaid whore out there! … Here! Try this!"

He placed a bowl of steaming water on the floor then pulled a wooden chest towards the camp bed sitting down heavily on it while pulling two tiny cloth bags from his purse.

"The surgeon sold me these." He said, unwrapping one of the bags containing opaque, irregular shaped crystals. Picking up a horn cup from the floor by the bed, he scooped hot water from the bowl. Dropping the crystals into the water, he stirred them with his finger before pulling it out quickly, cursing and shaking it vigorously to cool it. He sniffed the potion, his nose wrinkling and eyes blinking quickly.

"Baal's breath! This should clear your head and help you breathe."

Baldor accepted the cup and cleared his throat to speak. "What is it?"

"Camphor laurel he called it, it's some kind of tree? The crystals are dried resin from it."

Baldor closed his eyes and sniffed hard at the swirling steam. He twitched his head away quickly from the vapour and sharp odour as they pervaded his sinuses, groaning as his head exploded in pain from the sudden movement.

"Breathe it in! Breathe it in! If it's unpleasant it has to be good!" Armaco chided, steering the cup back under Baldor's nose. "Baal almighty, Baldor! You're a bit of a mess." He said, seeing Baldor's face more clearly.

Baldor sniffed tentatively at the potion, still grimacing at the sharp odour but persevering as he felt some relief to his nasal passages.

"Helping?"

Baldor nodded slowly.

Armaco looked pleased with himself. "I told the surgeon about your injuries see; he reckons you'll have a headache as well, a bad one! Like you've been in a drinking bout with Bacchus."

Baldor nodded again then supported his head with his hand as the movement sparked more pain.

"He's a veritable genius this surgeon!" He muttered, the heavy sarcasm missed or ignored by Armaco.

"I've got this for your headache." Armaco held up the other bag grinning all the while. "You drink this one."

Baldor just groaned.

Picking up another cup and filling it from the bowl, Armaco sprinkled the bag's contents into his palm then dropped a pinch of the fine green-yellow powder into the water and stirred it with the same finger. He passed it to Baldor.

"It's Butterbur." He said pre-empting the question. "It's as bitter as a cheated whore and tastes like stale piss but it'll ease your head." He carefully tipped the remaining powder back in the bag and placed it in his purse. "That'll keep for the next time we drink too much!" He chuckled softly.

Baldor's face twisted up as he sipped the liquid.

"You liken everything to whores, very intuitive and descriptive! You obviously have great knowledge of such?" He managed a smirk as he said it causing further pain to his face prompting him not to tease his benefactor further.

Armaco missed the veiled sarcasm again and continued. "Never mind the big words, it sums it up for me, you know what they're like; cold, hard, bitter, soft, warm …" He smiled mischievously.

"No, not really I lack your worldly experience."

Armaco looked like he was about to expand on the subject when Baldor raised a halting hand. "Yes, yes I get the picture." He cradled his head again.

Armaco shrugged. "Anyway, message from the Captain." He said as he rubbed the muscles at the base of his neck then stretched as he stood. "The General wants to see you."

Baldor closed his eyes and turned his head away, sighing deeply.

"And before dark he said! Come on man, you're not dying, yet!" He picked up Baldor's corselet and weapons belt dropping them with a clatter near his bedroll, Baldor cringed as his head throbbed with the noise gathering the sympathy session was over.

"Sniff that potion as you dress and quaff the other but move your arse, it doesn't do to keep a General waiting! Moreover, while you ready yourself, you can enlighten me as to what happened on the field … all of it! I'm your friend remember and I'd like to know?" Armaco grinned sarcastically.

Just before dark the two men were almost at Hannibal's tent with Baldor scrubbed, tidy looking and his white corselet cleaned of dirt and most of the bloodstains and his bronze helmet polished. To his surprise, he could now breathe relatively well and his head was easing from hammer blows to a dull ache. However, as he'd unfolded his tale he'd found himself having to repeat the sequence of events from both his childhood and the battle more than once, the one-eyed warrior shaking his head in disbelief and asking questions which didn't help his condition or patience.

"Baldor Targa to see the General." Baldor announced quietly to the tent guard who nodded and disappeared within.

"I'll wait for you out here." Armaco said stepping to one side.

"There's no need, I …"

The guard returned, beckoning Baldor into the tent; assisted by a gentle push from Armaco, his objections cut short.

The tent was warm but gloomy and smelt of old cloth and damp rushes. The fabric walls flapped as the occasional wind gust battered it. A servant busied himself lighting miniature oil lamps placed in bronze stands around the canvas room, in the corner a young man sat at a desk working diligently beneath the glow of a large lamp already aflame above him. Baldor, having removed his helmet cradled it in the crook of his arm and stood quietly waiting for the other to finish his work and acknowledge him.

Hannibal finished writing and taking a wooden shaker sprinkled fine sand, pepper like over the document drying the dark ink. Flicking the parchment to remove the sand he applied a lamp flame to a wax stick, the molten drips forming a glutinous crimson pool on his parchment, turning his hand over he pushed his seal ring into it. Folding it he repeated the process, sealing the letter closed while nodding in satisfaction; his task completed, he stood to receive his guest.

"Baldor!" He said warmly stepping across the room smiling and offering his hand. "It's good to see you again!"

"General, sir!"

Each gripped the other above the wrist, their other hand clenched in a fist over their heart. A warrior's handshake and salute from one soldier to another, Baldor bowing his head in additional respect.

At twenty-eight, Hannibal was only eight years; Baldor's senior and similar in looks and build but not so tall, being of more medium height. Like Baldor, he was clean-shaven and wore his black hair in thick, loose curls to the base of his neck, a purple headband, the only sign of regality upon him kept his hair in place while denoting his rank. He had a straight nose with a firm, angular jaw and large eyes dark to the point of black but strangely full of life and warmth. His skin was naturally swarthy from his Phoenician heritage, though darkening further to the shade of tanned leather from exposure to the elements.

"Baldor!" He said with quiet empathy. "My condolences and sorrow for the loss of your friend and my prayers for a swift entry into Elysium for him. From what I hear he was a great warrior and a good man." This time Hannibal dipped his head.

"Thank you sir, he was that and more to me."

Hannibal nodded gently and walked to a long, plain wooden bench picking up a bronze wine pitcher and two horn cups, he raised both gesturing to Baldor if he wished a drink.

"Yes, thank you sir." He nodded.

"Come … come." Hannibal invited kindly, indicating with a flick of his head to an area deeper in the tent. Turning on his heel with the pitcher and cups in hand, he walked into a smaller but better lit room off from the main one in which they stood. Now, in the stronger light Hannibal saw clearly the ruin that was Baldor's face. "I trust you're recovering well from battle?" He intimated Baldor's broken face and multi coloured bruising.

"Yes sir, thank you."

The smaller room, being Hannibal's private living quarters had patterned rugs on the floor compared to the brown, faded rushes of the other. The furniture however remained simple and practical though cloaks and animal skin throws had been cast over it giving added comfort; in the corner on a cross-shaped wooden stand, Hannibal's corselet and weapons belt hung with the helmet perched above it.

Gesturing Baldor to sit, Hannibal poured him a cup of wine.

"Your recovery and future good health!" He said, raising his cup in salute. "And absent friends."

"Absent friends." Baldor echoed quietly while standing and raising his cup and the pair drank. Hannibal quickly refilled them, urging Baldor to sit again. Walking to a small table he picked up the bloodied sash then sat down close to Baldor.

"Tell me Baldor?" He said conversationally. "Tell me if you will … about this." He said, placing the cloth between them.

Baldor picked up the sash and stared at the heavy staining, his face showing the sorrow his heart felt. He took another drink before clearing his throat to speak.

"The sash belongs to Publius Cornelius Scipio, the …"

"Scipio! Scipio, the Roman Consul?" Hannibal cut in, looking surprised.

"Yes sir, he slew Gestix … my friend." He clarified when Hannibal looked lost. "I went to help as I saw Gestix fall, I attacked the Consul …"

"Baal almighty! Did you kill him?"

"No sir! No, I would have … but …but for the intervention of his son." He said bitterly.

"His son? How do you know these people?"

Baldor peered from out of his swollen, blackened eyes that had now misted.

"The Consul slew my friend sir and … and so help me, as sure as the sun will rise tomorrow, I … I will have my vengeance." His voice suddenly unsteady and husky. "Even if it takes the rest of my life, I will have it."

A tear rolled over the purple and mustard coloured bruising of his cheeks that he wiped savagely away, wincing as his hand brought fresh pain to his face.

"How do you know these people Baldor?" Hannibal repeated patiently. "How can you be sure? There would be others of high rank on the field."

Baldor sipped his wine taking the moment to compose himself.

"In truth sir, before the battle I'd no idea of who they were. But the son, Cornelius … he … he and I have been acquainted before, when we were children."

Hannibal looked lost again

"You're not making sense Baldor; else I can't pick up the threads of it yet?"

"It's a long story sir." Baldor said as though it was trivial and not worth the effort of telling.

"Well, I'd like to know and we have all night … and the wines not so bad!" Hannibal grinned and motioned Baldor to stay where he was, as he stood and walked towards the main part of the tent.

"Guard! Dinner for two of us in my quarters, we're not to be disturbed thereafter."

Returning to his seat and placing another pitcher of wine on the small table between them, Hannibal motioned Baldor to begin again.

"From the start Baldor, leave nothing out, I'm intrigued."

Baldor took another drink and settled back into the chair.

"It began when I was but a child of ten, General I …"

"Lets leave the sir's and General out of it Baldor, its only you and I here, we can dispense with formalities eh?" Hannibal flashed his warm enigmatic smile. "Let's just talk as men, friends I think?"

Baldor nodded, feeling a little more relaxed he continued.

"I'd gone with my father to Gades, in southern Spain; we were visiting shipyards there, as you already know our family business was shipbuilding. While my father talked business I roamed the yard taking in the sights, it was quite something to a boy of ten who'd never left Carthage before." Baldor's face lightened as he reminisced. "I met some boys, all much my age, we played at marbles. I wagered a bracelet against this." He undid the gold wrapped marble from his throat and passed it to Hannibal.

"You won?" Hannibal smiled, nodding in admiration as he examined the quaint bauble.

"No … no, I lost." Baldor said slowly, a little smile playing on his lips as his mind raked over the memory. Hannibal frowned as if not understanding. Baldor swirled the wine in his cup then took a sip before continuing.

"In truth, the game was over, I was defeated and my bracelet lost, it was then a Watchman from the yard appeared and chased us, promising us all a thrashing when he caught us. Typical boys we were, playing where we shouldn't have been, high up on the stone wharf. There was pandemonium as we tried to run, we all pushed and shoved eager to be gone. The boy I'd lost the game and bracelet to was knocked from the wharf into the water below, smashing his head against the pier edge as he fell. Everyone was scattering, trying to escape the Watchman. I think I was the only one who saw him fall so I jumped in after him, to help him. They fished us out …"

Hannibal looked lost again. "Who's they?"

"Men, men came to help, Carpenters, Shipwrights, Servants and such like I suppose and … and the boy's father, the boy whom I'd helped in the water."

"The Scipios then? … Father and son?" Hannibal said piecing the story together.

Baldor nodded slowly. "Yes, though I didn't know it at the time. We were lifted from the water, puking and shaking and the father … Scipio, he was … was kind to me. He wrapped me in his cloak, held my head as I vomited while offering me anything in his power for helping his son." Baldor paused, his head down, a melancholy look on his face. He sipped again at his wine. "The son, Cornelius, he gave me that marble in gratitude for his life, he said it was his greatest treasure, his 'Vulcan's fire' he called it, that's what he'd wagered against my bracelet. He kept the bracelet though; said it was to remind him of our tie." Baldor managed a tight sardonic smile as he finished.

"But he … they never said who they were?" Hannibal asked quickly.

"No, they were about to, would have I surmise but my father coming to see what had happened to me found out they were Roman and would have none of them. He dismissed them and their entreaties harshly, so though they had my name and city, I had no notion of who they were … until yesterday."

A servant appeared bearing a tray laden with food and a platter of fresh bread, Baldor paused from his story as the food was served, taking the time to sip his drink and moisten his throat. As the servant bowed and left, Hannibal motioned him to eat. With the smell of the food assaulting his taste buds and his empty stomach rumbling in anticipation he remembered his hunger. Having not eaten since breakfast the previous day he eagerly helped himself to the hot lamb and flat baked, camp bread while Hannibal recharged the wine cups.

"Yesterday, you said ..." Hannibal, repeated; prompting him to continue now the servant had departed.

"Yesterday, when we clashed with the Roman cavalry I saw Gestix attacked from the side by the Consul Scipio."

"You recognised him?"

"No .... No, I had no idea who he was, other than the enemy. I attacked him driving him away from Ge ... but I was too late ... too late." Baldor put the meat down as the words stuck in his throat, his appetite suddenly forgotten. He stared at his wine cup then turned it slowly with his fingers; he began again slowly, the words coming out mechanically and monotone. "I fought him ... fought him to his knees." Baldor's eyes flashed with maloevence as his voice took on a husky bitterness. "He was beaten then and I about to finish him when I was attacked by his son."

Hannibal nibbled on the bread and sipped his wine, though he never took his eyes from Baldor.

"He and I fought then. First with swords and then hand to hand ... he desperate to save his father from me and ... and me desperate to slay him ... to slay them both."

"You would not have known they were father and son then though?"

"No ... no, I neither knew nor cared, I thought him just one Roman trying to save another ... he fought well." Baldor said grudgingly, pointing to his face. "But, hatred's a powerful weapon and vengeance the strength to wield it. I had him near choked to death when I saw the bracelet on his wrist ... my bracelet! Which we'd played a game for all those years ago. I let go of his throat, demanding his wherewithal of it. By this time he'd recognised the marble around my neck and we ... we, ceased fighting, I ... I let him go."

Baldor stared at Hannibal as if expecting a rebuke for his act of mercy. His look that of a little boy lost; lost in affairs and fates he could neither control nor understand. Hannibal however said nothing; he took another drink and nodded slowly, inviting Baldor to continue.

"As we separated I returned to looking for Gestix but had to defend myself against half-a-dozen Roman cavalry, I surmise they'd returned to the field in an attempt to take the Scipios off it. I fought against them."

Hannibal looked on in almost disbelief. "How did you …"

"Survive? … In truth, I'd also be dead now but for the son. He called them off and had them take his father from the field, thus he spared my life, making our life debt equal he said. It was only then, when I asked him his name that I learned who he and his father were."

Hannibal settled back in his chair now that Baldor's tale seemed complete; lifting his plate onto his knee, gently shaking his head in wonder.

"I tell you Baldor; the God's guard your footsteps and you have the mark of destiny about you. You save this boy's life, you save your friends lives in Spain when we fought the tribes in the forest, then survive a murder plot against you and …"

"And fail to save the best friend I ever had." Baldor cut in sourly.

Hannibal heard the bitterness and saw the abject sadness in his eyes as he continued.

"The Gods! …" Baldor laughed bitterly. "If such fickle entities do exist they don't guard my footsteps, they haunt them! I am I fear a curse, a plague, a harbinger of doom. All who befriend me, love me or become close, perish!" Distraught and downcast; he pushed the meat around his plate his appetite completely gone.

"Don't blame the Gods for all your ills Baldor." Hannibal replied somewhat sternly, then moderating his tone. "It is only by suffering that we become better men. You'll emerge a better, stronger man from these troubles, of that I'm sure."

Baldor was about to interrupt but Hannibal held up his hand silencing him. "And a better man is what I need, someone I can rely on, someone trustworthy, honest and brave. These are qualities I see in you, Baldor Targa." Hannibal pointed at Baldor with a lump of meat juice soaked, bread. "I need such to strengthen the ranks of my junior officers."

Baldor looked up from his misery, eyes wide.

"Tell me Baldor." Hannibal said lightly changing the tone. "Do you speak Gallic?"

"Yes sir, fluently ... Gestix taught me from being a child."

Hannibal nodded, smiling to himself his suspicions confirmed.

"I will have you away from Captain Balaam and onto my staff ..."

"But sir! I'm under contract to the Captain! I've signed to serve!"

"My need is greater than his." Hannibal said firmly and grinned. "I'm sure he'll understand."

"But I have little, no experience."

Hannibal huffed as if in disbelief and grinned again.

Baldor looked as though he was about to continue his objections when Hannibal placed a hand on his shoulder looking him straight in the eye. He spoke quietly but firmly, "Baldor, I command it!"

"Yes ... yes sir."

Hannibal offered his hand as if to seal the order, Baldor slowly, tentatively giving his.

"Good! It's settled then ... now eat, Hypolokhagos."

"Hypolokhagos!" Baldor exclaimed.

"It's Greek Baldor, Greek for Lieutenant."

"I know sir; my Father insisted I learn the language!" He replied in Greek, his voice however full of dread.

Hannibal raised his eyebrows and continued in Greek. "You are a truly amazing man, Baldor Targa ... truly, now eat ... please."

Chapter Three

Light snow had fallen since dawn, blowing in small flurries that swirled and drifted silently on the wind. It settled in the sheltered places first, between the rows of the animal skin and canvas tents and in the lee of carts and equipment, then as the flakes grew in size, gradually covering the grass and stone of the plain.

The Carthaginian camp was quiet, men choosing to huddle under cover in their canvas homes only venturing out for their ablutions or to throw more timber on the fires. The patrolling sentries were swathed in cloaks against the bitter cold, stamping their feet as they walked they took every opportunity to warm frozen hands by the glowing braziers at each guard post.

Baldor sat quietly in the corner of the tent, wrapped in furs and working a whetstone slowly and methodically along the edge of his falcata, his other swords and broad bladed dagger laid in front of him. He paused every two or three rasping strokes holding the heavy blade up to eye level sighting the edge for any remaining nicks and imperfections. When finally satisfied he rubbed the blade with lanolin using a scrap of unwashed sheep's wool as an applicator. He applied a little oil to the throat of the scabbard before sliding the sword in and out repeatedly, ensuring a smooth unrestricted action.

Rising from his cross-legged position, he rubbed his chilled and stiffened limbs then walked to the tent door, peering through at the fire that crackled and burned within its circle of stones. Content there was sufficient wood to keep a decent blaze fed awhile yet, he returned to his place and began work on his second blade.

Just as he began the first stroke, the tent flap pushed aside and Captain Balaam stepped in brushing snowflakes from his cloak as he came. He slipped the woollen hood from his head revealing short black hair and a goatee beard crowded by a week's growth of whiskers. His nose which was twisted and bent was blotched and reddened at the tip from the cold, his cheeks above the stubble pinched white and the skin drawn tight highlighting the dark rings around his eyes. Despite the frozen, weary look, his sapphire blue eyes shone like ice caught in bright sunlight.

"Bloody snow! I damn well hate it!" He stamped his feet to shake the flakes from his boots and help restore circulation. "Where's the rest of the laggards?" He asked suspiciously, as he looked around the empty tent then at the pile of furs that was Baldor.

"On patrol sir! I won at straws so am to stay home to feed the fire and prepare the food."

"Hah! Fair enough boy! How're you feeling anyway?" He pointed at Baldor's face.

"Good sir ... thank you, it's coming right."

Balaam nodded. "Good! Right, two things boy." He looked somewhat uncomfortable despite his brusque matter of fact manner.

Baldor put his sword and whetstone down, retracting both hands back into the warmth of his robes ready to listen.

"I'm sorry ... sorry about Gestix." Balaam managed awkwardly, rubbing his hands together as much to hide his discomfort as to keep them warm.

"Thank you sir, you did tell me yesterday."

"I didn't think you were all there yesterday, so ... well, there it is again." Balaam interrupted, speaking quickly his voice tetchy, almost snapping. "He was a good man and a damned fine warrior, probably the best I've seen ... and ... and he was my friend." His last words dropped to quiet sad reverence.

"Thank you sir." Baldor repeated, sensing Balaam's awkwardness and embarrassment at displaying his feelings.

Balaam sat next to Baldor, while pulling a soft, leather bag from under his cloak. Setting it down, he undid the hide drawstrings opening the neck. Fishing inside his corselet, he produced a folded piece of ivory coloured parchment, holding it up he looked Baldor in the eye.

"Gestix's last wishes." He cleared his throat to hide his sadness as Baldor reached tentatively for the missive. "And his affects." He offered the bag to Baldor with his other hand. "It's all for you boy, the possessions that is. He left us money enough to buy some good wine and decent food for the six of his comrades that remain." He waved the parchment. "We're all named here see: Harbro, Armaco, Marko, Malo, you and I. The funeral feast if you like, aye … aye that's what it is." His voice tailed off.

Baldor nodded, taking the parchment and bag putting them into a small wooden chest that held his own belongings.

"Don't you want to check the contents against the list?"

"No sir, I'm sure that's not necessary." He replied quietly.

"Fair enough boy, here!" Balaam dropped a leather purse into Baldor's hand. "That's the coin! See what you can get for us in the way of food and wine. Good wine mark you! He was a bloody good man!"

"Yes sir."

Balaam nodded in respect and seemed relieved that the personal matter was concluded.

"Now, to business! I hear from the General that you've been promoted and …"

"It wasn't my choice sir, I …"

"Don't interrupt me boy! I've told you about that before." Balaam's voice had all the surety and confidence of command again. "Hypolokhagos eh!" He smirked.

Sensing a piece of Balaam's usual sarcastic wit Baldor's face clouded. Balaam however, anticipating the prickly pride of the young warrior carried on quickly.

"You're worth that at least, boy! I just want to ensure you live long enough to enjoy it. Your courage and fighting ability I don't doubt but experience and wisdom you could suffer more of … agreed?"

"Yes sir … and agreed." Baldor's face lightened again.

"So, me and the General see, now that he's come around to my way of thinking, we've decided you should remain under my command, for a little while longer, at least till you find your feet so to speak, agreed?"

"Yes sir, agreed."

"Good! From today onwards, you're to become more involved with orders and responsibilities. Apprenticed if you like, to Harbro, Armaco and me so watch and learn boy, for the General tells me he sees potential in you. His plans will eventually take you onto his staff and away from us; I want to ensure that you're as good as you can be when that time comes."

"Thank you sir."

Balaam waved the thanks away.

"I didn't want to go sir. I was, am happy to stay, now you are … all of you are, the only family I have left!"

"Well families come and go boy, nothing stays the same!"

Seeing Baldor's head drop, Balaam realised he'd touched a raw nerve, he looked at the boy trying so hard to be a man. He saw the hurt, the anger, and fierce pride that burned his eyes bright like fanned coals, as he fought to hide his emotions. Perhaps seeing a reflection of himself when younger, Balaam sighed deeply and paused to pick his words.

"Look … Baldor." He began quietly.

Baldor looked up, taken aback by Balaam calling him by his name instead of 'boy'.

"Take the opportunity when it comes eh? That's what I'm saying … you're different to the rest of us. I think I knew that the day I met you in the market square at Icosium, when you defeated that Adharbal. … I've never seen two blades used so well … and then when you changed the fortunes of us all for the better at the battle in the forest, well …"

Baldor looked embarrassed and was trying to interrupt again despite his warning. Balaam waved him to silence and continued.

"The General's right Baldor, the Gods or …" He held up his hand again, anticipating Baldor's reaction, knowing well the disdain with which he held the divine. "Or something? Fate? Whatever follows you? Then this business with the Roman Consul, it's not just coincidence; I think the mark of greatness is upon you."

Both men fell silent and stared at one another intently; the crackle of the fire outside was all that was to be heard. Balaam found his tongue first.

"Right!" He said, clearing his throat as if to signify the subject closed. "If this snow eases by tomorrow we're out recruiting amongst the local tribes, so your knowledge of Gallic will be useful. With the current casualties, sickness and other duties the company's down to twenty men including Harbro, Armaco you and I. So we'll split into two patrols, you with Armaco and eight warriors and Harbro with me and eight, understand?"

"Yes sir."

"Good! We'll have that feast when the patrol's over. I'll see you and the lad's at first light." Balaam nodded, rose quickly and ducked out of the door.

Baldor returned to his blade maintenance his thoughts ranging from Gestix, the funeral feast, preparing food for his comrades and now the prospective added burden of command. What would Gestix have done?

****

Morning came with a chill that cut to the bone like a knife, it pained the lungs to breathe so cold was the air. The sun had just climbed into full view after clearing the peaks of the distant mountains, its rays colouring the snow and the assembling men a watery orange. The horses already had riding blankets over their backs and the men's equipment secured in place. The breath from animals and men bloomed in white clouds as they milled around trying to mount, the horses skittering as they tentatively found their footing on the ice-crusted snow. The usual sounds of harness and metal muted as the warriors were swathed in cloaks and furs, the horses having additional blankets over their hindquarters and necks in a bid to stave of the clinging cold. With the rest of the camp still asleep, it was silent commands that moved the men into column riding southwards parallel to the Trebbia River. Crossing at a ford well south of the Roman camp they headed east toward the distant hills. With the early start and the cold, men had little to say and were busy adjusting cloaks to cover any bare flesh and wrap scarves around mouths and noses.

Midmorning found the sun radiating a little warmth as it gained height, the skies also remained kind being clear of clouds and washed topaz blue. The warriors reined up at the edge of the forest that began just up off the plane. Spreading backwards into the gently rising hills it covered the higher ground in a mixture of pine, larch and fir along with a scattering of hornbeam and chestnut. Balaam studied the area for some time as the men sat their horses quietly, eventually he whistled and having caught Armaco, Harbro and Baldor's attention waved them forward.

"We split here, Harbro with me. Armaco, Baldor! Take your eight and work up through the forest, the locals say there's a village up there somewhere, find it and see if you can drum up some recruits. Avoid trouble if possible, we need to gain men not lose them!"

"Sir."

"Yes sir."

Balaam glanced at the sun and the distant mountains then back to his officers. "We've less than half a day of light left I reckon, be back here ere the sun passes over that tallest peak, no later! That way we return to camp in the light. Got it?"

The men nodded assent and Armaco and Baldor turned their horses and the small column split into two, Armaco's arm pointed towards the forest at the walk. Despite their intended peaceful mission the warriors were heavily armed, all carried a fighting spear, and a shield slung on their back or fastened on the horse's trappings. Some painted with images of animals, objects or mythical creatures; others bore an image with particular association to its owner or a symbol or letter denoting his city. All wore helmets of bronze in the Greek style with decorative crests of feathers or a brush of tufted, dyed horsehair with a long tail falling down past the wearer's shoulders. Instead of their customary thigh length tunics worn over bare legs, the men wore leggings or long trousers of calf leather or patterned wool in the Gallic style to protect from the cold. Their chests encased in leather corselets with bronze discs or studs riveted in place, giving additional protection as well as decoration and worn over padded linen or leather shirts. All had a scarf wrapped about their neck, in some cases continuing around the wearers face protecting the soft skin.

As the horses entered the shadow of the trees, the gloom amplified the cold. Above them however, the thickly needled, pine boughs formed a roof and the ground bore only a light sprinkling of snow and made for better going compared to the plain. The sharp freshness of the air was enhanced by the pungent smell of pine gum mixed through with the earthy odour of forest floor mulch and timber. The horses' hoof falls, muted on the carpet of needles made almost no noise as they followed each other in single file. With visibility reduced to less than a javelin throw, Armaco signalled a halt gesturing they should wait and listen. The warriors peered into the trees tilting their heads to listen as the wind rustled gently through the top canopy causing the odd protesting creak and groan from the limbs beneath. As it died away, the cooing of roosting wood pigeons could be heard along with the occasional yowling call of peacocks, all else was quiet. Despite the icy chill, some men slipped their scarves from their faces for the trees at least kept the dry wind at bay or perhaps it was to ease the claustrophobic feeling of the scarf and the thick, encroaching trees.

For the umpteenth time Baldor loosened his swords in their scabbards on his back then leant forward doing the same to the one fastened on his horse's withers.

"Gestix taught you well eh?" Armaco said.

Baldor managed a smile and a nod from his swollen face, the damage accentuated from being squashed inwards by the helmet cheek pieces. His cheeks had coloured a muddy yellow mixed with blackened, purple shades like over ripened plums as the bruising came out on his skin. His eyes were narrowed from the swelling and the lids blackened as if they'd had Kohl applied thickly to them, his swollen nose however felt better for being free of the chafing scarf.

"Maybe you should've kept that scarf on Baldor, you'll scare folk!" Armaco quipped along with a smirk.

"I'll recover from this, what's your excuse?" Baldor replied smugly.

The talk was cut short as a scout trotted towards them to converse quietly with Armaco; he pointed ahead indicating a track emerging from their left to join the trail they were following. Armaco walked the column on and looked down to where the trails converged.

"Horses! Those marks look reasonably fresh I reckon, Malo! Take a look."

The Nubian slipped soundlessly from his mount and squatted beside the tracks studying them intently. Tracing a gloved hand over the prints, he quietly counted to himself, nodding his head slightly as he mouthed each number.

"Fifteen, maybe twenty horses passed through here judging by the hoof prints, they're going southeast the same as us." His pointed, ebony, goatee beard bobbed on his chin as he looked up to talk.

Removing his gloves, he pushed his fingers into the disturbance in the forest floor testing the print depth against finger length, scooping up some dirt and rubbing it between his fingers he stood to face Armaco. "Going by the depth of the tracks sir, the horses are carrying heavily armed men, they passed sometime earlier this morning, no longer I'd say going by the softness of the dirt, the cold's just beginning to firm it, see!" He crumbled some of the hardening crust between his fingers to illustrate his point. "I'll go in front sir; I may be able to learn more if I see the tracks undisturbed?"

Armaco nodded and Malo walked ahead leading his horse by the bridle but keeping it slightly behind him.

"I'll go with him." Baldor also dismounted and walked after the former hunter, turned warrior.

Armaco turned to Marko. "Bring up our rear and make sure no ones' on our tail."

"Sir." The older man replied pulling his mount around giving it a gentle dig in the flanks to move it.

Armaco looked back along his small column holding his finger over his lips, warriors turned to pass the silent message back. Baldor caught up with Malo but held back half a pace; he knew from past experience the Nubian liked a clear field to study the ground.

The column made its way onward, continuing at a steady walk alongside the tracks that went in the same direction as they themselves intended. Moving in relative silence, the only sounds other than the rustle of the wind in the treetops was the muffled thump of hooves and the odd snort or whicker from the horses. Suddenly Malo put his hand out stopping Baldor, halting himself, he raised an opened hand to immobilise the column. He squatted again beckoning Baldor down to him as he ran his fingers over the ground.

"Here's where it becomes interesting." He pointed at the hoof prints counting softly to himself again moving his finger over the tracks as he did so. "Going by the number of prints this is the same group whose trail we've been following south-eastwards, now they've doubled back and swung off north." He pointed to the trail swinging away. "And see? ... Boot prints." He whispered while tracing an almost invisible outline for Baldor's benefit. "Someone dismounted and walked over there." Malo pointed off the trail, Baldor could see the prints now they'd been pointed out, though they were very faint.

"How do you know he was mounted to begin with and not on foot?" He asked.

"The prints show metal studs." Malo pointed at the faint, tiny indents in the earth. "If the man had been walking some of the damper soil would've stuck to the sole around the studs obscuring them, his boots are clean so he's been riding." Malo followed the tracks then stopped, pointing to a tree. "Huh!" He snorted. "He dismounted for a piss."

A white barked larch still bore a wet stain just below knee height from the ground. The Nubian crouched pushing his fingertips into the earth at the base of the tree.

"Still wet!" He wiped his fingers on the hem of his cloak. "He pissed earlier this morning that stain's no older than that."

Baldor could see the stain but would have missed it had the shallow prints leading to it not been pointed out. "How do you know it's a man?" He asked incredulously.

"The size of the foot and these are military boots, Roman boots I'd say with that pattern of hobnails! … And women squat to piss!" The Nubian flashed a smile as his face crumpled into a soft chuckle.

Baldor felt stupid for asking the obvious and looked to redeem himself with a sensible question. "Where did he dismount?"

Malo looked closely and pointed to the disturbed needles again drawing the shape of the foot with his finger, he walked back following the tracks. The tracks faded then disappeared giving Baldor a cold shiver down his back as he recalled an earlier experience in Spain, again while tracking with Malo, when the enemy had eluded them by travelling in the trees. Malo tapped him on the arm to draw his attention.

"The grounds too hard here for prints, see the trees have opened and the weather's getting in." He pointed to the open sky and the wider spaced trees. "Don't move till I pick up his trail again."

Passing his reins to a relieved Baldor, he walked slowly in the direction the tracks showed before they disappeared. He squatted again and thumped the ground; he looked back at Baldor. "See, frozen!"

Baldor nodded agreement as he stubbed his boot gently against the rigid carpet of needles. Malo continued walking away squatting every so often to press his hand against the ground. Eventually he summoned Baldor forward, the small column following in their lee.

"Here, he dismounted here!" He indicated an area with his hand. "The grounds softer here as there's cover again from the trees. There's the hoof prints, see how they become shallower as the rider dismounts and the weight comes off? And there's his boot prints, he dismounted to the right side, see how the left foot came down first? All the body weight on the one foot momentarily."

Baldor nodded as he took the information in, it was like watching the events unfold before him. Malo meantime had walked further away and was kneeling again.

"Our friend with the full bladder is part of the same mounted group."

Baldor looked at the trail and saw the hoof marks leading southeast then the mix of prints as the returning animals walked back on their previous trail, the prints became clearly directional again as they swung off to the north. Shading his eyes, he looked out over the top of the trees, northwards.

"Look!" He hissed, pointing at a spiralling column of grey and black smoke smudging the clear sky like a dirty stain.

Malo looked up then back to Armaco and the column; he whistled softly beckoning them forward. Indicating the smoke, he explained the back tracks and the time since the party had passed by, going from when the man had urinated.

"Should they be of a concern to us Malo? I'd imagine warriors moving about anyway with the disturbance from the last battle, local men maybe, checking their area or such?"

"Maybe sir but there's something else. One at least is wearing Roman Legionnaires boots … those hobnail patterns are unmistakeable." He added, as Armaco looked at him quizzically.

"But they've fallen back on the eastern bank of the Trebbia, what'd they be doing this far south and up here?"

"Baal knows sir!" Malo shrugged his shoulders. "It could be just as you say? On the other hand it seems like a lot of men to be checking the area, and the boots, how do you explain them and that smoke?"

"Roman cavalry don't wear hobnails in their boots." Baldor said, joining the conversation. "So they belong to a Legionnaire and as Legionnaires' don't ride, the boots could be stolen?"

"How far to that smoke Malo?" Armaco asked bringing the talk back to the swelling dark cloud.

"Hard to say sir ... perhaps five stades?"

Armaco thought for a moment.

"Right! ... Malo, Baldor, find out what that smoke's about. Once you know, Baldor you backtrack to us, I'll be bringing the men on."

"What about the main village?" Baldor intimated with a nod of his head up the trail.

"In time. I'm not happy with these tracks, nor the Roman boot prints or the smoke on our flank, find me some answers."

"Sir!" Came in unison from the pair who were already mounting and turning their horses northwards. Armaco signalled the remainder of the column to him.

****

Before long Baldor was heading back up the trail at a steady pace, steering his horse in and out of the trees towards his advancing colleagues. He signalled to Armaco, urging him forward but quietly.

"What have we got Baldor?" Armaco asked as he reined in next to him. The anger and disgust etched onto Baldor's face and the distant shouts and screams hinted at his message.

"A small settlement sir, hardly a village at all just some huts and shelters, fisher folk and such going by the drying nets and the boats on the riverbank." Baldor gasped a breath in. "The place is being raised by a party of Gauls along with murder being done and ..."

"Huh! It'll be some bloody tribal dispute, best we keep ..."

"There's a Roman there too!"

"A Roman! Is he in command?"

"He seems to be, the others look to him for direction though he does little other than watch."

"How many men altogether?"

"We've counted fourteen including the Roman; though there may be more in the huts ... they're raping the women by the screams." His voice tailed off.

"No warriors fighting back? Where's their men folk?"

"The few there was, all dead from what we've seen. They weren't warriors though, just simple folk, some boys and old men."

Armaco grimaced, his tone bitter "It's not our fight Baldor; this isn't the main village we're looking for and if it's not Legionnaires' raising havoc its best we keep ..."

"You're not going to do anything?" Baldor's eyes went wide. "For pity's sake Armaco they're murdering villagers down there … women and children!" He pointed back down the trail, his voice rising, his tone incredulous.

"What do you expect me to do?" Armaco snapped. "We're not on some save the innocents campaign! We have our orders …" A shrill scream echoed through the trees cutting him short.

"Damn the bloody orders!" Baldor replied bitterly, twisting away.

"Baldor! Fetch Malo, we leave now!" Armaco growled through gritted teeth.

"And damn you!" Baldor snarled, casting a contemptuous look at Armaco as he pulled savagely on his mount's bridle forcing it around and back whence he'd came.

Armaco controlled his response and ground his teeth in anger. As he turned his mount back up the trail, he saw his men's faces.

"What are you lot gawping at? … It's not our business, come on!"

The men remained where they were but looked away when Armaco glowered at them; Marko spoke quietly from the rear.

"Sir, they're doing murder down there."

"So! Haven't we all?" He snapped bitterly.

"Not like that sir!" Marko ventured, though keeping his tone civil.

"This patrol is not a bloody Greek democracy!" Armaco growled while scowling again at his men. Though none spoke, their thoughts and will were clear from their grim expressions. "Come on!" He waved the column back down the trail.

None of the men moved nor sought to argue further, they just returned his stare as he looked around their faces. He swore vehemently causing his horse to bridle.

"I'll remind you all this is mutiny!" He pointed a gloved finger around the men. "Do you want your hides nailed to crosses? For that's what you risk."

The warriors looked awkward but continued to hold his angry stare.

Seeing neither movement nor compliance to his orders, he nodded slowly, a slight sneer curling his lip. "Alright then, alright! You soft-hearted bastards! But we do it my way … come on!"

He kicked his horse around again and the small column followed to where Baldor had already disappeared back into the trees.

Chapter Four

The rush of water was audible to the approaching mercenaries long before the tiny settlement was visible through the trees. The river, which ran at right angles to the buildings, was a fast flowing upland torrent some eight-spear lengths wide that raced and boiled over its grey boulder bed on its way to the plain below. Out in the current in the deeper vees of the rapids, vertical ash poles pushed into the riverbed held fishnets in place. Dragged up on the shingle bank were three coracles made of hides stretched tightly over willow frames, stacked next to them were wicker baskets full of brook trout and mountain char.

The buildings were of logs or whitewashed wattle and daub thatched over with faded straw, some of which were lightly sprinkled with snow. Opposite the huts was a long, windowless, rectangular building constructed from the river rock. It's gently pitched roof, clad with thickly sawn timber boards and from which tendrils of pale grey-white smoke leaked through the overlaps and belched from purpose made vents on the apex, the building being a curing shed. The smoke rose lazily upwards carrying the reek of smoked fish with it joining the billowing black and grey smoke cloud coming from the burning hut.

The snow between the curing shed and huts was churned from hoof prints and dotted with bodies of men and children, some without their heads. Bright, crimson blood leaked from the torso's staining the snow, standing out starkly against the whiteness, splashes and trails of red led to where the heads had rolled. A large hunting dog howled mournfully as it dragged itself along the ground trailing blood from a severed leg. Most of the attackers had dismounted leaving their mounts with two of the youngest warriors while they busied themselves looting or dispatching any that still drew breath, others dragged screaming, struggling women towards the huts. One woman frantically clawed and gouged her attacker's eyes and succeeded in twisting free from his grip. She ran towards the tree line but was seized again just in front of where the Carthaginians hid in the shadows. The warrior caught her by her hair felling her with a vicious backhanded slap sending her spinning sideways to land in a dazed heap. Following her, he kicked her hard in the ribs sending her rolling over the ground. Standing over her, he loosened his trousers then bent down and tore off her dress.

Amongst all, a man wrapped in a crimson military cloak and wearing a Legionary helmet sat his horse drinking from a wineskin, calmly watching the rape and murder.

Armaco arrived behind Baldor just as he was preparing to ride into the village.

"You!" He hissed, pointing to Baldor with his spear. "Stay there!"

For a moment Baldor looked as if he was about to ignore the command. However, he remained where he was as Armaco continued quickly.

"Malo! Have you your bow with you?"

"Always." The Nubian replied, easing the bow from its case and unhooking the quiver of arrows from the horse's trappings.

Armaco pointed to the warrior who'd caught the woman and was now on his knees struggling with his victim and forcing her legs apart. "Start with that bastard! Then kill the ones out on the perimeter, as many as you can without alerting the others. Leave the Roman for now I want a word!"

Malo nodded then slipped silently behind a tree laying an arrow on the bowstring as he went.

"Baldor! Take half the men and work around opposite us. Don't attack until you see us break cover or one of those bastards raises the alarm. Understood?"

Nodding curtly, Baldor led his four men quietly away. Meanwhile the kneeling raider grunted as an arrow thumped into his back, the short range and the power of the bow driving the shaft through his ribcage, lungs and heart killing him instantly and pitching him forward over the woman. By the time the Carthaginians were all in position a further three of the raiders were dead in the snow with arrows sprouting from their bodies.

One raider swaggered from a hut drinking from a wineskin and pulling his trousers back into place, seeing his comrade's bodies he dropped the wineskin grabbing for his sword. Before he could draw it, an arrow smashed into his breastbone bursting his mail shirt apart knocking him backwards into the hut. Armaco didn't wait for the alarm to be raised. Whistling loudly he kicked his horse forward as Baldor and his men erupted from the trees opposite. With a dull rumble of hooves the Carthaginians swept into the settlement. Shouts and curses were already coming from the hut where the dead man had fallen. Hearing cries of alarm and the noise of arriving horses, warriors emptied from the huts fumbling at their trousers whilst trying to draw weapons, most were killed before they knew what was happening. One or two threw down their swords in surrender, they died where they stood either ridden down or feathered by Malo's arrows. Two mercenaries secured the Roman before he could escape, he dropped the wineskin raising his arms slowly, showing open, empty hands in surrender.

The burning hut crackled and roared as the flames claimed it. The thatched roof collapsed sending a shower of sparks and black debris spiralling skyward floating on the belch of smoke. As an eerie calm descended, the Carthaginians reined up looking around for any remaining raiders.

"Baldor! You and your men, two groups of two! Search the buildings."

The warriors dismounted quickly, hanging shields on the horse's trappings and sticking their spears in the snow. Drawing falcatas and daggers, they disappeared into the darkness of the huts.

Armaco signalled the remaining men to dismount. "Marko, with me! Malo with Baraan. We kill anyone that comes out armed."

Soon, more shouts and curses came from within the huts followed by the clang and rasp of metal and the crash of breaking furniture. Baldor and another warrior emerged from the first hut their swords reddened and helping two stumbling, sobbing women whom they'd wrapped in blankets. The two other warriors slipped into the second hut where there were more screams and sounds of a scuffle. A wounded Gaul exited the doorway at the run. Seeing the bodies of his comrades and the waiting mercenaries, he recognised his plight and dropped his sword raising his arms shouting for quarter. Armaco hurled his heavy fighting spear, hitting him in the stomach driving the wind from him and bending him double. He staggered under the impact then dropped to his knees. Gasping for breath, he groaned horribly, his face a twisted mask of agony and shock. His hands grasped the spear shaft trying to pull it free, he howled as the embedded blade tugged at his intestines. Remaining on his knees he pitched forwards as far as the shaft would allow, holding his agony and spitting blood.

Baldor and his partner made for the next hut. As Baldor slipped through the door, the warrior following him paused raising his falcata to dispatch the speared Gaul.

"Let the bastard bleed! Get on with the search!" Armaco called gruffly.

"Yes sir!"

The warrior left the wounded man and followed Baldor into the hut. He had to back out as Baldor stepped into the daylight carrying a bundle of blankets containing a frail and gaunt looking old man. He laid him down gently, propping him upright with his back against a tree. The man coughed, spraying the blanket with frothy blood and spittle, he gasped for breath while mouthing words to Baldor his hand gripping the young man for support.

The warriors escorted the weeping women and a limping man to stand with the others. The women holding their tattered clothing to their bodies and in various stages of distress from shaking and weeping to stony, bitter silence. Whilst the mercenaries brought cloaks and blankets to cover them and bandages to treat the injured man Armaco counted his warriors.

"Baraan!" He shouted taking a step forward, looking from the huts to the bodies in the snow. "Baraan!" The call echoed through the trees, the mercenaries looked up from their ministrations as Armaco paced towards the huts. Hearing a noise from the furthest, he doubled his speed while drawing his falcata and disappeared inside, Marko following quickly after him.

A loud thumping and crack of splintering wood saw the wattle panel wall that was one side of the hut burst outwards, spraying pieces of dried mud and wattle screen into the snow. From out of the hole and cloud of swirling dust, a giant warrior stepped, wiping at his eyes and brandishing a huge Gallic broadsword in front of him ready to fight. Armaco moved towards the destroyed wall having to step over a dying Baraan on the way. Baraan was sitting up, leaning heavily against the hut wall; he nodded slowly as Armaco stepped over him. He held his hands over his groin as dark, plum coloured blood oozed through his fingers pooling on the floor between his legs, Armaco motioned Marko to stay and help him.

"I'll get the bastard, don't worry!" He said quietly and winked at Baraan.

Hearing a quiet gurgling noise like soup coming to the boil Armaco looked to his left. On a wooden pallet bed a woman laid, her naked body twitching spasmodically, the blood from her slashed throat still pumping onto her breasts. Looking through the smashed wall, he saw the huge warrior out in the sunlight and with a low growl stepped through the missing wall section after him.

"Over here!" He called stepping clear of the wall debris.

 The huge Gaul however was looking to his front watching Baldor and the other mercenaries as they tended the injured, his sword pointing forward his legs braced apart setting his balance.

"Over here, you murdering bastard!" Armaco shouted louder.

The Gaul turned his massive head towards Armaco. Looking him up and down and snorting disdainfully, he gave a mocking laugh beckoning him eagerly onwards with his hand.

Armaco faltered momentarily when the enormity of the man became apparent. He was head and shoulders in height above Armaco and built like a draught ox. His hair washed white with lime and tufted into long, drooping spikes that reared a palms-width in height above his head like porcupine quills. Excepting for a broad white, drooping moustache his face was scraped clean of bristles showing milky-white skin like that of a week old corpse, his pupils a demonic, pink-red. His mail shirt fitted tightly over a huge, barrel chest with leather trousers covering his tree trunk, thick legs.

Armaco felt an involuntary shiver as he took in the unearthly appearance. Mumbling a prayer he flexed his sword arm, rotating the falcata fluidly in his wrist while slipping his dagger from his belt, then crouching a little he stalked the giant.

The mercenaries paused as they also took in the giant's manifestation. Everything seemed to stop, no one spoke and other than the rush of the river and the roaring flames from the burning hut silence reined. Armaco, seeing the awe and tinges of fear on his men's faces stepped forward bravely.

"You … freak!" He called pointing to the giant with his falcata. "Spawn from Hades! Come and fight a warrior instead of women and old men … if you dare?"

The giant gave a cavernous, hollow laugh and spat contemptuously then struck like a lightning bolt, swinging the double-edged broadsword in a wide whistling arc at Armaco's head. The cut bore little skill or finesse but compensated with lightning speed, more than one mercenary grimaced expecting to see Armaco decapitated. Armaco felt and heard the rush of air from the swing as he dropped low beneath it. He too had moved as the giant attacked, going forward then feinting to one side of the Gaul. Rotating his body like a child's spinning top he swerved around him. His falcata sliced back and low to hit one of the thick legs behind the knee chopping ligaments, tendons and hamstring into bloody ruin. The giant took a step further before the leg buckled beneath him.

"Not so easy fighting a warrior is it … freak!"

The giant roared like a wounded bull as he tried to stand on the useless leg. Falling back heavily onto one knee, he forced himself around to face Armaco while pointing his sword at arm's length to keep the mercenary away.

"Back!" Armaco barked, gesturing the mercenaries away who had drawn their own weapons and edged forward as the fight started. "No! He's mine!" He called to Malo, seeing the Nubian had another arrow on the string and raising his bow to aim. "See to the people, this carrion will be back in Hades shortly."

The giant watched Armaco as he edged closer changing his footing as he came, trying to wrong-guess him when he attacked. Watching and waiting for the Carthaginian to rush him, he saw the calm confidence combined with the cold stare of a professional killer and read his doom on the Carthaginians face.

Armaco sprung forward but this time drawn up to full height pressing his advantage of mobility, for despite being on one knee the Gaul was still taller than he and appeared to have plenty of fight left in him. Blades clanged and scraped, the metal ringing like iron worked on an anvil as the giant fought desperately to keep the mercenary away. As the swords parried high, Armaco kicked hard catching the Gaul in the lower stomach. The air left his lungs like punctured bellows and he folded forward from the waist just as Armaco stabbed upwards with his dagger seeking the giant's throat. Armaco's aim was off and the blade struck the giants shoulder instead. The dagger went deep as the man's weight and downward force pushed it through his mail shirt, the blade jamming between his clavicle and first rib. Armaco stepped back quickly out of sword reach. He watched the giants heaving chest as he sucked in precious breath and pulled at the bloodied blade with his free hand. The Gaul raised his head once more still pointing his sword blade forward; Armaco saw the look of agony and noted the slight tremor in his arm.

"Hurts eh? ... Good!"

The giant muttered something Armaco didn't understand though the look of fierce hatred conveyed the message. The mercenary launched forward again, swinging his falcata in a circle and catching his adversary's blade on the underside hooking it from his grasp sending it spinning away. The giant roared again and powered upwards on his good leg, his arms outstretched. His paw sized hands and long fingers hooked into claws, seeking Armaco's face and throat. Armaco was surprised at the speed of the attack but stabbed savagely upwards with his falcata. He felt the point burst through mail ripping stomach muscles, pushing into soft flesh and guts beneath. The giant shuddered as the sword went deep but fuelled by adrenalin and hate he continued scrabbling for Armaco's face and throat. His talon like fingers missed Armaco's good eye and face but ripped down his neck gouging skin into bloody furrows. They hooked into the neck cloth giving a good purchase and he twisted the cloth around them tightening it, dragging Armaco towards him. With Armaco off balance, the giant locked his hands around his neck pushing his thumbs savagely into the thorax. Armaco resisted the urge to wrestle the giant's hands away. Instead, he clamped both hands firmly around the falcata hilt, twisting and working it viciously in the man's guts, forcing the blade deeper.

With their faces close, Armaco could smell the giant's fetid breath as he looked desperately for signs of life fading from the demon-like eyes. The huge thumbs however continued to push inward and Armaco felt his throat collapsing and senses going awry. His vision flickered, going from spasmodic yellow flashes to blackened shades and shadows as his air supply cut off. Franticly redoubling his efforts he worked and sawed the blade in frenzy as he felt his throat about to burst under the huge strength. Suddenly, he felt an easing of the pressure on his throat as death crept into the giant's body. Drawing rasping, laboured breaths while redoubling his efforts with the blade he finally felt the pressure come off. He struggled free but lost his grip on the blood-slimed hilt as the giant fell forward on both knees a low growl coming from his throat, his hands trying to prevent his guts spilling out. Armaco saw the Gallic broadsword laid in the snow and staggered towards it. Snatching it up then swinging it high above his head, he stepped in closer driving it down with terrific force against the back of the man's neck.

A dull crack, like that of a breaking bough followed. A second blow cleaved through muscle and tissue and saw the white head roll into the snow. Blood fountained in crimson arcs from the severed neck as the huge body rolled to one side. Dropping the broadsword Armaco lurched drunkenly gasping for breath. He sucked air in huge noisy gulps while coughing dryly as he massaged his bloodied throat. His face splashed in ruby droplets and his hands red to the wrists while his corselet and tunic were wet and stained dark with the giant's blood.

The mercenaries looked on, dumbstruck.

"Baal almighty! … Are you alright sir?" Marko asked as he rushed to aid Armaco.

"Fi… ne!" Armaco croaked dryly while supporting himself by bending and resting his hands on his knees. "What … what of Baraan?"

"Dead sir!"

Armaco nodded grimly. "Tie him on his horse … we'll take him home with us." He paused to massage his throat as his voice faded. "See to these folk and then we're gone … we've that village to find yet."

"Yes sir." Marko turned shouting orders to the men.

"Marko!" Armaco rasped.

"Sir?" Marko turned again.

"Bring that Roman pig over here, I want a word! And fetch … fetch Baldor … he'll be able to interpret one way or another."

Marko whistled to the men holding the prisoner signalling them forward. Armaco pushed his foot onto the giant's chest and worked at the blade still lodged deeply in the tripe bowl that was the man's belly. He wrenched it free with a loud sucking noise just as Baldor arrived in front of him.

"Do you speak Latin?" He asked aggressively as he wiped the blade on the giant's trousers.

"Not enough to …"

"Try Gallic then!" Armaco snapped cutting him short, his voice rasping like water over a shingle beach. "He must be able to speak it to have been with this lot."

As the Roman was marched towards Armaco, some of the women recoiled and screamed as he passed near. One ran to attack him, her face twisted in hatred, a feline growl in her throat. Lashing out wildly with fists and feet, she rained blows on the cowering Roman, having to be pulled away and restrained by one of the mercenaries. Armaco waved the warriors and prisoner away.

"Keep the bastard out of the way for now …" He paused for breath. "Or we'll be here all day trying to get some sense."

The Roman shook his guard's arm loose and pushed towards Armaco beginning to speak. The mercenary escorting him twisted his hand into the man's cloak pulling him backwards sharply, cutting off his protests while kicking him in the back of the knee so he fell. He was dragged by the neck cloth, choking and coughing out of reach of the women.

"Are you alright Armaco?" Baldor asked stepping up as the Roman was hauled away, his voice full of genuine concern.

"I'll live." Armaco replied sourly. Waiting until Baldor was close he looked around ensuring the others were out of earshot. His face darkened as he pointed a bloodied finger accusingly at Baldor's face, his lips twisting into a canine snarl.

"If you ever disregard me or disobey my orders again in front of the men …" He paused for breath. "So help me, I'll kill you where you stand …"

Baldor stepped back at the venom in Armaco's tone, tried to speak but was shouted down.

"Do you understand?" His face screwed in anger the words hissed through gritted teeth.

"Yes … yes sir, I understand." Baldor replied quietly dropping his eyes from Armaco's baleful stare. "I'm sorry."

"No more Baldor! … Friend or not, I'll tell you no more! … You hear me?" Armaco banged his bloodied fist hard on Baldor's shoulder strap emphasising his point, his tone however somewhat moderated as the ready apology soothed the anger. "You're an officer now … whether you like it or not." He added quickly as Baldor looked up about to object. "The men will look to you for direction and leadership! Remember, there are more lives than just yours to consider … mind it!"

Baldor nodded slowly, his head hung shamefully again.

"Right, let's see to these people … find out what prompted this attack and ask where their folk are?"

Armaco steered Baldor towards the villagers huddled together under the trees. Baldor squatted alongside one of the younger women who recoiled fearfully from him. He removed his helmet making his appearance less threatening, slowly raising empty hands showing peaceful intent and spoke quietly in Gallic. "Do you know why these men attacked you? … We need to know where your people are. We're looking for a village hereabouts we surmise it must be yours? … Please."

The woman still turned away from him. Her dark hair in disarray, her bruised face buried in another woman's chest as she sobbed and shook. The woman slowly stroked her hair and rocked her gently whispering softly, reassuringly to her. She looked up at Baldor through eyes burned bright with anger, her own face swollen and bruised where she'd received a heavy blow, her lips split and bloodied. She answered in the weeping woman's stead.

"I don't know who they are …" Her voice was unsteady and shaky as she began, though hate forced the words out. "Other than Gauls with a Roman master." She swallowed hard trying to compose herself. "They rode in killing all they could catch. Our men tried to fight but they weren't warriors … they, they slew them and the children, us they … they …"

"It's alright! … It's alright now; no one will hurt you anymore." Baldor cut in quickly but gently as the woman succumbed to the stress. Her eyes flooded with tears as she turned her gaze away and back to comforting the still sobbing woman. Baldor looked at Armaco shaking his head slowly; Armaco chewed his lip glancing around the pitiful group.

"Try the old man, see if he knows anything?"

The man was the one Baldor had carried from the hut. Baldor knew he was dying from the stab wound to his belly. His head lay to one side, his eyes closed, blood and spittle ran from his mouth staining his white beard and blanket red. Baldor thought him dead until he saw the eyelids flicker. Kneeling to one side, he helped him to a more comfortable position gesturing to Armaco for water.

"Here … drink, drink!" He whispered as he placed the water skin to the man's mouth. "Its only water but it'll help." Baldor had heard of the terrible thirst that accompanied stomach wounds, the old man stirred as the cold liquid moistened his lips and sluiced his mouth.

"Where's your village? Can you tell us?"

The man coughed, spraying water and more blood. "Let me see the sun lad, if you will? … The sun."

Baldor eased him around towards the sun, the man groaning as he moved, the light reflecting off the snow causing his eyes to blink and close. Baldor placed his hand over the man's eyes as a sunshade.

"Try now."

The eyes flicked open and adjusted to the light, staying open as he looked around. He coughed again and brought up more blood.

"It's, it's a beautiful day …" He whispered then sat up involuntarily as he convulsed, the agony forcing a groan and more thick blood from his mouth.

"Let me have a look, we can help." Baldor said trying to ease the blanket away.

The old man panted to ease the pain and managed a faint smile whilst easing the blanket back into place.

"It's alright lad … it's, it's my time is all …"

As the old man's words echoed those of Gestix as he died on the field of Ticinus, Baldor felt his anger rise. Despite the bitter cold, his body flushed hotly, his throat tightening to an aching lump. The old man wrapped a cold, clammy hand over Baldor's forearm, gripping tightly as the pain seized him again.

"Epona, ble … ss you la …" He sighed deeply as his grip slackened and the hand fell away.

Baldor felt the anger in the pit of his stomach knotting his guts. Running his fingers over the man's eyes to close them, he covered his face with the blanket. Rising quickly he looked at the terrified and weeping women, the bodies of the children and the blood spattered snow then strode across the clearing towards the Roman. His wide steps almost a run as he closed on the man, he gestured the two mercenaries aside with a flick of his head then gripped the man by the throat dragging him towards Armaco. The man struggled and slapped at Baldor's hand shouting in protest but all that came out was strangled gasps and broken words. Baldor punched him hard in the mouth knocking him to his knees.

"You murdering bastard!" He shouted in Gallic as he landed a vicious kick into the man's stomach pitching him side-wards. The man groaned as the wind was driven from him. He tried to stand but Baldor kicked him twice more in the chest breaking some ribs. Seizing him by his neck cloth, he pulled him to his knees again while slipping a falcata point against the man's neck.

"Who are you? Who were the scum with you and why did you slaughter these people?" He leant down to the man's ear. "I know you understand me! … I'll count to three and if you don't tell me, you die here! One!" … He pushed the keen blade into the skin drawing blood. "Two!"

The heavy blade was already cutting deeper, the man wild-eyed and forcing his neck back from the honed edge, straining against Baldor's grip. Seeing Baldor's face twitch and his eyes look away, he realised death would follow in a heartbeat.

"Lucius Machus!" He shouted desperately in laboured gasps. "My name is … Lucius Julius Machus … of Rome." He tensed, still expecting Baldor to drive the blade through his throat.

"Keep talking!" Baldor maintained the pressure on the falcata as blood ran along the blade then dripped off.

"The … the main village …" The man fought for breath. "Is … is to the south … we came from there."

Baldor kept the pressure on the blade, the deadly message letting the Roman know more information was required.

"We were seeking recruits from the tribe … they … refused …ohhh." He groaned as Baldor renewed his grip and pulled him closer.

"So you chose to murder these people in retaliation?" Baldor's face was taught in anger, his words forced out, and his voice low giving added menace.

"It was Magalus's idea, he …" Lucius saw the blank look on Baldor's face. "Magalus, the white haired giant your officer slew!" He clarified.

"Let him loose Baldor, he can talk easier." Armaco said pushing Baldor's sword from the Roman's throat and pulling the man to his feet. "Make it quick Roman; his temper's as sharp as the blade."

Lucius looked quizzically at Armaco not understanding while struggling with his balance as Baldor released him.

"Why the slaughter?" Baldor continued in Gallic.

"They refused to …"

"You said that! Why the slaughter?" Baldor looked away as he spoke, idly spinning the falcata in his hand.

"Magalus said to make an example of these … people." He laboured with the last word as if 'people' was the wrong word and the Gauls less than human. "Terror teaches people to obey."

Baldor whipped around quickly raising the falcata to strike. Lucius cowered, raising his hands to ward off the blow. Armaco's arm shot out like lightning, gripping Baldor's wrist stopping him from any destruction.

"Leave it Baldor! Let him finish."

Sensing Armaco's authority Lucius changed tack moving from submissive to assertive.

"I'm a Roman citizen not a soldier! I've nothing to do with the military; I work as an interpreter! You must hand me over to the Roman authorities now! … Without further harm!" The Roman groaned loudly as the exertion pulled at his ribs.

"You're here working for the military attempting to coerce others into this war." Baldor argued.

"What makes you so different?" Lucius countered quickly. "You're invading our country inciting scum like these into rebellion against us."

"We're different because we don't slaughter women, children and old men … and they're not scum!"

Lucius shrugged as if it was insignificant.

"You must hand me over to the Roman authorities, I'm a civilian!" He shouted desperately.

"So were these people!" Baldor's voice was also a shout as his temper flared then snapped. He drove the Falcata into the man's belly and twisted it viciously. Lucius groaned deeply, his eyes rolled in shock as he staggered under the force of the thrust pulling the sword from Baldor's hand. He fell to his knees holding the blade and looking up at Baldor in disbelief.

"I … I … was unarmed."

"So were these people!" Baldor snarled as he reached for his second falcata. Drawing it smoothly he backhanded the weapon in a quick, fluid curve, slicing hard under the Roman's chin. The heavy blade chopped through flesh snapping the spine cleanly sending the head, still encased in the helmet rolling into the snow, the body remaining upright on its knees. Baldor delivered a heavy flat-footed kick, knocking the body onto its back where he stood on it to lever his first blade free. Retrieving the sword, he looked up to find everyone watching him. Again, other than the crackle of the burning hut and the sounds of the river, the settlement was deathly quiet, the women had ceased their weeping and his comrades looked on dumbstruck.

Armaco broke the silence. "I guess we continue southeast!" He said quietly before raising his voice to his men. "Bring the folk with us; we can leave them at the village." He turned to find Baldor picking the Roman's head up. "What in Hades name are you …?"

His question fell short as a commotion started again as the mercenaries herded the women towards the horses, they pointed back to their dead babbling hysterically and crying.

"Baldor! Tell them we'll send someone from the village to collect the bodies, we haven't … What the? …"

Baldor had found a sack and was pushing the Roman's head in it. "I have a message to deliver sir! … I heard you, I'll tell them."

Soon the mercenaries were ready to move out with the women somewhat calmed from Baldor's words and mounted now on the raider's horses to the columns rear. The more distressed among them choosing to ride two up, hugging their sisters back. Baldor led his horse to the front of the column where he removed his helmet cradling it under his arm. He bowed his head before looking directly at Armaco clearing his throat. He spoke loud and clear ensuring all the mercenaries could hear.

"Sir! Sir, a moment if you please? I'm sorry I disobeyed you! It was wrong what I did. My actions could have caused all our deaths. Baraan's death is on my hands and conscience. I will answer to the Captain for it when we return and to the Gods hereafter. I beg your pardon sir."

He bowed his head again saluting as he did so, his sincerity leaving no doubt as to his remorse. Armaco, mollified by the impromptu declaration and feeling somewhat vindicated in front of the men remembered why he liked Baldor. He resisted a smile as thoughts ran through his head of foolish boys with notions of honour in a world where it didn't exist. He sufficed with a curt nod of his head and a gruff …

"Let's go!" He waved his hand forward.

The column had not cleared the settlement when the rumble of hooves echoed through the trees.

"Form up on me!" Armaco shouted pushing an arm into his shield straps and hefting his spear. "Baldor! Shepherd the women in behind."

"Sir!" Baldor dragged the bit hard pulling his mounts head around turning it. Digging heels in its flanks, he rode it hard to the rear ushering the women in tightly behind the mercenaries.

More Gauls were spilling from the trees in front of the column blocking the trail while others materialised on the right flank.

"Steady lads!" Armaco's mount reared as it saw the other horses in front of it. "We go straight through them, keep tight!"

Drastically outnumbered, Armaco knew they were doomed. There was not enough ground for the horses to gain speed to force their way through and there was nowhere to run. Surrender however never crossed his mind as he eyed what looked like the Gallic leader and gauged the distance for his spear throw. Metal chinked and harness creaked, swords rasped from sheaths as the Gauls spread out blocking the path and preparing for combat.

Chapter Five

A heartbeat before battle joined one of the women from the rear of the Carthaginian column shouted frantically, trying to draw the attention of the leading warrior of the Gallic horse as she and Baldor rode up the side of the small column.

"Hold! … Hold sir!" Baldor bellowed above the drumming of the hooves as he reined in alongside Armaco. The woman continued on to the advancing Gauls holding her hand up in a halting motion.

"It's their folk sir! Their folk have come!" Baldor continued.

"Aye! Let's hope they listen then, they've seen the bodies, look!"

The Gauls on the flank could see the dead still littering the ground to the mercenary's rear and were pointing and shouting. Armaco saw the angry, vengeful looks on their faces and then the rider's legs flare outwards kicking the horses into action, weapon-laden arms beginning to rise, telling him the time for talk was over.

"Baal be merciful!" He muttered under his breath before shouting hoarsely. "Make ready lad's, they're coming! Baldor! Stay by me." He hefted his spear sighting the Gallic leader for a mark.

Baldor drew a falcata and pulled his shield across his chest as the first of the Gauls started forward. Suddenly a long, low drone flowed across the clearing; the brassy notes of a carnyx seemed to roll over the warriors into the frost-hardened trees. The Gauls, already just paces from the mercenaries tried to rein up forcing their mounts to a whickering, sliding halt but not before two horses collapsed dying with Carthaginian javelins in their chests tipping their riders into the snow.

"Hold lad's! Hold!" Armaco yelled above the din when he saw the Gallic leader also trying to pull his warriors back. His spear arm upright to halt his men, his words barely audible above the bellowing notes, the rumble of hooves and ring of metal.

On both sides horses stamped, reared and tossed their heads as the riders struggled to curb them, the odd curse and the clash of metal resounded as men collided.

"Ho …ld damn you!" Armaco bellowed again.

The two thrown warriors were on their feet and edging away from the Carthaginians, one limping as he dragged a twisted leg using his spear as a crutch. One horse lay still while the other thrashed and writhed kicking up snow and colouring it crimson. Relative calm descended as men brought their horses under control and both sides pulled back watching one another, the air charged. The woman talked quickly to the leading Gaul, pointing first to Baldor then to Armaco. The man nodded and walked his horse slowly forward, sheathing his sword as he came.

"With me Baldor! Let's see what he has to say. The rest of you stay ready!"

Armaco nodded forward and the pair edged their mounts toward the oncoming Gaul, stopping and meeting him halfway between the two forces. Reining up, both parties took a moment to study the other. The Gaul, like most of his race was tall and solidly built, he bore the same fierce, indomitable pride which emanated from his carriage and bearing. He wore a simple bronze helmet, the top crested with a chased image of a leaping boar. The rear of the helmet swept inwards, protecting and following the curve of his neck to his collar; huge scalloped cheek pieces covered his jaw and squashed his face. A thick, russet ponytail protruded from beneath the neck guard, falling down his back to below his shoulder blades. His facial features were large and coarse with pronounced reddened cheeks and a broad flat nose; a huge moustache framed his mouth and grew to the base of chin. Around his neck was a heavy torque fashioned of individual twists of bright gold. His short sleeved, knee length, mail shirt was slit from hem to waist allowing for easy riding and gathered at the waist with a broad leather belt to support its weight and carry his weapons. A second coating of mail lay shawl like over his shoulders, giving an added layer of protection and fastened closed with leather straps and burnished bronze buckles. Beneath the mail, a padded, black leather shirt patterned with bronze studs for additional protection and long sleeved against the cold. His woollen trousers were of a mustard and black chequered pattern, on his feet he wore doeskin boots to above his ankles bound in place with leather straps. Typical of his culture he carried a double-edged broadsword and round shield.

The horses were calming from the excitement but still blowing clouds of white vapour as they settled their breathing. Despite the bone-chilling cold the Gaul's horse gave off small wisps of steam from its coat, it blew heavier than the Carthaginian mounts, been ridden hard and fast. The river seemed loud as silence settled over the clearing once more, the tension taught as a bowstring. Men watched and waited, hands flexing around weapon hilts and tightening on shield straps, ready, should the order come to attack. The Gaul calmed his horse with a pat as a twitching nerve in its neck caused it to toss its head.

"I am Andulas, son of Gundulas son of Antulix of that ilk." His deep voice boomed across the clearing.

"Greetings Andulas, son of Gundulas!" Baldor replied, bowing his head respectfully. "Armaco Salamar and Baldor Targa of Carthage." He indicated Armaco then himself in turn.

"You speak our language well Baldor Ta...rga." The Gaul struggled with the unfamiliar name.

"I learned from a good man!" Baldor replied quietly.

"Fhina!" Andulas pointed back to the woman who'd spoken to him. "Fhina says that I've you and your warriors to thank for stopping the slaughter of our people, all would be dead now but for you." He paused as Baldor translated. Andulas looked directly at Armaco inclining his head in respect. "She also says that you slew the albino giant, Magalus of the Cenomani, as easily as if he were a child? He was known as a fearsome warrior among our people, he has slain many."

Baldor heard the awe in the man's voice then translated again. Armaco, tactless as ever grunted that he'd fought more fearsome and skilful drunks. Thankful of the language barrier, Baldor explained Armaco's words away as a mild boast.

"They came to our village seeking support for the Roman cause and that one said …" Andulas indicated the headless remains of the interpreter. "That your people would slaughter us and burn our villages and that we should commit to Rome for protection. My father would have none of it, he remembers the Romans and their talk of protection from times past and we sent them away. They departed easily enough, too easy when I think on it." He shook his head slowly as though in regrettable hindsight. "I thank you … thank you for what you've done." He bowed his head to Baldor and then Armaco.

Seeing their leaders conversing quietly the tension eased on both sides and men lowered weapons and relaxed a little, each side however watching the other. Andulas barked orders and some of the warriors sheathed their weapons and dismounted beginning the grisly task of sorting the dead. The raider's bodies were stripped of weapons, mail, helmets and anything of value, then thrown unceremoniously into a sprawling heap of limbs and severed heads. A Gaul picked up a long shafted felling axe from a nearby woodpile trying its weight. Pointing to a nearby tree stump, he took his stance next to it; resting the axe against his leg he spat on his hands then gripped the shaft anew. The bodies that retained their heads were thrown over the stump one at a time, their heads lolling over the edge like fish on the fishmonger's slab, the axeman removing them with huge swings. The thwack of metal cleaving flesh and the dry snapping noise of severed spines carried across the clearing, the bodies hurled into the still burning hut. It took four men to heave the giant's carcase into the fire while others added extra timber from the woodpile ensuring a good blaze. Another warrior collected the heads wrapping them in a cloak; he paused to spit on the albinos head then knotted the cloak closed. He shouted to Andulas, indicating the heads and raising his fingers as if tallying, he pointed to the burning bodies and raised his fingers again shaking his head.

Andulas turned to Baldor, "We'll deliver the heads back to the Cenomani as a warning but he says he's counted one more body than a head?"

Baldor hefted the bloodstained sack from his horses back. "I too have a delivery to make … back to the Romans."

Armaco, picking up the gist of the conversation rolled his eyes while muttering beneath his breath. "Baal's teeth, Gestix! What have you created?"

Andulas smiled grimly at Baldor. "This was our fishery, our village lies further in the hills." He indicated south-eastwards. "Our home and hospitality are open to you and your men."

Baldor interpreted for Armaco who looked to the sky while calculating time and distance.

"Thank him but we best get back while the light holds, we've tarried overlong already and the Captain will be chafing, wondering where we are. Tell him we'll return to see him though, as we need to speak to him and his people about fighting for us."

"Sir, begging your pardon but I wouldn't want to offend his sensitivities with a refusal!"

Armaco huffed and muttered to himself as he looked back along his small column using the time to think. "Alright, take Malo and go with them, I'll take the lads back to camp, be there tomorrow morning."

"Yes sir. Malo! On me." Baldor raised his hand and the Nubian cut out of the column and trotted forwards.

"See what you can manage in the way of recruitment eh?" Armaco said wearily. "Try and salvage something from the day, right now we've nothing to show for our efforts other than chilled bones, blood and poor Baraan."

Baldor's head fell as he remembered Baraan. "Yes sir! I'll do my best."

"See that you do!" Armaco nodded to Andulas then swung his horse to one side, waving his arm down and forward calling his men to follow on. Baldor explaining to Andulas as the mercenaries trotted off retracing their steps.

Andulas's warriors reverently collected their dead, bodies and head's reunited and wrapped carefully in blankets then laid on the floor of a wagon hitched to a spare horse. The children's corpses were gently gathered up as if they were but sleeping and deposited alongside the adults. Baldor grimaced as the little forms were loaded; he bit his lip hard when a small white arm tumbled from the blanket and flopped loosely in the air. He growled low in his throat and felt the terrible anger rising again, the desire to kill those who'd murdered came once more.

"There'll be a reckoning, all will be settled." Andulas said matter of factly and interrupting Baldor's thoughts. When Baldor looked up, he found him staring blankly as the bodies were loaded.

"Yes, all will be settled." He repeated.

****

Andulas questioned Baldor along the trail back to the village; his manner though inquisitive, remained open and friendly as he offered a wine skin to both Malo and Baldor, the three sharing it as they rode.

"So, what brings you far from your camp and into the hills in weather like this? Methinks it was not chance that brought you up from the plain." Andulas asked politely but bluntly as if already knowing the answer.

"We're seeking recruits from the local tribes and were told your village lay up here." Baldor replied just as politely and bluntly.

Andulas smiled, his suspicions confirmed. "Is the whole world to be set on fire then? You have many thousands of men already, as do the Romans, how many more will you need?"

He asked of Carthage and of Hannibal of whom he'd heard much of late and what brought an army through the mountains in the dead of winter. He was fascinated that a nation from across a sea could be so bent on war with another when their lands did not even join to cause dispute. Why fight? He asked. If no blood feud existed and the need was not one for slaves or riches … was the world not large enough?

Baldor chose his words carefully as he knew the Roman yoke was heavy on these people at times and didn't wish to imply that Carthage could perhaps replace Rome as masters or overlords should she conquer Italy. Answering the best he knew, he spoke of past offences by Rome with her expansionist policies in Sicily and Spain and which had started the first war. Andulas struggled to grasp the concept that City-States warred over land removed from them and over which they had no rights other than that of conquest, the mountain warrior through no fault of his own seeing everything in local scale. Baldor knew enough from Gestix however not to disregard these people as stupid, uncultured barbarians. Simplicity and childlike innocence was their trait as was shrewdness and intelligence. When they asked blunt, direct questions, they expected the same by way of an answer. Thus when Andulas asked what Hannibal would do if he defeated Rome, he answered truthfully that he didn't know.

"Is this Hannibal, your Chief, that you must do his bidding without question then?" Andulas asked.

"No, I'm here of my own free will, it was … it was what I wanted." The last words stumbled out with a bitter twist as he remembered it had been his decision and one that had affected Gestix's life and later his death.

"You fight then because you enjoy it? You should have been born a Gaul!" Andulas smiled then looked serious again as he saw Baldor's head drop. "Baldor, I mean no insult."

Baldor's face betrayed the sadness the words had awoken. In truth, the memories of Gestix had already been stirring in his heart and mind from the murder at the village, the garb of the Gauls, their simple acceptance of life and death and finally the intelligent reasoning of Andulas, all brought back the ghost of Gestix in varying degrees. Baldor found himself telling Andulas of Gestix, and his death and how he now had a personal blood feud with Rome.

"You will wage war on a whole nation to avenge your friend?" Andulas nodded approvingly seemingly genuinely impressed.

"A whole nation and one man!" Baldor replied bitterly.

"How will you find one amongst so many? These Romans are more numerous than ears of corn at a good summer's harvest."

"The man I seek is one of their leaders or Consul as they call him, I nearly slew him at the Ticinus … but for his son I would have done."

Andulas heard the hatred rattle in Baldor's throat as if the words would choke him and saw the distant, vacant look in his eyes as his mind conjured up pictures of revenge. Intrigued, Andulas was tempted to ask further but sensing the raw nerve he'd touched and seeing Baldor's descent into a silent, private world changed the subject.

"You learned our language from your friend, Gestix?" He asked genially.

"Yes … yes, he taught me that and many other things." Baldor answered snapping out of the dark world he'd momentarily lost himself in. "Gestix … Gestix was my father's greatest friend and … the brother I never had. He returned to Carthage with my father and lived with us after the last war with Rome ended. He was there when I was born and helped raise me, he is … he was, my family." Baldor corrected himself.

Andulas nodded. "Ah, family, I understand better now!" Seeing Baldor still trying to hide his grief and upset, he changed tack entirely. "What of Malo then?" He inclined his head respectfully as the Nubian looked up at the mention of his name. "What country does Malo come from? Does he hate the Romans as you do? … You are different in skin." He rubbed at his face to emphasise his words. "And from different tribes yet you fight together, how is this?"

Malo smiled as he saw Andulas rub his skin but typically made no attempt to ask Baldor to interpret. When Baldor asked if he wished to know what was said or reply, he consented for him to continue with a gentle wave of his hand. Baldor was left to explain as best he could about Nubia and where it was in the world. Respecting Malo's like of privacy he passed off his reasons for fighting also as that of revenge.

"I cannot comprehend such vastness, is the world really so large?" Andulas answered, somewhat in awe. Baldor suppressed a smile when he saw him look to the sky knowing he was considering the same question Gestix always had, 'what holds the sky up?'

"I've never left my hills and mountains here and though you come from a world away we have the same enemy in Rome. These Romans are powerful people to make war upon!"

"Yes, but not undefeatable as we proved at the Ticinus." Baldor answered quickly.

As they exited the shelter of the forest, they saw the village sitting further up the hill and still some five stades away. Snow covered the ground, roofs and road in a blanket of white blending the scene into an indistinguishable winter landscape. The ground surrounding the village was cleared of bushes and shrubbery and the larger trees felled. Only squat stumps, tangled briar and clumpy weeds remained, denying any cover for attackers and giving unrestricted views for the sentries on the encompassing wall. The village was large considering its position so remote and high in the hills, even at this distance the great hall or longhouse of the Chief was visible by its size and prominence upon a raised knoll above the rest of the buildings. Built of the same grey stone as the smoke house it differed by its larger size, small shuttered windows and a thatched roof of darkened straw. It was surrounded by circular wooden huts all encompassed by a timber palisade standing three spear lengths in height and fashioned of delimbed tree trunks. These being dug into the ground and lashed together with hide strips, their tops sharpened to points. The village had expanded over time and some huts now sat outwith the protective walls nestled alongside the vegetable gardens.

Innumerable columns of thick smoke eased through the thatch rising vertically into a windless sky adding to the drab grey clouds. With the exception of the patrolling guards on the walls, there was no sign of life, the harsh weather keeping animals and birds undercover and folk indoors by their hearths.

Snow began to fall heavily and Andulas called to Baldor and Malo.

"Come … come, let us out of this weather to the warmth of the fire, I've wearied you enough with questions."

He urged his horse to a trot calling the column on as they headed across the last few stades to the village.

****

Baldor and Malo were quartered in the Chiefs longhouse in a room off to one side of the feasting hall. It was a family room going by the number and varying sizes of beds and a family of substance judging by the quality of the furnishings. The floor was covered in clean, dried rushes over which orange-red deerskins were scattered, the beds covered in brightly coloured, woollen blankets topped with a mixture of black and brown bearskins. The windows shuttered against the weather and covered by heavy, yet decorative tapestries to keep draughts at bay. Wicker settles were draped in throws of plaid and colourful checks, small wooden tables were placed around the room with bowls and plates of bronze upon them, some inlaid with swirling patterns of amber. Nearest the wall on a table of honey coloured pine was an elaborate wine flagon of silver, circular and narrow based it rose to a swelling shoulder only to narrow again forming a neck with a flip top lid. An angled spout, finished in a chased, dragon scale pattern formed a mythical creature's neck with horned head and rubies for its eyes, its snarling, open mouth being the vessels pourer. The vessels handle, fastened at the shoulder and neck formed the shape of an animal this time a leaping wild boar.

Nearby, a silver tray held pieces of jewellery, torques and bracelets of gold and necklaces of amber.

Malo was most interested in the bearskins, he ran his fingers over them in wonderment then sniffed them before lifting them to assess the size the animal had been. Baldor was mesmerised at the craftsmanship in the jewellery, though he'd seen torques before they'd been designed for men and thus heavy in form. The ones before him were delicate and intricately detailed, these and the amber necklaces obviously the property of a woman.

"I think Andulas has given us his family rooms and it would seem we're to be trusted." Baldor gestured to the jewellery while slipping off his helmet and weapons belts. "I think we can dispense with these for now."

Malo nodded and disarmed himself, habitually however both men laid the weapons in easy reach. A knock on the door was followed by two women, the first bearing a tray with cups of steaming, mulled wine and a plate of cold meats and hot bread. The cinnamon and cloves in the wine scented the air and the aroma of the bread set the men's stomach's rumbling, neither having eaten since dawn. The second woman struggled with a bundle of furs; placing her weighty load on one of the beds, she picked up the topmost garment and with an effort that almost unbalanced her gave it a flourishing shake. A black bearskin cloak unfolded which she laid across a chair. She began undoing the lacing of Baldor's corselet shoulder straps, taken aback by her forwardness he tried to manage himself, gently pushing his hands away she continued. Undoing the side lacing, she gestured him to take it off; as he slipped it over his head, she hefted the bearskin onto his shoulders. Feeling the weight of the skin, he ran his fingers over it admiring the softness, next she produced a brooch of chased gold with green enamel inlay, the two elements twisting and scrolling together forming a beautiful pattern. Pulling the cloak together at Baldor's shoulder, she threaded the brooch pin through them tying the garment together. She did likewise for Malo; he smiled as he saw her discreetly but purposely wipe his skin then glance at her fingers to see if his colouring had come off. She bowed her head to both before directing her words at Baldor.

"The cloaks and brooches are a gift from the Lord Andulas, in gratitude for your bravery."

Baldor went to speak but politely shushing him, she carried on.

"They're yours to keep, my Lords."

Baldor tried to speak again but she bowed and disappeared as quickly as she'd arrived.

Despite the cloaks and the peace and beauty of the room, it was still bitterly cold. The pair electing to return to the main hall to warm themselves by the fire burning in the pit at the centre of the room. The hall was lit by the glow of the flames and pitch soaked torches positioned around the wall, their oily smoke creeping up the walls joining that from the fire before filtering through the thatch. The smell of wood smoke and rushes mixed with the tantalising scent of roasting meats and baking bread drifting through from the kitchens at the rear. Slaves and servants were busy setting up feasting tables, the head table set upon a raised timber dais with individual seats of varying size and elegance placed along its length. The tables at ground level were transverse to the main one and instead of chairs had benches placed parallel to them on both sides.

Baldor heard chanting outside and eased a shutter ajar to peer through. Although only early evening it was already dark outside with stars alight in a cloudless sky. The glow from torches and braziers in the courtyard showed people thronged around a dozen wooden pyres. Men in belted white robes, heads adorned in circlets of mistletoe moved between them pouring liquid from golden flagons over the kindling and timber which Baldor imagined to be oil. Others carried baskets and reached in to throw handfuls of dried leaves and flower petals over the bodies, scattering them liberally. As the chanting fell away men picked up torches and stepped up to the pyres setting flame amongst the structures. The elder of the robed men or priests, raised his hands throwing back his head to the heavens praying aloud, the crowd lowering their heads while he spoke. As the flames grew in intensity and began to roar he changed from spoken prayers to a melodic chant, every so often by way of a chorus the assembly joined in.

"They're burning their dead." Baldor said quietly while closing the shutter. Malo nodded; pulling his cloak tighter about him, he held his hands up for warmth in front of the fire.

"I'm ready for the summer Baldor, I can't keep warm. This cold seeps into my bones."

"We should be eating shortly and hopefully something hot this time; that'll put some warmth into you eh?" He grasped Malo's shoulder affectionately. "It smells good, to boot!" He said sniffing hard.

The singing reached a higher volume before coming to an abrupt halt. There was no more noise until the hall doors swung open and Andulas entered with an elegant woman at his side, his warriors, their wives and families following behind. Folk seated themselves quietly as if the arrangement was known and habitual. Andulas graciously ushered Malo and Baldor to the dais, seating them together and to his right, to their right he seated the woman. Baldor was about to speak to her when he saw her eyes were still full of tears and red rimmed from weeping, she maintained a proud vacant stare and looked at no one, holding his piece he decided to wait until he was spoken to. When all were seated and silence descended once more, a side door creaked open and a warrior dressed in full war gear stepped in. He spoke loudly in announcement and as the name, 'Gundulas' was uttered, seats and benches scraped back and people rose. A stately man swathed in a beaver cloak stepped into the room, the warrior continuing his diatribe as the man made a dignified progress towards the dais and the largest chair upon it. Baldor heard the name Antulix and realised the man's genealogy was being advised to all. Heads dropped respectfully as he passed the benches, the two warriors that pulled out his chair also bowing their heads as he was seated. The orating warrior continued his discourse and only when he'd finished and bowed his head did the rest of the hall sit.

Malo whispered into Baldor's ear. "Is he their King?"

"No, from what Gestix told me they don't have Kings. Chief of the tribe I'd say ... the nearest thing to a King hereabouts though."

As a low buzz of conversation began servants appeared bearing huge platters of steaming meat and oversize wicker baskets laden with bread, serving the raised table first then continuing along the others. Fish was brought, both fresh and smoked and hot or cold in choice, the fresh fish lavishly seasoned with herbs, nuts and oatmeal had been cooked by wrapping it parcel like in woven rushes that contained the flavour and stopped the flesh crumbling as it was served. The meats wafted appetising smells as they were placed on the table, Baldor recognised pork, lamb and chicken amongst the selection, his stomach rumbled and his mouth watered as the aromas assaulted his taste buds. More servants appeared carrying jugs of mulled wine and beer that they dispensed around the tables. No one touched the food, speaking in low whispers whilst casting furtive glances at the top table.

There was a scraping of wood as Gundulas pushed his chair back and stood, whispers ceased as all eyes looked attentively at their Chief.

Gundulas was tall but age was curving his back causing him to stoop. An old battle injury made his left shoulder sag a little, leaving his arm noticeably stiff and awkward in the position in which it hung. His hair was silver like a finely wrought blade and grew past his shoulders; it was tied back from his face in a thick ponytail.

"Good people! … My people …" His voice thundered as he looked around the room as he spoke. "We have suffered a grievous loss this day, a loss of our youngest and eldest folk, slain … nay murdered by the albino, Magalus of the Cenomani and his Roman masters." A growl like rolling thunder spread around the room, he held up his hand for quiet. "There will be … there must be, justice done and recompense sought for our dead!" A murmur of assertion grew loud around the hall again and he had to quieten them once more to be heard. "The families of the slain demand it! … Our warriors demand it!" His voice rose as the assembly grew more vocal. "My son demands it! … I demand it! … Our dead cry out and demand it!"

The Hall was now in uproar with warriors on their feet thrusting clenched fists in the air while others drew swords and pointing them skywards called for vengeance. Gundulas held up his hand for quiet but the noise continued and seemed to grow as if the previously controlled grief had finally erupted like lava from a volcano, his calls for quiet lost in the hubbub. Finally, drawing his dagger he hammered the pommel on the table repeatedly, the force sending crockery bouncing to smash on the floor spilling food and drink onto the rushes. People quietened as the noise pervaded their shouts. They quickly silenced their friends still caught up with the moment and soon a respectful silence claimed the room again. Gundulas laid the dagger down waiting for the power of silence to take affect; he began again but with his voice notably lowered.

"We have honoured our dead; we will now honour these two men." He gestured to Baldor and Malo. "For without their and their comrade's bravery and help to our folk, I'm told we would have more to mourn … tomorrow we plan our revenge."

He picked up his goblet raising it to Baldor and Malo, then looked around the hall ensuring his folk were doing likewise while gesturing them to their feet, when all had a drink in their hands he turned back to the two men.

"My thanks and my people's thanks, may Epona bless you."

There was a moments silence as goblets raised in salute then drained, Baldor and Malo bowing their heads in respect to their hosts. Gundulas seated himself and reached for the bread and meat, taking this as unspoken permission to eat the folk in the hall began their repast.

Chapter Six

Baldor and Malo followed the lead of the other diners and helped themselves to the food and drink. Both were ravenous and ate heartily washing the food down with mouthfuls of wine and dark, cloudy ale. Amidst the clatter of knives and platters, the low drone of conversation spread around the hall as folk discussed their Chief's words and their projected impact on their lives.

The half dozen hounds laid about the floor idly scratching and grooming themselves abandoned their previous apathy and now watched the diners with interest, hopeful of scraps being thrown down to them. The dogs varied as much in size as they did in breed with grey and black wolfhounds with long legs and sleek bodies covered in dense, curly matted coats. Greyhounds with bodies as lean as street beggars, their frames carrying not a trace of fat and their large rib cages curved upwards into a non-existent belly that tapered to flattened loins giving them the shape of large skinned rabbits. Predominately white in colour each bore patches of grey or brindle colouring on their coats or as a mask over their faces. Their whip like tail curled downwards between their legs; their heads like their bodies narrow and streamlined finishing in an elongated muzzle. Their sleekness spoke of breakneck speed and the long snouts of a ruthless, efficient killing ability.

In sharp contrast was a hound the size of a month old calf, its coat predominately black. Only huge tan coloured paws, legs, and traces of brown around its muzzle prevented it from being mistaken as some denizen from the underworld. Heavily muscled, it was thick of body and wide shouldered, its bull like neck supporting a head as broad as it was long. It yawned lazily; making a creaking sound as it stretched its maw wide. Shaking its head side to side, thick dollops of stringy saliva flew off its choler's towards the tables much to the disgust of the diners that it splattered. The dogs looked on expectantly, hoping for the first scraps of the night. Some wagged their tails slowly, watching with sad, soulful eyes, others just stared and panted. The smallest dog of the group, also smooth haired worked its way forward from the rear of the pack, slipping casually and easily through the larger dog's legs positioning itself at the front of the group where it sat studying the diners. The little dog watched intently for a moment before giving a low grumble in his throat which droned and rolled, not quite becoming a bark but nor did it drop to a begging whine, eventually he drew some interest from the folk at the tables nearest it. Their attention caught, he raised himself on hind legs into a begging position and gave a sharp singular bark. Gaining an audience it stood high on its hind legs barking again as it walked stilt like, parallel to the tables. Before long, a lump of meat was hurled and fast as a startled hare the little dog leapt, catching the morsel before disappearing under the tables and out the door. The larger animals seeing the departing meat and dog tried to follow, causing commotion as they pushed under the trestles, their larger size rocking and upsetting tables, platters and the diners who shouted and kicked the dogs away.

Baldor, watching intently nudged Malo.

"Did you see that?" He smiled and pointed with a chicken leg after the fleeing dog. "The little one worked for that."

Malo however was not listening; he'd been studying faces around the room and was exchanging smiles and a gentle bow of the head to two giggling young women at one of the lower tables.

Andulas leaned across, gnawing at a steaming pork rib as he spoke.

"Once we've eaten and heard the eulogy we can politely retire and I'll introduce you to my father and family but first eat and drink your fill, anything we have is yours for the asking."

Both men bowed their heads while muttering thanks through full mouths.

Baldor looked around as he ate, counting the heads on one table and multiplying the figure in his head by the number of tables, reckoning there was upwards of five hundred people dining. He noticed many faces were turned in his and Malo's direction, and he picked up nods, smiles and quickly pointed fingers, they were obviously the topic of much conversation. As the feast continued and the drink flowed the talk gained in volume. However, laughter and raucous behaviour, the usual partners to a feast didn't materialise, the underlying aura of grief and loss seemingly still holding all in check.

When the empty platters were cleared and the honey coated oatcakes, nuts and dried fruits served, an old man shuffled into the hall carrying a lyre under his arm. He was small in height and slight of stature, markedly different to the men who sat at the tables. His head was devoid of hair and his skin coloured a pale milky-white as if he never ventured forth into the sun or wind. An intricate, blue tattoo of three entwining chains began between his eyes and advanced up his forehead across his bald crown disappearing into his tunic collar at the nape of his neck. His parchment like face was creased and lined with age and fixed with rheumy eyes. His iron-grey, goatee beard formed a plait that hung to his waist, its tip secured in a small golden tube, the beard swung pendulum like as he limped past the benches towards the firepit where a small wooden stool was being placed for him.

A slow banging of hands on the table began, uncoordinated at first but becoming a cohesive, rhythmic thumping, which gained in speed and tempo until the man reached his chair. A servant stepped up and reverently removed the man's cloak, draping it carefully over the stool. The old man's gaze slowly circumnavigated the room, he paused occasionally to bow his head or raise his hand in acknowledgement to his greeting. The noise stopped without being requested and silence descended. A barking dog was quickly hushed as all eyes fell on the old man; he in turn raised his eyes to Gundulas. The Chief dipped his head by way of ascent and the old man sat, positioning the lyre in the crook of his arm the base resting upon his thigh, flexing his fingers he plucked gently at the strings. A slow, melodious tune filled the room, the music flowing like honey poured on a hot summer's day, warm and rich in texture enveloping all with its sweetness and purity

He closed his eyes as he played, humming softly before changing to a low chant. Baldor strained his ears to pick up the words but the dialect was thick and localised.

Malo leaned in close whispering to Baldor.

"Can you translate?"

"No, not well, the odd word or two here and there but it's difficult, the dialect's strange. I think it's more like prayers or rites than everyday language."

Malo nodded sagely, Baldor continued to listen then tapped him gently on the arm.

"Wait … it's changing."

Baldor translated in a whisper as the old man plucked soulful notes from the lyre then half sang, half talked, uttering words in accompaniment, the audience listened enraptured.

The peace it is shattered like blows to an anvil,
The innocent bore the brunt of the soon coming war,
The forest and plane is devoid now of laughter,
The Gods cry out for the children of the forest.

Our youngest and eldest have been taken from us,
And they nurture now at Brighde's breast,
Our eldest and youngest, our past and our future,
The children of the forest.

The dark warriors came from the land of the sun,
Mithras's sons, both true and brave,
They slew the Albino and his murdering minions,
For slaying the children of the forest.

Now we will ride to ruin and hell,
And the earth will shake at our coming,
Red is the colour we will carry before us,
For slaying the children of the forest.

Bright metal will ring and the horses will thunder,
Smiting our enemies ruin, cleaving mail and buckler
Death will come to those who have murdered,
For slaying the children of the forest.

His voice grew in power as the liturgy progressed, the notes becoming louder and more vibrant as he built to the finish. A heartbeat after the last words disappeared into the hall's rafters warriors jumped to their feet wrenching swords free, brandishing them aloft calling for vengeance. Some of the women joined in seizing knives from the table or making small, tight fists punching the air above their heads. Gundulas let them have their head for a moment then stood with his arms outstretched for quiet, this time the crowd obeyed his command and quietened quickly, sitting back in their seats, they looked to their Chief.

Gundulas waited until the scrape of benches subsided, when he had total silence he began.

"A most worthy rendition, Alaunus! A suitable eulogy for our fallen … we shall give weight to your words." Nodding his gratitude to the man with the lyre, he turned to the tables. "Andulas, Eoghann, Tuireann." He eyed each man as he called his name. "Meet me on the morrow for our council of war." The three men dipped their heads in acceptance. "My people!" Gundulas said, turning back to the main assembly. "My people, rest well! … Our dead have been respected, their spirits revered, they are safely on their way to our ancestors and the next world. We have done what was required of us as a family should, we can do no more until the vengeance trail begins tomorrow. I bid you all goodnight."

The two warriors stationed behind Gundulas's chair pulled it back allowing him to exit the table, as he turned to go he spoke quietly to Andulas.

"Give me a little time then come to my chambers and bring our guests with you, there are things I would know before tomorrow."

Baldor bit his lip to hide the tremble. His eyes however were full, he cuffed at the run away tears wiping them quickly away trying to hide his embarrassment when he found Malo looking at him. The black warrior merely bowed his head respectably giving a knowing, sad smile then looked away. Baldor stared at his plate, deep in thought. He quietly marvelled at these people the City-States casually termed 'barbarians' and wondered at the hypocrisy of it. These people lived and behaved like a large family. When one was hurt or endangered, the whole tribe responded in their defence. When they lost someone, the whole tribe mourned and it seemed planned vengeance even if it meant going to war to make the wrong done, right. What was so barbaric in that? In Carthage, he knew grief to be a more private affair associated to immediate family only. He sneered when he thought of the Senate and their attitude to vengeance or recompense for their people or the prospect of war even, for they would venture neither unless there was a profit in it.

The Gallic mentality and behaviour touched a raw nerve and he thought once more of Gestix. He'd always considered the Gaul family, reasoning it was because he'd been there since he was born; now he better understood the big warrior's attitude toward himself as he experienced Gallic culture first hand. His heart ached and his eyes filled again as he thought of his friend. He remembered his earliest days and being placed upon Gestix's shoulders and the big man's fierce love for him. The time and patience given to him in teaching whether it was aid with etiquette, life skills or martial arts, Gestix had always been there to help, to guide and love him like a brother. Cursing himself, he thought of his harsh words when he'd disagreed or argued, or the wasted time when his temper held him back from speaking because of foolish pride. How he wished the big warrior was here now.

****

Andulas escorted Baldor and Malo from the great hall to Gundulas's private chambers; he tapped respectfully on the door before stepping inside ushering the men after him. The room was grand in size; heavy curtains covered the shuttered windows and magnificent, colourful tapestries dotted the walls. Butter coloured pine furniture was set about the room and strewn with bear and wolf pelt throws with deerskins and bullhides covering the plain wooden floor instead of the usual rushes. The overlying smell of timber was strong, mixing with the musty tang of the animal pelts and the aroma of hot oil from the numerous lamps scattered about the room.

On a burnished tray, wine jugs and goblets finely wrought in chased silver and delicately inlaid with patterns of amber, haematite and topaz gems resided, the reflection of the lamps caught in their polished sides. Despite a glowing brazier, the room was cooler than the feasting hall and the two warriors thankful they'd elected to bring their bearskin cloaks with them. Gundulas sat in a high backed chair fashioned of pink-red, sheoak, not a throne as such but a finely wrought chair never the less. He was flanked by two titan sized, heavily armed guards, who stood with hands resting upon sword and dagger hilts and blank, unblinking stares at some point on the wall behind the incoming party.

Andulas stepped to one side and faced Gundulas then bowed his head.

"My Lord! May I present your Guests?"

He turned back to the two men gesturing with one hand towards the seated Chief the other indicating each man as he named him.

"Baldor Targa, warrior of Carthage … Malo, warrior and bowman of Nubia … this is Gundulas, son of Antulix, son of Arlen, keeper of the river and the forest. Lord and Chief of the Lingones … my father."

Baldor and Malo bowed their heads low, each holding the position for a respectful moment before straightening up.

"Welcome warriors! Warriors of Hannibal, I trust you're well fed and rested?" The older man said.

"Thank you my lord. Yes, we've been well cared for, your son is a most genial host." Baldor replied in Gallic.

"Ah, so you speak our language and well, your fluency tells of many years of learning, you learned from being young, yes?"

"Yes my Lord."

Gundulas nodded thoughtfully. "And Malo?" he struggled a little with the name.

"No my Lord, Malo speaks only his native tongue of Nubia and my own language of Carthage but not Gallic. If you have questions for him I will interpret."

Gundulas nodded and continued. "I'm told that many of the albino's men were slain by arrows from his bow, he has my thanks and blessing."

Baldor translated, Malo smiled and bowed his head again.

"And you, young warrior, When you arrived today, I saw that you carried two swords? Fastened thus, across your back." He gestured behind his shoulders as if reaching for two imaginary hilts.

"Yes my Lord."

"You fight with both at the same time?"

"I can my Lord, yes, though in battle it usually pays to use but one and a shield. As you will know there's not always the room to move and fight such."

Gundulas nodded. "Where did you learn? Who taught you?"

"I was taught from a young age for I've no preference for either right or left." He gestured with one hand then the other. "Either is comfortable for me to use. Thus, my father … and my … my friend, Gestix." His voice dropped at the mention of Gestix. "Taught me, encouraging me to use both hands and weapons together."

"Gestix, a Gallic name? Your friend's a Gaul then?"

"Yes my Lord, he was my father's friend and my friend, my brother in all but name, he taught me much."

"Hmm, And where is …"

"Dead my Lord, slain at the battle near the Ticinus a few days past." Baldor's voice thickened with emotion and despite himself, his eyes filled.

Gundulas nodded and looked away pretending not to see Baldor's grief.

"Romans then?"

It was Baldor's turn to nod.

"The Gaul in you will be seeking vengeance then, for your anger and hatred will run deep! From which tribe was your friend?"

"Of the Boii my Lord, north and west of here." Baldor's voice strengthened again.

"You're twice welcome then Baldor Targa, for no blood feud exists between the Boii and us the Lingones. You will realise though I trust, that the albino's people, the Cenomani will have declared feud upon you for your aid to us?"

"I do my Lord and I welcome it, for I've debts of my own to settle with them." His voice had all the anger and fire back in it once more.

Gundulas nodded appreciatively.

"Now, young warrior!" Gundulas said conversationally, Baldor however picked up an underlying tone. "There are things I would know … and let us be honest with each other, as friends or potential allies should be. If you weren't seeking recruits amongst our people would you have done what you did? I wonder, would the burning of a small fishery and the murder of its folk so far from your homeland have mattered to you? Why risk your lives for people you don't know?"

He looked directly at Baldor as he finished, watching intently for signs of fabrication or pretence.

Baldor returned the testing look, gathering his words before speaking.

"I was raised by a Gaul and thus taught to speak the truth regardless of whether it's palatable or not."

Gundulas shrugged. "My direct questions won't perturb you then, young warrior? Speak freely."

Baldor continued, his tone as level as he could make it.

"Thus, I can only answer for myself. I'll not stand idly by and watch women, children and old men slaughtered. I would risk displeasure, insubordination even, against my superiors … aye, even death itself, before I'll do nothing. But know you this, the men who rode with me, and Baraan, the man we lost, all came of their own free will."

Gundulas was about to interrupt but Baldor continued. With his integrity and honour up for question his voice dropped low as his indignation deepened, his temper beginning to flare. Folding his arms he looked Gundulas straight in the eye, his words forced from between tight lips.

"And unlike many men we need no reason to do what we did, other than to undo an evil deed. Not all men place reward or gold above all else, not all are slaves to greed, self-seeking …"

"You're mercenaries, you fight for money! …" Gundulas said matter of factly.

"Father!" Andulas interjected sharply.

Both men ignored the interruption and carried on the exchange.

"Yes I fight for money! Does that mean I'm without honour? Does that mean I have no principles? No scruples? No thought for the weaker amongst us? I think my Lord that you should ask the Romans the same question. Though they fight for their country and their homeland rather than monetary gain you saw the style of their honour and mercy today!"

Malo looked at Baldor. Though not understanding the diatribe, he'd noticed Baldor's ire and seemed poised to move. Despite the heightening tension in the room, the two guards remained as immovable and disconnected as before, Andulas looked uncomfortable and embarrassed. After a very awkward silence, Gundulas nodded.

"So oo! Twould seem we've honest and honourable men in our midst as well as brave!" He said at last, his tone sincere. "Now I'm impressed as well as thankful."

Baldor stared, searching for mockery. Gundulas noticed the look. Shrugging his shoulders and grinning he offered his hand to Baldor and Malo in turn.

"I was but asking … you know our culture? Or should from your Gallic friend! We speak directly, see and say it as we see it, call a spade a spade. I see a complicated mix in you Baldor Targa, this part Gaul, part Carthaginian and perhaps a dangerous one. You have the honour, pride and temper of a Gaul mixed with a most strange understanding, which I take to be Carthaginian." He laughed softly. "And no, I'm not laughing at you!"

Gundulas offered the couch and the chairs to Baldor and Malo bidding them be seated. He gestured to Andulas, then the wine jug and cups. Once the cups were full, Gundulas raised his to the two men.

"Our thanks!"

There was a moments silence as the men enjoyed the drink. Though no wine authority, Baldor knew this was no local pressing but most likely an expensive import if its sweetness and clarity were anything to go by. Feeling vindicated and somewhat honoured, he savoured the taste pushing it around his mouth with his tongue. As the wine warmed, it released a smooth, heady sensation into his nose and throat easing his ire and placating him somewhat.

"You would wish the support of our tribe in this coming war with Rome then?"

"Yes my Lord." Baldor sipped again. "And in the spirit of plain talking." Baldor smiled. "It could be a war of long standing and huge proportions, not something to consider lightly or quickly."

Gundulas grunted and nodded. "We'll decide our course of action tomorrow, after I've spoken to my son and my Captains." He gestured to Andulas. "I think however my son's already decided and will fight regardless of the decision reached but that is his choice and his right, he has his own men and knows his own mind."

The men looked around at each other as they continued to sip their drinks.

"Our problems though are twofold; on the one hand is Rome, a powerful and unforgiving neighbour, a neighbour with a long and vindictive memory for any slights or insults given, either real or imagined and I've seen Roman retaliation before …"

"With respect my Lord." Baldor interjected. "By your sending their envoy away does that not already invite their wrath?"

"Perhaps? And as he's now dead, more than likely." Gundulas sniggered, before becoming serious again. "But I'll not be dictated to or threatened in my own hall by some base born, arsewipe sent by the Roman Senate. Especially one that keeps company with the likes of the albino and his scum. This brings us to the second problem, the albino! Or rather, his brother, Lugobelinos and his people, once the heads are returned, and returned they will be! They'll be seeking revenge, war with us and feud with you."

"So, you've already decided upon that path?"

"I have! Murder has been done, vengeance and recompense are necessary, my people are not to be harried, abused and slaughtered and us to do nothing. I am the leader of my people, Lord of the Lingone but before we go to war as a tribe more voices than mine must be heard. I'll seek the council of my Captains tomorrow before setting plans in motion."

Baldor interpreted for Malo, as he finished Gundulas continued.

"As you say, we must consider carefully. We could have a war on two fronts, one here at home with the Cenomani and the second with Rome. I reason therefore, before risking war with Rome, we must ensure the safety of our homes and folk, thus the Cenomani must be brought to heel first. That would be sound military sense, do you not agree, young warrior?"

Baldor sipped his drink buying himself time before responding.

"I'm no master strategist or tactician my Lord but if I was in your place yes, I'd put my people and home above all, a safe and secure base is a must. For as I said, I believe the war with Rome will be long term."

"Will your General help rid us of the Cenomani threat first then? Thereby freeing us to march to war with you?"

"I'm sorry my Lord I'm not in a position nor do I have the authority to answer that, you must put it to the General yourself."

"Why must I go to him?" Gundulas's tone changed abruptly. "I'm Lord of the Lingone, when men seek aught of me they come to my hall. And, young warrior, if you cannot answer for your General then I must ask what position you hold to be talking to me as an equal?"

Baldor realised too late that he'd fallen into the mire of Gallic protocols and hierarchal pride and silently cursed himself that he should've known better, Gundulas would be expecting to treat with someone of at least his own standing. Thinking quickly he tried a new though reluctant tack.

"My Lord, It's true I hold no lofty status by birth but I am proud of my lineage, fiercely proud! Like you, I can name my ancestors back generations. It's also true that I'm no General; I hold only the rank of Hypolokhagos, a Lieutenant or rough equivalent of your Captains I surmise. However, as young as I am my weapons and skill add weight to my words, I've fought individual duels and five major battles. I can count Carthaginians, Iberians, Romans and Gauls among the slain in my list of victories and if needs must, I'll fight the champion of your choosing for the right to speak and treat with you!"

"Ah! The Gaul speaks again!"

Baldor looked for sarcasm in Gundulas's words. The old Chieftain just smiled and offered Baldor a refill from the wine pitcher.

"Fair enough young warrior. I deem you fit to speak with me and I doubt not your words, nor do you need to prove them with your blades, as much as I would like to see them used. I see the truth in your eyes and hear it there in your heart." Gundulas pointed to his eyes and tapped his heart with a closed fist. "My son will go and meet with your General; he'll carry the answers back for me."

"Thank you my Lord!" Baldor replied, sinking back into his chair hoping the meeting would soon draw to a close, bodily tired and mentally weary from the exchange he was seeking his bed.

Chapter Seven

Baldor and Malo's Gallic escort turned back southwards just after the party exited the steep sloped forest onto the Trebbia river plain, Andulas reined up in front of the pair offering his hand.

"Your camp's this side of the river; continue directly northward and you should reach it safely by midmorning. If my father and the council agree we'll be down in your camp the day after tomorrow or at the very latest the day after, weather permitting." He indicated the skies, which were greying over as the cloud banks thickened and built, threatening snow again.

"May your Gods protect you, fare you well till I see you next." He grinned while pulling his horse about to follow his departing warriors.

"Before I return to camp I've a message to deliver." Baldor said in a hard flat tone while lifting the bloodied bag in answer to the question forming on Malo's lips.

The Nubian looked at the skies and then in the direction of the Roman and Carthaginian camps respectively, as if gauging distance and time.

"We'll have to cross the river again then, we forded just after we left their village they obviously thought to put us on our side of it."

"I know, perhaps I should have said but …"

"Well, whatever we do, best be quick about it. I'm no expert on the weather hereabouts but looking at those skies I think there's more of this snow coming."

Baldor looked up and nodded agreement. "You head back Malo, I'll do this and be home shortly after you."

The Nubian looked blandly at Baldor. "Would you let me go alone?"

Baldor stared deeply into the dark eyes, appreciating the sentiment. "I …"

"Come on." Malo interrupted. "It won't take long." Kicking his horse forward, Baldor could only follow.

The pair headed north-eastwards across the plain, the horses' hooves crunching through the snow's frozen crust or ringing on bare, iron hard ground. The going however remained reasonable as the ground bore only sporadic patches of snow compared to the thick, even carpet at the higher altitudes of the village. They came upon the river just as the first flakes of snow drifted down.

"If this is the Trebbia, the Roman camp won't be far from the other bank."

"It's the Trebbia." Malo confirmed. "And this'll give us a little cover at least." He held his hand out to the blizzard, catching snowflakes on his glove.

The pair looked up and down the riverbanks as if preparing to cross a bustling city street, seeing no one and with visibility dropping to a grey-white blur, they steered the horses tentatively down the bank. Near the water's edge a pair of shell ducks ceased their preening, watching warily as the men approached. Malo gestured Baldor to give them a wide berth leaving them undisturbed and hopefully on the ground. The ducks continued their attentive vigilance until they perceived the men no threat and as the horses began fording the river the birds returned to their grooming. The fast flowing water had an iced, blue-green shade to it and was crystal clear; making it easy for the riders to see the bed and guide their mounts while remaining safely in shallow water. The river wasn't a single flow but numerous swift flowing, arterial like streams of varying widths and depths, spread across a wide boulder and shale covered bed. With an unseasonably dry autumn and midwinter, yet to come there had been neither heavy rains nor snowmelt to flood and join them into one huge torrent. The width of the riverbed however bore testament to the size and volume of the deluge it had held in the past. In most places, the water remained just above the horse's knees but come the spring thaw or heavy rain up in the hills it would be a much different story. As they cleared the rocky beach and scrambled up the bank to the Roman side the snow brought visibility down to less than half a stade and looked to worsen. Baldor became a little anxious as to directions and cast furtive glances back the way they'd come.

"It's alright lad, I'll get us back." Malo said confidently sensing Baldor's sudden unease. "I don't think we've much further to go anyway, listen!"

Malo held up his hand for silence and the pair reined in to listen.

The sounds of hammering and chopping of wood mixed with the odd shout drifted through the blizzard.

"We're here." Malo said from beneath his scarf that swathed his neck and face to just below his eyes.

Baldor nodded and lifted the sack. Malo looked around again before speaking quietly.

"We walk the horses in quietly under cover of this blizzard, when we're closer drop the head and we ride out fast! If they have cavalry patrolling we may have to make a run for it, so you stay close to me … alright?"

Baldor nodded. "Let's go."

With ears straining they walked their horses forward calmly and quietly as possible. As each hoof slapped the ground, Baldor expected to hear a shout of alarm. His mouth went desert dry, his heart beat quickened and his stomach heaved and tightened in trepidation. This skulking and subterfuge stressed and tore his nerves in the same way an argument or the wait before battle always did. He longed for the simple action of combat when all talk, hopes and fears were replaced by adrenalin pumped focus and preservation at any cost. Some men feared battle, for Baldor the fear came in the sword rattling and the empty boasts and the waiting for hell to break loose. Thus, it was a tense, bowel loosening few moments as they edged closer towards the sounds of work and men's voices, each becoming more distinct as the distance closed. Malo put his hand up and stopped him.

"Listen! …" He said in a muffled whisper. "They've stopped what they're doing, that's close enough methinks!"

At that very moment they clearly heard orders rapped out followed by the clatter of weapons being readied.

"Now Baldor! Now! Then we're away!" Malo hissed, already pulling his horse around.

Baldor wheeled his mount roundabout in a tight circle, throwing his burden laid arm out wide like an athlete about to hurl a discus, gaining impetus for his throw. As the horse came full circle, its hooves stamping and kicking up snow and it whickering in protest, he heaved the bloodied sack into the whiteness and the direction of the shouts, grunting with the effort.

"Leave the villages be! Or suffer the same fate!" He shouted in thick, accented Latin then kicked his mount hard around again, driving it after Malo.

The pair had only ridden a stade when they heard the sound of horses in hot pursuit. They dropped lower on their mounts, tucking heads and shoulders into their horse's necks shielding their eyes from the driving snow, making themselves smaller targets for any javelins. With the pounding of his mount's hooves and its snorting, gasping breathing in his ears, Baldor couldn't hear if the pursuers were gaining on them. With the poor visibility, he dared not look behind him lest he put his mount into a hole or they fall headlong over the edge of the riverbank.

Suddenly, Malo sat upright tugging at his scarf; pulling it away, he waved his hand to the front and shouted anxiously in his own tongue. Baldor saw other horsemen materialising out of the blizzard in front of them and recognised the small, sand coloured ponies of Numidian cavalrymen as they approached on a collision course. Malo continued to frantically shout, wave and point behind him. Baldor's mind went from relief at the sight of the Numidians to horror as he saw lack of recognition on their faces as to who he and Malo were and javelin-laden arms pulling back ready to throw. A moment later and with a sense of reprieve he saw the faces were looking past him, they'd either understood Malo's shouts or recognised them as allies, else seen the Roman cavalry closing on their rear.

Continuing their headlong gallop, Baldor and Malo thundered through the Numidians ranks after which the dark riders split into two columns that fanned out on the Roman flanks. The Roman horse, following closely on the fleeing pair's heels were partly blinded by the driving flakes and perhaps didn't see or realise the seriousness of their situation and were caught in a deadly crossfire of whistling javelins as their column funnelled between the flanking Numidians.

The first screams and sounds of falling horses and tumbling men allowed Baldor and Malo a moment to rein in and turnabout. Baldor was drawing a falcata and pulling his shield into place across his chest as the horses came to a wheeling, stomping change of direction. Malo snatched for his bow then stopped as he saw the majority of the Roman cavalrymen were already unhorsed or hit. Injured and dying horses went down in leg flailing, wild eyed, whickering ruin, thrashing and rolling in the snow, having thrown their riders and crushed others as the dazed and injured men were too slow to move. Some died instantly from the javelins, others as their mounts tripped over the dead as they in turn fell, only to be speared as they tried to gain their feet. A few riders folded backwards as javelins hit them in the chest sending them somersaulting over their mounts hindquarters from the force.

"Leave it Baldor!" Malo called. "Leave it! They can manage by the looks of it. Come on! Let's cross the river back to camp before we attract another patrol or this weather worsens."

Sheathing his falcata, Baldor saw the remaining one or two surviving Romans turnabout and gallop back in the direction they'd come with the howling Numidians in hot pursuit. The ground littered with over a score of bodies both animals and men, most now laid still. One or two of the fallen horses managed to struggle to their feet and stood about as if waiting further commands, of the men, only one was trying to get up. As he staggered about in small circles, either disorientated or badly injured a Numidian cavalryman materialised out of the blizzard and stabbed him in the chest with a javelin. The man clutched at it, howling like an animal caught in a trap as he pirouetted pulling fruitlessly at the wooden shaft before falling to his knees and pitching forward. Meanwhile, the horseman had already disappeared back into the blizzard.

"Sweet Tanith, that was lucky!" Baldor gasped, his heart banging in his chest and his pulse racing. "For a moment there I thought we were dead."

Malo however was already disappearing down the riverbank into the whiteness. Fearing to become lost, Baldor raced after him having to steer his horse at frantic, breakneck speed. Malo was already down onto the riverbed and waving him urgently onward. The pair blundered into the water but found it deepening quickly and the current very strong. The horses whickering and unsettled as their hooves slipped and moved on the stony bed. Malo's mount stepped into a deep hole, the water rising up its flanks and it floundering, swept sideways with the strong current.

"Out Baldor! Get out! It's too deep, too risky to cross here!" Malo shouted as he swum his horse back towards the stone covered beach. The moment the animal's hooves touched solid ground it erupted out of the water in a shower of spray tossing its head in panic.

"We'll try ... try ... further upstream." The freezing water stole Malo's words.

"Shit! ... It's so, so c ... old it burns!" Baldor yelped as the water reached his thighs and groin.

He backed his mount out of the deepening water. The horse, as shocked by the cold as its rider, twitched and skittered almost losing its footing as he pulled it around. With the horses soaked to the withers and the men wet to the waist they guided the animals back up the bank trotting them northward looking for a safer and shallower place to cross.

Some five, freezing stades upstream, Malo signalled they should drop down to the river's edge again. Hazarding the steep, snow-covered bank, they clattered over the stones and into the first stream at speed. Anxious, almost panicking to quit the Roman bank they kicked their shying horses hard driving them onwards, churning the water white spraying it high around them. They quickly forded another two rivulets that took them halfway across the river course then over a large raised area of dry ground. Heading back into the water they were stopped once more by the plunging depth and strong current of the third stream. Backtracking to the raised ground, they rode upstream where the island began to widen and rise in height. The snow dusted rock and shale beach gave way to a bank of hardened mud and silt populated with clumpy grass tussocks and patches of brown, dead gorse. Malo pointed to the far side of the island nearest the Carthaginian side of the river and they made their way over. They found the island widened again and rose in height forming a small hill.

"We must have missed our original crossing place." Malo sounded disgusted with himself.

Baldor was about to reply when Malo hushed him.

"Horses! Coming along the bank!"

The pair looked behind to the Roman held bank finding the visibility improving as the blizzard eased and the flakes diminished in size, the area becoming clearer by the moment.

"Damn it to Hades! We'll have to cross! Swim the horses if necessary, those could be Roman or Numidian cavalry." Malo pointed to the bank behind and the direction of the noise. "We can't afford to wait to find out; we don't want to be caught in the open."

"Over here … here! Look! This way!" Baldor urged Malo back from the water while sawing on his reins and turning his mount towards the hillock.

The hillock rose in height before splitting in the middle to form two breast like humps, Baldor urged his horse into the open gap with Malo following closely behind. As they slipped through the cleft, they lost sight of both riverbanks and pulled the horses up to wait quietly. Moments later there was the thunder of hooves from the bank they'd just left, the noise grew louder then faded away as the horses galloped along the bank heading northwards.

Malo shrugged and whispered. "Whoever they are, best let them go by, then we make our way home."

Baldor nodded and shivered at the same time, he was soaked to the skin from feet to waist. His trousers were sticking to his legs and groin and his toes were already going numb. Malo too was wet through and faring worse than Baldor as he was now shaking violently.

"We'll g…ive them some … some ti … time, then we…we'll have to move, else we'll die here." He stammered, as the cold snatched his words, Baldor just nodded.

The snow was still falling but not as fast and in smaller, fewer flakes, the skies however remained wolf grey, the morning light resembling early evening dusk. It was now strangely peaceful with only the noise of the water flowing and slipping over the stones, other than that the land was deathly quiet once more. The two men looked around as they shivered in silence and waited for the unknown cavalry to distance themselves. The cleft opened into a large, flat-bottomed basin some half stade in width and covered in a profusion of driftwood, rocks and clumps of dead looking grass, which was attempting to colonise the area. Baldor reasoned the basin would remain dry throughout the summer months, hence the grasses and weeds, then when the floods and spates of winter came the water would rise and course through the cleft carrying the debris and stones before it. The rising sides forming the edges of the basin were thickly covered in grass and stunted trees, the vegetation there surviving better as only exceptionally wet years would see the waters rise to cover the hillock. At the far end of the basin, perhaps some four to five stades away the two hilly ridges came almost together again but for another gap formed by exiting water as it overflowed the basin and forced itself out.

With the cold taking hold on their bodies, they could wait no longer. Departing from whence they'd entered and walking their horses upstream, they finally found a shallower place to cross the remaining half of the river. The ride back to camp made worse by the wet clothes chilling and burning their skins, allowing the cold to seep into their bones and finally numb their senses.

By the time they reached the camp, their clothes were stiffening and freezing on their bodies and they had to be helped from their mounts, their comrades placing them near the fire whilst removing their clothing. Wrapping them in warmed, dry cloaks, they massaged and rubbed warmth into their skin and limbs.

Malo fared the worst, his dark skin and pronounced features had radiated his body heat away rapidly. He'd ceased shivering but was now strangely incoherent and dozy, his body movements slow and stiffened like those of a walking corpse. Eager hands continued to rub him while others talked, forcing him to answer in order to keep him awake while holding a steaming bowl of mulled wine to his lips encouraging him to drink. Baldor shook uncontrollably with the cold, his teeth chattering so violently that he could hardly speak, as he too was force fed hot wine.

Chapter Eight

"Move your bloody arse Optio! You're wanted at the Consul's tent now!" Centurion Gaius Laelius shouted as he shook Cornelius roughly. "Come on! You can't sleep forever! Time enough for that when you're dead! Come on!"

Cornelius raised himself trance like from the low camp bed. Swinging his legs over the side while pulling the coarse-woven army blanket around his shoulders for its precious warmth, his aching body protesting at the enforced movement and his eyes refusing to focus. He massaged his throat gently, grimacing at the sudden pain his fingers created. As he stood his thigh muscle announced its displeasure with a deep-seated, toothache like pain, he eased his tunic up to view the front of his leg that was a multicolour of black, blue and yellow bruising.

"It matches your throat!" Gaius quipped with a small laugh. "Come on, you'll live! It's only bruises; wait till the real fighting starts."

Cornelius rolled his eyes as if he'd heard it all before and continued massaging his throat. His thorax felt tight and ached terribly when he swallowed, he tried to speak but only a low gravely sound came out, his throat felt as if it had been crushed in a vice.

"Here!" Gaius passed a steaming goblet of wine to him. "Get that down you, there's cinnamon and herbs in it, which should help a little."

Cornelius sniffed the brew, inhaling the spice-scented steam rising from it then sipped tentatively. Relishing the taste he tried to swallow, his cheeks filled and he nearly spat it out as the pain in his throat prevented him from swallowing most of it.

"Steady man, sip it! … Sip it!" Gaius chided him. "You'd best get dressed whilst you drink it though, they want you up there, at the Consuls tent!" Gaius pointed behind with his thumb.

"Why … me sir?" Cornelius rasped dryly, somewhat surprised that he could speak at all.

"Because that's the orders."

"What could they want with me?"

"How in Hades should I know? I'm just the messenger boy! Consuls aren't in the habit of explaining their reasons or orders to the likes of me, though I'd hazard a guess it's something to do with you saving the Consuls life I shouldn't wonder."

Cornelius managed to pull his padded shirt on, Gaius helping him into his mail shirt as he continued.

"The Consul may be your Father, Cornelius and most sons would do what you did because of that but he's also one of the first men of Rome! Either way, saving his life isn't the sort of thing that happens everyday."

Cornelius looked disinterestedly at Gaius while changing the subject. "How are the men?"

Ignoring him, Gaius passed him his belt of leather pteruges and his greaves. Tut, tutting when he saw blood stains on the bronze, he spat on the marks before rubbing them vigorously with his tunic sleeve before continuing.

"Our lads are alright, one or two wounded is about it, we helped hold the bridge while the army withdrew across it and then as the engineers destroyed it and that was it. Some of the engineers managed to get themselves speared though; those Numidian savages came out of nowhere. As you know, we never had a chance to become involved in the main battle, if you can call it such? It was more of a large cavalry skirmish really; the whole thing over before we even had a chance to engage. In fact, the infantry weren't involved at all, except the Velites and they apparently ran without even throwing a javelin … chicken-hearted bastards! They're not real infantry you know! There are calls for the punishment of some as an example to others."

Gaius passed Cornelius his weapons belt as he talked.

"The cavalry took a thumping though, we lost over two thousand, three hundred men they reckon, with a good number wounded."

Cornelius nodded sadly. "I think we under … estimated them." His voice fading as he spoke.

"Not so much underestimated as they're better equipped, and they fight differently to us, they have two cavalry arms, heavy and light."

Cornelius looked puzzled, which prompted Gaius to elaborate.

"It's the same principle as heavy and light infantry Cornelius, to increase the chances of success you need one to support the other. You know the way we work, or are supposed to! The Velites cause disarray in the oncoming ranks with missile fire, helping to break formations, us heavy boys step in and exploit any gaps making them larger. The Velites should then support us by attacking the enemy wings, cavalry need to work the same! That's what they were doing and doing well … bastards!"

Cornelius just nodded and continued to stare blankly as Gaius continued.

"Of course I'm just taking a simple, Centurion's perspective on it." He said in mock sarcasm. "But it makes good military sense to me. Another thing, their mounts are bridled therefore have to be easier to control; even those Numidian devils have a rope about their ponies neck whereas most of our cavalry have nothing. Their shields are smaller and more manoeuvrable than ours, which also helps. They send those damned Numidian savages out on their wings as light cavalry to harass and wear our lad's down. We have nothing to answer them with and can't catch them either, our cavalry all being heavy."

Cornelius fitted his helmet and tied his neckerchief, grimacing sharply as the knot contacted the bruising on his throat.

"Right, you look tidy enough, off you go." Gaius clapped him on the helmet and pushed him towards the tent door.

Cornelius slipped out of the relative warmth of the tent, turning his face down and away from the biting wind; crossing the snow-covered camp towards the Consuls command tent. The mule and goatskin tents were pitched in perfectly straight rows, dictating orderly roads through the camp as well as parade ground areas, baggage parks and horse lines. Although only a temporary marching camp, there was an earth embankment surrounding it complete with wooden stakes forming a fence some three cubits high sprouting from the top of it. On the outer side was a ditch five cubits wide and two deep, complete with sharpened wooden spikes protruding from its bottom. He passed Maniples of infantry practicing formation manoeuvres or training with weapons and smiled as he saw huge clouds of body vapour rising from them as they were drilled hard. Centurions rapped orders and in some cases enforced them with a swipe from their vine canes across the legs or backs of slovenly Legionnaires. Cornelius noticed that though the men went through the motions their air of confidence and drive seemed to be gone, their normal vigour, tenacity and sheer bloody mindedness they usually displayed was missing. The greatest military machine in the world had suffered a small but terribly significant defeat and thus a serious setback to its morale.

He paused outside the command tent to adjust his weapons belt and check his appearance, satisfied, he announced himself to the guard. He was ushered in removing his helmet as he went, then led to the side of a long table lined each side with over a dozen senior officers. Halting, he stood rigidly to attention awaiting acknowledgement. Seated at the head of the table was his father, Publius Cornelius Scipio, Consul of Rome. After the icy outside temperatures, the tent was pleasantly warm and filled with the scent of mulled wine mixed with warm humanity. His eyes stung then watered from the swirls of wood smoke from a glowing brazier. The table was littered with maps, helmets, gloves and wine goblets; off to one side a black robed scribe perched on a stool was scratching notes with a wooden stylus into a wax tablet. Most of the seated men were raven or brown haired with swarthy, olive coloured skins and dark eyes, all were clean shaven after the Roman fashion and their hair cropped short in the Legion style. The Consul stood out, being blonde haired and pale skinned like his son. His hair, thinning on the crown with middle age, was ash blonde as if time was fading the colour allowing fringes of pepper-grey to creep in at the temples. Cornelius's hair, although fine in texture like his father's was the colour of burnished gold. He was small and slight of build compared to the elder and bore the look of his mother with lively green eyes, high cheekbones and a fine sculptured face with a small mouth. In contrast, his father was tall; his height causing him to stoop and rounding his shoulders, his features coarse with a large hooked nose, a broad flat face and square jaw, the simple, earthy look of a peasant farmer.

Publius also had bruises on his face from battle and his right arm bandaged and strapped in a sling; beneath his scarlet wool tunic, his chest was swathed tightly in linen bandages supporting broken ribs and collarbone. Thus, he held his head and shoulders stiffly, as he looked up he saw Cornelius.

"Optio, Cornelius Publius Scipio reporting sir!" Cornelius managed in a broken, husky voice. He inclined his head while holding his right fist over his heart in salute looking first at the Consul then repeating the gesture to the seated men. The men pushed back their chairs and stood returning the salute.

"Hail Cornelius!" Came from one and echoed by the rest.

Cornelius was taken aback. These proud veteran and class sensitive, senior officers did not normally defer to the likes of an Optio. Still dumbstruck at his welcome, his father eased carefully from his chair and came to meet him grasping his forearm in the warrior fashion and embracing him. With his good arm over Cornelius's shoulder, he turned to the men at the table.

"Gentlemen, I present my son, to whom I owe my thanks and my life. Without his bravery and intervention on the field of Ticinus yesterday you would be seeking another Consul in my place."

The tent erupted in sudden uproar as the men cheered Cornelius, snatching their goblets raising them in salute. Cornelius blushed and looked awkward as the cheering continued and each man offered his hand to him. A chair was placed at the opposite end of the table facing his father and he gestured to sit. Only when he'd placed his helmet on the table and was seated did the others take theirs. A fresh goblet was brought for him but the slave serving the wine was waved away as Publius himself took the pitcher, filling his son's cup.

The Consul returned to his chair, his careful movement and awkward posture hinting at the extent of his injuries, seating himself carefully he addressed his son.

"Optio, Cornelius Publius Scipio. I trust you're well?"

Cornelius smiled and nodded gently. "Yes sir, Thank you, and yourself?"

"Recovering and alive, thanks to you!"

Publius kept his voice steady and serious despite the corners of his mouth turning upwards in a smile.

"Optio, we've summoned you here regarding your actions and bravery in the face of the enemy, beyond any call of duty and for saving your Consuls life without thought for your own. It is the wish of myself, as Consul of Rome and of these men here as senior officers and staff of this army, that your deed be recognised. Thus, you are to be awarded the, Corona Civica."

Cornelius looked stunned, his mouth falling open his face flushing hotly, the men banged their goblets on the table, the independent thumps becoming cohesive and timed as a chant broke out "Cornelius! Cornelius! Cornelius!"

Eventually, Publius stood, raising his arm and his voice to restore order. Snapping his fingers a waiting slave stepped forward bowing his head and holding out a red satin cushion upon which rested a golden circlet adorned with intertwining oak leaves. Looking at an embarrassed and very bashful looking Cornelius, he gestured.

"The floor is yours Optio!"

With all eyes upon him and the unexpected turn of events Cornelius just stared, his mouth moved but no words came out. Seeing the men peering as if trying to hear him speak, he moistened his lips and cleared his throat.

"Sir … sir!" He repeated as the words dried in his throat.

The men closest to him urged him to drink in order to help him speak. Raising the goblet, he saluted them all then drank slowly, taking small mouthfuls as the pain still pulled at his throat with every swallow. Rising from his seat, he inclined his head to the Consul again.

"Consul, sir, Legate, Tribunes, officers I … with the greatest of respect, I cannot accept this great honour you wish to bestow upon me, as much as I would desire and value it."

It was Publius's turn to look nonplussed. "Why's that Optio? Have you not a right to it? I show you no special favour because you're my son. It was these men here." He gestured around the table. "You're commanding officers who've requested it, an award from them and this army in recognition of your bravery, a gift from a grateful city to a brave and deserving soldier."

"In truth Consul had it been other than you whom I'd saved, I would most gratefully accept this honour."

The seated men furrowed their brows and looked at one another then back to Cornelius for an explanation all mystified at the refusal, Cornelius continued.

"Sir, with respect I cannot accept the Corona Civica when the result of its earning is I feel, the greater reward in itself."

As the men digested the words and grasped their meaning, they leapt to their feet cheering once again. All, making their way to Cornelius slapping his back heartily and offering their hands once more. Publius beamed at his son, nodding his head slowly the pride and respect on his features clear for all to see, he raised his goblet in salute and drank. Food arrived for the table and Cornelius found himself included in the repast, his thoughts and concerns over the men's humour lightened as he recognised the usual fortitude and resilience among the officers. Despite their shock defeat and their men's sombre disposition they remained gregarious and on a positive footing. As he listened to their discussions and ideas as they planned the next steps of the campaign he was heartened by their enthusiasm, despite ready acknowledgement of the poor start and acceptance of a sore lesson learnt. The 'she wolf' may have trouble in her den and her tail had been singed but let those that harry her beware, for when she howls and turns to snack there'd be a reckoning.

With the meal over the men took their leave, Cornelius also preparing to retire. Publius laid his hand on his sons shoulder.

"A word if I may, Optio."

"Yes sir!"

Publius waited until the last man had left then gestured Cornelius to pull his chair up close to the brazier, he called for more wood then dismissed the slaves leaving the two of them alone. He topped up the goblets and eased himself into his chair.

"That was nobly done my son but you'd earned the right to the Corona, Father or not you should have taken it."

Cornelius smiled and sipped his drink. "Father, but for the actions of another, neither you nor I would be here now to discuss the Corona."

"Another? … From what I'm told, there was only you with me on the field until the arrival of my bodyguard, whom you'd shamed into belated action? What have I missed? To who else am I indebted and also owe my thanks?"

"None amongst our men father but there's much, much that you should know."

Publius furrowed his brow not understanding, he was about to speak when Cornelius began.

"Cast your mind back some eleven years father, when you took me to the shipyards in Gades in southern Spain."

As Publius recollected Cornelius continued.

"Do you remember how I got this?" He pointed to the white lumpy scar on his temple, recognition and memory began flooding back to Publius. "And this?" Cornelius lifted his arm showing a child's bracelet of copper and brass wire twists fastened tightly about his wrist.

"I'll never forget that day Cornelius, never! I thought I'd lost you but what has that ...?"

"The boy that saved my life that day, father ..."

"Baldor ... Baldor Targa!" Publius interrupted. "Yes, yes I remember his name, a brave boy and ..."

"It was he ... he who tried to slay you yesterday."

Publius sat back hard in his chair as if struck.

"He? Why? ... How on earth do you know this?" He looked wide-eyed at Cornelius shaking his head in disbelief.

"He was pressing you hard when I attacked him ..."

"He was a heartbeat away from killing me when you attacked him." Publius corrected him.

Cornelius didn't deviate he just unfolded his story as if needing to be rid of it.

"He and I fought and in the end it came down to a hand to hand struggle. I hurt him badly, breaking his nose and face with a head butt, he in turn punched my groin. We ended up on the ground trying to choke the life from one another, he was hell bent on killing me, and you for slaying his friend."

"Slaying his friend? Who?"

Cornelius shrugged and paused to moisten his throat again. "I don't know father, I can only presume you slew someone on the field that was close to him. However and in truth, for all he'd fought much longer than I that day he was still the stronger and despite the blow I dealt him, he had the better of me. He would have slain me then and come for you before your bodyguard arrived. Of that I'm sure."

"How did he recognise you? Or you him? What stayed his hand?"

"He recognised this, my, his bracelet." Cornelius raised his wrist again. "I in turn saw my Vulcan's fire about his neck."

"That large marble of yours? Your favourite possession that …"

"That I gave to him in gratitude for saving my life when we were but children, yes! … Seeing the bracelet he let go of my throat and just sat back on the ground, he … he looked then how I feel now, lost! We … as …" Cornelius's eyes moistened and tears fell as he recounted his tale. "As he left me to recover I came to help you, seeing that he attacked again, calling that you were to die for the death of his friend. But for him tripping and falling and the arrival of your bodyguard I imagine you and I would now be dead and he shortly after, the guards would have slain him then no doubt."

Publius poured more wine into Cornelius's cup then leaned over patting him reassuringly on the shoulder; Cornelius wiped the tears away, cleared his throat and collected himself trying to hide his embarrassment.

"While he was distracted defending himself from the bodyguards I helped you. But he'd already slain two by the time I had you mounted and interceded to stop the fight"

"Slain two?" Publius asked in disbelief. "But he was on foot and sorely hurt you say?"

Cornelius nodded. "He slew one man with his own javelin then killed the second one's horse beneath him, the man himself never got up. The rest would have had him no doubt; he was outnumbered and must have been weakening. I intervened at that point, intervened to spare his life, despite all." Cornelius's head fell forward; he sighed deeply and shed more tears as his emotions got the better of him again.

"Bear up lad!" Publius said quietly. "I think, I think the Gods are cruel to cast the dice so, they must …"

"I think the Gods are malicious to play with men such, what were we supposed to do, kill one another? I would have tried to slay him if he'd come for you again but I couldn't leave him to die at the hands of the bodyguard, despite what he'd done to you. Despite all, he is brave and … and … it runs deep this strange bond we have, deep!" Cornelius wiped the tears again and collected himself. "We are even now though, I told him so. I told him that he must decide when next we meet what our course is, whether we turn away or whether we fight."

Publius looked thoughtful but offered no suggestions.

"I'm angry father, angry at this Baldor Targa for his attack on you and angry and confused as to the games the Gods are playing with our lives … and saddened also, that it's come to this."

Publius got up and embraced his son. At that moment he hated the war, hated all the hot-headed fools who'd willed it and prayed for it to happen, hated even the Gods for their meddling and playing in men's lives. Consul of Rome and a General of her armies he may be but above all, he was a father first and he loved his son. His son was everything a father could wish for; loyal, loving, brave and dutiful, no man could ask for more. A lump formed in his throat as he watched Cornelius wrestling his emotions and rights and wrongs of his actions, it was distressing to see the young man in such state. The father in him won out and he slipped his arm about him hugging him hard, he put his good hand atop Cornelius's shoulder and held him at arm's length where he could see his face.

"You did the best you could my son, the very best! Jupiter knows I'm grateful, the army's grateful and no doubt, Baldor Targa himself will be grateful. Believe me! There's no coincidence here. I surmise greater things at play that will shape both yours and this Targa's destinies. After all, every war needs its Achilles and its Hector."

Chapter Nine

The following morning the Roman camp was brought to abrupt wakefulness before first light by the wailing notes of the cornu. The haunting drone drifting over the snow-covered landscape, the brassy echo reverberating off into the white covered foothills of the Apennines. Men awoke instantly, as this was no usual reveille call but a warning of approach to the camp by a large force.

Centurions hurried to their allotted marshalling areas tying themselves into their armour as they awaited their men. Optios dashed from tent to tent, bawling for Legionnaires to 'stand to' whilst strapping themselves into their armour and sorting weapons belts as they went. At the horse lines, mounts stomped and whinnied, the animals tossing their heads as they picked up the scent of other horses and the heightening activity and tension from the men. Flints struck sparks to torches and soon hundreds were aflame, casting dots of light around the camp like swarming fireflies. The torches cast a smoky, orange light around the parade grounds and roads as Centuries assembled; messengers carrying the burning brands like Olympic runners as they went from command to command, relaying orders. Field artillery was readied, the crews groaning and cursing profoundly as sleep dulled muscles racked the engines throwing arms back in readiness.

Soon the thump of feet and the rattle of metal ceased with men formed up and awaiting orders, the hubbub replaced by an eerie, tension filled quiet. The ranked men blinked sleep from their eyes and eased chilled muscles as they waited. Clouds of breath vapour from the serried ranks rose upwards into the still, frozen air. Only calls from gate lookouts relaying information back to the watch commander broke the silence. Cornelius fell in beside Gaius.

"All present sir! And ready!"

"Very good Optio. Now, let's see who our early morning visitors are … bastards whoever they are! I was happily dreaming of that big titted whore back in Ostia." He muttered under his breath causing Cornelius to chuckle slightly.

A runner came loping over the white covered ground, the night's frosted, snowfall crunching under his boots. Saluting Gaius and Cornelius, he delivered his message in low whispers whilst pointing back to the camp gate. Gaius cursed loudly then turned and strode towards the road; Cornelius stepped forward to address the men.

"Consul, Tiberius Sempronius Longus approaches along with his Legions." There was a distinct sigh from the ranks at the anti-climax and mutterings of discontent relating to lost sleep and rude awakening.

"Silence there!" Cornelius barked. "You will form up in ranks on the Centurion and flank the road. You will present arms as the Consul passes … now, advance to the road, and move!"

The men drew themselves up at the roads edge shuffling and adjusting their distance from each other as if on parade. Cornelius began a quick inspection of them as they waited for the Consul and his Legions entrance to the camp. After sorting minor details such as neckcloths not tied correctly, helmets un-strapped and one case of a spear held upside down, he presented himself next to Gaius who was standing a few paces to the left of his men.

"All tidy sir!"

"Pompous, overstuffed, shitbag!"

Cornelius looked blankly at his Centurion. "Beg pardon sir?"

"Not you Cornelius! Bloody Tiberius! He probably turned up at this time just to wake us and so he could swan about looking superior. I tell you, he's a bloody fool marching in the dark when he doesn't know where in Hades the Carthaginians are, he could just as easy have blundered into them as found us."

"You don't like him then?" Cornelius said sarcastically.

Gaius however remained serious. "Jupiter knows why we have two Consuls." He said shaking his head gently. "I'd follow your father into Hades if I had to but I wouldn't follow Tiberius into the latrine."

Cornelius couldn't help but snigger but he did look around to ensure no one had heard Gaius sounding off. Gaius however continued his diatribe talking aloud to himself and still on a serious note.

"Fancies himself as a soldier he does, all he'll manage is to get lads killed, mark my words!"

"Begging your pardon sir but I would keep it down a little, just in case someone hears you."

Gaius huffed loudly but to Cornelius's relief said nothing further.

As the men waited, the first streaks of grey appeared in the east followed by large flakes of snow; Gaius huffed again, raising his eyebrows at Cornelius. By the time Tiberius had cleared the gate and made his way into the camp the waiting men had a covering of snow over their shoulders and helmets, many were shivering with the cold.

"Cornelius! Pull one man from each rank, detail them to tend the fires, I want a good blaze going and water on the boil ready for these lads a hot drink once we're stood down … quickly, before they get here."

Cornelius promptly detailed the men then returned to his position alongside Gaius.

The approaching Consul was pre-empted by two outriders whom ensured his horse had a clear road, the likes of; Tiberius Sempronius Longus was not to be hindered in his progress. Mounted on a resplendent grey and white dappled stallion; it nodded its head proudly as it walked, raising hooves in exaggerated plodding as it stepped out. Tiberius was resplendent in a bronze helmet with a heavily reinforced and decorated rim that shaded his eyes, the bowl richly embossed with images of Jupiter and Mars, flying eagles and lightning bolts. A tufted crest of purple horsehair sprouted upwards just back from the rim, traversing the bowl to the rear where it cascaded tail-like halfway down his back. Huge cheek pieces covered his jaw pushing his face inwards accentuating his large aquiline nose. His head tilted back like a fighting cock hinting at the haughtiness and the superiority that he emanated and no doubt surely felt. He was wrapped from the morning cold in a beaver lined; crimson cloak, which trailed from under a wolf pelt stole covering his shoulders, the cloaks trail lying across his horse's hindquarters.

Behind him rode his senior officers, themselves only a little less grand than their General. They were followed by Standard-bearers declaring Legion and Maniple numbers and the letters S.P.Q.R. denoting the Senate and the People of Rome. At the very top of the standard were golden eagles with wings raised and outstretched, their talons clutching a number of Jupiter's lightning bolts. After them came musicians with their swirling cornu followed by Signifiers with their banners, all of which were furled and wrapped in leather covers protecting them while on the march. The Legionnaires followed, fronted by the Hastati with the Princeps and Triari in their rear. The rhythmic thump of the marching grew as they approached causing the ground to vibrate making it impossible to hear individuals speak. Cornelius watched Gaius for any signalled orders, though he received none he noticed a fleeting but contemptuous sneer from his Centurion as the command group passed by.

Just as the paleness of dawn spread in the east, Tiberius halted his horse outside the command tent. A groom ran forward taking the mounts bridle while he dismounted. The cornu droned again but this time from a number of them in fanfare as he stepped across the snow towards a waiting Publius. Hiding his dislike beneath a painted smile, Publius walked to meet his fellow Consul while extending his good arm, his hand open.

"Well met Tiberius! I trust you're well!" He asked amiably.

Tiberius strutted the last few paces ignoring the offered hand. "What's to do Publius? ... What happened to you man?" His tone loud as if addressing a subordinate, his look disdainful, bordering on contempt. "I thought you'd have these Carthaginian savages brought to heel by now!"

Forcing himself to be civil in front of his men, his hand still extended, Publius swallowed his response as if bitter bile. Tiberius, either uncaring or oblivious to the slight he caused reluctantly shook the offered hand, grimacing suddenly as it was gripped vice like. Startled, he looked up to see a hard stare from narrowed eyes.

"Not in front of the men, Tiberius ... inside!" Publius hissed through tightened lips while nodding towards the tent, keeping his voice low so no others could hear.

The pair stepped into the Consular tent with Publius curtly ejecting the slaves and servants then dropping the flapped doorway to give some privacy. His face clouding like a gathering storm, he turned on Tiberius, his anger bursting forth like a torrent from a breached dam.

"Have you no damned sense man!" He said in an aggressive but enforced whisper. Tiberius was about to respond but was cut short as Publius's anger vented. "The men are already downcast from losing the first encounter, don't heap shame upon it!"

"Your men! Your first encounter!" Tiberius bridled, his mouth twisted in a belligerent sneer.

"Yes! And my shame not my men's!" Publius paused making a herculean effort to calm his temper and moderate his tone. "We … we need to take care lest it happen again."

"There is no we!"

"What?"

"There is no we! Do I not speak plain enough?"

Publius stared, his features expressing thoughts that went from confusion to disbelief. "Surely … surely you don't intend that we pass singular command from day to day, do you?" He asked, his voice trailing away to a disbelieving, sardonic laugh. "The Carthaginian will chop us to pieces and feed us to the crows."

"You've had your chance at glory Publius, now it's my turn. I'll show you how to deal with this Hannibal, I'll assume command of both Consular armies tomorrow and will hand over to you the day after and so forth."

"Tiberius! For the love of … you're running mad, man! We need to operate as a joint command, the men will …"

"The men will do as they are told or suffer for it. I'm exercising my Consular right to singular command of this army on alternate days. You have no choice!"

"We are playing into the Carthaginian's hands, can you not see it? We need a united front! We can't afford to lose the next encounter!"

"As I said Publius, there is no we! You've have had your chance, now I'll have mine. I bid you good day!"

Tiberius turned on his heel making for the tent door.

"Damn you for a bloody fool then, Tiberius Sempronius Longus! Damn you to Hades!" Publius called after him.

Tiberius did not look back as he exited the tent but strode across the snow calling savagely for his mount to be fetched. Gnaeus Servilius watched Tiberius and guessed from the brief meeting, the man's strained body language and peacock like strutting that trouble had broken out between the two Consuls. As Publius's senior officers headed towards the closed tent door he stepped in front of them placing his hand over the flaps.

"Gentlemen! Gentlemen, I ask you kindly to give me a moment or two alone with the Consul, if you will?" He asked, his tone quiet and conciliatorily.

Gnaeus was not known for his decorum or demure character, being usually direct and forthright by nature, the officers taken aback by his placid approach and sensing a hidden issue deferred readily to his request. Gnaeus stepped inside to find Publius pacing the floor muttering and scowling. As the tent flap fell back into place Publius looked up, his eyes glaring, his face reddening with anger at the imposition.

"Excuse me sir, can I help?" Gnaeus asked quickly but quietly before Publius found words.

Publius bit back his reaction to bawl the man out for his un-asked for intrusion; however, Gnaeus's unruffled and sincere manner brought him some calm.

"That man's insufferable! Insufferable I tell you! He's deluded and madder than a March hare if he thinks he alone can outthink or outsmart the Carthaginian."

Gnaeus let him vent, busying himself finding cups and wine for them both.

"I should not have committed to the fight at the Ticinus, I should have been more cautious, I …"

"You had no choice sir; the fight was thrust upon you." Gnaeus interrupted cautiously. "We did the best we could with what we had and …"

Publius shook his head slowly then continued but as if he was speaking aloud to himself, rather than to his most senior officer and friend.

"I should have done what I always do and prepared. Prepared thoroughly, I was wrong, wrong to look for a quick victory, I …"

"Publius … please, we've lost but one battle, not the war and our casualties were light, we are reinforced now, now we …"

"Aye Gnaeus, as you say it is but one battle, one skirmish even. Ordinarily I wouldn't be over concerned but it's the significance of the loss and the possible consequences from it that worries me."

"How so sir?"

"It was Hannibal's first encounter on Roman soil and he with his army half-starved and decimated after forcing the mountains! How do you think the charlatan soothsayers, mystics and the like will view it all back in Rome? What portents of doom can they read into it? Aye, and the mob, they'll be howling for our blood along with the Senators that sit on their fat arse's and talk while we fight to keep them there."

Publius paused to draw breath and adjust his sling while gesturing towards the wine jug on the table. Despite the seriousness of Publius's concern, Gnaeus couldn't help but smile at the last comment but seeing his Consul's fears continuing unabated, he hid it while turning to pour the wine.

"The mob is ever fickle Publius, you know that. They'll damn you one moment then sing your praises the next."

Publius didn't seem to hear him and carried on with his own thoughts, speaking aloud.

"Singular command huh! What worries me most of all is how our men will see it? What about them eh? … What about them?"

"So ooo, he's exercising his right to alternating days of command." Gnaeus now looked troubled. "Surely we can work it so you're in command when battle comes? All will be well then! The men respect you, revere you even! They'll fight for you and fight well."

Publius sipped his wine, his features bitter and sad looking.

"Tiberius is glory hungry Gnaeus. All he sees is a victory parade through the streets of Rome with him as the centrepiece. It would be easier to piss against the wind than to keep him from battle, he is set upon it I tell you! He sees himself as another Alexander." He huffed then smiled grimly. "Hannibal will destroy him and this army along with him." The smile suddenly faded away.

Gnaeus saw he was making no headway in alleviating Publius's concerns, though he drew comfort that the anger was slipping from his voice and his friend becoming rational again.

"The officers Publius, they'll want to see you." He ventured. "They'll want to know what's happened, can I bring them in?"

Publius swallowed his wine and sighed resignedly. He cleared his throat and collected himself, regaining his former air of command.

"Yes Gnaeus, yes bring them in!" He said slowly, smiling. "I'm still in command of this army, at least for today; I'd better be seen to be so!"

With the addition of the second consular army, some two regular Legions and two auxiliary Legions in support, the camp area required extending. Before mid-morning, the army's engineers were relaying their plans to the Centurions and the Legionnaires committing to the work. As a precautionary measure, a protective screen consisting of three Maniples of infantry deployed across the plain as cover for the labouring men while the rear camp wall was removed. A turma of cavalry was also deployed beyond the infantry screen to give ample warning of any Carthaginian movement or suspected incursion, with a single cohort of Velites as the supporting force between both. Cornelius found himself, Gaius, and their Century as part of the screen.

The snow had not slowed its fall, the flakes increasing in size, drastically lowering visibility across the plain. The wind whipped the flakes in all directions, swirling them around the men driving them into their eyes and beneath flapping cloaks to chill their skin further. Cornelius pulled his cloak closed across his chest as he walked along the lines of his Maniple. Dropping his head to shelter his eyes from the blizzard, his breath vaporising in white clouds as he called for the first line to move. To stop men freezing, Optios moved Maniples from one position to another, the activity helping to keep blood circulating and hopefully some warmth in the men.

Gaius shivered as Cornelius came alongside.

"I tell you Cornelius I'd happily dig or swing a pick instead of this; at least you can work to keep warm."

"Yes sir, I take back all my gripes about blisters and backache, guard duty's not a good place to be on a day like today. I doubt we'll see anyone anyway, who would be out in this?"

"Well, you never know. I've heard of stranger things than battles in the snow, lad and if your father thinks we should be out here that's good enough for me."

"If Tiberius had ordered us out here you'd be cursing him!" Cornelius smiled as he teased his friend.

"Aye that's true! But see ... see, there's the difference." He pointed to a small group of mounted men. "Your father!"

Cornelius shaded his eyes from the swirling flakes and saw his father working his way amongst the Maniples exchanging words with the men as he went. He felt his back stiffen and a feeling of pride emanate in his heart, who would complain now that their commander was out here with them sharing their hardship, he made a mental note as to his father's conduct and the hearty response he saw in his men.

Suddenly there were voices raised above the wind and the furthest away Maniple came smartly to arms, closing ranks tightly and locking shields. Almost immediately, other Maniples followed suit, the command group splitting up with officers riding to and standing alongside each Maniple as Legionnaires shuffled to close and form battle lines. Legionnaires disappeared behind long oval scutums and with spears sticking out and over their ranks took on the appearance of a porcupine under attack. Gaius and Cornelius quickly fell in alongside their men, waiting.

"Steady! Hold the line there!" Carried across the plain from one of the front Maniple, Centurions.

"What's happening? I can't see anything, can you?" Cornelius drew his Gladius as he spoke to Gaius.

"Nothing!" He replied as his eyes narrowed, peering to see what lay beyond the swirling snow. "I can't see a bloody thing for the blizzard, shields up lads!"

Wood rattled and clattered as the Legionnaires hefted scutums higher then silence fell again. Gaius stepped out front of his Maniple, his vine cane pointing down oscillating in small tight circles, his other hand on his sword pommel, looking to the front and waiting calmly. Silence reigned. Gaius tapped his greaves with his cane as if waiting for a parade to begin, his brave indifference to the situation setting an example to his men.

Men's ears strained and some held their breaths as they waited.

"Horses to the front!" Gaius shouted, unhurriedly sliding the cane into his belt and drawing his gladius. "First rank! Ready pila!"

Like the rustle of wind-blown leaves on summer trees, arms retracted and the small, barbed javelin points angled skywards awaiting the order to loose. Silence came again along with a nerve tingling tension as men waited to see what or who materialised out of the blizzard. There was a dull thud as a hessian sack bounced on the snow in front of the forward Maniple, the snow stopping it rolling further.

"Leave the villages be or suffer the same fate!" The shout came in heavily accented Latin from out of the blizzard, echoing lightly.

Cornelius looked to Gaius, seeing if he would order the pila loosed. There was the muffled sound of hooves that faded and then silence again. The sound of many hooves came next as Roman cavalry appeared to one side of the Maniples. One of the officers from the command group kicked his mount across to them pointing in the direction of the shout and urging them to follow him while forcing his mount around. The cavalry departed with the officer and were soon lost from sight in the veil of snow. Gaius waited until the noise of the horses disappeared then gave the order for the men to stand down. Walking to the bundle, he pushed it tentatively with his boot. Seeing dark stains over most of the sack and feeling the weight against his foot he sighed as if in recognition then reached down to undo the cord ties. Upending the sack, the helmeted head of Lucius Julius Machus rolled out into the snow. Gaius cursed to himself and stooped to pick the head up by the small brass knob on the helmets crown. The eyes were wide and staring as if in disbelief as to the heads fate, the mouth twisted open into a gruesome shape as if the scream of death was frozen upon it. The skin was now devoid of blood and white as the snow upon which it had lain, having dried and cracked like that of an ancient corpse from some dry, musty tomb.

"Who is it sir? ... Any ideas?" Cornelius asked, swallowing hard in horror at the grotesque sight and stepping back a half pace.

"None! ... None at all, other than someone who upset the locals." Gaius muttered with a hint of sarcasm. His tone changed again to one of sad resignation. "And so it begins" He said aloud but to no one in particular.

"What do you mean, it begins sir? The war's already begun."

"Not the war Cornelius, that's not so bad, it's the murder and the slaughter that goes with it and I don't mean on the battlefield. Once that starts amongst the local tribes or in the villages, pay back's not too far away." He raised the head as if to emphasise his point. "Patrols will go missing, sentries and scouts will be murdered, water will be fouled, food poisoned. The war will not just be fought on the field."

Chapter Ten

"Get out! … Out! You good for nothing whoreson's!" Balaam shouted as he burst through the tent door like an approaching hurricane. "Baldor! Malo! Bide were you are, I want a bloody word, now! The rest of you get out!" Balaam physically pushed the slower of the men out of the tent door flinging the canvas flap door closed with a sharp crack.

Inside the tent was pleasantly warm with the heat from the men's bodies, the air however, stale and stuffy from so many being crammed into the small place. The smell of cooked meat and fresh bread vied with the overlying odour of unwashed bodies and mixed with the sharp tang of dirty, sweat tainted clothes. Balaam seemed not to notice the warmth or the smell and pointed an accusing finger at Baldor whilst continuing his enraged diatribe.

"Damn you boy! Damn you for an empty headed, idealised fool!" He spat the words like a stream of venom as he strode further into the tent. "What in Baal's name were you thinking, eh? I could have you flogged for this! … And you Malo! I …"

"Sir it wasn't Malo's doing, it …"

Balaam's face contorted and reddened in rage. "Baal almighty! I'm not finished boy! How many times must I bloody tell you about interrupting me?" He screamed into Baldor's face then snatched at his neckerchief rolling it in his fist pulling him closer, the flecks of spittle from his incensed outburst spraying Baldor's face. He paused to gather his breath and control his temper, letting loose of Baldor.

Baldor stood to attention as he was addressed; abandoning the plate of food he'd brought for Malo to the floor by the camp bed. Though he never moved, his eyes watched Balaam intently as he'd never seen his Captain so enraged, he looked as if he could commit murder. Making an effort to control his temper, Balaam began again struggling to keep his voice steady and level.

"Tell me, why I'm one man short and why I've no recruits? And tell me, if you value your hide, what in Hades name you thought you were doing using my warriors to sort a feud between Gauls?" His voice rose along with renewed fury as he finished his sentence.

Baldor knew better than to attempt to justify his actions or try to reason, electing to take his dressing down without comment other than to offer an abject apology.

"I'm sorry sir."

"Not as bloody sorry as Baraan, I'll warrant!"

Baldor felt as if he'd been struck at the mention of the dead warrior. Already blaming himself for the man's death, he silently cursed himself for not having offered up prayers for his soul since returning to camp.

"This isn't some damned Greek myth we're embroiled in! I don't need high-minded heroes searching for glory! I need able, thinking warriors who'll do as they're told."

Baldor bridled at the insinuation of glory seeking but wisely held his tongue as Balaam continued his overflow of anger.

"I'll tell you this boy and mark my words!" Balaam stabbed his forefinger into Baldor's chest emphasising his anger. "General or no General, plans made or no, I'd have killed you where you stood had you defied me in front of my men!"

Baldor felt the raw anger that was so evident on Balaam's face. Despite the hot-tempered outbursts he noticed Balaam's eyes were devoid of emotion and cold, piercing, like pieces of sharp blue ice, he didn't doubt the threat for a moment.

"And before you think Armaco came running to me with tales, he didn't. I had to give him a swearing to find out what in Hades had gone on and where in damnation you and Malo were!"

Again, Baldor had to control his tongue. Wanting to say that he wouldn't accuse his friend so, but thankfully, the lessons of not interrupting Balaam finally seemed to be holding, he just looked forwards while the Captain continued. Balaam's anger however was subsiding as he vented and his voice was lowering.

"What happened after you left Armaco?"

"Sir, we went to the village with Andulas and his men and …"

"Leave out the minor details. I'm not interested in niceties and whether or not you humped the local harlots! Can we expect any recruits?"

"I think so sir, Andulas and his father Gundulas said …"

"I hope so for your sake!" Balaam cut him off. "Now! What took you so long to get back here? You would have left the village at first light yet you didn't arrive here till well after midday yesterday?"

Baldor swallowed hard, readying himself for another dressing down when he explained the dalliance for the head delivery. However, before committing to further trouble, Malo spoke up from the bed.

"Craving your pardon sir, we … we became lost as we came out of the hills back into the valley."

Balaam turned quickly towards the bed.

"You lost! I've never known you lost, ever!" He snapped, sounding incredulous while looking suspiciously at both men. "I don't believe it!"

"Sir the blizzard was heavy, the visibility poor." Malo protested, sounding convincing.

Balaam looked intently from one man to the other; tilting his head slightly as he studied their faces searching for signs of half-truths and fabrication. Baldor tensed, wondering how much Armaco had imparted to Balaam regarding the dead Roman's head and hoping that Malo's weak defence and fibbing wasn't going to lead to further trouble.

"So, you were lost enough to be on the wrong side of the river as well?" Balaam stared directly at Baldor as he spoke, his tone heavy with sarcasm.

"Well, we …"

Malo interrupted venturing further. "Sir, I crossed us over to avoid Roman patrols, they were operating on our bank as well."

"It strikes me as strange that the Numidians haven't reported such and they've been probing the Roman camp these last few days! They say contact's only come on the Roman side of the river!" Balaam looked thoughtfully at the pair as he asked his loaded question.

"We had to dodge patrols on our way back which is why we also ended up soaked ... sir." Baldor added as confidently as he could.

"H'mmm, Is that so?" Balaam left the question hanging, his eyes however never left the two men, as his look lingered Baldor felt a nerve in his eyelid jump. "I may be growing older and slowing down somewhat but there's nothing wrong with my wits and I smell a rat here?"

After what seemed like an eternity of taught, pregnant silence Balaam huffed then continued.

"What condition are you both in?"

"I'm alright sir." Malo almost chirped, relieved to be on another subject. "I've finally warmed up, the lads have got the heat back into me though they struggled for a while, it was a Gallic healer who'd seen the condition before, he ..."

"Whatever! Spare me the details, you're fit for duty?"

"Sir."

"Baldor?"

"I'm ready sir."

"Right, the pair of you report to the General's tent now. You can start by adding details to his maps of the area, of what you saw when you were lost!" His last words heavy with sarcasm. "And I mean now! So move!" He stormed out of the tent as forcefully as he'd arrived.

Abandoning their meal, Malo and Baldor dressed quickly then presented themselves at Hannibal's tent. They were directed off to an awning that passed as a map room. Braziers were scattered amongst the tables allowing the men a source of warmth to keep their fingers operating whilst they worked. They found Armaco already working with the cartographers and scribes to fill in details on the huge parchment maps. Shaking hands quickly, Armaco indicated with a slight flick of his head towards Balaam who was bent over another table discussing a map, Baldor raising his eyebrows in silent acknowledgement.

The activity in and around the tent was hectic; scouts arrived regularly, relaying verbal reports to scribes who scribbled notes and figures onto wax tablets. Messengers brought written reports from their commanders, depositing them with adjutants who prioritised them before passing them to the General's secretary. Numerous squadrons of Numidian horse arrived and departed at the horse lines and it was noticeable that many came with injured warriors and rider-less ponies in tow.

"Harassment tactics." Armaco offered as he saw Baldor counting the empty mounts. "They're probing the Roman defences; the empty ponies are the price they pay."

Baldor nodded as he watched a wounded warrior lifted from his mount by his comrades.

"It keeps the Romans under stress and we learn about their deployment and response times, it also keeps those black skinned demons gainfully employed. No offence meant to you, Malo." He added quickly.

"None taken." Malo replied quietly. "They're Numidian!" He shrugged as if to imply they came from a different world. "Raiding and killing is what they're born to do, best leave them to it."

The men worked until early afternoon adding further details to the maps, Malo's eye for detail and recall of the lay of the land complemented by Baldor's grasp of distance and relevant scale. The work was interrupted by Hannibal and his Generals breaking from their meeting in his tent. The officers crowded the tables, some asking questions regarding features, others discussing the maps amongst themselves. Hannibal studied without input and when asked for comment held up his hand for silence, deep in thought. Picking up a pair of divider's and setting them to the scale lines marked on the base of the map he walked them the length of the island drawn on the river course, as reported by Malo and Baldor. He raised his eyebrows as if in disbelief at the measurement.

"This here." He tapped the dividers on the island. "An island in the river?"

"Yes sir" The cartographer answered. "These men were on it yesterday." He indicated Baldor and Malo.

"Ah! Good day to you Baldor." Hannibal said genially, recognising Baldor between Malo and Armaco. "Tell me of this interesting island." He smiled warmly gesturing for Baldor to explain. Baldor coloured under the attention.

"Yes sir. It's about six stades long and just under a half wide."

Hannibal nodded agreement with his own measurements.

"It's formed of two long ridges with a hollow middle like a valley, sir." Baldor drew in the air with his hands. "The ridges are maybe, three or four times spear height and grown with small trees, grass and gorse. The valley's flattish but covered with stones and driftwood where the river washes through."

"It's wet then, in the valley part?"

"No sir, it's dry at the moment but heavy rainfall or snowmelt in the hills will change that I imagine."

Hannibal glanced out at the sky finding it clear and cloudless then looked back at Baldor. "You're sure of these measurements?"

"Yes, sir."

"How deep's the water around it?"

"Around knee deep on our side as the river bed is very wide and flat, on the Roman side however it's deeper, maybe waist height?"

"So, it would take a reasonable period of heavy rain you think, to swell the river before the valley would fill?"

"I, I imagine so sir, yes. The river bed at this point's very wide and half a cubit lower in level than the valley floor" Baldor looked at Malo for support.

Before Malo could contribute, Hannibal cut in.

"Show me, take me and show me now!"

Mago immediately called for horses and Hannibal's bodyguard to be summoned.

"Thank you brother, but no! That amount of men will only draw attention to us, Baldor and his companion here will take me."

There were immediate calls of support to Mago's recommendation and protests for Hannibal's reconsideration regarding his safety, all of which the young General cordially brushed aside.

"I'm not going dressed like this." He smiled and intimated his smart camp dress and purple cloak.

"Either way, I'm coming with you!" Mago added gruffly.

"No Mago, you're not! You're in command here until I get back, Baldor and his companion will be my guards and guides."

The command group all looked at Baldor. Seeing the grizzled, scarred faces of seasoned warriors, veterans of many campaigns, leaders of men and most old enough to be his father, he coloured again under their scrutiny. He read their looks, which said what they did not. 'How can this boy protect you?' Mago as usual couldn't restrain himself and huffed contemptuously. Hannibal cast him a filthy look to quieten him deigning not to rebuke his brother publicly.

Baldor, already deeply embarrassed smarted under the scorn and coloured deeper. Finally, with his fierce pride needled beyond sufferance he lost his self-control and found his tongue.

"General! It would seem I'm judged incapable of the task." He spoke to Hannibal but glared at Mago. Armaco groaned deeply.

The huge, bearded warrior hooted. "Listen to the puppy yap! I but say what we all think, you're just a boy!"

"Boy maybe, but man enough to teach you some manners!"

"Mago! Baldor! Enough! This is a council of war not some Inn room in which to brawl!" Hannibal said loudly before the pair could argue further, he pointed to both in turn. "I'll suffer no argument amongst my officers in my presence … or out of it." He added as he saw the murderous looks being exchanged between the pair. "Am I understood?"

There was a fleeting hesitation before both men grudgingly acquiesced with nods and quietly spoken, 'Yes sir's'.

"Good! There's an end to it! Shake hands and no more of this childish bickering."

The command group shuffled to let the pair approach and shake hands. Baldor felt his hand crushed by Mago's huge paw, gripping back as hard as he could he looked past the painted smile into the hard eyes that said, 'later boy, later!'

"Fetch my horse! Mago! See to matters here, you're in command until my return, Baldor …" Hannibal looked at Malo inviting him to give his name.

"Malo, sir." He saluted as he spoke.

"Malo, lead on."

"General! General! Excuse me sir." A guard called to Hannibal. "Sir, there's a party of Gauls to see you."

"Later! Allot them a camp space and escort them to it, I'll see them upon my ..."

"Tanith, Mother of Heaven!" Maharabal interrupted and nodded towards an incoming party of horsemen, Hannibal and the command group also looked up.

The horsemen rode in column five abreast and numbered over fifty. All dressed in the full panoply of war they followed behind a Standard-bearer and carnyx player, in front of them rode the reason for Maharabal's exclamation. The leader of the column sat his horse as if it were a child's pony. His thick legs hung low, his feet extended well past the animal's belly, his bear sized torso with a pumpkin sized head resting upon it seemed massively out of proportion with the animal and everything around him. No one from the command group spoke, even Hannibal seemed lost for words. Baldor whispered quickly to Armaco.

"Lugobelinos? … The albino's brother! It has to be."

Armaco looked at him not understanding.

The column halted in front of the command group. The giant looked at them with casual disdain as if surveying inferiors, recognising Sergatatonix as a fellow Gaul he directed his words to him.

"I am Lugobelinos! Son of Maponos, son of Teutorigos, Lord of the Cenomani." He announced his lineage loftily, his voice booming. "I'm here to see your General Hannibal on a matter of honour, one of his men murdered my brother."

Sergatatonix apathetically translated for Hannibal and the assembled men. Hannibal looked puzzled and glanced around his officers seeking clarity. Meanwhile, heavily armed camp guards arrived, flanking the Gauls; the mounted men watched them assemble then looked away as if it was of no matter.

"We're at a disadvantage, friend." Hannibal said affably, opening his hands in a lost gesture. "We know not to whom or what you refer."

Sergatatonix translated for the mounted giant while Baldor explained to Armaco in whispers. When another group of horsemen trotted up flanking the first, all talk stopped again. Recognising the foremost rider Baldor exclaimed too loudly

"Andulas!"

All eyes turned to him, Balaam in particular glaring as if demanding an explanation.

"Captain, this will be some of the recruits you looked for from our mission three days past."

"All of them?" Balaam indicated both parties of Gauls.

"Err, no sir, the ones arriving now are recruits the …"

"And the others?" Balaam snapped

"The others sir …" He said with hesitant regret. "The others, I surmise are brother and kin to the men we slew for murdering the folk at the fishery."

Meanwhile Andulas and his warriors had recognised Lugobelinos and his men. Curses and insults flew and hands began reaching for weapons. Balaam's reply was drowned in the chaos as a dozen voices spoke, while Hannibal called for order. The pandemonium ended with the rasp of metal leaving leather and brought the command group to cohesion; drawing their own weapons, they screened their General.

The Carthaginian guards were already forcing their way between the Gallic parties, swords drawn and shields raised as they pushed them apart. With horses skittering and rearing, men left their weapons to control their mounts. Hannibal and Mago were also directing and commanding. Finally, Hannibal had his signaller blow his horn and as the wail cut above the mayhem men quietened and a semblance of order returned.

Hannibal called quickly for Sergatatonix to translate then turned back to the two mounted parties.

"You! You! Dismount." He pointed and growled at Lugobelinos and Andulas. "My tent now! Have your men dismount or I'll have them speared where they sit. Sergatatonix, Baldor, on me!"

The separate groups did as they were bidden, albeit with hesitation. Meanwhile, the guards between the antagonistic groups were rapidly reinforced with extra men who thickened and widened the screen between the rival factions.

Hannibal strode into his tent with his adjutants and scribes scurrying after him, the summonsed men following on somewhat guardedly in his wake, Lugobelinos having to crouch low beneath the canvas door head. They found themselves before a seated, stately seeming General who glowered darkly at them from beneath furrowed brows. To each side of him were two scribes, wax tablets and styluses in hand while the tent walls were lined with heavily armed guards. Baldor saw the anger etched into Hannibal's face and him wrestling to bring his temper into check before trusting himself to speak. His own feelings were also in turmoil and somewhere between anger and dread. He cursed himself for his damnable pride and lack of restraint toward Mago and the trouble it would no doubt bring but mainly for his behaviour in the forest, which had brought this sorry matter to a head. He also wondered briefly at the wisdom of Armaco and Balaam's words of leaving Gallic feuds to the Gauls. With all gathered within the tent, Hannibal ran his eyes slowly over the assembly. Urging Sergatatonix to translate he turned his gaze back to Andulas.

"And you sir are, whom?"

Andulas raised his head higher as Sergatatonix asked the question.

"I am Andulas, son of Gundulas, son of Antulix, of the Lingones."

Hannibal said nothing; he waited a moment before pointing to each man in turn and allotting a place to stand before him. After an awkward, taught silence and lethargic movement from the two belligerent Gauls, Hannibal cleared his throat then taking a deep breath spoke quietly though firmly to the giant.

"You have a grievance regarding my men!"

It was a statement not a question. Sergatatonix turned towards the giant to speak and found that despite his own considerable height the man stood head and shoulders above him, forcing him to tilt his head to see his face. Lugobelinos was draped in a sumptuous, high collared, bearskin cloak fastened closed at the neck with a brooch of gold and amber loops. His mail clad chest and shoulders were the width of two men and his arms which he held folded over his chest as thick as an infantryman's thigh, his skin the same pale, milky-white as that of his brother. His bright copper hair was tightly bound in two heavy plaits, which fell from the rear of his high domed helmet half way down his back. His bushy eyebrows and wild, straggling moustache and beard were coloured the same as his hair. The contrast of his hair colouring against his skin gave him a ghostly pallor and the same corpse like look of his brother Magalus.

"Your men attacked mine, slaying all and killing my brother." He said accusingly to Hannibal.

Baldor was about to interrupt then thought better of it, though he noticed Andulas about to interrupt anyway.

Hannibal held up his hand to silence Andulas and spoke to all.

"Before we go further can anyone tell me what happened and what all this is about? Time is short my patience already worn thin!"

"General, I can explain." Baldor said regretfully then turned towards Sergatatonix. "I can translate if you wish? I speak Gallic."

The Gallic warlord shrugged disinterestedly, indicating Baldor could do as he pleased. Baldor began his tale from when they'd picked up the raiders tracks. He spoke first in Phoenician then repeated in Gallic and surprisingly he was left to speak without interruption. The only movement in the tent was Hannibal's head as he looked at each party as they were mentioned in the rendition. As Baldor finished his tale and before anyone else could speak, Lugobelinos announced hotly.

"I will fight this Armaco now, bring him to me."

As Baldor translated, Hannibal jumped up from his chair his composure gone, his brows knitted and his mouth twisted into a snarl, barely in control of his anger.

"How dare you sir? This is a military camp! My camp! Not some public arena for fighting or debate! I give the orders here. I can have you and your men killed here and now and as easy as that." He snapped his fingers. "Do you understand?"

The giant never flickered at the outburst; he calmly eyed Hannibal as Baldor added the words to his Generals very apparent body language.

"And …" Hannibal continued. "With this Roman envoy previously in your retinue it would seem you've already chosen sides. We should crucify both you and your warriors as Roman spies."

Baldor looked up quickly at Hannibal, then at the guards.

"Tell him! Every word." Hannibal snapped.

Baldor swallowed hard and did as he was told. Lugobelinos slowly unfolded his arms, the first movement he'd made since the talking began. All around the canvas room men tensed. The guards ceased their unseeing stares, fixing their gaze on the giant, looking for signs of movement that would pre-empt a bloodbath. Lugobelinos slowly lowered his arms, bringing his hands to rest atop his weapons hilts and the tension rose another degree. Baldor felt his skin beginning to itch then glow hotly. His muscles tensed as he calculated the time needed to draw his falcatas' and bury them in the giant's chest before he could draw his broadsword. The Gaul however, left his hands resting on the weapons pommels and nodded gently then laughed softly.

"Another day General, there will be another day for all of you." He stabbed a thick forefinger at Andulas and ran it accusingly around the assembly. "And this Armaco." He paused to spit on the floor. "I will find him and send him to serve my brother in the afterlife."

Baldor translated and seeing Hannibal growing angrier expected a command to arrest Lugobelinos when the man continued.

"I'm told you're a man of honour, General. I came here under the white spear and I believe you will let me leave under it."

As Hannibal listened to the translation, he looked around at the men before him his face betraying nothing of his thoughts. The atmosphere remained tense and Baldor and the guards still eyed the giant for signs of trouble. Hannibal eased back into his chair but stared hard at the arrogant colossus who seemed to dominate the room.

"I am an honourable man, Lugobelinos of the Cenomani! So take yourself and your men and get out of my sight and camp. Go back to your mountains or your Roman masters I care not which. However, make sure you are gone far from here forthwith, for if I set eyes upon you or your men again you'll be killed where you stand, there'll be no second chance, no mercy! That's my final word and warning."

As Baldor translated, the giant scowled at the mention of Roman masters and his lip twisted as if to speak. Hannibal however, motioned his guards that the audience was over and to remove all from the tent.

Outside, the Cenomani horsemen prepared to depart. Baldor watched as Lugobelinos mounted, noting how the horse slumped under his tremendous weight. The giant pulled savagely on the bit turning the animal around in its own length, commanding his column onward and out of the camp but at a slow, arrogant walk. Two squadrons of Carthaginian heavy cavalry and a supporting squadron of Numidians were dispatched in the Gauls rear to ensure they kept heading away from the camp. A hand tapped his shoulder and Baldor turned to find an adjutant.

"The General will be ready to ride as discussed before the intrusion but first he wants you to translate for the other Gauls whom he believes are joining us?"

Baldor nodded and made his way back into the tent finding Andulas standing quietly in front of Hannibal.

"Baldor! Translate for us if you will."

Hannibal smiled as he spoke, his anger gone and he clearly back to his normal, affable self.

"I bid you welcome, Andulas son of Gundulas, son of Antulix of the Lingones. My apologies for the unlooked for discourse with the unwelcome guests and into which you became embroiled."

Hannibal rose from his seat offering his hand in friendship, the atmosphere in the tent now more convivial and relaxed. Andulas nodded acceptance of the apology and replied.

"Thank you General. I'm also here in regard to your men. Had it not been for this man and his comrades" He indicated Baldor and smiled. "My folk at our fishery would all be dead, thus we are in your debt. As a sign of faith and gratitude I have brought myself and one hundred of my own warriors to enlist in your army."

Baldor translated and Hannibal smiled while nodding his head and saluting Andulas graciously.

"Thank you again, Andulas."

"We can put a further five hundred warriors under arms and under your standard, General but my father sets conditions upon their use." Andulas said bluntly.

Baldor translated and Hannibal looked thoughtfully at Andulas.

"What conditions might that be, Andulas?"

"The head of Lugobelinos, General. His village to be raised to the ground and his warriors slaughtered the people of the Cenomani given over to slavery and bondage."

Hannibal looked thoughtful, his mind calculating and planning. He reasoned Andulas's people had little choice; they would have to fight Lugobelinos and his people now that the blood feud had escalated. Also, there was the added risk of Roman intervention or support for Lugobelinos, so to whom or where else could Andulas and his people turn if not the Carthaginian's? However fostering a small war between the two tribes could be advantageous, it could remove potential allies and support for Rome while bringing much-needed recruits for themselves. The action may even be seen as useful propaganda with the Carthaginians seen to be removing Roman tyranny and safeguarding the smaller, weaker tribes. Far better, he thought to have many of the smaller tribes flocking to his banner than the odd larger one or two, smaller was easier to control. Andulas interrupted his thoughts when he continued.

"With this renewed enmity between my people and the Cenomani we dare not commit to the war wholly and leave our village unprotected. Especially while Lugobelinos and his men are under arms and ranging at will in the hills. We don't ask you to fight our battles while we stand by General, only to help us rid ourselves of the giant and his people. The Cenomani are a more numerous tribe than we and have plagued us over the years with raids here and there, our folk slaughtered or carried off to slavery even held to ransom. We would end it this time, once and for all."

As Andulas finished, Hannibal nodded sagely. "It will be so. First, I must break this Roman army on the other side of the river, once that is done, we'll remove the threat of Lugobelinos and his people from these hills forever. You have my word."

Chapter Eleven

Baldor and Malo escorted Hannibal south-eastwards, retracing their path to the Trebbia and where they'd seen the island. The weather held cold but fair though the skies were once more ash grey with the promise of blizzards. The temperatures remained below freezing and a hard, frosted crust had begun to form on top of the previously fallen snow. Water in wells and buckets at the horse lines had long since frozen and in the river itself, where the flow eddied and slowed near the bank side, ice was beginning to form. With the late afternoon slipping towards evening the trees, bushes and taller grass began developing a coating of powdery, white crystals as a thick, hoar frost began to form. The three men all wrapped in furs and leather gloves and swathed in heavy campaign cloaks against the weather. Noses and mouths hidden beneath scarves as they strived to keep the moisture stealing wind from cracking their lips and softer skin of their faces.

Despite the bitter cold and the lateness of the day, there was still much activity on the river plain. News now of Roman incursions onto the Carthaginian bank saw numerous patrols of Numidian and Roman cavalry racing up and down the banks like groups of soldier ants. They fought and chased one another and Baldor noted disturbingly that the Numidians appeared to be coming off worst. More than once the three had to dodge back from the bank and hide within the cover of the trees as groups of horsemen galloped past. Baldor was particularly on edge, with Mago's scorn still ringing in his ears he felt solely responsible for the safety of his General. Ever mindful of Gestix's teaching he constantly loosened his weapons in their scabbards as he rode, his head moving cockerel like in all directions as he searched for Roman patrols. Sound rather than sight alerted the men. Hearing the muffled rumble of hooves further downstream had them once more seeking the blue-black shadows of the trees a little way back from the bank. The arriving Roman cavalry were about to ride past when one man noticed the men's tracks swinging away from the bank and called a halt. The turma slowed and stopped to examine the trail leading into the trees.

"They're becoming bolder." Malo muttered softly beneath his scarf while easing his bow from its case. He laid an arrow across the string, his bow hand holding two spare shafts in readiness.

Baldor drew a falcata slowly, the snake like hiss of the blade leaving the leather sounding deafeningly loud to all of them. Hannibal too reached for his sword then stopped, placing a restraining hand first on Baldor's then Malo's arm, cupping his hand to his ear indicating they should listen. A faint pounding became a thundering rumble then a score of Numidians appeared from the same direction they themselves had come. The Romans snatched for weapons kicking their mounts forward into the path of the oncoming warriors, concerns over the tracks forgotten. Whoops and battle cries rent the frigid air as the two sides raced headlong towards each other. Just before contact the Numidians hurled their javelins into the oncoming Romans hitting the leading horses and dropping them into the snow. Animals and men fell and slid along the ground smashing the javelins that impaled them, the sound of snapping wood and men's screams punctuating the rumble and thumps. Despite this success the Numidians wheeled about, retreating whence they'd come. The Romans, recovering and regrouping quickly, rode around their fallen and followed but at a more respectful distance.

"How much further Baldor?" Hannibal asked calmly.

"Around the next bend I think, sir." He looked at Malo for reassurance.

Malo Nodded. "Nearly there General and this coming darkness will help us reach home much safer once we're done." He indicated the last chink of light disappearing behind the distant mountain peaks.

With the skirmishing patrols gone and silence returning they emerged cautiously from the trees. A further two stades of riding downstream they found the island rearing up in dark silhouette from out of the middle of the river. They forded the first of the multiple streams, the horses skittering as the icy water reached over their knees. Emerging onto a raised gravel bed, they stepped out sprightly glad to be free of the freezing water. Their hooves scrunched on the gravel and rang hollowly on the larger stones as they made their way towards the next stream and the long, large hummock. The creeping darkness turned the world to gloom and the riders curbed their speed lest the horses turn an ankle, letting the animals pick their own way tentatively over the riverbed. Finally, they splashed up the shingle beach of the island, crossed the tussock-covered ground and rode through the gap into the valley behind.

"I'll keep watch from here sir, just in case anyone's afoot." Malo said quietly slipping fluidly from his horse, landing softly. Taking his bow and quiver, he tied the reins to a tree bough wedged just inside the gap that marked the entrance between the ridges. Slipping behind its tangled branches, he squatted down.

Baldor and Hannibal walked their mounts into the main valley, picking their way around rocks and debris left by the previous flood, the ground whitening from the earlier snowfall and the fast forming frost. The valley sides rose sharply, the sporadic clumps of winter-dead gorse standing up darkly from the white blanket, as the bank height increased the clumps multiplied, thickening into stands. On the crest, stunted willow and silver birch trees rose above all, denuded of leaves their branches black and skeletal in the gloom. Hannibal halted his mount studying the valley, with the height of the ridges it was impossible to see either riverbank, even the gurgle and rush of the water was muted.

"This might just suffice." He muttered beneath his scarf.

"Beg your pardon sir, what was that?"

"Nothing Baldor, I'm just talking aloud." Hannibal's eyes narrowed as he peered along the length of the valley whilst patting his horse's neck settling it. "The exit there …" He continued, pointing to the gap at the far end of the island. "What's beyond it?"

"Similar to where we entered sir, a spit of land made up of gravel and rocks then the main riverbed again."

Hannibal nodded. Seeming pleased with what he'd seen he turned his horse about. "Come, let's collect Malo and head back to camp."

"Is it what you expected sir? Does it help us?"

"Greatly Baldor! Greatly! The pair of you have done well."

Baldor sensed Hannibal was not to be drawn on the subject but detected a glint in his Generals eye and an excited eagerness in his body language, which he took as signs of satisfaction. Collecting Malo, they made their way homeward through the dusk and the now heavily falling snow. They encountered no more patrols but passed numerous bodies of men and horses stiffened in death and slowly disappearing beneath the falling snow, becoming irregular shaped lumps.

No one spoke as they rode, their heads down, tucked against their chests to keep the driving snow out of their eyes; it was only when the pinprick glimmer of the Carthaginian camp fires appeared out of the darkness that Hannibal broke the silence.

"It was a most worthwhile trip, my thanks to you both. This island suits my plans and purpose exactly. Be at my tent by first light, all will be explained then. Pray to the Gods that the weather remains cold and dry, for much will depend upon it."

Before Baldor or Malo could respond, Hannibal kicked his mount to a trot. "Come, we can risk a little speed now."

****

It was a muffled and fur wrapped group of officers that approached Hannibal's tent the following morning. The men shapeless beneath heavy fur cloaks that fell to their ankles with scarves swathed about their necks, only their exotically plumed helmets, worn as much for additional warmth as denoting status labelled them as men of rank. Amidst clouds of breath vapour and crunching snow underfoot, the men filed through the flap door held open by a servant. Inside, the tent divided into three zones; a main meeting area complete with long table and chairs for twenty, to the rear a small living space complete with simple furnishings and a camp bed affording Hannibal privacy to rest and relax. Lastly, a curtained section secreted a small area for prayer complete with miniature altar, incense burners and a bronze statue of Baal Hammon. Slaves heaped wood into braziers while poking the embers vigorously to produce more heat. As the flames roared and consumed the wood, sparks spat and fizzed in all directions. The incoming men ignoring the hazard and the thick effusing smoke, holding hands up to the warmth arranging themselves around the fires. Servants served goblets of mulled wine to warm them through, the aromatics in the wine vied with the other smells of the tent, the fresh tang of newly split wood, the musty scent of rushes and the reek of woodsmoke. The pungent odour of unwashed humanity failed to register amongst them as all had been without a bath for some weeks. Shaving was also a luxury few had lavished upon themselves, beards and hair were bushing and lengthening giving the men an unkempt look, the growth however offered some protection from the incessant wind and cold.

For all they'd been outside the tent first that morning, Baldor and Malo entered last of all feeling distinctly uncomfortable in close presence of their senior commanders. They waited respectfully as the officers were ushered in, wined and seated, before positioning themselves just inside the door. Mago saw Baldor enter and fixed him with a cold, hard stare. Baldor held and returned the look for a moment as his own anger stirred but sensing a scene, lowered his eyes and moved quietly to the opposite side of the tent. His heart rate increased and his chest tightened as a mixture of injured pride and repressed anger swept over him. Remaining respectful of Hannibal's commands to end the row he recollected the previous insults and quietly fumed. Momentarily lost in his own world with thoughts and regrets he missed the call to attention, it was Hannibal himself calling his name sharply that snapped him from his reverie to find all eyes upon him. Embarrassed at being caught daydreaming he mumbled his apologies and stepped towards the table. His eyes involuntarily flashed towards Mago to find him sneering back at him and shaking his head in mocking disgust before saying something to the officer next to him. Baldor couldn't hear the talk but from the looks of contempt, he knew it to be at his expense; Hannibal however had begun explaining his plan and missed the exchange.

Referring to a parchment map tacked to a wooden mount and suspended from the tent frame, he began with simple details; the position of both camps, times and distances from one to the other and from the camps to the river, to the edge of the plane and finally to the mountains. He paused, seeking understanding among the men and asking for questions. With none forthcoming, he broke the map down further into features of terrain, river widths, depths and bank heights, vantage points, wooded and clear areas. He seemed relaxed, happy even, smiling as he spoke while carefully involving all in the discussion, using their names and prompting them for opinions, finally he drew their attention to the island.

"This, gentlemen." He tapped his finger on the shape. "This is the lynch pin of my plan."

He smiled again watching the faces as they peered quizzically at the shape he'd pointed out. Baldor was bemused by Hannibal's casual manner, as if he was discussing a game or a hunt, not describing the geography for a battle.

"I'll return to the usefulness of the island shortly though I ask that you bear it in mind." He smiled with boyish mischief a sparkle in his dark eyes. "You now know the lie of the land, but first let's discuss our adversaries." He sat down resting his chin on clasped hands. "Opposing us are some forty thousand men, two Consular armies, along with two Consuls!"

There was an audible in taking of breath around the table.

"That means they've upwards of ten thousand more men than us!" General Gisgo growled into his goblet as he savoured the wine.

"True, true!" Hannibal nodded and sipped his own drink then laughed softly.

"They flatter us Gentlemen, flatter us with their numbers and such a prestigious gathering, which tells me one thing, they fear us! And since when has being out numbered ever bothered you, good Gisgo?" He asked in a playful, mocking tone.

It was the turn of the men around the table to smile and laugh. Gisgo grumbled and smiled then shrugged good-naturedly as those closest jostled him.

"Underestimating them however, I do not! They're a formidable and well-trained army, well equipped, armed, and ably led at Maniple level by Centurions and Optios. It has to be said they're battle proven and probably the best in the world, bar us!" He flashed a wicked grin.

Loud acclaim and thumping of the table followed which he had to quieten before continuing.

"They've a number of weaknesses however; the first is their unchanging and unimaginative battlefield manoeuvres. For example, their continuous … no, permanent reliance on heavy infantry to engage, hold and crush the enemy. Whilst this gives them power and momentum, it also gives their second serious weakness, which is lack of flexibility. We know heavy troops need light ones for manoeuvrability and support; they however, ignore their Velites after using them in preliminary skirmishing. This same weakness is true of their cavalry arm; as here they have only heavy troops and as you all know, for cavalry to operate effectively you need both heavy and light brigades. Thirdly, they fail to operate their cavalry in affective combination with the infantry, these are lessons we can teach them to their cost."

He paused to drink again letting the men digest his words.

"Their fourth weakness lies in their senior command structure. Usually the two Consuls operate an equal joint command, how can this work? It's seldom that two will agree as one. A ship, like an army has many officers but only one Captain. I need each and every one of you to drive this campaign but the ultimate responsibility and final decision is mine, come what may. At present, the Consuls are passing ultimate singular command from day to day. You may think that better …? However, not in this case. Happily, for us, Scipio and Longus are at each other's throats. One is experienced and cautious where the other is amateurish, pig-headed and reckless, this recklessness is what I intend to exploit." He tapped his finger to his nose intimating a secret and chuckled softly. "Two Consuls then; Publius Cornelius Scipio and Tiberius Sempronius Longus, two very, very different men both in abilities and character. Both are in the final month of their term of office and would no doubt stand to gain much by crushing us. We routed Scipio at the Ticinus but despite his defeat there, do not discard him, he's the thinker, a seasoned soldier and a brave one at that. Wisely for them but unfortunately for us, he has, as yet, refused to be drawn into pitched battle, declining our formal calls for combat and ignoring our probing stings at his camp and men, other than to fight us off attempting to keep us this side of the river. He was also buying time, time until he could be reinforced by his fellow consul, Longus."

"Shouldn't we have forced the fight then sir?" Maharabal asked. "Before he was reinforced? Now we have twice the amount to kill."

"That was my thoughts too General, initially! Strike while the iron's hot, destroy them a piece at a time while their morale was shaken, while the advantage of our victory at the Ticinus lay with us … but reason this! While their Consul refused to fight, their men must surely chafe and wonder why? Their morale and confidence must be sapped! They've lost battles in the past but that's never stopped them taking the field again and quickly. I tell you Gentlemen; the ordinary Legionnaire will be asking what it is that their commanders' fear?

As for us? Well, Baal knows our men need the rest and why not? They've earned it; having fought their way over mountains in the grip of winter, gone hungry and damned near froze to death on the way. Any time the Romans are willing to grant us will put some meat back on their bones and help them back into shape. In contrast to the enemy though, our morale is high and growing as surely as it diminishes for them. Also, the longer they procrastinate the more insurrection grows among the Gallic tribes, daily they throw off the Roman yoke and come over to us. News travels fast that the unbeatable Romans have been beaten; talk inflates the victory at the Ticinus and spreads like a forest fire of this Roman indecisiveness, their fear! The tide turns Gentlemen and we need do nothing but paddle to hold position." He smiled again.

"However, you're right General." He said turning to Maharabal. "This waiting will mean there are more to kill but this also I ask you to consider. When you trap a wolf, do you not then seek her cubs? And then? ..." He looked around the table gesturing for an answer.

"Hannibal, pray enough of the fables, what is it you wish to tell us?" Mago grumbled his patience short as ever.

Hannibal ignored him and looked at his men, his face suddenly serious, his smile gone and his voice cold and hard as winter frost. "You kill them all is what you do! The wolf and the cubs, sparing none, then burn out the den. The work's over and done with one effort and that's what we'll do. We'll destroy the Roman field armies and when they're no more, the city of Rome itself."

His voice changed to harsh monotone as if repeating some secretly held vow that could finally be spoken and made public. His gaze fixed on the flaring brazier but without really seeing, unless in his mind's eye he saw not a brazier afire but Rome itself in flames. His voice thickened with the passion of his conviction, the hatred flowing into the words like venom.

"This war will not just be until the Romans capitulate and seek terms, I'll give them none! None, save blood and iron, it will be to the end, the very end! This carbuncle on the world that is Rome will be raised to the ground as if it's never been. Rome and anything Roman will cease to exist, any memory of her will be erased as if it never was, as this world is not large enough for the sons of Baal and the sons of the she wolf."

The men stared at their General a little askance. All knew of the hatred that burned within him for Rome and were not surprised by his harshness to that end, what disturbed them was the change from the rational, level headed commander they knew to what sounded like a ranting madman. It was either their silence or the sudden loud crack of the burning wood that brought Hannibal back from wherever his thoughts were. As if waking from a dream he glanced around the room, and then recollecting his thoughts and words prior to his diatribe, he cleared his throat.

"Forgive me Gentlemen, I digress." His voice once more light and rational, the brightness back in his eyes.

"Firstly, we need Scipio out of the way; our intelligence already reports him injured at the Ticinus."

Smiles, chuckles and low voiced banter broke out around the table, Baldor coloured slightly at the thought of the information he had passed to Hannibal in that regard.

"Injured gentlemen but neither seriously nor like to die anytime soon, he remains the man to watch along with his brother Gnaeus. Gnaeus remains in Spain, a thorn to our rear but neither he nor his brother are my concern for the moment, nor the crux of this plan. Tiberius Sempronius Longus is our man of interest. He's the man who'll give us victory here at the Trebbia if I've judged him aright? Longus is a brave man but his weaknesses are vanity and hunger for glory, by nature he's intemperate and overly sure of his abilities and I'm told he rates us poorly."

Smiles and laughter changed to snarls and grumbles around the table. Hannibal smiled, raising his hands gesturing for calm and quiet.

"Bear with me Gentlemen, bear with me, it's a good thing this Consular arrogance! I would that all Romans rate us so, for it makes their defeat surer and easier to bring about. Longus thinks we're but fleas that crawl on the she wolf's back and can be easily picked off. We'll make him suffer for his temerity though, he'll have good cause to curse us all, aye and himself for his rashness, mark my words! Like most of these Consuls, he soldiers purely to raise his political ambitions, to further his name, wealth and his prestige in Rome. He has some military experience but nothing like that of Scipio, nor does he think like him. Caution, common sense and reasoned strategies are not his style, blunt unimaginative manoeuvre with hammer like blows are his trade mark but now we'll turn the hammer on him!"

The men were very quiet, even Mago had no comment, all were deeply impressed at the depth of knowledge Hannibal displayed concerning his enemy.

"This arrogance extends even to his own people, I'm reliably informed that he and Scipio have argued and now neither speaks to the other. Their joint command is thus divided, supreme command of the whole army passes from one to the other on alternating daily basis. This foolery, aided by Longus' intemperate character will bring us victory.

You'll have noticed the constant harassment tactics by our Numidians against the Roman cavalry? We appear to come off worst because that's how I wish it to seem! The Numidians were ideally suited to this task in the way they fight; sting and fall back, sting again and so on. Over this last week I've noticed a pattern developing, in that the days when Longus commands the responses to our sorties are larger and more aggressive compared to when Scipio holds sway. This Longus has something to prove Gentlemen, he's hungry, wanting! I'm happy to help build his confidence, let him think they're superior, to fill his head with thoughts of a quick and easy victory then draw him out, to a place of my choosing, and then our hammer blow!" Hannibal punched the palm of his other hand with a loud crack.

Pausing to let them absorb his words, he poured a drink while the seated men talked excitedly among themselves.

"So, I've been steadily baiting the trap. Until yesterday I was unsure of how to spring it until these two men presented me with the ideal opportunity."

He gestured towards Malo and Baldor. When all turned to look in their direction, Malo managed to remain impassive, Baldor however colouring under the attention shuffled awkwardly.

"And here's how I propose we do it." Hannibal walked to the map and the men turned back to watch.

"Scipio is in command tomorrow so the response to our attacks will be muted and purely defensive. The day after however, when Longus is once more Kingpin I'm turning the Numidians loose on his camp again but this time in force. As dawn breaks, they'll launch a heavy, more determined attack than usual. Once they have the Romans attention and hopefully a substantial response they'll fall back. However, with the numbers I'm committing, it should look like a major attack which is failing and dissolving into a large-scale retreat, a retreat that Longus will view as a sure sign of victory should he pursue it. I want him to turn his whole army out this time; I want him snapping at the Numidians heels as they cross the river back to our camp.

I want our men up before dawn and breakfasted. Issue oil so they can warm and rub it into their skins to guard against this damnable wind; we need them fed, warm and ready for action. We do this quietly mind! No trumpet calls, no shouts! With this done I want them in battle formation on the plain in front of our camp just back from the river, I'll cover actual troop deployments shortly." The men erupted with questions, as usual Mago's gruff voice rose above the others.

"What if Longus doesn't take the bait, brother?"

"If he doesn't we've but risen from our beds over early for nothing, is all! No harm done, other than some lost sleep for us and a rude awakening for the Romans." Hannibal shrugged and smiled as laughter broke out.

"However! … However." He repeated raising his hands for quiet. "I'm sure I've judged my man aright, I warrant he'll be chivvying and harrying the Numidians tail all the way, he wants a battle and he wants a victory. The Numidians will be carefully briefed to wreak havoc not just at the Roman horse lines but throughout the camp, wherever and however they can! I want the whole Roman army mobilizing and coming down on us. Importantly though, the Numidians must retreat northward back along the Roman bank and only cross when they're opposite us."

Using a charcoal stick, he circled the Roman camp on the map then drew a line parallel to the river back towards the Carthaginian camp.

"They cross here." He drew the line over the river. "We'll be formed up and waiting for them here!" He drew another circle in front of the Carthaginian camp. "The plain's relatively flat which suits our pike phalanx as well as allowing all to see what's happening. The bank slopes quite steeply to the water, not too much to put the

Romans off but enough to tire them further as they exit the river. We let them cross and form up then hurl them back into the river."

"Why let them form up General? Would it not be better to kill them as they struggle up the bank?" Sergatatonix fingered his moustache thoughtfully as he spoke.

"Undoubtedly! However, I don't want to discourage them from the attack. I want them all on our side of the river so we can kill thousands, not hundreds!"

"I see what you're doing, sir but there's much we cannot control, much that is left to chance in this: firstly we have to hope they mobilize and follow us; secondly it has to be the full army that does so; thirdly, they have to cross the river where we want them to."

"Granted, General Maharabal! All that you say is true! But is warfare not a game of chance like any other? Excepting the stakes are higher, the losses crueller but the rewards greater? Here though, we instigate, provoke and guide then hope the Gods smile upon us. However, if they don't there's no real risk to our men, lost sleep and wasted time is all. Trust me! I haven't brought you all this far to gamble on an outcome."

Hannibal clasped Maharabal on the shoulder and chuckled.

"Where does this island come into the plan, sir?" Gisgo asked without looking away from the map.

The rest of the group ceased the talk and looked at their General.

"The island gentleman is our Trojan horse."

"Not more Greek stories Hannibal?" Mago rolled his eyes in exaggerated impatience.

"Yes brother, and knowing your Homer better than I? Remind me and the others what decanted from the horse?"

Mago looked bashful then suspicious as if he was being setup for a fall.

"Men … warriors!"

"Yes brother! A handful of warriors, whom at the right time brought about the destruction of Troy, the greatest city on earth! In our case though, we'll use more than a handful. In fact, a thousand heavy cavalry and a thousand foot to attack the Roman rear. The infantry to punch a hole, the cavalry to exploit it but only when we're fully engaged on the plain, not a moment before! Timing will be of the essence, too soon and the Romans may recover from the shock, too late, and they may try to withdraw. Thus, the distance and time from the island to the battlefield needs to be carefully considered."

Hannibal drew another line on the map indicating the advance of the ambush party from the island, up the Carthaginian side of the river into the rear of the projected Roman position.

"Cavalry and Infantry, brother? Two thousand! How large is this island?" Mago stood up, leaning forward on his fists to scrutinise the map.

"You'll soon see, good Mago for I want you to command and lead the attack."

Mago supported his chin with his hand looking thoughtfully at Hannibal.

"Now, there'll be many questions I'm sure?"

"How and when do we place the ambush party sir?"

"Tomorrow evening as the Romans bed down we begin our move. Their patrols are virtually non-existent after dark. Apart from a few outriders in immediate vicinity of their camp and their usual sentries near their palisade, it goes quiet. We'll wrap the horse's hooves in sacking and enter the island from our side. The island has high banks obscuring its centre from view; once ensconced within we should be safe from Roman eyes.

Those that make up this ambush party will have the hardest job of all for they need to be in place tomorrow night, remaining there until battle joins the following morning. Have the men each heat river-rocks and wrap them in cloths to take with them, these will have to suffice for warmth for there can be no movement or fires and with the weather as cold as it is … well, I need not elaborate on the challenge this presents."

The men around the table nodded agreement

"Well brother, I know where I'm going to be; freezing my balls off, chewing dried meat down by the river. What work have you for these other reprobates?" Mago gestured to the table and the seated men. Sniggers and mocking moans broke out.

"I have work for all Mago, worry not! … Baksaal! Markers for the troop dispositions if you please."

Chapter Twelve

Closeted in the corner of the wind slapped tent, Baldor stared blankly into space as he pushed the wooden spoon around his mess bowl, most of the greasy lamb and vegetable stew was gone, Armaco having browbeaten him until he'd eaten it. He belched quietly as his nervous and nauseous stomach digested the food then grimaced at the hot, bitter reflux that rose to the back of his throat making him reach for the hot water and honey to swill away the sour taste. He'd sharpened his weapons to perfection, checked his harness a dozen times, cleaning and oiling the leather and rubbed goose grease into his boots, the work at least taking his mind away from his fear of the coming fight. Would it always be like this he wondered? This fear, this gut wrenching, hollow feeling that shackled mind and body, loosened his bowels and dried his mouth. Having fought five major battles he'd expected the preliminary lingering to become easier, the fighting, killing even, he knew he could handle but this waiting, this nerve jarring waiting he could only suffer.

His mind was full of thoughts and regrets and far from focused on the coming combat. Thinking of both Gestix and Baraan and whose deaths he believed he was guilty of; he thought of his insolence to Armaco while in the forest and cursed himself again. Armaco, like Gestix before him deserved better treatment from him. Then the most painful memory of all assailed him, his self-imposed guilt from what now seemed a previous even surreal life, the guilt for Aiticia, his wife, his beautiful, spirited Aiticia. The love of his life, the most precious, most beautiful creature he'd ever known and loved. When had he last spared a thought for her?

Pushing a hand inside his shirt, he found the leather cord upon which hung the cameo, disentangling it from his neck scarf he lifted it out. The silver was warm from the heat of his body; he gently almost reverently rubbed his thumb over the delicately chased lines. This precious keepsake was the only possession he had to remind him of her. A lump formed in his throat that he couldn't swallow away, his stomach flipped, feeling oily and heavy, his chest felt as if there was a hole the size of his fist where his heart should be. His eyes smarted then filled as his memory conjured pictures of her and the former life they'd shared. She'd been dead just less than two summers now, paying he believed, the ultimate price for loving him. Her death he'd also added to his long list of personal blame and reckoning, reasoning his pride and black temper had killed them all and nearly done for Armaco at the fishery as he fought the albino. Now he and Mago were on a collision course. What in Baal's name, had he been thinking? Picking a fight with a General and Hannibal's brother no less, this damnable pride and temper would surely see him killed one day. Perhaps … perhaps, that would be a blessing, he reasoned bitterly while cuffing away the tears amidst an angry sneer and a shake of his head in abject disgust at himself for his self-pity.

A shadow blocking the lamplight snapped him from his dark thoughts and looking up he found Armaco standing above him, he pushed the cameo back into his shirt.

"It's nearly time Baldor." He said quietly.

Baldor stood, placing his mess bowl on the seat.

"May the God's protect you" Armaco said clasping Baldor's forearm. "I'll see you on the field or when it's over."

Baldor nodded slowly, a sad smile playing on his lips. He gripped Armaco's arm using it to pull the one-eyed warrior closer before flinging his other arm over Armaco's shoulder, embracing him tightly. Armaco, somewhat reserved in showing his own affection was taken aback by the demonstration of concern and affability, tentatively returned the gesture. Then standing back a pace, cleared his throat and punched Baldor on his shoulder strap speaking with mock aggressiveness.

"Look to yourself, you hear? Stick with Malo, no heroics! Just kill the bastards as they come at you, no quarter!"

Baldor nodded then slipped his helmet on, the lamplight reflecting from his oil-covered face. He flicked the broad, hinged cheek pieces down, the metal cold against his fire-warmed skin. He fastened the chinstrap as Armaco passed his cloak. He went to speak then stopped; looking embarrassed, he sought the right words then spoke quickly the words coming out in a rush.

"I'm sorry, sorry for my temper and harsh words that day ..."

"It's forgotten! Buy me a drink to make it up once we've beaten these bastards! Just worry about staying alive, nothing else!"

Baldor looked around the tent at Marko and Harbro, bowing his head and offering his hand to each, they in turn offering a blessing and similar advice to Armaco. Malo ducked into the tent bringing a blast of cold night air with him, he bound his scarf around his face as he spoke.

"I've brought the horses Baldor, we'd best move."

The men filed out into the darkness where Armaco undid the reins from around a planted spear shaft, throwing them back over the animal's necks, holding both by their bridles while Malo and Baldor mounted. Harbro passed shield and spear up to Baldor.

"See you tomorrow lad, when it's all done eh!"

"Tomorrow." He echoed managing a smile.

Marko passed shield and spear to Malo, the pair exchanging a handshake and words that were lost on the wind. Just as the men turned their horses away from the tent, Balaam appeared out of the darkness a flaring torch in his hand.

"It's a good night for it! Virtually no moon!" He said, flicking his head towards the sky and grasping Malo's hand as he spoke; Malo bowed his head in respect. "This weather will keep most under cover and the sentries near the braziers." He shivered as he walked to Baldor's mount pulling his cloak tighter about him. "Baal's breathe its cold as a witch's tit out here! Remember your lessons from Gestix, Baldor. Stay out of trouble eh! Fight and come home, on the morrow, lad!"

Baldor bowed his head and shook his Captain's hand. The men stood clear as the two turned their mounts to leave. The wind whipped their cloaks, stretching them out sail like behind them as they kicked the horses into motion. They trotted towards the camp exit passing the one thousand strong, heavy infantry already on the move. Moving the animals to a canter, riding along the side of the cavalry column they reined in next to Mago and his officers at the columns head. The infantry walked in a purposely, broken step less the cadence of a thousand pairs of booted feet be picked up by the enemy. The horses' hooves were wrapped in sacking muting their ring and thump on the ground; the men's weapons hilts and metal of their harness swathed in cloth to prevent tell-tale scrapes and rattles, their shields shrouded in their leather covers. Animals and men had been well fed and the horses draped in blankets covering their rumps, backs and withers. Gloves, scarves and cloaks had been found for all the men and they'd rubbed warmed oil into their skins. Each man carried a heated river stone wrapped in cloth and placed in their pack along with dry rations, for their next hot meal was likely to be late the following afternoon at the earliest.

"Come on Armaco, there's nothing we can do now, the lad will be alright! Malo will see to him. Let's get some sleep if we can, we've only a short time till we're up and moving ourselves." Harbro said, putting his hand on Armaco's shoulder steering him gently towards the tent. The one-eyed warrior was clearly agitated and replied.

"One of us should be with him Harbro; he's too bloody young, too hot headed! He's as like to pick a fight with General Mago as the Romans."

"He won't have time for anything like that; by the time they're into position and settled, they …"

"You didn't see the pair of them in Hannibal's tent! I tell you, they'd have set about each other there and then if the General hadn't intervened, Mago's as bad as Baldor!"

Harbro sniggered then laughed, Armaco looked at him suspiciously.

"I'm sorry Armaco; but you sound like his mother." Harbro laughed louder and pushed Armaco though the door into the tent. "Don't judge me wrongly, I care for him as much as you, perhaps more so, as he saved my life that day in the forest, but at twenty summers he's a man for himself, young yes but how long had you been at war by that age?"

"Huh! Too bloody long!" He grunted. "I know." He shrugged. "I know, you're right! Right in what you say but I was wise to the ways of the world, hardened. I'd have bladed you and emptied your purse before your shade was by the Styx, he's still got notions of honour like bloody Achilles!"

"Aye! And by the God's he fights like him too, I wouldn't like to take him on."

"No, not in a one to one fight but you know how battle is."

"Aye I know, push and shove the blade under the shield, the horse hamstrung under you." Harbro pushed a goblet at Armaco and motioned him to sit, "Marko! Drink?"

"Make it a large one!" The tall, olive skinned warrior answered. "It may be my last."

Harbro groaned loudly. "Tanith, mother of all that's holy, help me! What a bloody pair! An old woman and a harbinger of doom! Is there anything else you two want to worry about or can we have a drink, tell some lies, boast a little and make one another laugh?"

****

Only a sliver of moon showed beneath the banked cloud, keeping the night black as a sealed tomb. Other than the shuffle of feet and the odd blowing horse, the column pushed silently on following Malo and Baldor's lead. Malo was riding well out front, appearing every so often out of the darkness like a cloaked spectre relaying directions to Baldor who was bringing the column on and riding in uncomfortable silence next to Mago. With no stars to see or steer by, Baldor strained his ears against the wind listening to where Malo rode ahead of them. Mago had glanced up momentarily as Baldor first came alongside but said nothing returning his gaze into the blackness ahead. As they passed copses and small thickets, the wind blowing through branches and rustling pine needles helped hide the noise of their passing. A glimpse of the moon through a chink in the dense cloud cast a weak, wan light over the plane and the column, the gusting wind however drove another cloud over it returning the world to blackness. Despite the deliberate slow advance, one of the foremost horses tangled a hoof in a rabbit hole snapping its fetlock, the animal falling whinnying and wild-eyed to the ground, twisting and thrashing in panic pinning its rider beneath it. The cry of surprise then a grunt of pain put the column into a state of alarm as men held their breath listening for signs that they'd been heard. Mago cursed under his breath, gruffly calling for men to dismount and see to their comrade. The horse couldn't stand, its hoof remaining lodged, its leg badly broken. Whickering loudly it flailed its other legs wildly as it struggled to gain its feet, churning the snow and scattering the men as they dodged the deadly hooves while trying to free their comrade, he groaning in pain as the horse rolled and thrashed crushing his trapped leg and hip.

"Shut them up!" Mago hissed. "Kill the bloody horse before the noise brings the Romans down on us!"

A dry rasp, like snake scales across a stone floor told of a sword freeing its sheath, followed a heartbeat later by the wet thwack of cleaved flesh. The horse's scrabbling and snorting rose to a new level for a moment before it shuddered, gasped and lay still, its rider muttering from between gritted teeth to pull it off him. It took four men to lift the horse and two to drag the injured man clear, a quick examination found his hip broken, his knee dislocated and his leg badly smashed. He was also bleeding badly from where the shattered shinbone had punctured his skin.

"Tie him over one of the spare horses. Gag him or give him something to bite on I want no more noise. We'll patch him up when we're in position, move! Damn it! Damn it to bloody Hades!" Mago cursed then snapped at Baldor. "How much further to this island, boy?"

"Not far sir, five stades at most."

The gurgle and rush of the river announced itself before the men could see it but as they approached the bank the moon appeared; the light, although weak seemed to illuminate the valley as it reflected back from the dark water. Mago held the column in the shadows until the cloud closed over quenching the light once more. He dispatched two columns of cavalry into the river, edging their way tentatively across the current small plodding splashes from the hooves marking their movements. They formed two lines across the river to the island, the first a breakwater upstream from the crossing point with the second, half a stade downstream acting as lifeguards for any man losing his footing in the swift current. Meanwhile, he turned half his infantry about face, forming a defensive rear-guard crossing the rest of his cavalry over first. The rush of the river was amplified by the sound of water flowing around and against the cordon of horses, though the water only rose belly high on the animals the flow was strong and fast and the stones of the bed slippery. More than one horse stumbled and some fell with one or two needing recue by the lifeguards, the others managing to swim or flounder their way to the island.

Once across the river, Malo directed them through the gap in the hillocks into cover and relative safety of the islands valley. At Mago's command, Baldor took orders to the infantry to fall out and begin crossing the river a company at a time. With silent precision, the rearguard withdrew, shrinking ranks line by line but leaving a shield wall of men facing outward in all directions. At the river edge, men removed their helmets, trousers and boots, those who still wore tunics hitched them up and removed their leggings, stowing their gear along with their packs in the inverted bowl of their shields. Resting the shield on their heads and supporting it with one hand, they headed to the water, using spears as wading sticks. Like porters bearing goods in some desert caravan they eased into single file entering downstream of the cavalry breakwater, wading cautiously into the black, icy waters. Sharp intakes of breath and muttered curses told of freezing water rising up their legs and occasionally reaching groins and waists as some stepped into deeper holes. On the island, officers quickly and effectively marshalled the arriving troops sorting them back into their companies. As each reached its correct number, they marched off into the confines of the valley and allotted space, safe from sight. Officers checked every man of their company for injuries and ensured wet clothing was removed and that the warriors dried themselves with the cloths they carried in their kit.

Infantry and cavalry were separated, the infantry placed around the slopes of the valley with the horses tied to rope lines within the flat bottomed centre, each rider allotted a space in front of his horse ensuring that if orders came to mount quickly there'd be no delay or confusion.

Despite the efficiency of the manoeuvres and the efforts to keep quiet there was the unavoidable bustle associated with movement and settling of two thousand men and a thousand horses in darkness. Relief came as the hubbub dropped away as company by company, they settled and peace and quiet returned to the valley once more. Baldor and Malo along with Mago and his two senior officers were the last to enter the valley. Mago tapped the shoulder of the man next to him and whispered softly.

"Get the officers over here."

The man mimicked a screech owl, sending an eerie call across the valley that reverberated as a slight echo. Within moments, officers arrived out of the darkness assembling quietly alongside Mago and his senior commanders. Mago listened as the numbers of missing and injured were relayed. In total, seven men were missing presumed drowned; three horses had been destroyed having fallen and broken their legs. Injuries were surprisingly light considering a night march and bad weather, amounting to a dozen twisted or broken limbs, the biting cold and wet clothing was now the main worry. Mago listened to all without interruption and was about to issue orders when snow began falling heavily.

"Humph! More snow! A blessing and a curse." He muttered, looking up while pulling his cloak tighter about his shoulders.

"How mean you sir?" One of the officers asked.

"It'll cover our tracks and the dead horses making them indistinguishable from any others and the chances of any of the drowned lads being spotted should be remote, for apart from us mad bastards few others will venture out of camp in this weather I'll warrant."

There was some muted grim laughter to that.

"However, if this snow keeps up all night there'll be fewer of us left to fight come the morning."

There was no response to that.

"Separate the injured, place then in the centre next to the cavalry, all of you, back here just before dawn breaks."

Baldor and Malo settled amongst the cavalry; Baldor ferreted in his bag whilst unlacing his sodden boots. His horse had stumbled into deep water and his feet and legs were wet. He grimaced as he removed his boots, the cold air on his wet skin felt as if he'd been scalded; he massaged his numbed toes trying to rub life back into them then rubbed briskly with his cloth, drying his feet. His leather trousers were damp to his knees but the dubbing he'd rubbed into them had kept most of the water at bay.

"Are you dry Malo?"

"Yes, but I'm stiffening up with this unending cold. I swear before holy Apedemak and his brother Amun that I'll never curse the heat and dust again if I could just feel some warmth on my body, how long till spring?"

"Three moons or so, we haven't had the midwinter solstice yet." Baldor replied as he wrapped his feet in dry linen and pulled his damp boots back on, lacing them as he spoke. "How long till dawn?"

The Nubian looked at the sky gauging where he'd seen the moon last.

"Not too long I'd say, but we could be here till midmorning anyway, that's presuming the Romans take the bait and go to battle. And I don't imagine the warmth will be any greater just because of daylight."

"At least it'll be light; I feel like we're sitting in some pharaoh's tomb, it's so dark."

"At least we'd be warm, wrapped in all those bandages." Malo chuckled causing Baldor to snigger.

The pair sat quietly thereafter, back to back supporting one another, heated rocks wedged between chest and knees, only moving to flick the thickening snowflakes from their cloaks and to blow warm breath into their gloves. Eventually they tired of both and just sat, waiting out the time until they had to report again. The snow continued to fall without pause and build in depth, the huddled bodies blending into the whitened landscape as the snow blanketed all.

****

Just before dawn agitated talk erupted in the valley bringing men to their feet, some however did not rise. Officers moved swiftly amongst their men urging them to help their comrades up. The befuddled, stiffened warriors who made it to their feet shook those still seated and found some as stiff and lifeless as stone idols. Baldor discarded his cooled stone and struggled to his feet amidst numbed and aching limbs, his balance awry. His cloak was stiff and standing off from his body and he felt weary; his arms and legs slow to move, his very bones seemed to be chilled. Lethargically, he rubbed his hands and arms trying to restore warmth, his movements clumsy and uncoordinated. Realising that Malo hadn't moved he reached down to shake him.

"Malo! … Malo! Get up, up! Come on!" He whispered hoarsely as he shook the Nubian. He noticed a corpse like stiffness in the man's shoulders, his concern turning to panic when he received no response and he shook him more violently.

An officer came past urging men up and gesturing them to rub each other's arms and legs. Baldor physically hauled Malo to his feet, relieved to find him coming to; he wobbled and staggered as if drunk, Baldor having to steady him,

"Malo! Malo! Can you hear me?"

Malo was covered in snow and his cloak, like Baldor's was stiff and stuck out at an angle. He looked at Baldor but without seeing.

"S … so, so co … cold!" He managed from between stiff lips. Baldor rubbed Malo's arms, his movements far from fluid and still clumsy. He worked on one arm then the other, the action helping his own body to warm; he moved to Malo's legs and began work there. The officers were assessing those that hadn't got up, more of the prone bodies were dragged to their feet; others however, stiff as two day old corpses were pulled to one side, help having come too late.

While the warriors struggled dawn broke, pale and grey then slowly turning pink as it spread from the east washing the retreating clouds pink-red. The snowfall had stopped earlier but left a fine covering, causing the men further problems as they slipped and fell while they tried to warm themselves. Baldor heard the screech owl call again and saw the officers making their way back towards the mouth of the valley and Mago.

"Come on Malo, we have to report." Baldor continued to rub the still shivering Malo as he talked. Mago was already issuing orders as they arrived, with the morning light coming full he pointed to various points around the valley to illustrate his commands. The officers returned to their units and immediately set their orders in motion. Companies began swapping positions, shuffling to their new locations as the previous occupants moved to another area. They paused only long enough to form up and be counted before moving on again, the enforced movement hopefully restoring circulation and bringing some warmth to their bodies. Their commanding officer remained in the original position as an assembling point for the newly arriving unit; the company Hypolokhagos however went with the troops to keep them moving and help marshal them anew. As part of the manoeuvres one company at a time went down among the horse lines, the men removing their gloves and slipping hands under the animals blankets seeking what heat they could from the horses skin to help warm their own. Slowly the confusion eased and the men's movements to flow as warriors learned what was required of them. The deployment was beginning to warm most of them through, a few however, Malo included, still struggled. Baldor was still helping him when Mago turned to him.

"You! Walk me around this frozen hole. Now that it's light we can plan our exit and hopefully through shallower water."

"Yes sir."

Seeing Baldor still helping Malo while he listened and answered, Mago motioned his adjutant forward. "Help this man while we take a walk."

The adjutant took over ministrations from Baldor who had to stride quickly to catch Mago up. Mago stopped suddenly looking skyward causing Baldor to do likewise. Thick columns of grey-black smoke climbed high and straight into the morning sky, casting an ugly stain across the now wine red colouring.

"It's begun! The Numidians are attacking the Roman camp." Mago said turning back to speak to his adjutant. "Pass the word along and have the men begin weapons checks, we could be moving anytime."

"Yes sir."

"Right boy!" He said turning to Baldor again. "Show me what you know."

Baldor felt his insides knot as he fell in alongside Mago; he indicated they should walk towards the entrance of the valley.

"The other entrance is back that way sir, more towards the Roman side of the river." He indicated over his shoulder. "Its best we use the same ford as last night when we leave, it twists and turns but the daylight will make it easier for us."

Mago nodded acknowledgement as the pair slipped into single file and pushed through a patch of dead gorse. Mago cut an impressive figure, though not as tall as Baldor he was broad shouldered and thick set. A powerful, 'bull' of a man, encased in black helmet and armour and wrapped in a thick bearskin cloak, which only added to his imposing appearance and width. Despite his size and no doubt considerable weight, Baldor noticed he moved nimbly and with a light tread. Their feet scrunched on the fresh snow as they walked, their breath ballooning in the morning air, the atmosphere between them as warm as the weather. The ground levelled as it neared the river's edge. Mago broke the silence, speaking while still looking forward not bothering to look at Baldor.

"When this is over, we'll have matters to discuss, will we not?"

Baldor cleared his throat, using the time to form his reply, he'd half expected the question or at the very least further reference to their disagreement. He struggled with his anger, the usual hot, quick temper battling with the rationale he'd promised himself to exercise.

Mago turned to Baldor. "Well boy, lost your tongue? It …"

"No sir!" Baldor's voice wobbled slightly as he spoke though not from fear but a mixture of anger and regret at himself. "No sir!" He repeated firmly. "Our disagreement needs to be settled."

"Good! So though intemperate, you're a man of honour at least! After this battle then? Baal willing we're both spared."

"Yes sir."

"Away from the camp and my brother, you and a second and myself and a second, to the death."

"Agreed sir!" Baldor replied sombrely then chuckled quietly to himself.

Mago heard the out of place mirth and looked scathingly at Baldor.

"What is it you find so amusing?"

"Nothing amusing sir, rather ironic I'd say, fit for a Greek tragedy."

Mago stared intently seeking signs of mockery. "How mean you?"

"It strikes me as ironic sir, that you ask Baal Hammon to spare us in the coming battle so we can try to kill one another when it's over."

"Death doesn't frighten you then, boy?"

"My death? No sir! Perhaps, perhaps it would be a release but your death yes! That thought frightens me; it frightens me greatly, for I fear what I will have to tell your brother."

Mago looked at Baldor his eyes narrowing until he picked up the grim satire in the words and then smiled.

"You know boy it'll almost be a shame to kill you, your wit's as sharp as your tongue and temper."

Baldor just smiled, the pair walked on cautiously in silence as they neared the valley entrance and the view to the river.

Chapter Thirteen

Baldor and Mago cautiously exited the valley mouth onto the shingle beach. Feeling distinctly exposed they moved into cover of a narrow, dead ended recess. Crouching low at the front of the moss covered rock and grass alleyway they peered warily up and down the river for signs of life. All across the water a low hanging mist floated just above the flow like steam rising from a simmering pot. Everything seemed peaceful; the silence undisturbed other than the natural noises of water over the stones and the stilted, chattering cries of a moorhen from the far bank. Among the shallows and half-submerged stones, the water had turned to ice, its crystal fingers securing rock and water setting itself into white swirling shapes else freezing to a glass like finish. The marrow chilling temperatures at the waters side were even more biting than back in the valley, Baldor shivered as he felt the dampness creeping into his bones along with the cold.

A sudden, hollow sounding crack of hooves on stone and the rushing, splashing noise of water being waded through had both men scrabbling backwards into the recess for cover, flattening their bodies against the moss-covered sides. Holding their breaths in trepidation and straining their ears for further signs of the approaching horses they waited, motionless. Everything went silent for a moment, a fear filled moment that seemed to stretch into eternity. The silence dragged on and just as they dared to breathe again, they heard another clop of hooves but closer. Grimacing in anticipation of discovery, they slipped falcatas slowly from their scabbards. Light metallic clicks and the smooth rasping, hiss of oiled metal being uncovered announced the bright blades to the morning.

Low toned voices drifted along the bank, unclear and muffled; the clop of hooves on stone however grew louder. Both men pushed back into the mossy wall, flattening themselves wishing to become invisible, each holding his breath as the noise of hooves came still closer. Mago looked at Baldor and raising his blade slowly mouthed bitterly. "Romans?" Baldor nodded and crossed his sword-filled arms in front of his chest, the blades resting either side of his face. As cold as it was, sweat broke out on their faces sending tiny tendrils of heat vapour rising from their skin. Baldor felt his scalp itch and the hair at the nape of his neck rise as he waited grimly for discovery and no doubt, bloodshed. The clop of hooves stopped and a heavy thump told of a man dismounting. Words grunted in thick Latin were followed by footfalls crunching on gravel and coming closer. Both men tensed as the footsteps came around the corner. A Roman cavalryman stepped into view, yawning widely and pulling at his tunic below the waist. He turned to face the recess side, not noticing the two men standing just paces from him.

He groped under his tunic and then with the sound of splashing water and a low contented groan of satisfaction, he urinated against the wall.

The two men were stuck; once the Roman finished and turned back, he must surely see them. They dared not move, as he would hear them and raise the alarm before they closed the gap to kill him. The sound of other horses arriving forced their decision for action. Mago looked at Baldor one last time then nodded towards the urinating Roman whilst tapping his chest lightly with the tip of his falcata. A moment later he was halfway to the man who though not finished his ablutions was startled by Mago's footfalls and already turning around. He died with a shout forming on his lips and piss running down his legs as Mago slashed his throat. The heavy bladed falcata sliced deeply, destroying thorax and muscle, spraying blood like scarlet rain across the recess wall. Mago grabbed him as he fell, holding him by the folds of his cloak and lowering the gurgling, twitching body quietly to the ground, despite the effort the man's helmet clanged on a rock. Another horseman appeared at the recess entrance calling for his colleague while chewing on a piece of bread.

Seeing his comrade's body and Mago standing over him he was momentarily stunned but recovered quickly. Spitting the bread away and swearing loudly he lowered his spear while calling behind to warn his comrades. Another rider appeared in his rear and seeing the trouble, he too shouted in alarm. Baldor immediately moved in front of the first rider drawing his attention, causing him to kick his mount hard driving it forward aiming his spear straight for him.

The horse scrabbled and slipped on the snow and stones trying to gain traction, whinnying hard as the rider dug his heels cruelly into its flanks in urgent desire for speed. With the short distance between it and Baldor and the treacherous going under its hooves, it only managed to stamp its way across the snow and came slipping and side on at Baldor. The rider was disadvantaged as he lurched in time with the horse's staggering, irregular movements in order to keep his seat. His spear swung off target as Baldor jumped clear of the careering horse. He braced his legs, both weapons ready, one to deflect the spear the other to attack the rider. Another unpredictable slip of the horse brought the spear back on target and he had to side step again to avoid being skewered, spoiling his chance to get under the spear and at the man. His sword chopped the spearhead from the shaft as man and horse bore down then careered past him.

Mago, carrying just one sword pushed the fingers of his empty hand to his mouth whistling shrilly, then side stepped the second horse dodging the rider's spear. Realising there was no room to manoeuvre the rider dropped the spear and went for his sword, tugging frantically to pull it from its sheath. Seeing the panic and realising the sword was frozen to its sheath Mago smiled grimly. He stepped then half slipped towards the horse crashing into its flanks. The rider lashed out with his foot trying to push him off while he fumbled for his dagger. Mago grabbed the man's leg pinning it against the horse, powering his sword upwards he drove it half a blade length under the man's armpit. Mago grunted with the effort while the man gasped as the blade burst a lung; he crumpled and fell on top of Mago knocking him off his feet sending him sprawling onto the snow.

Baldor stepped after his adversary as horse and rider passed him, the man trying to fight to his rear, draw his sword and control his horse. Baldor slashed the back of the horse's legs before the man could turn it. With hamstrings, ligaments and most of one leg chopped through, the animal collapsed onto its hindquarters whickering horribly. Thrashing and screaming it fell onto its side crushing its rider beneath. As it rolled clear of its rider, its front hooves flailing, Baldor stepped over the half-conscious, broken man slashing at his lolling head, chopping the neck through to the spine. The blade lodged between the vertebrae and he snatched hard at the handle trying to free it. The sword however was stuck fast; he stamped his boot hard onto the man's shoulder while wrestling frantically to free it. Struggling wildly he contemplated abandoning it but with no shield he deemed he'd need the safety of both blades to survive. Glancing behind he saw more riders filling the entrance and grabbing for their weapons. Gauging the time before they closed on him he worked feverishly to free the blade. One of the riders was already attacking Mago, trying to spear or trample him as he was still on the ground trying to disentangle himself from the dead man.

With a dull click, the levered bone splintered apart and his blade came free, he spun around just in time to face the fast approaching horseman. Looking past the rider he saw Mago had struggled to his feet only to be knocked stumbling backwards onto the ground again as his new adversary's horse hit him hard with its front flank. The man pulled the horse around again, his spear arm rising ready to drive down into Mago's chest. Sprawled on the ground and with no shield Mago could only raise his sword in vain defence. Baldor switched his attention back to the oncoming horseman. Seeing the man's spear lowered and lining up on him, he hefted one falcata back over his shoulder as if to throw it. The man saw the move and veered sharply to avoid it, giving Baldor a moment's respite. With his view clear again, he saw Mago parrying and knocking the spear point away with his sword while trying desperately to get up. Without another thought, Baldor hurled the falcata at the horse and rider trying to trample and kill Mago. The heavy blade whooshed as it spun over and over through the air. A wet thwack of metal puncturing flesh was followed by a scream from the horse as the sword punctured its flank forcing the rider to break off his attack as it collapsed dying beneath him. With the pressure off, Mago powered to his feet and stepped in killing the man before he could disentangle himself from his dying horse.

Meanwhile Baldor looked to his attacker. With only one sword left, he was in trouble. He must rely on speed to keep out of the way but with ice underfoot; he knew his chances weren't good. Seeing the threat from the thrown blade gone, his attacker pulled his mount back into line heading straight for Baldor again, his spear lowered. Suddenly, he grunted like a stuck pig and pitched forward as if being pushed from behind. He slumped over the animal's neck, a brightly fletched arrow sticking in his back.

"Malo!" Baldor almost laughed with relief.

Baldor saw Carthaginian warriors were now surrounding the Roman cavalrymen, spearing and dragging them down. Mago was struggling to regain his breath from the fight while shouting orders and pointing across the river with his sword. Some warriors clambered onto the rider-less Roman mounts trying to turn them in the direction he indicated. However, the ponies had no bridles and the Carthaginians, unaccustomed to such were struggling. Malo was at the water's edge loosing arrows in quick, fluid motion. Baldor couldn't see what he was aiming at or if he was hitting his target but seeing the body language from the warriors on the bank he guessed he was being successful. Malo loosed the bow for the last time while Mago made his way to the water's edge rapping out orders to have the dead collected and hidden. Baldor made his way to his comrade and had to wait as others crowded him slapping his back and congratulating him. Baldor looked across the river seeing four rider-less horses, two stationary on a raised part of the riverbed, the third wading back across the river towards them following another bringing its dead rider slumped over its back. He saw one body lying prone on the island and another two washing over the shallow rapids, all had arrows sprouting from them.

The Carthaginians were now out in the river rounding up the horses, some had waded midstream and were hauling the dead men from the water dragging them back to the bank.

"Move the bodies and the dead horses out of sight! Bring the live ones back into the valley! Wash or cover those bloodstains, move it!" Mago strode amongst the men growling orders while looking for any sign of movement on the far bank. He paused to watch as the bodies came ashore nodding satisfactorily before approaching Malo.

"Well done warrior! Did you get them all?"

"I think so sir, I don't think there were any others in front of them."

Mago counted bodies. "Four in the river, two I killed, one the boy killed, that's seven." He looked around to see the other dead Roman that had attacked Baldor and which Malo had slain. "That's eight; you're good with that bow!" Malo bowed his head to the compliment. "I would expect ten troopers and an officer to make up a patrol. Are there any more bodies?"

Men looked around counting for themselves.

"Over here sir! Three more of the bastards." A lowered voice came back from where the Carthaginian infantry had joined the fray. "They've done for two of our lads' sir, and we've another two wounded. One won't make it sir … spear in his belly."

Mago swore and ground his teeth though he knew it could have been worse, especially if one had escaped.

"Let's get them and ourselves back into cover before another patrol happens along, come on! Move!"

Men slipped back into the island trailing the dead with them, others quickly washing away the bloodstains then sweeping the tracks in the snow using a branch as a brush. Mago looked around and saw Baldor wrestling his falcata free of the dead horse; snorting to himself, he made his way over. Despite his size, Mago moved almost silently on his feet, he stopped a few paces behind Baldor, unheard. With a loud sucking noise, the sword came suddenly free of the clinging flesh and Baldor stumbled backwards. His chest heaved for breath and his hands still shook moderately from the fight, scooping up a handful of snow, he scrubbed the blood from the blade while looking regrettably at the dead horse.

"That would be my blood being wiped off someone else's blade if you hadn't intervened."

Startled, Baldor whipped around and saw the bloodied sword in Mago's hand. His reflexes immediately took him to a defensive stance his weapons outstretched, his mind however telling him the language was Phoenician not Latin and that there was no threat. Recognising Mago, he immediately tensed again preparing to defend himself. Mago watched the differing thoughts playing across Baldor's face and smiled broadly.

"Relax boy! You think I'm offering this?" He held out his bloodied blade then lowered it changing it to his left hand.

"What I am offering is this …" He pulled his glove off with his teeth and stepped towards Baldor offering his right hand. "And my thanks!"

Baldor watched warily as Mago stepped closer, his hand still outstretched.

"You needn't have done what you did, you endangered yourself when you could have let that bastard kill me … or do you just want to fight me anyway?" The big man laughed and shook his head.

Baldor finally relaxed and smiled, pushing his right hand sword into the ground giving his hand to Mago. The pair shook firmly without the underlying menace of the last time.

"Thank you!" Mago looked Baldor in the eye as he said it.

"You're welcome, sir."

"Mago!" He corrected. When Baldor looked lost, he continued.

"You can call me Mago, Baldor; I think you've just earned the right." Baldor inclined his head respectfully. "Now, we best get out of sight."

The pair slipped back into the valley helping the warriors drag the dead horse in behind them.

Back where they started before the Romans appeared; they again looked to the far bank and up and down the river searching for movement. With glimpses of the sun through the cloud veils and the mist thinning the visibility was improving, thankfully the only disturbance seemed to be a pair of paradise ducks flapping and quacking at each other near the far bank.

"We might just have got away with it." Mago muttered. "By the time that patrol is missed it should be too late to make any difference."

****

Back in the Carthaginian camp, all was astir. Men had risen before dawn as commanded ensuring fires were stoked, breakfast prepared and flasks of oil set nearby to warm. Under torchlight, Quartermasters rolled supply wagons through the camp while slaves worked distributing extra rations of bread, meat and honey from them to all the men. The Numidian cavalry had already breakfasted and were now slipping away over the river turning southwards into the darkness towards the Roman camp.

The men breakfasted at leisure then began rubbing the warmed oil into their skin. Taking the luxury of another cup of hot water and honey as they worked, they pulled on their armour, their comrades helping lace them in. Swords were checked for ease of drawing then strapped on, harness buckles' and shield straps adjusted ready, shields, and spears placed in easy reach. Cavalrymen made their way to the horse lines ensuring the animals were fed and watered before fitting bridles and strapping on riding blankets.

"Baal almighty, it's colder than a whore's heart out here!" Armaco grumbled as he reappeared from the horse line and tipped oil into his palms rubbing it vigorously into his neck.

"Aye! And just as hard!" Harbro agreed. "Rub that into your face as well lad, it'll keep the wind from drying your skin and keep the warmth in. How's the horses?"

"They're alright; I've bridled and blanketed the three of them ready. Poor bloody things they must be frozen too, the blankets we put over them last night were stiff with frost."

"What about Baldor and Malo, poor bastards! I wonder how they've fared. I don't envy them last night in that cold … here, fasten these for me Armaco, my fingers aren't working yet." Harbro held out his wrists with the unlaced leather bracers as he spoke.

"No hot breakfast for them this morning either." Marko joined the conversation while turning sizzling lamb strips in a shallow pan. "Are you lad's hungry?"

"I can't remember not being hungry or not being bloody cold!" Armaco grizzled as he worked Harbro's lacings. "How's that honey and cloves doing?"

"Coming my Lord!" Marko quipped sarcastically tugging his forelock then genuflecting in exaggeration. Armaco grunted at the sarcasm.

"If your cooking skills were as quick as your wits we'd be better served!"

"I can serve you a thumping my Lord; would that serve? You'll find my fists as fast as my wits too!"

"Boys, boys!" Harbro interjected chidingly. "There's going to be more than enough folk to fight with today without starting with each other … when will that honey-water be ready anyway, Marko?" He chuckled.

Marko rolled his eyes. "Come back Baldor, all is forgiven I'm resigning from being cook."

The three laughed and settled down to eat, in the east the stars slowly dimmed as the pale grey wash of dawn crept into the sky. The campfires were kept roaring and as the repast finished; the men remained near the warmth, passing time as warriors do checking and cleaning their weapons.

Pillars of black-grey smoke became visible from the area of the Roman camp. With no wind to disperse them, they climbed high into the sky, Hannibal and his officers watching as they ate.

"I trust the Romans had a rude awakening and are not enjoying such a peaceful breakfast?" Hannibal joked, pointing to the smoke and raising laughter from around the table. "Or perhaps they've burnt their breakfast?"

This raising more laughter and comment, Hannibal however took the moment to watch his commanders, looking for signs of concern or hidden worry.

"Now, while we eat let's cover the battle plan one more time and as always: you're free to ask questions, comment and disagree as you see fit."

He flashed a warm smile as he walked toward the map board whilst chewing on a piece of oil-soaked bread, his manner as calm as if he was about to discuss a game. Most of his commanders were old enough to be his father, yet Hannibal held court and the undivided attention and respect of all in the tent. He oozed quiet confidence and control as he spoke, his tone, while remaining easy and casual was also precise and informative as he went over the main points on the map in detail again before moving onto the battle plan itself.

"So, all depends upon our Numidians raising enough hell in the Roman camp to tempt Longus out to fight."

"How can we be sure that Longus is in charge today sir?"

"Today is his day that I can promise you!"

"Baal willing, we make it his last sir!" Hasdrubal the elder quipped raising more laughter.

Hannibal chuckled himself then bit his bread and continued.

"Now! To business. Over this last week, the Numidians have repeatedly probed and skirmished around the Roman camp, hopefully stinging them to distraction. As you know these were only probing attacks and relatively light in troop numbers. Without making it too obvious as to our real intent, we've fallen back under each counter attack the Romans made to drive us off. However, we even won some of the skirmishes, forcing them to turn out a stronger force."

Some of the men laughed lightly.

"Thus, we've played cat and mouse with them and been seen to be the mice, thereby building their confidence again, fuelling their belief that we are weaker and they the stronger … invincible, the better men."

Groans and angry mutterings interrupted him; he smiled raising his hands for quiet.

"I told you, let them think it! What harm does it do?" He shrugged his shoulders; his arms open in a hapless gesture. "We know it's not so, as do our men and we'll prove it again today, and as I've always told you, too much pride and over confidence can be an army's undoing! First, however, we need to tempt them out … then the mice will turn.

With four thousand Numidian cavalry making up General Maharabal's sortie this morning, the Roman command will, I'm sure, construe it a major attack and respond in kind. Even if they don't, I'll wager it will be too much for Consul Longus's vanity and pride to ignore. With no steadying influence or advice being exerted upon him from Scipio or any other that Longus will heed, I expect him to take our bait and attack immediately with his whole army. I pray to Baal that the mice have pulled the cat's tail just too hard this time!"

"What happens if we have a patient cat, General? What if they just curl up and wait? Even just for better weather?"

This brought some light laughter from around the table.

"Then it's a cheaply won victory of sorts for us, for if they do nothing but sit and brood our men will see their inaction as fear and feed upon it, thus our men's confidence will increase as theirs diminishes. Doing nothing will erode the Roman's confidence in both themselves and their commanders, so either way victory will be ours, whether by action or inaction."

Hannibal paused to let his words sink in while helping himself to more bread.

Gisgo spoke first. "This flat ground bothers me sir, it suits their Legions well, if they cross the river and push us back they can effectively deploy their heavy infantry."

Hannibal chewed then swilled the morsel with a drink. He looked around the men's faces like a tutor studying his pupils when pushing for answers or to stimulate questions and discussion. He let them consider a while longer taking the time to dip the bread in his honey and water nodding in satisfaction at the taste.

"You're exactly right General Gisgo, the level ground suits their heavy infantry and sledgehammer tactics very well. However, for the same reason it also suits our elephants and pike phalanxes and my silver is on pike, rather than pila. Remember what Alexander's pike men did to the Persians and their Greek mercenary hoplites at Issus?"

The grizzled old General looked thoughtful then nodded. "Aye, true! I think you've the rights of it sir, pike with a good African warrior behind it will take pila!"

"So, as agreed at our last meeting, we let them cross and form up in reasonable order." Hannibal smiled at Sergatatonix who nodded sagely in return. "Then we have them where we want them, on the anvil and us ready with the hammer!

Deployment! I'll take the centre with the Gauls and the heavy Spanish infantry supplemented by our African troops. On our right and left flanks, the pike phalanxes. On the wings the heavy cavalry under you General Hasdrubal, I expect General Maharabal and the returning Numidians' will reinforce you to some degree. When they arrive, direct them out to your own flanks thus extending our lines further, this allows them the possibility of breaking off in pursuit again but without leaving gaps in the line, remember the Persian cavalry's mistake at Issus gentlemen?"

Heads nodded along with mumbled agreement.

"In front of us I want a screen of skirmishers and slingers to harass the Romans once they cross the river. To our extreme left and right the elephants, these will provide firing platforms for archers. I want the best marksmen placed there, their targets: Centurions, Optios, Standard-bearers and such, I don't want too many cool heads available to marshal their men when they finally reach our bank. The elephants should also be our shock weapon against the Roman cavalry. They I imagine will be placed on their wings after screening their crossing and as they haven't faced elephants before, the noise and smell should panic the horses and with no bridles, chaos should not be too far away!

Now, as you know for absolute success the timing of our ambush will be of the essence, which is where General Mago will play his part."

"What happens sir, if General Mago doesn't arrive on time? He has a way to travel and much can change on the field in a short time." Hasdrubal asked.

"We still win!" Hannibal replied confidently. "But not as easily, quickly or decisively as we would with him there. With the timing right he'll be our closing door in their rear, blocking their retreat, double envelopment! …"

Hannibal paused, looking around at the faces staring back at him. He nodded slowly.

"You think me presumptuous? Over confident? Brazen? All the things I've warned against?"

There was a quiet, mumbled disagreement and shaking of heads, Hannibal continued.

"I am confident, confident in your abilities, in my brother's and our men's abilities, for you are the best! Have we not proved it along the way from Saguntum?" He looked around the table to see heads nodding slowly. "My confidence is not over placed either, for we've planned and prepared well for this battle, believe me when I say this is no casual throw of the dice! Also, is it not we who have carried the fight to them this last while? They've not ventured to our side of the river in force as we have done to them. We choose the time for attack, not them! Our men are well rested and by now, well fed and guarded from the cold. They wait around the fires for the enemy to hurry themselves to destruction, so let them come, we don't need to steal a victory as they cross, let them come and we'll kill them all here by this Trebbia river."

The men's faces lightened as Hannibal drove his point's home. His quiet confidence and meticulous plans settling their minds and answering their questions.

Chapter Fourteen

Adharbal Samilcar thrashed and rolled on the sweat damp sheets of the divan like a man possessed of demons. The veins in his neck stood out like thick, corded ropes, sweat glistening in heavy dew like drops on his burning skin. He groaned and muttered loudly his words jumbled and incoherent, eyes wide and staring but not seeing. The two female servants at the bedside trying to bathe and cool him with dampened cloths had the water bowls knocked from their hands as his fevered convulsions reached new heights of agitation. His body relaxed suddenly as the kindness of unconsciousness took over and he fell back limply onto the damp linen, his chest heaving like an athlete starved of air after a long run. The women resumed their bathing of his brow and chest while at the bed head, two Kushite slave boys slowly wafted pole mounted, ostrich feathered fans, driving gusts of cool night air over his body.

The room was brightly lit from numerous oil lamps placed liberally on tables and ornate, tall bronze lamp stands. Smaller lamps burned beneath steaming dishes of aromatic oils, the scent of which fought to mask the nauseating stench of rot and decay emanating from the man's thigh. His leg, bandaged in white linen was wet with sweat and heavily stained with black blood and clay coloured, pus. To help ventilate and cool the room the doors were wide open to the gardens beyond, allowing the heady scent of jasmine in with the gentle evening breeze ruffling the drapes as it entered. The furniture was of high quality and plentiful; occasional tables, chairs and stools some delicately inlaid with ivory or tortoiseshell and made of African blackwood, rosewood and cedar nestled between padded settles and divans draped in colourful throws and an abundance of cushions. The floor was of creamy granite and littered with intricately patterned rugs woven in a multitude of colours. Despite the luxury, the room had a man's feel to it, the walls hung with weapons and a shield, and on a cross-shaped, wooden stand a warrior's corselet hung with a magnificent red plumed helmet sitting atop it. On the rear wall was a colourful, life size mosaic depicting Achilles and Hector engaged in their deadly duel outside the walls of Troy.

Whilst the man lay unconscious, the women unwrapped the fouled bandaging. As the wound was exposed, the sickly, sweet odour of rot seemed to fill the room causing them to gag and hold their hands over their noses and mouths. As the younger of the two took the stained linen away for burning the elder steeled herself, held her breath then washed and cleaned the blackened, puckered flesh. Despite the man's comatose state, his body twitched when the cloth touched the wound, sending his features into an agonized grimace forcing a pitiful whimper from his slack mouth.

Just as the girl returned with fresh linen the man cried out, his howl akin to an injured animal. He babbled then seemed to wake from his blackout and powered up from his prone position, sitting bolt upright and seizing the older woman's wrist in a vice like grip.

"Serfina! … Serfina!" He hissed. "Ser …fi …na! For the love …."" His shout echoed around the room as he crumpled and collapsed letting loose of the startled woman.

"We'd best call the mistress."

"And the Leech, I'll find both!" The younger answered as she dropped the fresh linen by the bed and bolted from the room.

Adharbal lay quietly again, allowing the woman to minister him with the damp cloth's, his body mercifully still, his breath ragged and irregular. His eyes opened again, the wild, deranged stare gone from them, he appeared coherent but there was no hiding the agony wracking his body. Another spasm shot through him and his eyes closed tightly, his mouth twisting into a grimace pulling his lips back baring his teeth. His hand grasped the woman's arm once more but this time the grip was just firm.

"My, my sister! … Fetch my sister for me." He managed.

"Zenobia's gone for the Mistress, my Lord. Rest you! Rest now." She replied gently. "She'll be back directly. Come my Lord … come, lie back now." She eased him onto his side, turning him so his injured thigh was uppermost.

Other than a white loincloth to protect his modesty, he was naked. As the woman dabbed the cool cloth over his chest trying to draw some of the fire from his skin and ease the fever, she couldn't help but notice and admire his muscular frame, which complemented his clean cut, good looks. He was only young she thought, so very young, such a waste. Working her way down to his thigh once more and seeing the suppurating wound leaking again, she focused back on the work in hand.

She knew from experience and the putrefying odour of the wound that he was dying, his body slowly poisoned from the infection and the flesh of the leg rotting. The wound, the result of a duel he'd fought in Numidia over a year ago where the heavy falcata wielded by Baldor had chopped into his leg and thighbone. Brought home on a horse litter on a journey of some hundreds of stades with only rudimentary care available, he'd arrived in a poor state. Initially the wound had seemed to be mending and the flesh beginning to heal, however the damage to the thighbone had allowed an infection into his body and over time, the wound ruptured. It had been treated again and again, seeming to improve only to rupture once more, each time worse than the last. Finally, putrefaction of the flesh set in and now the rot was spreading into his body, killing him slowly and painfully.

The sound of quickly approaching footsteps snapped the woman's attention back to her patient.

Three people entered the room, the young woman scurrying ahead of two men, gesturing them towards the man on the divan. The most senior of the party was an overweight, grey haired man, followed closely by a younger one carrying a leather-covered chest. Both paused momentarily just inside the doorway as the smell hit them. The man looked up from the bed and recognising the two newcomers groaned aloud to the woman.

"My sister! … For the love of Baal! Fetch my sister."

The grey haired man made his way to the bed and began assessing the injury while urging the younger to open the chest. An arm came up from the bed and he was pushed suddenly, roughly away, the injured man may be dying but his strength remained formidable.

"Leave me! … Leave me be, damn you!" He paused for breath. "I've had enough of your knives and you're poking … Serfina!" He bellowed again.

The two physicians stood back from the divan not sure whether to help or leave. Their uncertainty ended when an elegant young woman swept into the room. The physicians and the attending women all trying to speak at once, Adharbal however shouted them down.

"Serfina!" Gaining his sisters attention and the others silence he lowered his voice. "Serfina, for the love of Baal, send these two fools away!"

Serfina looked as if she was about to argue or reason with him but seeing the despair in her brothers eyes she turned quickly on the men.

"Out! … Get out, now!"

"My Lady, we…"

"Get out! I'll not repeat myself again." She snapped harshly while pointing to the door.

The anger on her face prevented further retort from the pair and they scuttled quickly away.

The two women and boys also looked at her, unsure as to whether they should also leave. Serfina seemed to notice the stench for the first time hiding her distaste with only a slight wrinkle of her nose. Taking the water bowl and cloth from the women, she dismissed them with a curt flick of her head. The two boys also went to leave but were brought back with a snap of her fingers and a sharp command of "Stay!"

Adharbal groaned but this time in relieved satisfaction as he lay back on the bed closing his eyes and catching his breath. Serfina settled herself on the stool and wrung out the cloth applying it gently to his brow, her face drawn in concern and her eyes filled with tears as she bathed her brother. Thankful of the air movement from the fans keeping the smell away she whispered softly, soothing him with her words and dabbing the cloth repeatedly on his skin. He seemed to settle as her presence and efforts brought him some peace and his breathing regulated and eased, eventually he turned his head and his eyes opened to look at her. He tried to speak but only a husky whisper came out, she immediately tried to quieten him, shushing him, her finger over his lips. He turned his head away slightly, moving the finger allowing the words to form.

"Serfina …"

"Shh brother, don't speak, just …"

"Serfina, listen … listen my time's short."

"Don't say that! Don't you say that, we …?"

It was Adharbal's turn to quieten his sister. "Listen, please." He said and managed a smile.

Serfina just stared; her lip trembled slightly, her eyes flooding with tears, which he wiped gently away with an unsteady hand. He tut, tutted while shaking his head a little, as if in remorse. Serfina Samilcar was a beautiful woman and in the prime of life. Not yet twenty-five years old, she was delicately featured with large doe like eyes, a small rounded nose and shapely mouth. Her raven hair wound into large curls and sat bun like on top of her head, held in place with four ivory combs linked with numerous tiny golden chains, the chains circled her hair, their sparkle adding to her beauty. Long necked, full breasted and elegant, her perfect hourglass shape and long legs were the desire of many a man in Carthage. However, her general disdain for men other than her father and brothers along with her legendary temper kept any would be suitors from the Samilcar door.

Adharbal cleared his throat and moistened his lips with a flick of his tongue.

"All is in order sister; I've had papers drawn up which hands over the family estates and businesses in their entirety to you and your care whilst Sakarbaal remains in his minority. Once he comes of age it's all to be shared equally between you …"

"Peace brother! Peace, you're not …"

"Shh … please sister! Listen, my time's short and there are things I must say."

She reluctantly acquiesced but continued bathing him.

"So, equal shares for you both. Now! When I'm gone, burn my body and …"

Serfina made to interrupt but Adharbal gripped her wrist while shushing her gently, he smiled sadly again as he saw her chest heave with sobs, her tears falling copiously. Her eyes were reddening the lids smudged and blackened as the delicately applied kohl mixed with the tears and ran down her face.

"Burn me Serfina and lay my ashes with those of our father and Carthalo."

He saw her face harden and brows knit, her eyes went from wide and tearful to narrow, darkened slits full of hatred. Reading the thoughts on her face, Adharbal continued though his tone changed from soft beseeching to firm command.

"Your hatred and thoughts of vengeance towards Baldor stops now! The matter's over and done, has been, long since …"
"How can you say that? How? When, when he's done this to you!" She gestured to his leg. "He's killed you as surely as he slew our brother and broke our father's heart!"

Realising she'd spoken her dread thoughts aloud; her hand flew to her mouth as if trying to stop the words escaping. As he heard, then saw Serfina's horror, Adharbal softened his tone and reached for her hand.

"He's not a bad man."

"How can you say that brother, how? He took Carthalo from us and now …" She left the rest unsaid.

"I heard his testimony in the Senate, before all." He replied quietly but resolutely. "And …"

"And you believed him? Sweet Tanith, mother of all that's holy! He slew our brother!" She looked incredulously at him, her temper flaring.

"Yes I believe him! I know he slew Carthalo but…"

"But nothing! He must pay! Blood for blood."

"There's already been enough blood spilt, Serfina: first Aiticia's, Baldor's wife, then our brother and finally me. It stops with me do you hear? It stops! For pity's sake Serfina, we've been through this so many times, you promised me!"

Serfina looked as if she would argue further but her brother's baleful stare halted her words. He began again; his speech slow and deliberate as if he needed to spell things out.

"Our father granted the loan to Baldor along with extended terms, I saw the agreement! He was making regular repayments in full and on time as the terms of the contract stated. Carthalo had no right to call in the loan against him and no right to go to his home unannounced demanding immediate payment."

"This war changed all that! The city empowered Carthalo to foreclose the loan."

"Yes! The city did! Should the lender wish to do so? But before our father took ill and the business dealings handed to Carthalo, he'd already agreed with Baldor that the original terms of the loan stood and would carry on to full term, war or not!"

Serfina had no answer to that.

"So truly sister, should you wish to lay blame for this sorry trail of bloodshed and misery we must point the finger at ourselves and blame Carthalo."

Serfina looked as if she was about to interrupt but Adharbal squeezed her arm to stall her then carried on quickly though struggling for breath.

"The fight between Carthalo and Baldor I blame both for. The death of Aiticia I believe to be accidental. As for me, it was I that attacked Baldor, he tried to dissuade me and explain but I'd have none of it, I wouldn't listen. Like you, I wanted blood for blood; he bettered me in the duel and could have killed me. Baal almighty knows! I'd have killed him without hesitation had I triumphed."

"I would that you had brother." Serfina said bitterly.

"It was Baal's will Serfina, we should not dispute that! Baldor and I fought and the God's favoured the righteous."

"He owes us and …"

"He owes us nothing, perhaps we owe him for his wife's life I think? Thankfully we've returned his home or rather the cost of it to him, but that's no recompense compared to the loss of his woman and livelihood."

Serfina's bitter sneer said what her words didn't. Adharbal paused to gather his breath again as his voice was slowly losing its strength.

"I loved our brother too Serfina but I also know Baldor very well, we were good friends as children. Whatever bad blood passed between he and Carthalo it should never have come to this."

She looked away as if neither interested nor listening. He gripped her arm tightly again making her turn to look at him.

"He's a good man; we'll leave it at that! … Do you hear me Serfina?" His words began to falter and his grip slackened on her arm.

Shocked at his sudden decline, Serfina snapped out of her apathy and blind hatred and grabbed for her brother.

He reached his arm up around her shoulder. "I'm so … so thirsty."

She reached for the water jug and poured him a cup, then supporting his head with one hand offered it to his lips. As he drank, he seemed to recover slightly and she fluffed the pillows beneath him aiding him to sit up more comfortably. He pulled the sheet over his lower body hiding his leg and the bandage then smiled at her, his own eyes moistening.

"Let our last words be not ones of anger sister? Do as I ask, I beg you? Life will be …"

She hushed him gently and hugged him then gave him another drink. However, he wasn't to be put off.

"Promise me you will …"

His words trailed off, his body relaxed and his eyes flickered.

"Adharbal! … Adharbal!" Her voice rose as her gentle shaking prompted no response. "Sweet Tanith please …" She mouthed.

Her words however were cut short as his eyes flickered then slowly opened. The wracked and drawn look that had lined his face for so long seemed to leave him; his body lost its rigidity and seemed to sink into the divan.

"Goodbye sister … give my love to Sakarbaal … he will …" The words faded to a whisper then stopped, he gave a long deep sigh and lay still.

Serfina sat back her hands over her mouth, her tear filled eyes wide and staring at her brothers body. Her body began to shake as she wept; she looked up at the two fearful looking fan boys, her face hardening.

"Leave us!"

The boys quickly put the fans down, bowed deeply and scurried from the room. With the room to herself, Serfina broke down and cried bitterly, she picked up and held her brothers hand to her cheek as her heartache poured out in a soft but relentless whimpering.

****

She wasn't sure how long she'd sat for her tears had long since dried and her weeping stopped. Perhaps it was the early morning chill on her body that brought her from her apathy or her brothers hand, still in hers but now ice cold. She gently laid his arm down, rising to her feet pulling the sheet up covering his upper body. Holding the sheet at his shoulders, she took a final look at his face; he looked peaceful at last, his eyes mercifully closed. Kissing him gently on the forehead, she laid the sheet over his head and turned away from the divan.

As she exited the room, she picked a small hand bell from the table and shook it thrice. Within a moment a sleepy looking guard appeared, upon seeing Serfina he immediately straightened his back and looked more attentive.

"Wake Zenobia and Metucosa. Have them wash and prepare my brothers body for his funeral. Rouse the scribe and have him come and see me, tell him to bring his writing materials for I wish him to prepare my brothers obituary and missive for the Senate.

"Yes my Lady." The guard bowed low and turned to leave.

"One more thing."

"Yes my Lady."

"Wake that idle maid of mine and have her fetch me hot water and honey, I'll take it in my room."

"Yes my Lady." The guard bowed quickly and left apace.

Serfina made her way across the still shadowy gardens to her own quarters. Hearing a lone blackbird singing and noticing the sharp chill, she looked to the east and saw the pale glimmer of light that heralded the new day. Realising she must have stayed with her brother through most of the night she understood why she was bodily tired and hungry. Her mind however was far from tired, full perhaps but not tired. She'd sat through the horror of her brothers passing and mulled over her grief, finally falling into a state of self-pity and that she hated. She had no time for pity, for either herself or others, pity was for the weak and weakness was not one of her traits. Despising herself for her momentary lapse, her hatred surfaced and found direction, channelled at the source, Baldor Targa.

Within moments of arriving in her quarters her maid appeared carrying honeyed water on a silver tray. Serfina picked it up and swirled the contents sniffing the sweet steam rising from the cup. The steam scorched her skin and with her short temper flaring again, she rapped out curt commands that cowed her maid. Realising a sense of normality she immediately felt more like herself and a little better.

"Prepare my bath and find out where that fool of a scribe is. I asked for him to be here! I shouldn't have to ask twice."

"Yes my Lady, which oil would you like in your bath; lavender, rose, chamomile or berg…"

"Lavender will do and lay out my black dress, veil and mourning jewellery and …" She hesitated slightly at the mention of mourning, then like the Serfina of old, she carried on forcefully. "And my hooded cape, the black woollen one, fetch that also."

The maid bobbed in deference then disappeared. Serfina sat back on her divan sipping her drink and thinking. She finished her drink as the first slaves appeared, entering in quick succession bearing buckets of hot water. They filed past her with a brisk step and their eyes respectfully down, tipping the water into the shoulder deep bath set into the floor while the maid added oil and fresh flower petals to it. Serfina knew it would take time for the bath to fill so made herself comfortable as she waited for the scribe to appear.

Moments later, he bumbled into the room spouting, stuttered excuses and apologies for his lateness.

Serfina glared then pointed towards the table; in his rush to accommodate, he dropped his writing materials then knocked the lamp stand from the table as he went to take a seat. Thankfully, with the morning light full, the lamps were safely extinguished. Serfina exploded in fury as oil swamped the tabletop.

"Tanith save us! What in Hade's name's wrong with you man? I didn't have you summoned so to wreck my house!"

He stooped quickly to clear up the mess while stammering further apologies but she silenced him with a sharp, 'Enough!' Then turning to the nearest water carrier, snapped at her to clear up the mess. Eventually the scribe was seated and ready to take instructions. Serfina paced as she spoke.

"To the Senate: the usual greetings and salutations, so on and so forth … The obituary for my brother, Adharbal Samilcar … Be it known that Adharbal Samilcar, second son to the Lord Hanno, of that house, brother to Carthalo, Sakarbaal and Serfina, has died of his wounds. Wounds incurred and suffered whilst seeking justice for his elder brother's murder. The funeral will take place one day hence. The Samilcar family will observe mourning for the next three moons."

She waited as the scribe scratched the words quickly into a wood framed wax tablet, when she looked curiously at the tablet he began to explain albeit in stilted, stuttering tones.

"I … I, can write fas …faster …in the, the wax, my Lady. I … ca …ca can copy it to parch… parchment later."

"I pray to Baal Almighty you write faster than you speak!" She answered caustically.

The man smiled weakly and said nothing.

"These are also to be taken to the Senate." Serfina dropped the bundle of rolled parchments that Adharbal had given her onto the table. "This is my brothers will and testament and needs to be lodged with the Law lords, make a copy for me to retain before you take it away."

The scribe nodded obediently while making more notes onto the tablet.

"Finally … Finally, seek out the original warrant for Targa's arrest. You have a copy, yes?" It was a statement not a question.

"Yes m … m, my Lady."

"Resubmit the warrant."

The scribe looked up, though he said nothing his face bore a puzzled look. Serfina ignored him and carried on.

"In support of the warrant you will make an addendum saying, since my elder brother, Carthalo's death, my father has also passed on, having died of grief and a broken heart from the loss of his eldest son. In addition, my younger brother, Adharbal as mentioned, has died of his wounds given him by the same criminal who murdered his brother.

Now I, a mere woman, remain to organise my family's affairs and care for my younger and only remaining brother. What is a woman to do?

My father served Carthage dutifully and honourably all his life and now his children are at its mercy and justice. Justice is what we seek for both our father and brother's deaths. As one of the first families of this city we respectfully ask the Senate that the man, Baldor Targa be recalled again from General Hannibal's army to Carthage to answer for my father's and Adharbal's death's."

The scribe worked quickly, his stylus vigorously scratching words into the wax. As he finished and looked up from his work Serfina asked him to read the threads of her words back to her. Nodding satisfactorily that all was as she'd said, she ordered the documents drawn up ready for her to sign by midmorning, curtly dismissing the scribe she summoned her maid.

"The bath's nearly ready Mistress, I …"

Serfina waved the words away cutting her short. "I'll take a massage whilst I wait."

Serfina walked to the private bath area where the steaming water gave off a pleasant heat and aroma of lavender, which filled the room and her senses. The maid hurried in front of her shaking a linen sheet and thick towels over a low stone table, adding a pillow for extra comfort.

Serfina stood alongside the table as the maid undid her dress then helped her onto the table. Completely relaxed with her nakedness, Serfina snuggled her face into the pillow enjoying the softness and the relaxing scent of lavender with which the pillow was laced.

"My neck, shoulders and back." She commanded as the maid laid a sheet over her buttocks and legs then rubbed her hands briskly with warmed oil before applying it to Serfina's skin.

The maid was gentle but skilful and delicately eased the stiffness from Serfina's muscles, even causing some small contented groans. After a short while Serfina found her mind drifting, the sleep she'd gone without was creeping up on her as her body and senses relaxed, lulling her to slumber. With a huge effort, she sat up abruptly, startling the maid.

"Enough!" She snapped, pushing her away.

"I'm sorry Mistress!" The girl looked horrified. "Have I hurt you? I'm sorry." She cowered backwards a pace.

Serfina ignored her. "My bath! … I have much to do, hurry girl!"

The maid wiped her oily hands quickly and slipped out of her dress. Holding out her hand to aid Serfina from the table then walking to the bath entered the water first. Waiting half way down the steps, she again held out her hand aiding Serfina into the water.

With the morning still young, Serfina was bathed and dressed, her make up redone and perfume applied. She looked into the burnished bronze mirror and liked what she saw. She was beautiful, that she knew but to see it after the last few days of pain and grief was a welcome relief. Despite the lack of sleep most of the stress and worry lines around her eyes had gone and her face free of the drawn, tense look she'd carried for so long. She needed to look beautiful today but also sad and vulnerable, men paid keen attention to all those traits and that's what she would use to obtain what she needed from them. Her hair was combed out from the high bun style that denoted a mature woman and head of her household and bound back into a ponytail making her appear younger than her years. Her eyes were kohl'd then lightly shadowed on the lids with a smooth paste coloured of autumn gold matching the olive tone of her skin. Her lips were carefully outlined and rouged and her perfume, though sweet, withheld from being heady or sensuous. As the maid held up a second mirror and moved it from side to side, Serfina practised dropping her eyes then peering upwards from a saddened face. She let her lips fall slightly open, completing the look of a beautiful young woman, saddened, lost, and needing help.

The maid laid a veil of black, gossamer lace over Serfina's head and face fastening it in place in her hair with black pins, swathing the surplus material about her neck. Serfina stood and pointed to her cloak, which the maid fastened over her shoulders.

A tentative knock on the door found the anxious scribe with the sealing waxes and parchments in his hands, which he timidly offered to Serfina to check. Walking to the window and holding them to the light she read the obituary, warrant and addendum. He kept his head down and fidgeted nervously as she paused, traced her finger over some of the words then nodded and read on.

"Excellent!" She snapped eventually and laid the parchment on the table holding out her hand blindly for a stylus to sign with.

Not believing his ears the scribe sighed in an all too audible relief his body losing some of its tenseness; Serfina's disparaging look however had him clearing his throat and quickly reverting to his previous apprehension.

"Meet me on the Senate steps." She snapped, while pushing her sealing ring into the pooling, molten wax then turned to the maid. "Call Panhessy and have him bring another with him, they'll escort me to the Senate then on to the temple. Have my palanquin brought to the front door."

Serfina was already leaving the room as the maid ran to do her bidding. By the time she'd crossed the gardens and reached the main door of the villa the palanquin was arriving at the foot of the steps. Carried by two huge Nubians, one placed at the front and the other at the rear, their hands supporting two long handles sprouting from each end of the wooden litter. To help carry the weight of the chair and the occupant, the men's shoulders were fitted with a heavy leather harness attaching them to the palanquin like draft horses to a cart. The palanquin itself was a flat, cedar pallet generously upholstered with a padded mattress over its base; resting on top of this were cushions and pillows allowing the occupant the choice of being propped up or lying down in comfort while travelling. To keep unwelcome odours and stink from the streets at bay both pillows and mattress had tiny bags of dried sweet smelling herbs and leaves discreetly sewn into them. Rising vertically from the corners of the pallet were round poles, again of cedar and ornately carved with intertwining flowers and leaves, giving shape and relief to the timber while adding a feminine touch. Atop each of the poles was a thin metal rod with a crescent moon the size of a woman's palm attached to the end of it, all were made of gold. A cloth roof of white linen stretched tightly between the poles acting as a sunshade. Hanging down, on all four sides were curtains of finely woven material giving the occupant privacy yet allowing plenty of light to enter. The hem of the curtain contained tiny lead weights preventing the material billowing as the palanquin moved along. Three of the curtains were already closed with only the side nearest the steps left open for Serfina to enter. As she descended the steps, Panhessy and another guard, both equally large as the two that carried the chair fell in behind her. Dressed in short white kilts and cotton shirts that barely contained their heavily muscled frames they were armed with a broad bladed dagger and heavy wooden club apiece.

As Serfina neared the base of the steps, a slave boy placed a footstool for her while another servant stood alongside offering his arm in readiness to help her onto the stool and into the litter. With Serfina seated, he bowed his head and closed the curtains, tying them in place. Once comfortable, she called the larger of the two, armed men towards her.

"Panhessy, I'm not to be detained or bothered on my way to the Senate. Keep the street life and the unwashed from my presence. Distribute these coppers as you think fit." She passed a leather purse through the curtains.

The mute giant bowed his head in acknowledgement then clicked his fingers and the small party moved off towards the city.

Chapter Fifteen

Being early morning the streets were free of crowds, making for unhindered easy progress of the palanquin and the small party. The shopkeepers and traders were just opening up for the day's business, pushing faded wooden shutters open and pulling canvas sun awnings into place. In the market square, makeshift stalls were being erected and reed mats thrown on the ground for wares to be displayed upon. Passing the waterfront, the fishing boats were already berthed and the days catch coming ashore in rush and wicker baskets to be weighed then sold at the fish market. Seagulls swooped and circled above the boats, their piecing cries competing with others who'd already touched down and now flapped and fought over pieces of fish offal. The salt smell of fish and the sea carried on the light on-shore breeze.

As the palanquin turned away from the water back towards the city, the stink of filth from pens crammed with unwashed people announced the slave market. Off to one side and away from the prevailing wind was the auction block, a raised platform of worn, sun-bleached cedar with steps set both sides and rows of seats in front of it. A canvas awning, supported and tensioned by tall wooden posts covered the seated area protecting customers from the sun. To the rear of the block was the holding pens, crammed to capacity with their human merchandise in anticipation of a brisk morning's business. The slaves were sorted by sex and age. Miserable and frightened faces stared from behind the cage bars, some huddling for comfort and more than a few cried or wailed until quietened with threats of a lashing. Others stood alone, dejected or silently resigned to their fate, some of the men glowered but whether their anger was directed at themselves or their captors for their state, only they knew. One pen held children no older than ten years of age, here the genders remained mixed along with race and creed; boys with straw-blonde hair and fair skin stood alongside girls with skin black as ebony with strange hair colourings and styles, either cropped and braided to their heads or long and decorated with coloured beads. This cosmopolitan mix; evidence of the Carthaginian empire and far reaching trade stretching across North Africa, Spain, Sicily and beyond. Slavers marched their captives' one at a time from the pen, stripped their ragged clothing then held them securely whilst others washed them quickly with sea sponges fastened to the end of wooden sticks. Sluicing them with buckets of water they pushed clean loincloth's or shifts into their hands leaving them to dress as best they could as they were bundled into another pen like prize stock prepared for sale.

Serfina's eyes caught three slavers pulling a tall blonde man from the adult, male pen. One slaver held a spear threateningly in front of the man's chest while the other two restrained him with leather nooses around his neck fastened to wooden poles allowing them to keep a safe distance. Despite this and the fetters on his ankles he walked proudly, his head held high. Ignoring their savage pulls with the noose as they walked him to the washing area, his pride and nobility setting him apart from the meaner men that held him captive. His muscled physique and Adonis like shape held Serfina's interest, which rose further as his tattered trousers and loincloth were ripped away leaving him naked, he stood proud and unashamed as he was washed in front of all. Admiring his spirit and his body, she smiled to herself as she thought of the bids that would be raised. Men would seek such as him for a bodyguard, women, perhaps for the same reason. However, for the rich women, the trophy wives, the ignored wives and the lonely wives whose husbands were engaged in the war with Rome, the added thrill would come in the other services he could render.

The thought of the war snatched her from her idling thoughts bringing them back to Baldor Targa and the reason for her journey. The flash of hatred and anger showed as her small hands curled into tight fists, a feline snarl twisted her face and she snapped sharply at her chair bearers for an increase in pace.

The small party, moving at double pace made quick progress and arrived at the marble steps of the Senate. Panhessy opened the curtains and standing like a black colossus offered a rigid forearm as an aid to Serfina as she alighted.

The sun was bright and gaining in height as she ascended the steps. Despite her regal and measured tread, being dressed all in black she drew the sun's heat, causing her to perspire lightly and breathe a little heavier. Wishing she'd brought her handmaiden and a sunshade she continued her climb while cursing Baldor Targa with all the vehemence her breath would spare her.

At the stairhead, she paused to catch her breath, adjust her veil and smooth the folds from her dress. She glided the last few steps to the open doors of the Senate, set back in the shade of the high-pillared portico offering welcome respite from the morning heat. The door guards came to attention as she entered, raising both shield and spear in salute, neither looked at her as she passed, keeping their eyes respectfully front. Serfina was met by a bowing official who seeing her mourning garb respectfully and quietly bid her a pleasant morning, gesturing her to the benches at the side of the hallway.

"My Lady, if you please you must wait here, you cannot pass into the Senate chamber itself, it …"

"It is only for men." She finished for him, making an effort not to snap or speak disparagingly. "And Senators only, at that." She managed in a quiet respectful tone.

He smiled warmly and bowed again. "My Lady, can I fetch you some refreshment?"

"Some cool water would be most acceptable, thank you." She said, dropping her voice as if distressed.

As he disappeared for the water, Serfina took stock of her surroundings. She was in the main entrance hall of the Senate; its marble panelled walls rising three times the height of a man to a vaulted ceiling of white speckled, black granite, the flecks in the stone seemed to twinkle back at her like evening stars. The width was such that two, four horse chariot teams could pass alongside each other and still not touch the walls. She looked further, into the debating chamber itself. The room was vast and circular in shape with marble benches placed in a semi-circle running concentric to the room and rising in successive elevated tiers back and away from the floor. The benches draped with colourful fabrics and plump cushions, giving a touch of comfort for the sitter against the hard stone beneath. Marble steps rose at both sides of the benches and as an avenue through the centre, allowing ready access to the seating. High above, long thin rectangular windows allowed the sunlight in. The vaulted ceiling was of white stone upon which huge, colourful images of Baal Hammon and Tanith, the mother or sky Goddess of Carthage had been painted, the two deities staring balefully down like stern parents at all in the chamber below. Inlaid in the floor in front of the tiered benches was the outline of a circle some twenty paces in width. Within its centre was the crescent moon of Carthage, both it and the circle were of pure gold.

Her study was broken by the sudden appearance of her scribe from a side door, seeing Serfina he immediately broke into a hurried but ungainly walk. Thinking he was late he stuttered excuses and apologies as he came to a stop in front of her, remembering where she was she raised her hand to silence him. He quietened quickly but fidgeted nervously picking at his fingernails as the official returned with the water for Serfina. As he bowed and left she lifted the veil to drink, keeping her face demurely lowered she spoke quietly.

"Have you registered the paperwork?"

"Ye …s."

She raised her hand cutting him short.

"All of it?" She looked at him as he nodded, then silenced him again as he began to stutter. "It'll be read today?"

He nodded again.

"Excellent! Leave me." She dropped her veil waving him away.

She sat quietly, watching the Senators arriving for the day's business. All were dressed similarly in plain white robes with an edging the width of a man's palm in either crimson or blue around the hem. The robes covered them from ankle to breastbone where they wrapped under the armpit and swept over the left shoulder, the surplus material being gathered and laid over their left arm. Some passed her without seeming to notice, others distracted by her beautiful but carefully covered figure smiled, else wished her a good morning. Eventually a middle-aged man at the head of a lively conversing group stopped, held up his hand to his fellows and spoke enquiringly.

"My Lady Serfina?"

Serfina raised her head slowly, stopping before her face could be seen fully, casting upward looks from beneath the veil from large, dark eyes.

"My Lady Serfina!" He repeated. "It is you! What brings you here? And so early in the day?" He asked kindly.

Keeping her face downcast and voice low she answered.

"I come, my Lord Banataar ..." She hesitated slightly. "I come, to ensure my brother's obituary is read."

There was an audible intake of breath from the waiting group.

"Your brother, Lady? The Lord Adharbal, he's passed on? I knew he was unwell but ..."

"He died last night my Lord ... of his wounds."

Banataar placed his hand comfortingly on her shoulder. "I'm sorry Lady, truly sorry! This pain will be doubly hard to bear when you've but recently lost your father."

Serfina nodded and looked down.

"Your father and I, we were good friends. Aye! Good friends! Is there anything I or we ..." He gestured towards his entourage. "Can do to help you?"

Serfina glanced up then down again quickly, looking awkward then unsure; she shook her head then nodded as if confused. She went to speak then stopped as if hesitant to divulge her thoughts.

"I ... I may need some help my Lord." She cringed inside as she asked.

Banataar tilted his head as if already listening.

Serfina cleared her throat and spoke quietly, hesitantly.

"My Lord, you'll realise that I'm now the head of my house. Of my three brothers, I have but one surviving and he is as yet, too young to assume the mantle of responsibility for the family estates. I've prepared our elder brothers obituary and arranged for ..."

"I'll see to the reading Lady, it's the least I can do for the memories of your father and brothers. Is there anything else that you need or we can help with?"

Serfina paused again. Sensing the pressure upon her, Banataar turned to his colleagues asking them to carry on into the chamber, they should give the lady a moment he said and he would join them directly. Inclining their heads respectfully to Serfina, they moved off to the chamber.

Banataar gathered his robes and sat next to Serfina.

"Come, my Lady." He said gently. "You're my oldest friend's daughter and I know that were he here and I gone and it was a child of mine before him, he would offer his help such as I do now."

Serfina felt her heart quicken as she saw her plan beginning to bear fruit. 'Caution' she told herself, 'caution.' She'd dangled the bait and the fish was nibbling, now to keep the interest until she could hook him.

"I have … I have my brother's instructions, his will and …" She gave a sniff as the words broke off. "My scribe has the papers to be read to the Law …" She slipped her hand beneath her veil, her fingers plucking a scrap of fabric from the neckline of her dress and dabbed her eyes.

"Come lady, come! … Bear up now! I'll see to your brother's instructions. You've done well, very well! I can see all is soundly prepared. Your scribe, he's here?"

Serfina nodded.

"Then I'll collect the papers from him and present them to the Law lords myself, think no more of it."

Serfina mumbled her thanks between sniffs and sobs and more wiping of her eyes. She bit her cheek as she prepared the final part of her plan, the pain helping with the tears she now wanted to shed, the pain, punishment to herself for having to show weakness.

"Can I have something brought for you? A drink? Some wine perhaps? Yes wine …"

"No, no thank you my Lord, I shall be alright, I … I am my father's daughter, he would wish me to be strong."

"Aye, but this, this business is for men to deal with." He spoke sadly as if he felt her pain.

Gritting her teeth Serfina began to cry softly. Banataar tut tutted and fussed about her uncertain of what to do, having no daughters of his own he was unsure of how to handle her heartache.

"Come now! Worry not, these affairs I can handle and see to. Take yourself off home and think no more on it, I'll settle things here and at the Courts and carry my report to you myself."

Serfina forced out another sob, followed by cautious, broken words. "Thank you my Lord, there is one other task you could do for me, if you would be so kind?"

"Surely lady, whatever I can do, I will."

"I've renewed the warrant for the arrest of the criminal who slew my brother, will you see to its action for me?"

She got the words out in a rush glad to be rid of them, her body relaxing slightly as she finished. Banataar looked puzzled and paused as if to recollect, he cleared his throat cupping his chin in his hand whilst tugging at his wispy grey beard.

"Your pardon my Lady but I thought that matter done with long since. The man concerned … Targa? Yes, Targa it was. I believe he returned from Spain when summonsed, was tried and acquitted." Serfina coloured beneath her veil. "Things … things have changed since, my Lord."

"But your brother dropped the charges my Lady! We heard him say so, here in this very building."

"Since … since then my Lord I've lost my father, succumbing to a broken heart over the loss of his eldest son." She added quickly as he went to interrupt. "And as my second brother lay dying he reconsidered his decision of leniency, begging me to redress the case. I have my Lord, now lost two brothers and my father to this Baldor Targa."

She allowed herself to sob then cry though the tears at least were sincere. Banataar placed his arm about her shoulders drawing her to him hushing her gently, his pity genuine for the burden she bore.

"It's too much my Lord, too much! I've no man to help me, yet I strive to do my brother's dying wishes."

Banataar looked perplexed. "I don't know that I can support a second warrant or what good it might do. The man's been tried for his crimes once."

"But it's different now my Lord, there are two more deaths that require atonement."

Banataar chewed his lip as he thought; he felt a warm tear on his shoulder and Serfina's body tremble as she sobbed again.

"But I was at the trial my Lady; I remember it … from what I saw and heard this Baldor Targa seemed an honourable man, a brave man. It would seem both the army and our Generals hold him in high regard. With my own ears I heard your brother drop the charges against him … I believe they were friends from …"

"If I was a man I would find him and kill him myself, he owes me thrice!" Serfina spat the words like poison as her carefully controlled hatred finally surfaced. "I wish my father was here, he would know what to do."

"Hush now child …" He said softly. "Hush, don't upset yourself."

Banataar felt his heart strings pull as Serfina continued to sob and cry softly and her body shake, the suppressed heartache seeming more pitiful than a loud outpouring of grief. The memory of his friends passing was still fresh and raw and now he held his friends child, her heart broken again. The enormity of the catastrophe struck him as he tallied up the loss to her family, a mother long since gone to the grave, albeit of natural causes but followed by the eldest son slain, the father and now the second son. All that remained of this prominent family was the daughter and a son in his minority. The fatherly instinct within him stirred, pulling Serfina closer he whispered quietly but regretfully.

"Let me see what I can do. I can't promise anything but let me see what I can do."

Her hand came up onto his shoulder and gripped tightly. "Thank you! Thank you my Lord." She managed between sobbing.

Seeing the Senate official dallying to the side, he clicked his fingers summoning the man to him.

"Have my Lady's escort called to the steps immediately, then find her scribe and have him report to me in the Senate."

"Yes my Lord." The man scurried away calling for help to perform his tasks.

Banataar gently eased Serfina up from the bench. "Worry no more my Lady, I'll see to things here. Come I'll help you to your escort. Come now; lean on me while we walk."

The pair shuffled into the warm sunlight and to the waiting palanquin. Serfina was desperate to ask how he would proceed but fearing she might overplay her hand let herself be quietly chaperoned. With Serfina safely away, Banataar returned to the Senate to be met by her scribe. The man bowed low offering the rolled parchment before him.

"M … my, Lord the pa … papers as you … you, requested."

"All are ready I trust." He said firmly.

"Y… yes, my … my Lord." The scribe bowed again.

Banataar dismissed him with a weary wave of his hand, striding towards the chamber and already regretting his involvement and offer of help.

It was late in the afternoon before the state matters such as the war with Rome concluded, along with city commerce issues such as tribute payments from subject nations and the purchase and shipping of grain from Egypt. By which time some of the Senators dozed, others looked apathetic while a few looked on with pretence at listening, their minds clearly elsewhere.

The Head Speaker banged his gavel and announced the Senate would move to matters of law. He read through the notaries of capital offenders and summary punishments to be meted out, then on through the mundane matters such as wagon delivery restrictions within the city during business times and the licensing of brothels. Banataar waited for a pause in the proceedings before signalling to the Speaker that he wished to speak.

Adjusting his robes, he made his way down the stairs to the open floor, stepping through the bright shafts of sunlight from the high windows he paused at the lectern laying the parchment over the wooden top. Holding the stand at arm's length and settling his posture, he drew himself up to his full height clearing his throat to speak.

"My Lords! My Lords." His voice boomed around the chamber. "It's late in the day I know but I crave your indulgence, I have matters of note that you will wish to know."

He waited as his prospective audience stirred from their apathy, when he considered he had enough attention he began.

"My Lords, I bear sad tidings from the house of Samilcar, my Lady Serfina, of that ilk has asked that I advise you all with the latest news."

He paused as the mention of the Samilcar family saw more of the Senators bestirring themselves and looking his way.

"My Lords, Adharbal Samilcar, member of this house, friend of many here and second son of the late Lord Hanno Samilcar, is dead. He died from the wounds incurred whilst seeking justice for his brother, Carthalo's death."

All knew of the fight between Adharbal Samilcar and his brother's killer and the terrible injuries he'd incurred and the consequential battle with his health since. Some remembered the court case and the decision granting a pardon, freedom and recompense to the assailant, none however knew of Adharbal's death and a low murmur spread around the chamber. Apathy vanished as men focused and shook and prodded their neighbours awake to listen.

"My Lady Serfina informed me but a short while ago that the Lord Adharbal passed early this morning, his funeral takes place on the morrow. Members of this house should allow time to pay their respects, for, as you know this is a prominent family, which has served this city passing well.

The Samilcar family estates and businesses are to be held in safekeeping of the Lady Serfina, until the youngest brother, Sakarbaal comes to his majority, from which point the property and monies are to be divided equally between them. The papers conveying Lord Adharbal's last wishes are both signed and sealed by him and available for inspection should anyone wish to do so?"

The chamber was deathly quiet as men looked at one another in dismay. Despite Adharbal's injuries being public knowledge, the news of his death still came as a shock to his peers. Adharbal, unlike his elder brother, had been popular in both the Senate and the city, his name synonymous with honour, truth and fair dealings. As the news sunk in chatter started up in earnest as men conferred.

"Further!" Banataar rapped his knuckles on the lectern to bring silence again. "Further … and of great importance, Lord Adharbal has cited a plea for the case of his assailant, Baldor Targa to be reopened as …"

Shouting and heckling broke out from a number of benches to which a response just as vibrant and agitated was taken up by another part of the house. The Head Speaker shouted above the din calling repeatedly for order, with his words drowned in the commotion he resorted to beating his gavel against the bench top.

"Order! Order! We will have order!" He bellowed, the hubbub died away and he lowered his voice as quiet returned. "Please continue, Lord Banataar."

Banataar waited a moment longer, taking time to look around the chamber; he glowered as if daring any to interrupt him further. He began again, repeating his words before the interruption.

"The Lord Adharbal has cited a plea for the case of his assailant, Baldor Targa to be reopened as matters have moved on from when the initial hearing took place here one year ago."

A man from the group of hecklers stood quickly raising his hand to speak, though he began without waiting to be invited.

"My Lord! This cannot be, the accused has been tried once and acquitted! We cannot try him again for the same crime, it would be hypocrisy!"

There was commotion as everyone tried to speak at once followed by further calls to order and the banging of the gavel. As silence claimed the room once more the Head Speaker cut in quickly.

"My Lord Banataar, you heard the opposition to your plea and it is a most valid point. Please, advise us, what has changed that we must consider this case anew? This is most … most irregular."

"I can and will sir! If you can but calm and quieten these dolts!"

The instant catcalls, laughter and loud rebuttals were drowned out as the Speaker hammered the gavel into the table. When silence was restored again, the Speaker looked back to Banataar.

"Please continue my Lord."

Banataar took time to look around the room again letting the silence take effect, his brows knitted and his face grim, he finished with a look of contempt towards the group of hecklers.

"It's true the Lord Adharbal withdrew his complaint and dropped the charges against the formerly accused, a one Baldor Targa of this city. It was felt at the time, that the accused and the Lord Adharbal's, elder brother, Carthalo were equally to blame for the fight which resulted in the deaths of Carthalo Samilcar and Baldor Targa's wife."

"Aye! And Baal almighty himself knows they'd not dare raise the matter again were the good Strabonus still alive and here!" Came from the benches where the first objection had arisen.

"Silence!" The gavel beat loudly. With quiet returned once more, the Speaker nodded in response to Banataar's request to continue.

"Since closure of the case, the Lord Adharbal's father, the Lord Hanno Samilcar has passed on. He was neither an old man, having attained but fifty-five years, nor was he unwell having recovered fully from his affliction. He died I'm told, from a broken heart over the loss of his eldest son and the crippling of his second."

The room erupted again and this time the divided political factions could clearly be seen. After repeated banging of the gavel and the Speaker beside himself to restore order, quiet settled over the room. The Speaker was the first to find voice.

"I see what's afoot here!" He pointed slowly and accusingly around the room. "And I warn you all now, this matter's not concerned with, nor is it to be aligned with the political factions and motives currently present in this house. Those favouring the war with Rome." He pointed to the loudest group of hecklers. "Or equally, those who follow the house of Samilcar and oppose it! This matter relates to blood feud and the need, or not, to re-examine the facts and judgement of a past case."

This time there was no uproar as men took time to consider the words. Banataar took the opportunity to finish his speech.

"Finally, we have to consider the plight of a helpless young woman left to pick up the pieces of her life, as well as manage the family estates until the youngest brother is of age to inherit and assume some control."

There was some hooting and muted, derisive comments at the 'helpless young woman' tag followed by restrained laughter but mostly manners and decorum prevailed. The Speaker looked to Banataar for a sign that he was finished so he could begin summing up, Banataar however signalled for a moment more.

"I should not need to remind you all that the Samilcar's are one of the oldest and most prestigious families in Carthage and have contributed greatly to this city. Over the years, they've given freely of their men folk, as both warriors and statesmen and this city has prospered from their selfless actions. We should bear this in mind when we consider if or not we come to their aid in this matter."

He nodded briefly to the Speaker indicating he was finished.

The Speaker rose to address the assembly. "My Lords, you've heard the plea put before you. An unusual request perhaps? And not one I've witnessed within my time in this house. However, that aside, as is the politics of the two factions present, pro-war and anti-war. Cast these thoughts from your minds for neither has any bearing on what I am about to ask you.

"Sir! I object!" A young man shouted as he rose to his feet. "And if the Lord Strabonus was here he would argue that this is most irregular, in fact he would say it was damned illegal, I …"

"Sadly sir, my Lord Strabonus is no longer with us to advise but if you feel your conscience or truth of the matter lies that way, then cast your vote as you think fit." He turned to the whole assembly. "As I said Gentlemen, place factions and parties aside. This matter is a conscience vote and the question is this; Do we or do we not revoke the past judgement and send once more for the man, Baldor Targa to answer charges anew?"

He left the question hanging, giving the chamber time to discuss and think.

Excited murmurings sprung up around the room as men huddled into groups and voiced opinions then argued or agreed with one another. The Speaker sat back in his chair, deep in thought himself.

Banataar remained at the lectern relieved that his duty was fulfilled; his own mind asking what he thought was the right course of action. The discussion continued until men settled back into their seats; the Speaker rose and tapped his gavel twice, an immediate hush followed.

"My Lords, Gentlemen, you've had time to consider, we shall now put the matter to the vote."

He motioned two officials to his side then looked to a scribe sat discreetly behind him; the man raised his wax tablet and stylus acknowledging readiness. The speaker stood. "Those favouring a recall of the formerly accused, Baldor Targa, and the subsequent retrial of the case, raise your hands."

Hands went up, some quickly others more slowly as men looked about to see who voted. The two officials began the count, each whispering their tally to the scribe who wrote both figures down, seeing the tallies matched he nodded to the Speaker.

"Gentlemen, those who favour the status quo, raise your hands."

Once more, the officials counted. The Speaker cleared his throat.

"Finally Gentlemen, those who wish to abstain?"

With voting complete, the scribe reviewed the figures then made his way to the Speaker passing him the tablet. The speaker stepped to the lectern.

"My Lords, Gentlemen, the votes are returned such; … we have four abstentions." He frowned and looked at Banataar. "With respect my Lord, I noticed that though you brought the motion you didn't vote?"

"Sir, I cannot. Despite bringing the plea and the fact that the Lady Serfina and her family are close to me, I beg to abstain." There was a buzz of talk around the room as they absorbed his words. "I listened to Baldor Targa's testimony when he was brought before us the day after war with Rome was declared. I believed then as I do now, that I saw and heard the truth, thus I cannot choose between them, therefore I choose neither."

The Speaker bowed his head in acknowledgment then looked back to the assembly.

"Those in favour of the status quo … one hundred and two. Those in favour of a retrial one hundred and six. A retrial it is."

There were no loud cheers, only a buzz of murmured conversation as the Senators took in the result, the pro-war or Barca expansionist faction looked disgruntled and heads shook.

"Surely sir, we'll not bring this warrior home when he's needed in the field?" Asked from the benches of the pro-war faction.

"The decision is the will of this house; our army will not stand or fall for the sake of one man. A messenger will be sent to General Hannibal along with the warrant, Baldor Targa will be extradited to stand before this chamber once more and Baal's will be done."

Chapter Sixteen

Before the first grey fingers of dawn lightened the sky, Numidian cavalry burst out of the shadows. Racing their ponies over the last stade of open ground towards the gate of the Roman camp, the rumble from the hooves strangely muted on the snow. The warriors were swathed in billowing, flapping cloak's their horses wrapped in blankets from the cold, the men's hooded faces as dark as the morning sky above them. The darkness and their clothing's drab hues rendered them almost invisible in the gloom thus they seemed to float across the ground like spectres from a fevered nightmare.

The sentries huddled around the brazier near the gateway looked up from their chilled apathy gazing unbelievingly at the horsemen bearing down on them. Weary from their nightwatch and with senses numbed from the cold they were too slow to realise what was happening. Before they'd gathered their wits, the first man was already dying as a javelin whistled out of the darkness hitting him in the chest, flinging him backwards against the wooden palisade. As he slumped down the wall, the others finally came to their senses and found their voice.

"Attack! Attack! We're under attack!"

A shower of javelins rained down on the remaining sentries. The thuds from the missed javelins hitting the timber mixing with the cries of agony and dull clatter of armoured bodies hitting the ground. Dozy and slow, shocked and unsure of what was happening, the guards died where they stood, their cries briefly rending the morning air, the killing over as suddenly as it began.

Despite the sentries cries the camp remained strangely quiet. Using the precious moments before further alarms sounded or cohesive resistance materialised, a dozen Numidians dismounted lashing ropes to the spiked, trestle like barriers across the entrance. Mounting again, they kicked their horse's savagely forward, using the animal's weight and impetus to drag the obstruction clear. Sporadic shouts came from inside the camp as sleep fuddled men roused themselves. A cornu blew an emergency 'stand to', it's long brassy notes echoed moments later by others across the camp, torches spluttered into life as men looked to who or what assailed them.

Like a deluge from a ruptured dam the Numidians poured through the gate, a seething torrent of horseflesh and warriors, they slowed only to light torches as they rode past the braziers. Drowsy Legionnaires were exiting the tents in ones, two's, and small groups and snatching up their weapons. Those that ran onto the roadway were ridden down as the high-speed wave of wraith like horsemen charged along the main thoroughfare of the camp. The Numidians kicked over braziers, throwing torches and small pots of naphtha into tents, wagons and anything capable of ready combustion; soon fire sprang up and started to spread. Burning men staggered from tents, falling or rolling on the ground in an attempt to extinguish the flames. Unable to quench the clinging naphtha their movements spread the fire further, their howls and screams adding to the hell like scene. Unarmoured and confused the Legionnaires still fought back valiantly, throwing themselves at the horsemen but attacking without cohesion and any real numbers, they made easy targets for the short javelins. Voices of command trying to instil order and a structured defence were drowned by the thunder of the hooves and the screams of the dying. On the opposite side of the camp, the other gate had been similarly forced and the roads quickly filling with small desert ponies and their spectre riders.

The fire took a strong hold at the wagon park, sending tongues of orange-yellow flames roaring high into the morning sky that spread quickly to others in close proximity. Horses fastened at the rope lines bucked and kicked wildly, jerking their tethers as sparks and smoke blew towards them.

Centurions and Optios grabbed at panicking men as they spilled from tents and ran from the flames. Bellowing orders and enforcing them with their vine canes they coerced, pulled and pushed the men into line, slowly forcing them into a semblance of order. With signs of command and structure becoming evident and with dawn breaking in the eastern sky, discipline and being able to see, removed some of the fear from the men.

"Form up! Form up on me!" Gaius roared, his voice hoarse from smoke inhalation and the effort to make himself heard, his words vying with the crackle of flames, thundering hooves and the din of battle. He slapped his vine cane repeatedly on his greaves shouting for order as men assembled in front of him with Cornelius pushing and barking at them to fall in. Counting quickly as he paced, he estimated seventy Legionnaires, most of whom were only half dressed with no helmets or armour but all at least seemed to have snatched up shields and spears. Thinking quickly he rapped out orders whilst directing and pointing with his cane.

"First two ranks!" His cane pointed. "You're with me! I want a shield wall blocking that road. Cornelius!"

"Yes sir!"

"Place the remainder of the Century either side of the road! As the horses shy away from us they'll have to ride through and around the tents, if we can split them up it'll be easier to kill the bastards, we'll send them to you."

Hearing more horses approaching he glanced behind to see a squadron of Numidians racing past. A wildly flung javelin whistled past him, hitting one of his men, a second one thudding into the earth a pace away from him. Calmly picking it up he tossed it lightly in his hand as if assessing the weight then hurled it after the departing horsemen now some forty paces away. Grunting with the effort, he was rewarded when a bundle of dark robes went suddenly rigid, threw up its arms and rolled sideward as the javelin buried itself between the man's shoulder blades.

A ragged cheer broke out from his men as they saw the Numidian fall.

"Come on!" He roared as he ran for the road. With spirits lifting the men followed him.

Excepting the dead, the road was clear for the moment. However, a second squadron of Numidians were already bearing down it at speed, their ranks packed tightly together. Gaius calmly stepped into the tent-lined road. Stopping in the middle and standing side on, he watched the Numidians while arraying his men in lines across it.

"Form up! Shields front!"

Bronze shield rims clinked dully, spear shafts rattled as a wall of flesh, blood, wood, and metal began to form, the men jostling into position while pushing spears forward over the shield rims. Years of discipline helped them draw strength from their comrade's closeness and they began to contain and control their shock of the surprise attack, eyes looked to the front and hands hefted spears. Ignoring the charging horsemen approaching behind him, Gaius walked the line tapping a shield here and there with his cane urging its holder to raise or lower it as necessary.

"Cornelius!" He called into the half-light. "Are your men in position?"

"Ready sir! Hold your formation but back your lines up till I call a halt, we have a plan!" Cornelius was already heading to the side of the road presuming his Centurions co-operation. Seeing his men's faces beginning to twitch and their eyes narrow as the horsemen closed, Gaius resisted the urge for questions. Placing his trust in Cornelius, he shouted his orders.

"Holding the line and facing front, withdraw one pace at a time … withdraw!"

The ranks edged backwards, the imbued discipline and training paying off as men backed up as if moulded into one. Bravely refusing to face front, Gaius watched his men move. The noise of the approaching cavalry however told him they were but moments away from impact, 'what in Jupiter's name was Cornelius doing?'

The men continued to step backwards their spears still pointing forward hedgehog like over the shield wall. He could hear horses snorting and blowing now and the hair at the nape of his neck began to rise. He saw his men's shields firming in anticipation of the impact and their faces setting into grimaces or mouths opening to scream defiance and war cries.

"Century halt!" Shouted from the roadside shadows.

Relieved, Gaius slipped his cane into his belt and drew his gladius turning at last to face the enemy, 'where the hell was Cornelius?' He saw him squatting low at the side of the road and now some ten paces in front of him. Cornelius held his hand up, palm open in a halting motion, his shouted words lost in the pounding hooves. Gaius set his mind to the cavalry, now only some twenty paces away and coming at full gallop. Mumbling a quick prayer to Mars, he slipped between the shields with his men.

"Hold lads! … Hold! … Hold!" He called, his arm held straight above him, gladius pointing skyward.

The men braced themselves for the javelins and impact while subconsciously shuffling tighter as fear heightened the need for a comrade's closeness. Suddenly, ten paces from the shield wall the first rank of horses tumbled forward and down, rolling headlong into the road. Like a wave breaking and crashing onto the beach, horses smashed into the road, bodies somersaulting; men flew from their mounts like stones from a catapult as horses went down like nine pins. Bones snapped, javelins broke and men and horses screamed as bodies of both slipped and skidded along the road slamming into the feet of the men behind the shields.

A rope, pulled tight and low across the road had tripped the leading rank. Tangled in the hooves and carnage of bodies it had dragged two Legionnaires who'd been too slow to release it. Three successive ranks tumbled over the first adding to the carnage and mess. The rear most rank narrowly managed to avoid the chaos as the horses slowed and the riders peeled away off the road into the tent lines. Again, not without loss as the sharpness of the turn and the snow covered ground claimed the less than sure-footed. With a shout and roar of battle cries, Cornelius's men sprang up from the ground, drawing gladius's and setting about the milling horsemen. Like wolves bringing down gazelle's, the Legionnaires leapt up and dragged the remaining riders down. With their speed gone and forced to fight at close quarters the lightly armed Numidians were no match for the Romans. Fuelled by shock, fear and blind hatred, hands twisted and knotted into robes, cloaks and horse blankets as Legionnaires hacked and stabbed at both man and horse, the ferocity of their attack testament to their fighting ability. Gaius advanced his first rank and had them stepping through the heap of mangled bodies dispatching any man or injured horse that still drew breath.

General Maharabal sat his mount quietly looking over his pony's ears at the camp that was now recovering from his men's assault. Recognising effective command and resistance coupled with marshalling troops he nodded to his subordinate commanders.

"That should suffice methinks, we've set fire to their tail enough to provoke a decent response."

A flash of white teethed grins came back from beneath the men's hoods.

"Call the lads off, we'll retire upstream as planned … but not too fast mark you! We need to entice our Roman friends for breakfast." He grinned as he turned his mount about and trotted towards the gate.

One of the Numidians raised a curled ram's horn to his lips and blew three short, loud blasts; he waited a moment then repeated the call before trotting after the departing command group. All around the camp the Numidians began to disengage or leave their looting and fire raising, guiding their horses back towards the gates.

"Turn out the horse!" Tiberius bellowed to his Tribune as he prowled in front of his tent like an agitated bear guarding its den. His eyes large and bulbous as if they would burst, his face twisted into a mask of fierce red anger and hatred.

"Kill the bastard savages!" He yelled, spraying saliva as the words hissed out.

"Sir, shouldn't we assess the situation first? We don't know if …"

Tiberius smashed his fist into the side of the man's head sending him staggering.

"I command here!" He bawled. "Now turn out the horse and support them with the Velites! Get after them murdering bastards now! Do it!"

The man was dazed by the sudden blow but regaining his balance mumbled a 'yes sir' relaying the orders to the signaller. A fresh loud blast blew from the cornu, a vibrant, rallying melody that sent men running to the horse lines or trying to catch the loose horses that had snapped their tethers.

"The Tribune's right Tiberius." Publius interrupted urgently as he approached while struggling into his armour. "We don't know who or what and in what strength lies beyond the gates."

"Not now Publius!" Tiberius snapped.

"By all that's holy man, think!" Publius said placing his hand on Tiberius's arm in a bid to urge restraint.

Shaking the hand free with a violent flick of his arm, Tiberius cast him a look of disgust and pushed past him.

"Out of my way, Publius. Stay in your tent if you've no stomach for the fight! I for one will not stand by and see my camp attacked and burned and do nothing about it."

"It's what the Carthaginian wants, can you not see it? Damn it man! … This, this is …"

"My day for command! Now get out of my way! We're going to best this boy that you're so fearful of, we'll teach him what it means to make war on Rome!" Tiberius turned away shouting to his servant. "My horse! Fetch my horse! Quickly, damn your eyes!"

Smarting from the rebuke Publius hesitated then his temper gave way and he stepped after Tiberius, his jaw set and his good hand reaching for his gladius. A restraining arm slipped quickly around his shoulder slowing his progress. He shook it off only to find it back again, this time firmer. The action followed by quiet words from Gnaeus.

"Let it go Publius, he …"

"Damn him to Hades I will not! The blind, overstuffed peacock! I'll not suffer that! I'll …"

"Please Publius; the officers are watching, please sir!"

Publius glanced about seeing the staff officers collecting near the tent and noticed how their eyes fell away as he looked at them, he swore viciously but quietly beneath his breath.

"I swear to Jupiter that if the Carthaginians don't kill him I'm like to do it myself and save them the trouble."

"We know sir, he won't listen, he's …"

"A vainglorious arse! And now better men must die because he's a prize fool without sense or reason?" Publius vented, at the same time making a herculean effort to bring his temper under control.

"Perhaps he'll be lucky sir? These raiders are running now, all he can …"

"Raiders!" Publius exclaimed in disbelief. "We've had raids these last two weeks; this is more than any raid. Don't tell me you haven't noticed the attacks are larger and more aggressive on the days when he's in command? I smell a rat here, we're being set up for a fall and that idiot is playing his part well." He pointed sharply at Tiberius's back.

Gnaeus paled and looked at Publius.

"If it's more than a raid why didn't they press their advantage and finish us once they'd forced the gates?"

"Because Gnaeus, Hannibal wants us out there, in the open."

"But we outnumber him, why would he tempt us out where we can operate at full strength?"

"Because we could operate better in here, despite the restrictions of walls and equipment! We don't need space, as close quarter combat is our expertise and he knows it, he wants us out there, so he can manoeuvre. He fights differently Gnaeus, his thinking and tactics are large scale, fast moving, they appear rash, risky even but believe me they're well thought out. Hannibal only gambles when he's sure of a win. He is numerically superior in cavalry to us and those elephants could be devastating if used correctly. We're predominately heavy infantry where he has a mixture of heavy and light, the same with his cavalry arm, he wants room to manoeuvre, to manoeuvre and then exploit his advantage and destroy us."

Gnaeus's jaw dropped his eyes wide with shock. "You don't think we can defeat them? Surely sir, you don't believe …"

"Yes we can beat them, but not now, not this way!" Publius pointed to the men running to their units, most were carrying their equipment or dressing themselves as they went. "And definitely not on the Carthaginian's terms, timing or ground of his choosing."

"That's what you believe is happening now?"

Publius nodded sadly. "I'd wager my last Denarii on it!"

Tiberius reined in alongside Publius, his mount stamping its hooves and tossing its head as it reacted to the surrounding tension, the smell of blood and swirling smoke.

"I'm leaving you with a Legion to guard the camp, I'm mobilising the whole army. This finishes today!"

Publius just stared at Tiberius then looked away. As Tiberius kicked his horse on, Publius beckoned to one of his messengers.

"Find my son! He's an Optio in the Boar Maniple with the Second Legion, tell him … tell him …" Publius waved the man into the tent gesturing him to wait as he searched his desk snatching up parchment and ink, writing quickly.

My son, I know you'll account yourself well in this coming battle. Look to your men and yourself, remember the glory that is Rome and the good name of our family. I'm ordered to remain in camp with a rear-guard; I will see you ere the battle's done. May the God's bless and keep you. '

Folding the parchment, he sealed it with wax, rolling his ring in the liquid then passed it to the messenger.

"Return to me here once you've delivered this."

He watched the man mount then until he was lost amongst the smoke.

The camp was emptying of Numidians, the gates choking as they funnelled through. Some Roman archers sent arrows into the retreating ranks, bodies pitched forwards as arrows found their mark. Isolated groups of Numidians were hunted down, caught between tents and amongst the baggage; with their speed lost they were hacked to pieces as the Legionnaires took their revenge and reclaimed their camp.

With tents and carts well ablaze, dense black smoke swirled and billowed spreading and hanging over the camp like winter storm clouds. With no breeze to dissipate it, it hung thickly, obscuring and darkening a still ashen sky. The smell of roasting horseflesh mixed with that of timber and the stench of burning men. Flames crackled, flared and roared devouring wood, canvas, oil and bodily remains. Officers organised men into bucket chains to fight the fires while others reformed units ready for any new attack.

The Roman cavalry were quickly mounting and forming into their thirty-man turmaes. The lightly armed Velites were also assembling, each armed with a handful of short javelins and buckler and carrying a short sword. They wore no amour other than a helmet, some of which were adorned in wolf pelts, quickly forming into their maniples they moved off at jogging pace shadowing their cavalry.

The Numidians fought a dogged rear guard action as they retreated northwards following the eastern bank of the river. Keeping their pace fast enough so the Velites could not close with them, they employed their hit and run tactics on the Roman cavalry. Tempting them on then turning quickly to shower them in javelins then racing away before the Romans could come to grips. Meanwhile the Roman army decamped, forming into maniples they marched in their comrade's wake, the trail clearly marked with blood, dead and dying men and horses was easy to follow.

****

By mid-morning, the weak and brief sunshine had given way to banking, dark cloud and the temperature was again dropping. The Velites jogged nonstop after their cavalry, behind them and at a forced march came the Legionnaires, drawn up in maniples but strung out in column over two miles. Very few had time or thought to pick up a water skin or some food, none had breakfasted having being roused to the attack, forced to fight and then mobilised. Hungry and thirsty, their Centurions pushed them onwards in the wake of the Velites and cavalry.

Chapter Seventeen

"Gentlemen, it's almost time." Hannibal eased from his chair while gesturing his Generals back to their seats as they tried to rise with him. Taking the wine pitcher from the servant, he walked around the table recharging each man's cup. Back at the table head, he smiled warmly, his eyes bright like splinters of jet reflecting the morning sun, his manner proud and confident. He raised his cup in salute.

"I ask Baal Hammon's blessings upon you all; victory and honour!"

"Victory and Honour!" Echoed in chorus as men stood and raised their drinks. Cups clattered back on the table and they took up their helmets and cloaks, shaking hands and offering words and prayers along with the odd grim jest as they left the tent.

As the men exited into the freezing air, a signaller blew a short vibrant tune on his trumpet. The notes relayed by others across the camp and soon the area was ringing to the repeated tones that commanded a 'stand to'. From around the blazing fires waiting men roused themselves and took up their arms, reluctantly shedding their heavy robes and furs, rolling and stowing them safely ready for their hoped for return. The clatter of wooden spear shafts and the cold chink of metal sounded loudly as they picked up shields and spears and loosened swords in their sheaths. Horses whickered and stomped excitedly as cavalrymen mounted and formed into units, trotting out towards their given position on the wings. Like worker bees from a disturbed hive the army came to life, sporadic and chaotic for a moment then amidst shouted commands, horn blasts and bustle sorted itself into organised and cohesive order, the men assuming their predetermined battle positions closer to the river. To the rear and unseen, a loud, piercing trumpeting sounded, causing more than one horse to skitter and prance. Again and again the shrill call came, growing louder until it was echoed back in a cacophony of pitches as the elephants advanced to battle.

As the Carthaginians waited, they watched the Numidian horse cantering along the opposite bank with turmaes of Roman cavalry and some Velites chafing their rear in dogged pursuit. Behind them and advancing at double pace but good order came the Legions. The Numidians kept up their relentless tactics of attack and withdraw, one moment pausing to hurl javelins into the oncoming Romans, the next, kicking their ponies about and racing away before the Romans could close. As sporadic shouts and sounds of battle carried across the river, the excitable Gallic infantry brandished their weapons beating them on shields as their battle frenzy began to mount.

Some four stades back from the bank, Carthaginian officers began forming Moorish javelin men and Rhodian slingers, some eight thousand strong into skirmishing lines. These loose order troops protecting and screening the main army behind them.

Meanwhile the first of the Numidian horse were fording the river amidst whoops and whistles, racing for the safety of their assembling army. Hundreds of horses thrashed the water white, kicking up clouds of spray as they crossed at speed, hooves churning the water as if it boiled and reducing the bank to a muddy, slippery ramp where they exited onto the plain. They were met by Carthaginian officers who steered the units left and right towards the outer edges of the already assembled wings of heavy cavalry. As General Maharabal drove his horse clear of the water, Hannibal himself met him. Hannibal beamed at his General whilst extending his hand in greeting.

"I bid you good morning General! I see you've brought breakfast guests!"

Hannibal laughed whilst quietening his horse as it whickered and tossed its head as other animals cantered past.

"Yes sir!" Maharabal smiled and saluted. He had to shout as the noise of the horses and the whoops of the Numidians drowned his words. "And I believe they come in force sir!" He pointed back down the opposite bank to the column snaking away into the distance. Hannibal looked to where Maharabal pointed and smiled again.

"Excellent, General! Excellent! We're more than ready to serve them as they arrive, though I doubt they'll like the fare!"

Maharabal grinned and nodded, his face quickly becoming serious again.

"We lost quite a few men in the camp sir, the bastards recovered quickly and fought back well considering the rude awakening we gave them."

"We'll repay them for that, never fear! You've done well General, very well! This is exactly what I wanted … At last!" He slapped his fist into his palm to emphasise his point. "I have the intemperate Tiberius right where I want him." Both men had to calm their horses again as the Numidians galloped past in greater numbers. "I've arranged food for your men as we have some time to spare before the Romans cross the river and form up, eat what you can."

Hannibal's horse stomped and turned round about as the excitement affected it once more, its ears pricked up, its head tossing and nostrils flaring, he brought it back under control stroking and patting its withers with his hand.

"Baal Almighty's blessings upon you General, victory and honour!"

"Baal Hammon be with you Sir!" Maharabal saluted again and kicked his horse away.

****

"Well, it's going to be an interesting morning." Harbro said to no one in particular, his eyes following the seemingly endless Roman column on the opposite bank.

"Interesting and bloody wet, likely!" Armaco grumbled flicking his head skyward indicating the iron-grey clouds. "What do you think, Marko?"

"Aye, I'm thinking you've the rights of it. Either snow or rain, perhaps both, who knows, I do know I'm heart sick of this dammed cold … I wonder how Baldor and Malo have fared? The poor bastards must be frozen to the bone; that was one bitter night to be away from the fire."

"Look! The Roman horse are crossing!"

Balaam's sudden call broke the conversation drawing the men's attention to the ford and the first of the cavalry already midway over the river. Positioned on the left flank five stades back from the bank and four stades to the left of the ford the men had to strain their eyes to see.

"Look behind them and back down their side of bank; I think we have the whole Consular army coming on." Armaco added soberly.

"Like you said Harbro, it's going to be an interesting morning." Marko quipped wryly.

The chatter dropped away as the men watched the first of the Roman cavalry exiting the river to deploy in front of the Carthaginians.

"Still no bridles on their horses eh!" Armaco muttered, shaking his head. "How do they expect to rule the world if they can't control their own horses?"

"Well I'm happy for any advantage we can gain." Harbro answered. "Bridles or not they're not bad soldiers."

"Aye! Till we make them into dead ones." Marko added.

There was a little laughter from the group before they quietened again, the size of the approaching Roman army sobering their thoughts. The Moorish javelin men trotted along in parallel to the arriving Roman cavalry, covering their movements ensuring they didn't venture too close. Seeing easy targets some of the slingers loosed their lead bullets, similar in size and shape to a bantam egg, they claimed a dozen Roman cavalrymen and some horses before being barked at by their officers to hold. To their rear, the Carthaginian centre consisted of heavy Libyan, Gallic and Spanish infantry, out on their flanks were African pike men drawn up in phalanxes' sixteen men wide by sixteen deep. Well trained and armed, each carried a pike with a small bronze buckler on their left arm, bronze greaves covering their shins and leather or mail corselets covering their chests; all carried a falcata and wore a bronze helmet. On their flanks, the heavy cavalry and newly arrived Numidian light cavalry massed and on the very edges of the field and slightly to the rear the elephants were drawn up in two lines.

"That's interesting." Balaam said pointing to more horsemen splashing across the river.

The men peered to see.

"Gallic cavalry, hundreds of the bastards!" Armaco spat bitterly. "How in Hades do we tell them apart from our own?"

"Well, they'll be coming towards us trying to kill us, not riding alongside us." Harbro chuckled as Armaco cast him a disparaging look. Harbro was about to poke more fun when his face suddenly hardened as he stared then pointed at the deploying Gauls, swearing under his breath.

"Baal almighty! Look at the size of that bastard out front! Look! ... Look over there, the one stopping to speak to the command group."

The mercenaries were already watching intently as the arriving Gauls joined the Roman cavalry, the intakes of breath and whispered exclamations betraying their awe as they caught sight of the giant.

"They're the Cenomani, they've thrown in their lot with the Romans and going by their numbers it looks like they've brought the whole tribe, barbarian bastards!" Balaam hawked and spat. "And I reckon that big oaf there is that Lugobelinos; see, the one too big for his horse, the one whose brother you slew, Armaco."

"Armaco! ... That big bastard? Is that the one whose brother you slew?" Harbro asked, his tone incredulous.

Armaco shrugged giving a disinterested response. "Could be?"

"Was his brother as big?"

Armaco snorted then grimaced tilting his head to one side as if assessing the giant.

"Probably."

Harbro whistled softly. "If I ever insult you again I apologise now, in advance. By all that's holy, how did you kill a colossus like that?"

Armaco remained casually disinterested and strangely modest. "Size counts for nothing Harbro, you know that. He was like a ploughboy the way he came waving his sword at me. He was easy to kill."

Harbro still looked suitably impressed, raising his eyebrows in exclamation to Marko who smiled wistfully and nodded as if affirming the truth of it all. In the Carthaginian centre, the Gallic infantry had also seen the Cenomani and insults, war cries and challenges were being shouted across the two stades that separated the armies, the hullabaloo drowning out further talk by the mercenaries.

The last of the Cenomani exited the ford, reining their mounts in next to the Roman cavalry already formed up opposite Balaam's men.

"Looks like you might have a chance to finish the job, Armaco." Harbro said.

A rumble of hooves had them looking up to see more Gauls arriving but this time marshalling alongside them, at their head rode Andulas. Andulas and his Lingone warriors were escorted by a Carthaginian officer, who reined in while talking and gesturing their placing. Andulas nodded then indicated his Standard-bearer and carnyx player into position behind him. His Lieutenants following his lead settled the men into ranks adjacent to the mercenaries.

The colour and splendour of the warriors was something to behold, for the most they were large men, heads held in-dominantly proud beneath ornate bronze helmets. The cheek pieces squashed and framed their faces accentuating the huge drooping moustaches or beards that seemed common amongst them. Nearly all wore their hair long, hung in thick plaits else tied into ponytails or loose and spilling down their backs. Most wore three-quarter length mail shirts, others clad in leather jerkins, heavily studded with small discs of bronze shaped into squares, circles or stars. They carried circular or elliptical shields of lime wood strengthened with a central spine and painted in bright colours, the facing showing devices of animals, plants or the intricate curvilinear patterns of their cultural art. All carried fighting spears and a spatha at their hip. As they settled into line, they saw the Cenomani directly across from themselves and shouted threats and curses started up in earnest.

"What were you saying about an interesting morning Harbro?" Marko asked.

****

"Optio! … Optio Scipio!" The mounted messenger bellowed as he reined in alongside the Boar Maniple of the Second Legion. The Legionnaires were moving at double pace, the noise of pounding feet mixing with knocking spear shafts and panting men drowning his words. The messenger steered his mount into the rear of the Maniple using its weight to force and push men aside until he came alongside Cornelius. The shouted curses from the displaced men added to the noise of their movement and again his words were lost. Eventually

Cornelius became aware of the man and his attempts to speak to him and he moved alongside the horse, jogging at the animals flank as they tried to converse.

"A message for you sir! From the Consul."

The man held out the small folded parchment, Cornelius looked askance, still not hearing or understanding. The messenger continued to shout but with the noise and Cornelius's helmet closing off some of his hearing, all he could do was accept the missive. Turning it over and recognising his father's seal, he nodded and pushed it inside his corselet.

"Any message sir? … Any message?" The man repeated loudly.

Cornelius smiled holding his right fist over his heart, dipping his head briefly before turning to face the front again. The messenger understood and turned his horse out from the ranks back towards the camp.

The Legionnaires finally slowed then stopped as the Maniples in front began queuing for their turn to cross the ford, their Centurions haranguing and marshalling them into order. Like some giant serpent, the Maniples stretched back along the riverbank following its bending contour into the distance. The men were a blaze of colour against the whitened ground and denuded, black trees. Their helmets topped with horsehair crests of red, white or black while others sprouted tall feathers, again dyed in differing hues. Huge oval shields, almost as tall and wide as the owner gave grouped blazons of red, blue, green, white or black facings, identifying each Maniple. Above their heads on poles of cornel wood, the Maniple standards showed emblems of horses, boars, eagles and bears haloed by a circle of interwoven, golden ivy leaves. Beneath, on a silver rectangular plate, the Legion number was engraved and below all, silver discs denoting the Legion's battle honours. The Legionnaires leant on their shields and caught their breath, the hot vapour from their panting rising in white clouds along with tendrils of steam from their sweating bodies. Some sipped at water skins others nibbled lumps of bread or a stick of dried meat. Most however had neither, as they'd gone from disturbed sleep into battle and then immediately on the march. With no time to collect anything other than weapons and their wits before being ordered into pursuit, thoughts of breakfast and a drink had come too late.

They looked on as the Velites splashed over the ford; they crossed easily at first the water ankle deep but which by midstream had changed to thigh and in places waist deep. The watching men groaned and cursed loudly as they saw the Velites encounter almost chest high water just before they reached the Carthaginian bank. Some stumbled, losing their footing on the stones or floundered into deep holes, submerging briefly then surfacing downstream as the swift current carried them. The risk of drowning for the heavily armed Legionnaires was thus a very real possibility. This fear went along with the realization and certainty they were going to be soaked through as well as cold and hungry. To add to their concerns and discomfort it began to rain heavily, the drops driven on the suddenly rising wind and angled such that they drove straight into their faces. The temperature dropped further and the torrent became a skin stinging, blinding hail. Visibility fell as the ice crystals descended like a grey veil, men held shields up taking shelter behind them, the heavy pellets bouncing and clattering off the wood like a storm of slingshot.

"God's above! They cannot seriously be contemplating attacking in this. We can't see where we're going!" Cornelius asked earnestly though keeping his voice low as he raised his shield against the weather stepping alongside Gaius offering him shelter.

"Don't discount it lad, there's been many a battle fought in the snow." Gaius replied in a measured tone.

"But we can't see! How in Jupiter's name can we fight? And the river, we have to get over that yet and then form up! We'll …"

"Calm yourself lad, one problem at a time eh!"

Cornelius marvelled at his Centurions steady and unruffled manner and made an effort to control his own misgivings and outbursts. Lowering his voice further and removing the concern from it as best he could he continued.

"This doesn't feel right sir; we're not prepared. We've force marched from camp, the men have had no breakfast, the …"

"We'll manage Optio, the march has stretched the legs and the men will be alright! Don't worry about food; they'll eat those bloody Carthaginians instead." He grinned causing Cornelius to smile. "You're correct though, there's something not right here those bastards are expecting us! They look all too well prepared to me." Gaius ranged his eyes across the Carthaginian deployment as he spoke. "Still, let's see what your father has in mind when he arrives."

Cornelius remembered the message and passing his shield to Gaius fished in his shirt for it. Pushing chilled fingers under the seal to break it, he scanned the parchment quickly. Not believing his eyes, he read it again. Feeling his heart sink he passed the message to Gaius, who was politely looking elsewhere.

"He, he's not coming, he has to stay in the camp, he …"

Gaius glanced at Cornelius not understanding then quickly read the offered paper before cursing savagely under his breath. Handing the message back, the pair looked at one another, their eyes showing a despondency they dared not speak. For a day that had started badly it had just become much worse. Gaius recovered first.

"We say nothing! The men don't need to know, they'll presume he'll be elsewhere on the field, we can still win this battle!"

His words however lacked their usual ardour and conviction, Cornelius sensing they were spoken in an attempt to dispel the foreboding they both felt. Gaius however was unable to contain himself further and tuned away from his men and the cover of the shield venting his anger and frustration into the wind and hail, cursing Sempronius with all the hatred he could muster. Cornelius had to calm him as his words were carrying on the wind. The young Optio looked troubled and suddenly afraid as he realised the faith and reliance he also placed in his father's presence. For try as he might, he could not recall ever hearing a favourable comment regarding Tiberius' abilities, either on or off the battlefield.

Further contemplation was interrupted as a cornu blast drew their attention. An advance party of guards cantered past, closely followed by Tiberius himself and his splendidly attired command group. Cornelius instinctively gripped Gaius' arm, his eyes locking with his Centurions beseeching he hold his peace. Gaius nodded slightly but grimaced as if he'd swallowed poison; both noticed however, the distinct lack of cheers from the watching soldiers. Within moments of Tiberius passing the order to march came. The accompanying fanfare from the cornu coinciding with an increase in the hail's ferocity and sounding to Cornelius as though it heralded their advance to Hades and their doom.

Gaius snapped from his despondent apathy and slapped Cornelius on the back, flashing him a wink and a smile then called the men to attention. Cornelius ran to the rear of the Maniple repeating the order as he went, the men shouldering shields and preparing to march.

Gaius prowled amongst them checking harness and weapons while calling them misbegotten whoresons and lowlife scum from the gutters of Rome. In the same breath reminding them that they were 'his' whoresons and 'his' scum and they were the best, pig headed, brave bastards he'd fought with. The men's fervour began to ignite and cheers for themselves and their Centurion started to ring out. They grew in strength as Gaius played to their pride and demanded that they cross the river and show how the Hastati from the Second Legion fight. As men's cheers rose, Cornelius joined in, attempting to hearten himself as well as his men.

The Maniple advanced to the river edge but had to wait again as the men in front tentatively made their way across the water. Cornelius moved up next to Gaius again, the pair watching in silence taking note of where the water seemed deepest and the current strongest. Gaius pulled a cloth package from his purse and unwrapped it exposing two sticks of dried beef, he offered one to Cornelius.

"Here Cornelius, I softened it up for you with my sweat, it'll add to the flavour." He laughed softly.

Seeing the jerked meat, Cornelius realised how hungry he was and went to take one of the sticks, then remembering he'd brought nothing, retracted his hand.

"Thank you sir but I've nothing to share, not even a drink. I neglected to bring anything other than myself." He replied sadly.

"Well, age brings experience and hopefully wisdom, Optio." He winked again. "Let's put the benefits down to that. You're only young, learn from the experience but eat anyway, it'll stop the worms nibbling your guts and you'll fight better with something on your stomach."

He offered the meat to Cornelius again who still hesitated; Gaius pushed the meat at him forcefully while mumbling 'eat!' through a full mouth. Cornelius acquiesced, accepting it gratefully.

They both looked up as shouts went up from the far side of the river where the water was deepest. Two men had stumbled, knocking into others causing a dozen more to flounder and some to disappear beneath the water. Some surfaced immediately splashing and labouring to find their footing, some emerged further downstream and others never surfaced anymore.

"Remember that spot Cornelius, I'm not planning on losing lads before we've a chance to fight." He lowered his voice. "We should've had two screens of cavalry across the flow, one acting as a boom the other as lifeguards, hah! He calls himself a bloody General!"

Shaking his head in disgust, he bit his words off as he felt his anger manifest again, putting it from his mind he concentrated on the job in hand, as he gave the order to advance into the river.

****

Hannibal watched as the Romans deployed. Despite their perilous crossing and soaking in the icy waters, they made a brave and colourful show as the Maniples formed into lines. The Velites were out front forming a protective screen while menacing the Moorish javelin men and slingers and setting a tense atmosphere of standoff. To the rear of the Velites, the Hastati formed the first ranks, followed by the Princeps and finally the Triari. Ringing blasts of the cornu saw each line dividing by Maniple, leaving a space the same size as themselves between them and the Maniples to their left and right. The Maniples of the line to their rear covering the space of the line to their front, when complete the maniples took on the form of squares on a chequer board.

Shouted orders carried clearly as the pounding of feet ceased and the rattle of harness quietened. The commands drifted across the plain to the Carthaginian army that watched and waited in silence.

Hannibal leaned back on his horse stretching his back and pulling his cloak about him as he viewed the deployment. The hailstorm had eased in intensity and was allowing a better view of the whole of both assembled armies. The Romans had deployed in almost mirror image of the Carthaginians with Velites screening their centre and their cavalry on either wing. The armies had a frontage of some nine stades with less than two between them. Hannibal placed himself at the centre and front of his heavy infantry; he smiled when he saw Tiberius had placed himself similarly.

'You may be a fool Tiberius but you lack not for courage.' He thought as he kicked his horse forward. Beckoning to a Spaniard and Gallic officer from his command group to follow him, he walked his mount along the front rank of his men.

"Interpret for me." He said as he removed his helmet, cradling it in the crook of his arm. "Is this the best that Rome can send us?" He shouted, pointing to the Maniples. "It would seem they must compensate with numbers for lack of ability and fighting spirit."

He let the words sink in and a low murmur started in the ranks.

"Large numbers tell only of low confidence and if they fight as poorly as they are led then this battle is already won."

Some cheers came back to him.

"Our enemy arrives too late for breakfast and too early for the midday meal, thus they've had neither. Now, we'll serve them some fare of our own!"

He paused again as his words were translated followed by a ripple of light laughter from the ranks.

"They come ill prepared these Romans, rudely dragged from their beds, unfed and soaking wet, though I cannot tell if their shivering is from the cold or fear of you."

Again, there was laughter and now some vibrant cheering.

"In the past we've all suffered from Rome's overbearing and oppressive nature, her interference and brutish indifference to her neighbours …"

He waited as the interpreters finished.

"I say we've suffered long enough! Today we begin to repay the injustices done to our fathers, our brothers, our women and our children … for all who've suffered at the hands of Rome."

Shouts and cheers reached new heights and swords began to beat on shields.

"We'll destroy them here, at this Trebbia River! Give them no quarter! Kill them! Kill them all! Slaughter them as they've slaughtered us!"

His words rose in volume and tempo as his feelings caught alight, the men's response came back with no less gusto and fire. Cheers and roars emanated loudly along the ranks, those that hadn't yet heard the words were caught up in the euphoria of their comrades and cheered anyway. Spears were shaken aloft, swords brandished or banged rhythmically on shields while men shouted war cries and for their General.

The Romans looked up as the noise and cheering spread along the Carthaginian lines. Rising in intensity as the small group that was Hannibal, his interpreters and commanders worked their way along the front of the army. Legionnaires looked to their officers who in turn looked toward their commanders and Consul. Tiberius also looked up then looked away and continued talking to his immediate staff.

"Come on you dumb bastard! You're ere the cockerel, now's your time to crow!" Gaius muttered as he looked at Tiberius then back to his men, all now soaked to the skin and shivering with cold, their faces set in grim anticipation of battle. "For the love of the Gods, talk to the men!"

Tiberius dismounted, followed by his bodyguards. He accepted a shield from his arms bearer as the group pushed themselves into the centre of the line not far from Gaius, Cornelius and their men. All was quiet on the Roman side.

"You bloody fool! You overstuffed, conceited fool! Your big chance to make an impression with the men and you let it go." Gaius mumbled shaking his head in disbelief.

He grimaced as he recognised men sorely in need of hearty words and encouragement before battle commenced. He thought only briefly before stepping forward and turning to shout.

"Maniple of the Boar! Men of the second Legion, your Consul stands amongst you and honours you! Show him how we can fight."

The maniple erupted in cheers. The men may not love their Consul but their Centurion was a man without equal and they responded to his call as if ordered to battle. The loud cheering was infectious and soon spread along the lines. Gaius inwardly despised himself for having bolstered Tiberius, as he disliked the man intensely and insincerity was not one of his traits. He balanced his feelings with the comfort that the men were at last being encouraged. He knew only too well you had to go into battle believing you can win.

Chapter Eighteen

"I think they've had enough time to deploy." Hannibal said with finality. "Have the Skirmishers loose javelins to drive off the Velites and the slingers concentrate on the Centurions and Standard-bearers."

With orders relayed, horns blared in fanfare along the Carthaginian lines and the battle at the Trebbia River began in earnest. The small scale, almost personal duelling and dog fighting playing out amongst the Moorish javelin men and the Velites instantly moved up in speed, size and ferocity. Showers of javelins loosed, followed a moment later by the whoosh, whine, and hailstorm of lead bullets from the slingers.

Men raised shields high for defence against the descending javelins and paid the price as the closely following salvo of slingshot punched into their unprotected bodies. All across the field men went down like skittles as javelins and lead did their deadly work. The second throw of javelins was very one sided as the Velites had already expended most of theirs in the fight with the Numidians earlier that morning. Drawing swords, they moved forward attempting to close with the Moors. The Moors stood their ground and released more javelins into the oncoming men, the slingers following on with deadly affect. As the Velites fell in droves, their lines faltered then stalled only to be hit repeatedly with more salvoes. Seeing the Velites plight and subsequent inaction Tiberius had the cornu sound their recall.

With the Velites withdrawn, another blast on the cornu had the rearmost three centuries of each Maniple; move to their right into the space between them and the adjacent Maniple. Advancing forward they came level with the three Centuries previously in their front. All along the Roman front line, the gaps filled, presenting a huge, solid wall of shields and protruding spears to the Carthaginians.

With the pressure from the Velites gone, the slingers turned their attention to Centurions and Standard-bearers. Neither of these officers carried a shield thus making softer targets, lead bullets shattered knees and ankles or burst un-armoured thighs open dropping men to the ground. Others fell as the shot hit them in the chest or stomach, the mail shirts prevented the shot's ingress but the tremendous impetus smashed bones like dry sticks and drove breath from men's lungs. The more deadly hits were those to the head, concussing or knocking men out when they hit helmets but where they hit faces they smashed them like breaking eggs, spraying blood and flesh, bursting open like over ripened melons, men fell never to rise again.

Angry cries arose from the Romans as they watched their officers falling. One of Gaius's legionnaires broke ranks rushing forward with a shield for his Centurion; he fell heavily as a low flying slingshot tore his kneecap apart. Struggling to raise the shield as he rolled on the ground, his head disappeared in a cloud of red mist as another shot destroyed his face.

"Hold the line there! Raise shields!" Gaius roared, contemptuously turning his back on the enemy and ignoring the lead screaming past to ricochet off men's shields.

The cornu blew again signalling a general advance. With shields locked together and spears protruding like a porcupine's quills, the Hastati moved forward in good order at slow step. Behind and still in individual Maniple form the lines of Principe's and Triari followed.

As the distance between the armies reduced, the Carthaginian skirmishers hurled their final javelins then melted away out to the wings, their work done. As the heavy infantry headed for collision the ranks shrunk inwardly as men on both sides instinctively closed tighter together, the need for closeness being some comfort for what they knew was coming. Men gripped weapons tighter as chilled, numbed fingers became wet and clammy, the cold forgotten as fear brought increased heart rates and mild perspiration. Men tried to make themselves smaller behind their shields and here the Roman Scutum helped, its length and width covering almost the whole body of its carrier. Thirty paces from the Carthaginian front rank the cornu wailed again and the Maniples stopped.

In that tense and terrible quiet both sides could clearly see the other in detail: uniforms and weapons, beards, moustaches and the faces with anger, hatred or fear etched upon them. Young men of less than twenty summers fighting their first action twitched nervously, eyes wide, saucer like, some vomited, and others shook or pissed themselves as the fear mounted. The middle-aged family men whom had fought before mumbled quick prayers while flexing fingers reassuringly about weapons and shield straps and the grizzled, unruffled veterans of many campaigns smiled grimly. All looked and wondered if the enemy ranks were the last thing they would see in this world. Muffled commands came from the shield-covered ranks and the protruding pila suddenly retracted. Shields pushed out and angled up as the Hastati leaned back, arms stretching behind them as they prepared to hurl pila.

"Raise shields!" Shouted and repeated along the length of the Carthaginian line. "Incoming!"

A moan, like winter wind announced the pila storm heading towards the Carthaginian infantry and masked the rasping noise of gladius's being drawn from scabbards. A short, loud blast from the cornu saw a sudden and intensifying rhythmic thump of Roman boots as they went to double step, telling of combat but a moment away. Thumps and rattles like hail on a tiled roof interspersed with screams and grunts as the pila fell into the Carthaginian ranks. Some bounced off shields others piercing and skewering the holder beneath, a few slipping unencumbered through careless gaps in the shields and finding flesh. Finally, within ten paces of the Carthaginian line, the cornu blew vibrantly again and with a roar, the Hastati charged, throwing themselves against the solid shield wall of the waiting Gallic, Spanish and Libyan infantry.

The deafening crash of shields colliding, snapping wood and clashing metal was heralded by an unearthly singular, loud grunt as flesh and bone absorbed the savage impact. The chilling screams of the injured and the dying rose as ranks buckled and wavered as men staggered or fell beneath the force. The Gauls, already in a state of battle fury exploded in ferocity, hacking and thrusting with herculean sword strokes at the Legionnaires and briefly pushing their line back into a deep concave bow. The discipline of the Legionnaires told as they held the frenzied sally, thrusting viciously at the exposed flanks of the Gallic line, gradually forcing them backwards until the opposing lines paralleled one another again. Cornelius mumbled a quick but very sincere prayer to Jupiter as he crouched behind his shield. Pushing forward, he grimaced as he stepped onto bodies of wounded comrades whom had fallen in the front ranks, his gladius at waist height to the side of his shield, ready to thrust and twist as he'd been taught.

With the infantry fully engaged, Hannibal signalled for the elephants' to attack the Roman cavalry on the wings. The lumbering beasts advanced, trumpeting loudly. Brightly decked in their own panoply of war with a scarlet leather sheet laid over their head and broad brow. Over it, a mail cover gave added protection against missiles from the front and above. Their tusks, tipped with bronze and reinforced midway along their length with bands of the metal. On each leg, numerous bronze hoops protected against weapon slashes. Over their back, hanging level with their belly was a padded quilt with a sheet of suede stitched onto the upper side giving comfort and grip for the riders. Being African forest elephants and only spear height high to the shoulder, they were much smaller than their larger cousins from the savannah and thus not capable of carrying a howdah on their backs. Instead, each elephant carried a mahout and two archers, arrayed in a row and seated splay legged across the animal's broad back. Using the elephants themselves as the weapon, the Mahouts drove them directly towards the enemy cavalry. Picking up the stink of blood, vomit and human excrement and the scent of fear from both men and horses they tossed their heads raising trunks and trumpeting loudly. The chorus amplified to a crescendo as their own excitement and fear mounted the closer they came to the Roman lines. With the wind coming from behind, their strong spoor blew across the field assailing the Roman horses sending them into a state of discord then blind panic. Horses broke ranks and bolted while others reared and bucked throwing riders off, the horses galloping away.

The Carthaginians were now fully engaged across their centre. Though fighting doggedly they had to relinquish ground to the intense weight and pressure of the Maniples that were pushing and driving them back. However, it was easier going for the Carthaginians as they gave ground. Having fewer dead or wounded bodies to surmount, their rearward ranks called them backwards or guided them by pulling on their harness; allowing the warrior to keep his eyes front. The Roman advance was hindered, having to clamber, step or trip over the dead and dying as they came. Their stumbles in some cases costing lives as spears and swords thrust out taking advantage of their vulnerability. As the Legions deepened their penetration of the Carthaginian infantry, the pike phalanxes swung inwards attacking the Roman flanks enveloping them on three sides. Oblivious to the danger it posed their Consul continued his drive through the crush towards the Carthaginian centre.

Hannibal was at the centre and slightly to the rear of his heavy infantry battle lines. Calling for his horse he mounted to view the battle unfolding about him. He raised his shield as javelins flew overhead, his bodyguards reined alongside adding their shields as further cover. Seeing the Legions fully committed to driving his infantry back, with only the Triari left un-engaged, he smiled. The remaining Equites and Cenomani cavalry were being driven from the field by his heavy cavalry. The Numidians had already disappeared from view hounding those that had fled while the elephants turned their attention to the exposed flanks of the Roman infantry. The Legionnaires, seemingly unaware of their cavalry's flight continued their dogged push against the Carthaginian centre. Satisfied, Hannibal dismounted and turning to a group of waiting messengers beckoned two of them forward.

"My compliments to General Mago, I ask that he comes now with all his forces and all speed. Immediately upon arrival, he's to engage the Triari in their rear, thus closing the door and preventing their escape." He gestured with his hands to emphasise his point. "Do you have it?"

"Yes sir!" The men nodded and saluted.

"You!" He pointed to the other man passing his reins. "Take my mount, report back to me once the message is delivered."

"Yes Sir!" The men led their horses clear of the press before mounting and galloping downstream towards the island.

****

As the Carthaginian heavy horse charged in the wake of the elephants, Balaam led his men directly at the shattered Cenomani cavalry. On the mercenary's flank, the Lingone horsemen howled their bloodlust and kept pace as they also bore down on the already decimated enemy. Catching the Cenomani almost at standstill they smashed into them knocking horses and men down like scythed wheat as the effective charge swept through them. Those that remained mounted were driven back towards the river, here the fighting intensified as the cornered warriors fought desperately for their lives. Horses slipped down the steep bank as they lost their footing while others fell as the edge of the snow covered bank collapsed under their weight. Unable to gain traction and seeing the carnage, some warriors dismounted to jump or slide down the banking into the river attempting to make their own way across.

The Cenomani remaining on the bank top were hemmed in like rats in a trap. Responding with the fury and ferocity akin to their desperate situation, they hurled themselves back at the Carthaginians like demons bursting from the gates of Hades. Here the advantage lay with the Cenomani for their mounts were in good condition and fit, in contrast the Carthaginian horses were already weary, emaciated and still underfed from their ordeal in the Alps. Thus, the greater weight and stamina of the Gallic mounts carried them through with Lugobelinos himself leading their frantic but haphazard counter charge. Colliding again with Balaam and his men to the sound of splintering spear shafts and clattering shields the charge dissolved into another stagnating melee of wheeling, terrified horseflesh and hacking, screaming warriors. As the Cenomani forced their way through the Carthaginian ranks the fighting intensified as men came close enough to reach out and seize one another. Their previous fear transformed into an unbridled ferocity coupled with the need to kill and survive at any cost. With spears broken or lost, men snatched for swords and daggers or used their shield as a weapon to beat at the enemy. With horses jammed flank to flank and the room for manoeuvre restricted, the shorter falcata came into its own over the longer Gallic broadsword. It was pushed and thrust viciously under shields and into the sides or throats of the Gauls to deadly affect. All would have perished there but for the berserk fury that incites men when trapped and which fuels them to almost superhuman strength in their need to survive, thus the Gauls fought back like Titans.

Despite this sudden upturn in the fight, Armaco coerced and forced his mount closer to that of Lugobelinos, his falcata held low.

"Come on you big bastard! I slew your brother; I'll send you to join him!" He shouted hoarsely.

His challenge drowned in the clash of metal, the cries of the dying and the neighing of the horses.

He stabbed and hacked his way through the mayhem, killing or wounding any Cenomani warrior barring his way, gradually forcing his way closer to the giant. Suddenly out of the chaos and madness, an unseen heavy blow cracked the rear of his helmet. The force snapped his head forward pulling savagely on his neck muscles and scrambling his senses. His vision, replaced by blackness lit only with tiny, yellow lights that flashed then vanished like dying miniature sunbursts, the deafening noise disappearing as his senses closed down. He came to a moment later, his mind sluggish as if drugged, his vision blurry the volume of the surrounding din going from deafeningly loud to quiet then back to loud again. His body slumped forward over his mounts neck, the smell of its mane strong in his nostrils, his falcata fallen to the ground when he lost consciousness. His empty hand scrabbled along the horse's withers, snatching clumsily for the hilt of the spare sword fastened to the animals tack. With his mind and body co-ordination awry, it was with difficulty that he tugged it free, flailing it blindly behind him in a desperate attempt to keep any enemy away. The blade sliced the neck of the horse nearest him stalling it giving him a moment to collect his wits. Forcing himself upright and finding his balance, he kicked his mount around to fight his attacker. The Gaul was struggling with the injured horse and raising his shield as Armaco thrust the falcata into his throat, the blood spray covering him and his mount in a warm shower of red droplets. Blinking his eye and wiping his glove across his face to clear the blood, he felt a warm wetness oozing from beneath his helmet down his neck; disregarding it, he drove his horse towards the giant once more.

Despite the close combat, Lugobelinos still carried a huge boar spear, thrusting it like a striking snake at any Carthaginian within reach. Recognising Marko's blue-feathered helmet as the warrior currently fighting the giant, Armaco edged his horse closer. He saw the spear drive in knocking Marko's sword to one side and bursting through his corselet, the force burying the head up to the shaft in his chest. Marko's cry died on his lips as the blade ruptured his heart and lungs. Lugobelinos heaved and twisted frantically at the embedded spear to free it. Such was his strength that Marko's body shook like a rag doll as he was dragged from the horse, the giant forced to release the spear as Marko's body fell.

"No… o! Bastard!" Armaco screamed as he forced his mount closer driving his sword at the giant's throat.

Seeing Armaco coming from the side and realising he couldn't draw his sword in time, Lugobelinos pushed out with his shield deflecting the sword thrust. As Armaco retracted his arm, the Gaul slammed the shield forward into his chest knocking him to the ground. The impact drove the wind from him where a further crack to his head from a milling, horse's hoof knocked him unconsciousness again.

****

The Carthaginian messengers thrashed their mounts across the river towards the island. The ambush party lookouts had already seen them and alerted Mago and Baldor who ran to meet them on the shingle beach. The messengers reined up sharply their horses shedding water, hooves crunching and spraying gravel as they slid to a halt. The first messenger already calling out to Mago as he took hold of the leading horse's bridle.

"Sir! Sir, the General asks that you come now, at all speed and with all your forces."

Mago looked to his rear catching the attention of his second in command. Raising his arm and clenching his fist, he pointed sharply back across the river. The man nodded and turned on his heel calling for stand to, the need for silence and stealth gone.

Mago turned to the messenger "Now, man!" He said coolly whilst stroking and settling the blown horse. "Calm yourself and tell me how the battle fares."

While Mago questioned the messenger, the second man saluted and took his leave. Jumping onto the spare mount, lashing its flanks with the reins and kicking it hard he set off back to report to Hannibal. Malo appeared with Baldor and Mago's mounts in tow, the two men throwing themselves across the horses backs and kicking them into the river while continuing to converse with the messenger.

After fording the river, Mago summoned his officers to one side.

"Gentlemen, battle's joined!" The officers leaned in listening intently. "Our heavy infantry are holding against the Legions though having to give ground."

Seeing the concerned look on some of the faces and questions forming on their lips, he raised his hand for silence. "Which my brother commands and requires them to do." He flashed a smile for the benefit of his officers, showing more comfort than he truly felt. "Their Equites and allied cavalry have been routed by the elephants and are currently being harried by our heavy and light brigades."

Some measures of relief registered with smiles and one or two thankful sighs.

"We're ordered to come at all speed and concentrate our attack on the rearmost ranks of their Triari. Mount the infantry behind the cavalrymen that will speed our progress and save the men's wind for battle. When we arrive, drop the infantry along the length of the Roman rear. Once they've formed up begin the attack. The cavalry will divide into two companies and attack their flanks. I'll take five hundred to their left, General Bostaar; take your five hundred to their right. Do you have it gentlemen?"

A chorus of 'yes sir' followed.

"Baal protect us all!" Mago shouted as he pulled on his reins.

With horses' stomping and men desperate to be moving blessings were quickly mouthed, the officers separating to organise their men. Mago flicked his head beckoning Baldor and Malo to fall in behind him. With infantrymen mounted alongside the cavalrymen, the double laden mounts set off retracing their tracks of the previous night. Mago holding the pace to a canter not wanting to tire the horses excessively.

Baldor's stomach began to churn and heave from the mixture of fear and apprehension, though there was a small measure of relief now the agonising waiting was finally over and action imminent. It did feel strange however, to be riding to a battle already half-done.

'Would they arrive in time?' He wondered. Would their meagre numbers be enough to make a difference? Pondering the questions, he reached over his shoulder loosening each falcata in its scabbard then the spatha on the animal's withers. Content, he settled back allowing the awkward postured and 'horse nervous' infantryman behind him to hold onto his waist. He knew now was the time to offer prayers for both courage in battle and salvation. His snort of contempt awakening a memory of previous disdain towards the divine and his rebuke from Gestix for it. The memory tortured him, part of it calling for and needing the belief of a higher being to look to, something or someone to offer guidance and support. To comfort and instil a sense of belonging and care, else surety of an afterlife and his shade's crossing of the Styx. Another part of his mind, the hardened resentful part reinforced the sneer, filling him with cold contempt towards the Gods, the Gods who'd stood by doing nothing to help despite what had befallen him. He remembered Gestix's words and the same council from Hannibal as they'd harangued him not to blame the Gods for his misfortunes and loss. With no one to talk to in these last moments before battle and share his misgivings, he suddenly felt alone, very alone. Contemplating his coming dice throw with mortality, he realised that should he fall there would be few to mourn his passing and within a short time, less who would remember him. If his comrades survived him, he didn't doubt they would see to his remains but eventually their memories would fade or most likely, their own demise would follow. Most of all, there was no one to carry his name forward; he was the last of his family, name and line. With sudden doubts and misgivings gnawing at him, he cast a glance at Malo then Mago. Malo's face was turned into his chest hidden beneath his scarf, away from the driving wind and spitting rain. Mago was staring fixedly ahead his mind intent only on their arrival. Hiding his angst and bitterness, he moved his thoughts back to Gestix asking of him the strength for the coming fight and the wisdom and understanding to become a better man should he survive.

The ambush party heard the sounds of battle long before they could see it through the rain, the hubbub of shouts and screams carried across the plain snapping Baldor back to reality. They encountered some rider-less horses and saw the first bodies of the fallen, all of which were Roman. Judging from the positions of the dead and the slush and mud tracks leading from the water, Mago calculated they were directly behind the Romans and gave orders to set the infantry down and form line.

The rain changed to sleet, blowing across the plane towards them in swirling grey veils, stealing their visibility but also masking their approach. The infantry formed into a broad rectangular phalanx with orders to adjust their line as required when they contacted the Triari. The cavalry divided into the two prearranged sections of five hundred and trotted out to the wings, the horses prancing and snorting as they detected the tension and stink of blood. The men were quiet for the moment, with no enemy in sight they kept their war cries and whoops in check, some closed their eyes and mouthed quick prayers while others exchanged nods and smiles. As the advance began, the sleet eased then stopped, the dense, grey curtain slowly lifting and bringing the rearmost ranks of the Romans into view. Less than one stade separated the two forces. Some of the Romans having heard noises behind them were already turning and pointing towards the Carthaginians while alerting their comrades, their faces and shouts showing shock and alarm.

"Hold the line there!" Was bellowed as some of the Carthaginian front rank infantry surged in their eagerness to engage.

"Shields locked! Stay tight damn you!"

The commands repeated along the ranks as officers strived to keep the lines dressed whilst adjusting its width matching the Roman formation. The cavalry were going to the canter and responding to command, closing their mounts together forming a wedge. The rear ranks of Triari were doing an about face, preparing to receive the Carthaginian infantry who's advance had already reduced the distance between them to half a stade. Moving to double step with war cries and shouts starting up in earnest they charged the hastily forming Roman shield wall. Despite the looks of surprise on the Romans faces their courage and discipline was faultless though their reactions slow. With cornu wailing an 'about face' and the Centurions and Optios shouting themselves hoarse, the Triari maniples turned themselves to receive the incoming charge which was only a heartbeat from impact.

Baldor found his legs chafing under the pressure from Malo's mount on one side and Mago's on the other as they moved tighter together and went to the gallop, his heartbeat increasing along with the pace. The closeness of his comrades combined with the now reckless speed of the horses giving him a bizarre sense of invincibility, his previous fears forgotten. With the horses forced onward and driven almost to madness with terror, the men too seemed to catch the insanity of it all and their howls, whoops and war cries broke out in a frenzy of hate. With blood pounding in his ears and time seeming to slip into a drunken slow motion, Baldor joined the hullabaloo and raised his war cry, his fear replaced with desire to kill. He looked up moments before the high-speed collision and as far as he could see in either direction, battle raged, ebbing and flowing like the tide of a boiling, restless sea. The brightly coloured ranks bending and shifting as if unruly wave crests, as ground was lost or won.

Moments later the horses punched into the loose, open sides of the Triari ranks. The Romans bowled over and crushed in a pandemonium of charging horseflesh, stabbing spears and spraying red mist. Baldor's spear lodged in the collarbone of a Legionnaire, the man reeling as the impact cracked bones and burst his shoulder apart. The shaft snapped and pulled from Baldor's grip. Reaching for the falcata at his shoulder, he set about driving the recovering Legionnaires back and away from his horse. The Triari ranks crumpled and collapsed inwards from the impact, the men falling and knocking their comrades over. Unable to raise their shields in defence many died from well-aimed spear thrusts to their faces and throats. Baldor kicked his mount hard driving the terrified animal onwards, trying to maintain impetus and reduce the chance of a spear or sword thrust at him. Meanwhile a deafening clash of wood and metal and a roar from hundreds of throats told of his infantry comrades clashing with the Triari frontage. The combined onslaught turned the ordered ranks into a scene from Hades. Men screamed and hacked, berserk fury overtaking many as the instinct to survive fuelled courage and sword arms. Fighting dissolved into push and shove, blades seeking throats, groins and gaps in armour. Those that fell wounded continued to stab and hack at ankles and knees until silenced forever.

With their outer ranks destroyed and the inner ones bending under the pressure, only the iron discipline of the veteran Triari saved them from annihilation. Refusing to accept defeat, they gradually rallied. Coerced and driven on by their Centurions and Optios they fought back to a semblance of order as they slowly recovered from the surprise attack.

However, with the steady drive forward from the Hastati and Principe's to their front they had to keep pace else be left isolated. Having to advance while fighting to protect flanks and rear proved too much and they bunched up tightly behind the Principe's, adopting defensive tactics to ward off the Carthaginians attack rather than aggressively embracing and fighting it.

Thus, the previously ranked Maniples closed up, congealing into an unwieldy, large mob. Which although still moving inexorably forward was intent on salvation and escape rather than fighting an enemy which attacked it now from four sides.

The Roman leviathan of flesh and metal eventually forced its way through the Carthaginian infantry to their front using sheer weight as the weapon. The Carthaginians having little choice other than to let them through but decimating their flanks and rear. Like lions picking off the outermost sheep from the flock, the Carthaginians wore them down, the dead and the dying Romans leaving a mangled trail of bodies marking their progress.

Despite their horrifying predicament and slaughter, the courage of the Romans saved many lives as they stoically refused to break under the intense pressure and flee. If they had done so they would have been cut to pieces by the Carthaginian cavalry and the now returning Numidians horse.

Chapter Nineteen

The front ranks of the beleaguered Romans broke through the Carthaginian centre away from the enveloping pike men into open ground. Recognising defeat, their battle fury began to ebb replaced by a no less fierce will to survive at any cost. They left behind a carpet of dead, thicker and more numerous than daisies in a summer meadow. Sporadic duels still raged between some as the armies eased apart, the Carthaginians driven on by an almost drunken sense of victory and a need to slake their thirst for blood with further slaughter. The Roman's rearward ranks continued backing away; fighting a stoic rear-guard action, that still offered death to those reckless enough to risk further violence.

Calling for no quarter, Mago urged his men onward harrying the retreating Romans, still hoping to unsettle then shatter their ranks forcing them to scatter, making easy prey for the cavalry to mop up. Most of his warriors however had lost or broken their fighting spears and horses and men were nearing exhaustion, so though they attacked again their ardour lessened. Forcing his mount hard along the edge of the ragged outer ranks Baldor saw a sea of grim, blood spattered faces glaring back at him over dented shield rims. Their features a mixture of emotions from a numbing combat weary fear, to steady unshakable defiance. Finally, those, where madness or the Gods of war still invested berserk fury and still wished to fight and spill blood.

Baldor's own fears had long been replaced with battle madness verging upon exhilaration and a strange provocative euphoria. Sensing victory, he roared his hate as he chopped his falcata down over the rising shield rims. Heads ducked and swords knocked his blade aside. Retracting and slashing again he felt the blade hack flesh then clatter off armour as he rode on. A shield thrust forward into his mounts flanks causing it to shy and rear. His sword chopping down in retaliation like a butcher working his block, his blade aiming at the exposed arm behind the shield. His savage slashes saw a man fall and another reel backwards spraying blood from a half severed neck. The dying were pushed from the line, the Romans desperately trying to close ranks. His own shield took repeated hits as the Legionnaires fought like madmen to keep him away, the heavy blows from their gladius's reverberating and numbing his shield arm forcing him to kick his mount away.

****

By mid-afternoon, the light was fading as clouds gathered promising more sleet or snow, the approaching mid-winter solstice aiding and abetting the gloom with shortening daylight. To the wail of the cornu, the Romans retired in battered but reasonable order heralded by a chorus of contemptuous shouts and jeers from the victorious Carthaginians. Aggressive pursuit ceased as the inclement weather and approaching darkness ruled the manoeuvre too risky. The Carthaginian infantry turning their attention to the systematic dispatch of Roman injured as they began looting the fallen. Mago slowed his cavalry squadron to a walk, shadowing the retreating Legionnaires while maintaining a respectful distance, satisfied now to herd the Romans onward and away. Men's breathing slowed as adrenalin-fuelled ferocity seeped away and rationale returned, albeit combined with jubilation as the realization of victory began to dawn upon the Carthaginians and their allies.

The Romans were forced to leave their dead behind when the injured died enroute, with darkness falling and a long march back to Placentia and safety it was impractical to carry the bodies with them. With flanking screens of Legionnaires protecting their withdrawal others sheathed their weapons to aid and carry what wounded they could. The howls and cries of the injured chilled the marrow and played on the already frayed nerves of those that remained whole. With the fighting done Baldor found his own feelings affected, despite his deep hatred of the enemy he still pitied their injured. Killing and death he readily accepted, the combat he realised he took a perverse enjoyment in but the tortured screams and wails of the injured churned his stomach and frayed his nerves.

"Halt!" Mago called reining in his tiring mount and holding up his hand to stop his men. He watched carefully as the Roman rear moved into a large copse. "Let them exit those trees first, we can't see them clearly."

As the Romans disappeared into the trees, the screening Legionnaires stopped and presented a shield wall towards the Carthaginians while others slipped from the ranks to aid the injured fallen on the road. The Carthaginians watched as the men formed pairs, placing one arm about the other's shoulder their other hands clasped together at waist height forming a seat, others helping the casualties into the human chair. The wounded howled and groaned as they were moved, others passed out as they were lifted into the makeshift chairs.

Squinting through the blue haze of twilight, Baldor watched one man in particular as he commanded and organised the wounded to be lifted and carried. Removing and discarding his damaged helmet, he exposed blood-matted blonde hair and a fair-skinned face stained red-brown with blood, his tender years belying his grasp of command. With the wounded safely away, he turned his attention to the watching cavalrymen. Another Legionnaire dropped back from the main group and came alongside quietly gesturing after the retiring column; the blonde man nodded, waving him away. He studied the Carthaginians for a while before slowly moving his hand to the hilt of his gladius.

"Huh! The game bastard!" Mago muttered while motioning to Malo. "For Baal's sake put an arrow in him, let's have done!"

As Malo nocked an arrow and lifted the bow the man drew his sword holding it aloft in salute.

"Hold! … Please sir, hold if you will?" Baldor implored Mago while un-strapping his helmet.

"What?"

"A moment sir?" He gestured towards the Roman.

As Baldor removed his helmet both Mago and Malo, cast him a puzzled look. Hanging the helmet on his mounts tack, he relished the tingle of the icy air on his head and the relief on his jaw as the pressure eased from the cheek pieces. He rubbed then flexed his jaw before he spoke.

"Sir, enough for one day?" He entreated to Mago as he flicked his head in the direction of the Roman.

Mago huffed again and raised his eyebrows, his arm waving Malo's bow down while continuing to stare at Baldor then back to the Roman, his features betraying his puzzlement.

Baldor bowed his head respectfully as his request was silently granted then urged his mount towards the Roman. Letting it pick its way at its own pace he kept his eyes on the now lone man. Halving the distance between them he stopped, the Roman watching his approach while maintaining his sword aloft. Baldor's mount whickered and shook its head while the Roman studied them intently before bringing himself smartly to attention. He smiled sadly bowing his head again and placing a closed fist over his heart. As he lifted his head, he sheathed his sword.

"Baldor!" He called, his voice husky and unsteady.

"Cornelius?" Baldor replied uncertainly as he peered trying to distinguish the man's features.

"You have the field and the day once more my friend, I salute you."

When Baldor looked blankly, Cornelius repeated his words in Greek.

This time Baldor dipped his head in acknowledgment and fidgeted with his reins as once again he found himself at a loss for reply. Staring and hoping the right words would come he saw the Optio was much battered and bloodied, his mail shirt hanging loose where the leather securing strap had been hacked away and his tunic sleeve beneath, bloody and hung in tatters. His hands, like his head and neck crusted with dried blood and his leg carried a deep slash above the knee. He looked as haggard and weary as Baldor felt. Despite his poor state and his army's defeat, he held himself proudly and smiled as he continued.

"You're hale and well I trust?"

When Baldor continued to stare mutely, Cornelius nodded as if answering his own question. "The God's are indeed good!"

Baldor looked for hints of mockery or veiled sarcasm and found none; instead, his feelings and thoughts became more confused. He'd sworn to hate this man and his kin as he'd sworn to hate all Romans. He'd rejoiced in the battle and killing and knew that in the heat of it he'd have slain Cornelius without thought had he crossed his path. Now he experienced a sudden, unexplainable longing to talk, to take time to come to know the man who smiled politely and paid his respects, he thought how easy but strange it would be to form a friendship. They'd survived yet another day of terrible slaughter while thousands had perished around them, now for them to meet again like this; surely, this was not mere chance, their paths crossing for the third time? Instead of speaking Baldor lost himself in his thoughts again. The Roman column and the screening Legionnaires had now exited the trees and the Carthaginians began walking their mounts on. Cornelius, seeing the horsemen advancing raised his hand in farewell and backed away.

"Farewell Baldor, may your Gods keep you." His voice fading as he ducked into the trees.

Mago reined in alongside Baldor.

"Somebody you know?"

"Yes … yes sir!" He replied hesitantly. "Someone from half a lifetime ago."

"Huh! Can't say I admire your taste in friends."

Baldor found himself uncomfortable with the conversation and fidgeted with his reins again, seeking a reply to close the subject.

"Not a friend sir, until the battle at the Ticinus I didn't know who he was."

"Sounds like a good tale to share over some wine."

"It's not that interesting sir, believe me!"

"You're too modest Baldor." Mago laughed and kicked his horse on. "Later!" He called from over his shoulder as Baldor continued to stare after Cornelius.

Baldor was snatched from his reverie by a whoosh and a thump, leaving an arrow quivering in his shield, his shock, unexpected movement and loud cursing causing his horse to rear in fright. The sound of another arrow coming towards, then past him, raised shouts of alarm with Mago calling for the advance to flush the archers out. As the horsemen pushed towards the copse, furtive dark shapes were seen disappearing deeper into the gloom of the trees. A horse's loud blowing and whickering had Baldor looking around to see Malo's mount sinking shakily to its knees. The second arrow had transfixed Malo's thigh up to the fletching, pinning it to the horse's side. Dismounting, he rushed to his aid, the horse collapsing and dying under him. Malo, fastened in place, was unable to dismount. His face twisted in agony as the convulsions of the horse shook him from side to side. Another warrior dismounted coming alongside to support him while trying to keep the horse from rolling onto its side.

"Snap it! Snap it off!" Malo hissed from between clenched teeth.

Baldor tried to break it but with so little shaft showing above his thigh the wood bent rather than broke. Blood leaked profusely and Malo groaned and gasped for breath as the pulling intensified the pain.

"Cut it! Cut it and then snap it!" The helping warrior called.

Baldor drew his dagger and ringed the shaft, each push and pull of his hand bringing another stifled moan from Malo. The wood was seasoned and hard and the dagger, designed for stabbing rather than cutting made little impression. The other warrior reached to his weapons belt pulling a small utility knife free.

"Here! This's sharp, pare the fletching off we'll slide his leg upwards and off it. Quickly lad! We need to stop that blood flow!"

Baldor set to work with the tiny blade, his heart thumping and his hands shaking, slippery with Malo's blood. He'd pared off the first fletching when the knife slipped and fell.

"Damn it boy, come on!" The warrior snapped.

Baldor retrieved the knife; wiping slicked hands on his trousers, then cut the remaining fletchings free. Other warriors dismounted to help hold the dead horse upright as Baldor lifted Malo's leg upwards, his brow knotted as the shaft disappeared from sight into his thigh. Malo slapped his hand onto the wound, blood oozing between his fingers, Baldor undid his neckerchief and pushed it under Malo's hand. The men lifted him clear, laying him down so the wound could be dressed properly.

"Are you alright?" Baldor asked frantically while adding pressure on the bloodied hole.

Malo nodded and panted a little.

"He'll live lad!" One of the attending warriors confirmed. "See! The blood flow's slowing."

Baldor wondered how the man could tell the difference as there seemed to be blood everywhere, his hands were covered and Malo's trousers and the ground were soaked.

"He'll recover, believe me! If it was more serious there'd be much more blood!"

Baldor stood back as hands more expert than his cut the trousers away and took over dressing of the wound; he patted Malo's shoulder in reassurance.

Numbed from the suddenness of the attack and his friend's injuries he collected his wits. Cornelius! Cornelius, damn him! He'd played him for a fool! He felt his anger rising as he remembered the farewell wave and time wasting talk. Talk that allowed an archer time and chance to loose. Snarling like an angry dog, he strode in the direction Cornelius had gone.

"Careful Baldor! There may still be an archer or two about." Mago called after him.

Baldor swept his shield up from where he'd dropped it when going to Malo's aid. Snapping the arrow shaft, he hefted it higher covering his body but didn't slow his pace.

"Baldor!" Mago snapped. "Baldor! ... Baal, Almighty!"

Baldor stopped. Nodding quickly to Mago in recognition of his command he filled his lungs.

"Cornelius!" He shouted into the darkened trees. "Cor...neli...us! ... I'm coming for you!"

The words sounded loud in the gathering gloom. Baldor felt his throat grate and his head rattle as his shout resonated hurting his temples.

"Do you hear me Cornelius? You ... Ba ... st ...ard! You're a dead man!"

The warriors in earshot stopped and listened as the threats rolled into the frost covered trees. All had heard threats and intimidation before but there was something in Baldor's tone, something primeval and marrow chilling. Something cold that told of broken words and treachery, which had them pause and listen. Baldor gasped in more breath before throwing back his head to shout again.

"I swear, I'll find you and kill you for this, Cornelius! ... If it takes till the end of my days!"

Baldor stared into the trees as if seeking a reply, his chest heaving and mouth twisted into a snarl. His hand knotted tightly into his shield straps, his heart pounding in his chest as his anger coursed through him, his mind full of hate and vengeance. With no response forthcoming, he strode back to his horse slinging his shield over his back. Hurling himself over his mount, it pranced and stepped quickly as he swung his leg over and took the reins.

"Baldor, leave it! I command it!"

Mago barked the order as he reined alongside Baldor snatching his mounts bridle. As the horse stopped abruptly Baldor glowered as if about to argue, Mago continued firmly, cutting short any protest.

"I command here sir rah! This is a military unit not some damned arena! Do you understand?"

Baldor sobered under the verbal onslaught and dropped his head.

"Yes sir." He replied quietly, his tone conciliatory. "I'm sorry sir."

Mago grunted then huffed.

"I'll lose no more men this late in the day; there'll be another, mark my words! … Revenge Baldor, is a dish best served cold."

Cornelius heard his name drifting through the trees and recognised Baldor's voice. He didn't understand the Phoenician dialect but the tone was clear. A moment later an archer appeared moving at a steady pace and casting furtive glances back towards the Carthaginians.

"Best keep moving sir! We've slowed them up somewhat and feathered one of the bastards to boot."

The words took a moment to register then Cornelius snatched the archer's shirt, rolling his fist in it. Tightening it on the man's throat, he pulled him close.

"What do you mean feathered one of the bastards? Which one? What in Jupiter's n…?"

Seeing the shocked and confused look on the man's face Cornelius ceased his diatribe. He swallowed quickly letting go of his shirt.

"Use your damned head man!" He snapped quickly, seeking to hide his misplaced concern. "Do you want to bring them down on us? They're content to see us off without further bloodshed."

The archer stared back into Cornelius's angry gaze.

"We were covering you sir, as you fell back, they were outflanking you! A captured Optio would be a fair prize."

Cornelius knew the man was correct. Feeling awkward, insincere and suddenly very young, he clasped him on the shoulder and hiding his misgivings behind a painted smile, steered the archer in front of him.

"Yes ... yes, you're right; we'd best move on, they're in the tree line now."

****

The Carthaginians continued to shadow the Romans, only when darkness was complete did Mago signal them back towards the battlefield then their camp. As they trotted in, they noted the starkly different temperaments of the men. Some, already drunk judging by their boisterous singing and revelry, others paraded or danced with their spoils, weapons, cloaks, helmets and mail shirts holding them aloft as trophies. In sharp contrast, men by the rows of fires stood quietly with heads reverently bowed, some holding fists over their hearts while others added fuel and oil as they mumbled prayers over dead comrades.

Despite the unmilitary seeming camp and free flowing wine, Baldor was reassured that control was still present and being vigorously exercised by the constant challengers levelled at them out of the darkness. Large, well-armed and very sober patrols were traversing the outer limits of the camp ensuring it remained safe and secure. Hitching their horses the men removed riding blankets, bridles, trappings and gear then set about examining and checking their mounts. Servants brought fresh water and spread bundles of dried hay and old apples in front of the horses, which they cropped hungrily, oats and grain still being in short supply. Meanwhile the riders dried and cleaned the sweat and dirt from their coats, grooming them before covering them with their night blankets to guard against the cold and frost.

"Captain!" Mago called across to one of his officers.

"Yes General."

"See to the men, issue food and wine to all. Furnish me with a casualty list from our ambush party; the dead, injured and the missing, horses and men, you know the drill."

Taking a torch from outside one of the nearby tents he held it in the direction of the cavalrymen still tending their mounts, the glow reflecting from the snow and driving some of the darkness back.

"There you are Baldor! Come, I need to report to my brother and I'm keen to hear how we've faired overall. From what I saw on the field methinks we've won a great victory and at relatively small cost, most of the fallen seemed to be Roman."

Baldor slung his shield over his back and picked up his blanket and water skins.

"Sir …"

Mago missed the hesitation in Baldor's voice and continued.

"Let's wash this Roman blood off then we'll see some hot food into our bellies at my brother's tent. Will you take a drink with me to celebrate our victory and as thanks for saving my life?" He asked as he walked towards the tents while shouting for his slaves and hot water with which to wash. Before Baldor could reply, Mago continued.

"Your friend will be cared for at the surgeon's tent, you have my word."

"Thank you sir, I should find my unit though, I …"

"How in Baal's name do you propose to do that in this darkness and bloody chaos? I'll warrant that until daylight comes we'll have little idea of where anyone is."

Baldor looked reticent and as if sensing another excuse Mago countered.

"Baal almighty man! Must I beg you to take a drink?"

Baldor quickly assessed the situation, Mago was correct, he had no idea where to begin looking for his comrades and the darkness would only add to the difficulty. He was aware of his bodily needs, having last eaten and drank just before dawn, lightening his thoughts he replied just as Mago turned away, his patience exhausted.

"Sir, sir! Thank you, I'll gladly take that drink and food and your company if you will, thank you!"

****

Armaco regained consciousness for the second time or so he thought, he remembered the shouts, screams, and din of battle but how long ago? Where? His sluggish, befuddled senses drifted between wakefulness and semi-consciousness, his eyelids flickering then opening slowly as if waking from a drugged sleep. Trying to focus, he could see nothing only black shapes, his hands instinctively rubbing his eye trying to clear it. The darkness terrified him, bringing him from his comatose stupor into what he was sure was clear consciousness. Where was he? … Was he still alive? … Had he been blinded? Was he dead and waiting by the haunted banks of the Styx for Charon to ferry him over? Was he already in Hades? Did this blackness harbour demons waiting only for his realisation that they were coming for his shade. Gathering his wits and fighting the icy fear of the unknown, he tried to move but found himself pinned to the ground by his leg. Discovering he was trapped added to his horror and he kicked with his other leg trying to push and lever himself free, he felt his foot connect on something solid which wasn't the ground. His exertions left him panting heavily and his fading strength forced him to stop, his trapped leg remaining immovable. Making a herculean effort to calm himself he listened for sounds of life around him, his laboured breath loud in his ears. Hearing nothing other than the wind and his breathing, he ran his hands slowly down his leg and touched velvet softness, quickly retracting his hand, he caught the scent of horse on his fingers. Like a blind man feeling his way he groped tentatively, searching for objects or something to help him understand where he was. His fingers closed on something hard and cold and as the tips felt a keen sharpness, he recognised the shape of his sword and snatched it up. His fingers closed around the hilt like a man thrown a lifeline in a raging sea, his heart rose in his chest and his feeling of helplessness eased a little.

A pain like a lightning strike pounded across his temples rattling and shaking his skull down to the roots of his teeth. Sourcing the pain, his hand found the cold metal of his helmet and the heavy dent in the side of it, then he remembered the blow to his head. His fingers traced beneath the dent and felt the cloying stickiness he knew to be blood. He tried recollecting what had happened in the last moments before losing consciousness, though trying to think and remember was like walking through dense fog. Reluctantly his mind gave up details, delivering them in pieces without sequence. He remembered the giant and forcing his way towards him. Baldor appeared next embracing him and shaking his hand, his face drawn with concern his eyes moist and fearful, childlike. The memory faded, changing to battle joined and he remembered Marko falling to the giants spear. The giant seemed terribly real and touchable and he involuntarily flinched away. He managed to link the scenes that brought him to the first blow on his head. Before long, he'd picked up the threads of his demise and reasoned that some time had passed since. He also knew that with night fallen help wouldn't come until daylight at the earliest.

Along with returning coherence and immobility came the feel of biting cold, so wrestling and tugging at the horse blanket beneath him he pulled it free wrapping it around his upper body. The plummeting temperature and seeping chill soon pervaded the blanket and had him seeking further layers. Remembering a spare blanket fastened to his tack, he groped for it, his numbed fingers struggling with the buckles to release it. Unrolling and wrapping it around his chest and shoulders, he reached inside his corselet for his gloves, blowing unsteady but warm breath into them he slipped them on. Laying his sword close to hand he settled down to wait for morning, they'd find him he told himself, as long as he didn't freeze to death before then.

Drifting in and out of dozes as the cold or his stiffening muscles disturbed him; he was brought awake by an agonizing ache deep in his thigh. Feeling with his hand, he recoiled in fright when his fingers squeezed hard but registered no feeling, using his other leg he pushed and heaved with all his might to alleviate the weight. Unable to move the horse he did relieve some of the weight and pressure from his thigh, before long however he had to rest and as the weight returned the pain started over. Easing into a better position, he removed his helmet, encountering more pain and difficulty from the liner where it adhered to his hair and dry blood of his wound. The freezing air helped clear his head and he unfastened and took out the liner refitting it to his head; half twisting his torso he laid flat on his back allowing more leverage for his good leg. He shoved and pushed at the dead weight and as the horse's body lifted, he pushed the helmet under it as a support. Resting a moment, he began again, pushing with his good leg while easing the helmet further under the horses flank, repeating the process until his reach was exhausted. The helmet supported some of the animal's weight and he was rewarded with the tingling, pinpricking that came from returning blood and feeling in his lower limb.

Wearying and forced to rest he heard footfalls and low voices carrying on the wind. Fighting the urge to shout for help he weighed up possibilities, who'd won the battle? These could be Romans or Carthaginians, however owing to the lack of torches and their animal stealth they were more likely looters seeking easy pickings. Legionnaires or looters? Either way, he would be dead before much longer. Straining his ears for their dialect, he thought it prudent to play dead for now; hoping dawn could not be far off.

Slowly loosening the blankets he relaxed his body, lying limp while forcing himself to take small shallow breaths so not to move his chest. He heard coarse whispers, which he didn't understand, and then rummaging as the shapes searched the dead for anything of value.

With his heart pounding so loud he thought the whole world must hear it, he held his breath. He sensed rather than saw the dark shapes coming closer; with a huge effort, he closed his eye. Suddenly a heavy foot slammed down on his forearm nearest his sword whilst a hand covered his mouth cutting off his cry of pain and shock, another pushed cold iron against his jugular. Words laced with the stench of garlic and ale hissed into his ear, he didn't understand the language but the blade beneath his chin made the meaning clear.

Cursing himself for a fool he realised others must have been behind him and heard him moving. A rope was fastened tightly around his wrists with another slipped about his neck, the horse pushed off him and he dragged choking and stumbling to his feet. He fell as his leg refused to accept his weight. One of his captors stepped over him and he heard the rasp of metal clearing its sheath. Surmising they thought him crippled he expected a deathblow and he lashed out desperately in an upward motion using his bound hands clasped as one. Connecting with what he thought was a man's groin he heard the sharp intake of breath and groan followed by a body hitting the ground. With desperation fuelling his body, he thrashed his arms wildly attempting to keep his assailants away while trying to get up, expecting at any moment to feel the blade that would end his life. Instead, feet and fists rained down knocking the wind and senses from him. Sharp but hushed commands stopped the beating followed by urgent chatter, half-senseless he was dimly aware of hands checking his leg. A vicious kick to his ribs stole his breath again then the rope tightened on his throat urging him to his feet. Managing to hold his balance, he was led from the field like a dog on a leash.

"Like warfare and time itself
Blood feuds and their recriminations
can be interminable"

Anon

Part 2

Chapter Twenty

The morning following the battle, Baldor received a summons to Hannibal's tent, the messenger advising that he was to come without delay. Despite the imperative command, he was reluctant to acquiesce as having been reunited with Balaam and Harbro late the previous evening he'd been told of the still missing Armaco and Marko. Despite repeated assurances from Balaam that the missing often turned up later, expecting the worst his heart was heavy. The orders came just as the three had mounted and were heading back to the field to begin searching anew.

"You'd best go boy and quickly, when the General commands it doesn't do to delay. We'll see what we can find out there. Baal knows they could still be lost and trying to get home. We were scattered every which way chasing those Equites and it was black dark ere we gave up ... go on, away with you! We'll find them."

Balaam gestured him away as he and Harbro turned their mounts towards the field.

Baldor presented himself at Hannibal's tent still in his armour and war gear, he was ushered in whilst being served a goblet of wine. Coming out of the chill wind and frost-keen air the tent felt luxuriously warm, two braziers crackled and spat as the flames devoured the wood, the smoke and sharp scent of green timber mixing with the heat and appetising smells of cooking food. Baldor slipped off his gloves and helmet while wiping his eyes as the heat and smoke made them water.

"Baldor! Here! Here, by me lad." Mago called.

Baldor blushed as Captains and Generals moved out of his way to let him through.

Mago clasped Baldor's hand warmly in welcome as he ushered him towards a seat while Hannibal called the room to order.

"Gentlemen! Gentlemen! Seats please. We'll breakfast as we talk." The twenty or so men seated themselves around the table. Servants deposited baskets of bread, bowls of olives and olive oil, slabs of goat's cheese and platters of sizzling lamb and goat meat along with plates of dates and nuts. Most still looked weary, their eyes black ringed and hooded from lack of sleep, their skin sallow and deeply etched with lines and creases. Their faces however scraped clean of bristles with beards and moustaches trimmed; some had even cut and oiled their hair.

Their tunics and corselets had been cleaned and repaired as best as possible, though many still showed ingrained blood and dirt stains. Despite their sombre appearance, the men smiled and laughed readily the atmosphere one of celebration and optimism. By comparison, Baldor looked unkempt having not shaved for weeks, sporting the straggling, sparse beard and moustache of a twenty year old and hair so long that it rested below his shoulders. His eyes were sunken from lack of sleep and his lips cracked and chapped from the dry, biting wind. His corselet, spattered with dirt and dark bloodstains and the bronze of his helmet and harness tarnished for want of a clean. His cloak was fraying in places and the Gallic style, leather trousers he wore were dirty and showing faded, ingrained creases from constant riding.

Hannibal clanged his goblet with a knife drawing his men's attention.

"Gentlemen, I bid you a very good morning!" The greeting was returned as enthusiastically as it was given. "I thank you all from the bottom of my heart for a battle well fought and won. The light of day has confirmed that which we thought, a great victory!"

The men cheered and clashed goblets together their hands slapping the table in applause. Hannibal saluted them, letting them cheer and have their head for a moment before raising his hand for silence.

"The cost …" He lowered his voice respectfully. "The cost to us is some two thousand five hundred men dead, with some three hundred and forty badly wounded. The elephants fared badly, of our thirty six, only six remain, four of which are in poor condition."

The men looked grim, eyes and heads lowered in respect with some mumbling a quiet prayer for the departed and injured.

"The loss to Rome however …" He paused for effect. "The loss to Rome is an almost unbelievable twenty thousand dead!"

The men looked up, their features brightening, their eyes widening in disbelief, excited chatter broke out as they absorbed the figures. Baldor couldn't believe his ears, Mago turned to him smiling and reassuring him that he'd heard correctly, the sons of the 'She Wolf' were scattered over the Trebbia plane, their bodies almost as numerous as the trees that dotted her banks.

Hannibal continued.

"We've faced the might of a double Consular army fighting on home ground and still come off best, we were outnumbered …"

"Aye! But not out General'd!" Mago shouted causing further cheers and applause and his brother some embarrassment as the men rose to their feet raising their goblets to him.

"Nor outclassed, outfought or outmanoeuvred either." Another added.

Again, Hannibal let them have their head, it was heartening to see them in such good spirits for the cold, hunger and privations of the last few weeks had taken their toll on all regardless of ethnicity.

The small victory at the Ticinus had boosted the morale of the weary and half-starved army but Hannibal and his Generals had known that the real test would come when they faced the Romans in a set piece battle. The Ticinus had been a hasty, almost unplanned large cavalry skirmish but the advantage had always lain with the Carthaginians with the speed and superiority of their cavalry arm and tactics. Now, having locked horns with the Romans at their excelling best, a set piece heavy infantry encounter and slaughtered them, they could truly say that they, the 'Sons of Baal, the Lions Cubs' where the better men. Hannibal rapped his knuckles on the table, drumming them until the men quietened and settled back into their seats. He smiled at them all.

"The Gods are good! Baal in his infinite mercy has granted us a great victory! A credit to you and to our men, well done to all. Pass my thanks and the numbers to the men for I believe it will hearten them further. Now, I've learned much from yesterday's battle.

Though the Romans fought with their traditional tactics as expected, I still underestimated their power and weight. Their forward impetus I have to say, is astonishing, I surmise that had we been able to hold their front and centre for longer we'd have slaughtered them to a man."

There were some downcast looks and mutterings.

"I'm not criticising!" He said sincerely. "Believe me I'm not! I'm most thankful to Baal Almighty for the victory but especially thankful to you all for making it so. I wish only to examine our performance and learn from it, for does the artisan not examine his work to improve, seeking perfection in his trade? Does the philosopher not always ask why?" Smiling his enigmatic smile he looked around the table and heads nodded. "The sooner we destroy their field armies once and for all, the quicker we return to our homes and wives."

"If you don't mind General, I'll settle for the hot young harlot I have in my tent! Not going home to an aging wife with sagging tits and a sour tongue makes fighting these Romans somewhat worthwhile!" Hasdrubal the Elder, the oldest man in the room quipped.

The men roared with laughter.

"Take the harlot home then General, three in a bed will keep you well warm in winter." Hannibal replied, his comment provoking more laughter. "Gentlemen, Gentlemen!" He called them to order once more though smiling at his jest and his men's happiness. "Before we discuss our next moves there's another matter I would acquaint you of."

The men looked up and quietened to listen.

"Once more it is a pleasing matter and again one which prompts my thanks to Baal Hammon for his mercy but most of all my heartfelt thanks goes to one who sits amongst us."

The men were all attentive and looking to see if anyone had any notion of what was to come.

"I'm told, but for the brave and selfless actions of one man here, that today I would be mourning my little brother."

He paused to let the words sink in; some smirked at the inference of little. Mago was younger by age but he dwarfed Hannibal, both in width and height; Hannibal continued.

"So today I have two reasons to rejoice, a great victory and my little brother still alive and well to enjoy it!"

Baldor shifted uncomfortably in his seat as Mago smiled and winked at him. Hannibal filled another goblet of wine carrying it towards Baldor offering him the cup in both hands like a gift.

"Generals, Captains, brothers in arms, I give you Baldor Targa, my brother's saviour, a brave and able warrior and a man whom I'm proud to name as a friend."

Baldor coloured at the praise and being the centre of attention, his heart pounding in his chest as the men slapped the table in applause. Taking the offered cup, he sipped the wine as Hannibal placed a hand on his shoulder and bowed his head. As the applause petered out, Mago stood, snapping his fingers at a servant who disappeared out of the tent door. Urging Baldor to his feet, he escorted him in the same direction; he paused briefly to excuse himself and Baldor, Hannibal gesturing acceptance while smiling knowingly.

Outside, the servant appeared leading a roan horse by a neck rope. Unlike the Carthaginian mounts the horse was well fed, its ribs and rump well covered its coat groomed and shiny. Its ears, mane and tail were of similar hue to its coat only darker in shade. It whickered lightly as it caught the new scent of the two men, tossing its head gently and twitching its coat. Over its back was a finely woven, black blanket, edged along its hem with a broad silver stripe and over which an iron grey, wolf pelt lay.

"A fine beast, do you think Baldor?" Mago asked.

"Beautiful sir! The colouring, the condition." He moved to stroke and examine the horse. Whispering softly to it he ran his hand up its neck patting gently; it turned nudging him gently with its head.

"Hah! A good match, you like him and he likes you."

"Is he yours sir? I take that it was Roman by the condition?"

"He was mine, the Decurion who owned it has no further use for it so it was given to me." He chuckled. "Now I give him to you."

Baldor gasped and stammered an objection along with a polite refusal; Mago held up his hand for silence and continued.

"I give him to you with all my thanks."

Baldor, lost for words just shook his head in disbelief.

"I think my life's worth at least a fine horse, even if it's a Roman one!" He offered the rope to Baldor who chewed his lip and nodded slowly while continuing to pat and soothe the horse.

"I don't know what to say sir, I … I …"

"You accept, excellent! Right we'd best get back in there, my brother will wish to continue."

Baldor reluctantly let go of the rope, passing it to the servant, the boy in him wanting nothing more than to go for a ride immediately. He felt a sense of the unreal as if he were dreaming; could his luck be finally changing for the better? A great weight seemed to be lifting from his shoulders, for the first time in what seemed like years he wondered if he was turning a corner, his sudden optimism even surprising himself. Returning to the table it was as if he floated over the ground, the men, his commanders, bowed or offered their hands as he passed; some clapped him on the back. Settling back into his seat, he sought his cup using it as a prop to stop his hands fidgeting raising it to his lips to hide his blushing.

"Now … my gift to you, Baldor, along with my personal thanks."

Hannibal placed a dagger on the table in front of Baldor. The hilt was of silver inlaid with gold. Narrow nearest the cross guard then widening midway before reducing again affording a tapering grip for the palm and fingers. The pommel was an inverted, deeply curved crescent moon, again fashioned in silver which while giving decoration also prevented the users hand from slipping off. The straight, broad blade was encased in a black leather sheath decorated with small silver crescents and circles formed into symmetrical patterns over its length. Though highly crafted it remained a practical and deadly weapon.

Baldor was in awe of its beauty; he picked it up almost reverently and slipped it from its sheath. Turning it to the light he saw the blade bore three marks like wisps of smoke hovering above a placid silver lake and which ran the length of the metal. The dagger hissed as it glided back into its sheath, the click of the hilt coming to rest snapping him from his trance. He mumbled an awkward thank you while bowing his head to Hannibal and the assembled men.

Hannibal smiled graciously then called for the map board. He sipped his wine while waiting for the men to finish the setup, his mind engrossed with thoughts and plans. He silently appraised the map, tilting his head a little while chewing some bread and following imagined routes across the board. He swilled his wine then called the men to attention.

"Gentlemen, Gentlemen! Pray carry on with your well-earned breakfast but your attention please. As you know we are here." He indicated the camp drawn by the side of the Trebbia, the many water courses of which seemed to radiate across the board like the veins in a man's forearm. "I'm for wintering hereabouts, it's late in the year and the campaigning season is really done."

"Aye, well done! For the Roman bastards!" Mago shouted and the men broke into laughter.

Hannibal smirked and held up his hands for quiet.

"Yes, well done I agree! Nevertheless, they'll regroup and they will be back. This was but the first hard lesson we'll be giving them, they'll need further teaching ere they realise they're done. Methinks however, they'll leave us alone until spring and the weather changes. Therefore, we have some time to put a little meat on the men's and the horse's bones and train for the coming season. As I see it, we have three options southwards when spring comes: we march down the west coast towards Pisae then southeast across the plain." He used his finger to trace the route. "Or take the eastern route skirting the mountains towards Ariminum or … or we can go directly south through the Apennines?"

The men took a moment to consider the options then turned to discuss with their neighbour.

"Myself, I prefer the …"

A servant appeared and sought to catch Hannibal's eye. "Excuse me General; we've a courier, a messenger from Carthage, from the Senate, sir. He awaits outside, requesting an audience as soon as possible."

"Can it not wait?"

"Sir, the weather's closing in again, he would be away homeward he says, he asks if you will but spare him some time at your earliest convenience."

Hannibal looked at his men, seeing Mago was particularly irked at the interruption and likely to voice it he managed a quick smile and added.

"Our City and Senate will wish to know our good tidings, we should grant this courier time then send him on his way for the news will hearten and please our people."

He turned to the servant, signalling the courier could be admitted.

"Baal bless and preserve all here." The man said as he was ushered in, his entrance allowing a blast of icy air from the open door.

A few mumbled a return blessing as he stepped into the tent and towards the table. He pushed the hood of his cloak back pausing to bow to Hannibal then to the seated men wishing them all a cordial good morning. His clothes were heavily soiled from the road, his face pinched white with the cold, removing his gloves he held his hands to the fire for warmth. Hannibal gestured to the servant to bring food and drink for him.

"How fares the City and people of Carthage, courier?"

"Well General! Very well! They're much heartened by your successful advance across the Alps and victory at the Ticinus."

Hannibal was surprised at the messengers reply. News had certainly travelled quickly to Carthage, no doubt from spies within his camp, even if they were on the same side he didn't like the thoughts of being watched. The courier gratefully accepted the steaming wine he was brought. Wrapping both hands around the cup, he sipped and breathed deeply of the cloves and cinnamon, savouring it as he acquainted all with the news from Carthage. In turn, he asked for further news of the campaign and the projected outcomes and time lines. His manner, being very respectful and polite didn't draw any hostility from the seated men as was usual towards such visitors. He offered a small leather satchel to Hannibal.

"Your correspondence General, both official and domestic."

Hannibal accepted the bag with a nod and a thank you.

"Correspondence for your staff, General; again official and domestic."

He passed over another larger satchel, which Hannibal passed to his scribe.

"Distribute this as required." He gestured towards the men around the table.

Hannibal had his reports and correspondence brought, already placed in secure, capped leather tubes, advising that they contained his undertakings until yesterday, again the man accepted gratefully.

"Can we not offer you a nights lodging? You've travelled far and fast and the weather's set to worsen."

"Thank you for your kindness, General but I'm already much delayed and as much as I would relish the chance of a dry bed, if I tarry another night I'll be yet further behind. The Senate behoved me to return at all speed, both they and the city anxiously await your news and reports."

He placed the satchels in his shoulder bag as he spoke.

Hannibal nodded offering his hand to the man while signalling to the servant with the other. The servant brought another bag containing food and drink and an extra cloak. The courier accepting gratefully.

"There is one final matter General."

He fished inside his tunic pulling out a folded, ivory coloured parchment bearing the red wax seal of the Carthaginian Senate offering it to Hannibal. Hannibal took the paper and laid it on the table intending to read it later.

"General, with respect I … I was told to remain until you read the message and have your answer to carry back to the Law lords and Senate."

"The Law lords?" Hannibal repeated as if he'd misheard.

"Yes sir."

The room fell quiet, the fizzing and cracking of the timber being the only noise. Hannibal eyed the man suspiciously while picking the message back up and pushing his fingers under the seal. Turning towards the light he began to read. Maintaining an impassive look, he read; then read again. He huffed as if realising the inexorable hand of fate then folded the paper placing it back on the table.

"What's to do brother? … What is it?" Mago asked, unable to contain his curiosity.

Hannibal didn't answer immediately, instead he stared vacantly, deep in thought then hearing his name called in question again he said very quietly

"They ask the impossible."

The messenger sensing a change in Hannibal's tone and manner said nothing but lowered his head and waited patiently for the General's answer. Mago and others were enquiring what was afoot, what had the Senate asked that had so upset him? Hannibal raised his hands for quiet and as the room came to order, he turned to the messenger.

"I'm sorry, but what they ask is impossible."

The look on the couriers face intimated that he had no idea of the message's content. The men however were becoming vociferous; demanding to know 'what in Baal's name' it was that the Senate wanted. Hannibal raised his hand for silence once more as he walked slowly along the length of the table; his hand cupping his chin, deep in thought, he paused by Baldor and Mago. With sadness etched into his face, he looked to his men sighing deeply.

"Gentlemen, this matter is of a personal nature, if you'll but spare me a moment. Please, take this chance to enjoy your breakfast at leisure."

The men consented to his privacy and turned to their plates and to talking amongst themselves. Hannibal intimated the courier should step through to his personal quarters at the rear of the tent. Stepping behind the heavy drapes that made a dividing wall, the men's voices at the table became muffled and lower in volume. Hannibal held up the parchment and keeping his voice low picked his words carefully.

"This I cannot do."

The courier looked unsure; was this a direct refusal to the Senate or was the task beyond the capacity of the General? He was about to ask for clarification when Hannibal began again.

"Baldor Targa, the man whose name's upon this warrant for murder, was injured in the battle at Ticinus and killed yesterday here at the Trebbia; we burned his body last night."

Hannibal's expression was one of abject sadness, the courier sensing the man's melancholy lowered his head.

"Baldor Targa died in the service of his city, as you can see his loss weighs heavy upon me, he'll be mourned by many here."

The courier was about to speak but Hannibal continued.

"Whatever his alleged crime is and I do wonder? For he was cleared and pardoned of any wrong doing before the Senate and the Courts in Carthage a year past. Now he'll have to answer for it in the afterlife. However, I tell you this and carry my words back to Carthage; as sure as sunrise tomorrow, there was not a better man amongst us, the city and this army has lost a great warrior. Thus my reply to the Senate is such, the matter has gone beyond the reach of mortal men to the God's, they alone now must decide upon his deeds and thus his salvation or not. Carry this news to Carthage courier, and tell them we need more men of his ilk, alleged crimes or no."

The courier nodded his head and bowed.

"You have the message?" Hannibal asked firmly.

"Yes General and you have my condolences." The courier held his fist to his heart and inclined his head. "With your leave General?"

Hannibal returned the salute and dropped a small leather purse into the man's hand. "May the Gods guard your homeward journey; I trust it will be both swift and safe."

The man bowed again and turned for the door.

With the courier gone, Hannibal laid the paper on his desk and returned to the table and his men. Quietly deferring questions in connection with the message, he returned to military matters. Continuing at length with his conversation prior to the interruption regarding the proposed routes south and the subjects of supply, training, reconnaissance and camp security. As the briefing ended and men stood to leave, he signalled to Baldor and Mago that he'd like a word in private. Dismissing his men with heartening words and smiles, he turned towards the pair, his face grave.

Baldor felt uneasy. Presuming the discussion could only be concerning the message and judging by Hannibal's reaction it wasn't good news. Why would he be included for matters of the Senate? What was it that Hannibal wouldn't discuss with the command group that he now wanted to discuss with him and Mago?

Hannibal passed Baldor the message indicating he read it; Mago looked on, clearly agitated to know what was afoot. As he read, Baldor slumped in his seat, the nauseous, oily feeling in his stomach combining with the tightness he felt in his throat, the colour drained from him leaving him white as the winter snow.

"For the love of Baal! Tell me what ails you both. What's that whoreson of a courier brought that can dampen your spirits so?" Mago growled in frustration.

Baldor remained dumbstruck, still looking at the paper. Hannibal intervened.

"The Senate demands …" His voice faltered a little, his expression causing Mago further concern. "The Senate demands … the re-arrest of one, Baldor Targa."

Mago couldn't hold himself in check any longer and leapt to his feet.

"Damn them! Damn the old, twisted, pox-ridden bastards! Damn them all to Hades!"

"That's enough Mago!" Hannibal snapped.

Mago was about to vent further, his face flushed and the veins standing out in his neck like engorged purple worms. Hannibal placed a hand on his shoulder gently pushing him back into his seat; he lowered his voice attempting to soften the rebuke.

"Enough brother, enough, if you please. I understand your angst but this command comes from our government, however misinformed, misled or mistaken they may be, they are our elected leaders and thus due some respect."

"Hah! You're not going to comply with this are you?"

Baldor looked on blankly still lost for words as the brothers discussed.

"No … no, I'm not, I …"

"How can they try a man for his crimes twice anyway? He went to Carthage." Mago stabbed a finger in Baldor's direction. "To the Court, he was acquitted, he …" Mago ranted.

"Do you think I don't know that brother?" Hannibal snapped with more ferocity than he intended. Quickly regaining control, he lowered his voice again.

"I'm not giving Baldor up for the Senate or anyone else, this army and I need him."

"Well, at least we're agreed then!" Mago said, calming himself.

"I smell a rat here." Hannibal said, looking thoughtful rather than directing his words to Mago or Baldor. "A rat from the family of Lord Samilcar."

"General … sir!" Baldor had to speak up to intervene in the conversation and break into Hannibal's thoughts. "I'm sorry that I've brought this upon you, upon us all. I thank you for what you did but I should return to Carthage to defend myself and my name again or leave this army else I bring more disgrace upon it or trouble to you."

Mago looked as if he was about to voice his opinion when Hannibal cut in.

"It's bad enough that I had to lie to the courier and thus the Law lords but I can live with that. You Baldor however, I won't be without."

Baldor coloured under the sentiment.

"I need every man I have, especially the likes of those that breakfasted here and of course you two but you're right Baldor, you will leave this army."

Pre-empting Mago's interruption, Hannibal held his hand up for silence; he allowed himself a little smile, which quietened the questions on the lips of both his brother and Baldor.

Baldor looked crestfallen as he contemplated life away from the army but was jolted from despair by a sharp dig in the ribs from Mago who was now grinning and pointing to Hannibal.

"You have a plan brother; I see it in your eyes!" He said knowingly.

"Yes, I have a plan and it doesn't entail any more visits to Carthage for you." He pointed to Baldor. "At least not until I can combat the sway and influence that the Samilcar's seem to hold within the Senate and Courts. For that problem though I believe we can let time aid us, this campaign will not be over quickly, as successful as we are and will be, Rome will be slow to learn her lessons. Much will have changed in Carthage ere we turn for home."

Baldor, seeing the brothers relaxing recovered some of his composure. Hannibal poured wine for the three of them and sat looking at Baldor while tilting his head from side to side as if assessing and contemplating options.

"Come brother, share your thoughts!" Mago said sharply but with a half laugh. "You're as wily as a fox, what have you up your sleeve?"

In answer Hannibal stood, asking Baldor to stand next to him, Baldor was a head taller than him. Nodding sagely he walked behind him, grasping Baldor's hair gently he gathered it back into a ponytail. Mago watched intently.

"You're fluent in Gallic, Baldor are you not?"

"Yes sir?"

"H'mm, your height along with your lengthening hair plus that beard and moustache …"

"Baal almighty! You're planning to turn him into …"

"Into a Gaul, yes! Why not? He looks the part and speaks the language, knows the culture! A change of cloak, shield and weapons will complete the transformation."

Baldor just stared, his head in a whirl.

"I said you'd need to leave the army and you will, you'll leave the Carthaginian army, for a while anyway and join the Gallic one! This also fits well with my plans to develop your command potential, along with the opportunity to fulfil a promise I gave to the Lingones prior to the battle yesterday. Most importantly there's a chance for us to rally more men to our standard."

He had both men's attention now.

"The Cenomani, these allies of Rome and troublesome neighbours come enemies of the Lingones, I want them removed. Their village, Victumulae they term it, be it palisade, town or whatever it is where they reside, must be located and razed to the ground. The warriors, kill them all; I've no wish to have to fight them again as auxiliary cavalry divisions of the Romans. The ordinary people, drive them off; if they won't go take them as slaves, then bring all the supplies, animals, carts, anything you can find that you think may serve us back here. Once the threat from this tribe's removed the Lingones will commit to us with all their men, this will also serve as a useful demonstration to other tribes not to ally themselves with Rome."

"Consider it done! When do we leave brother?" Mago asked his tone matter of fact.

"You don't Mago; I need you here for further planning and training of the troops. You, Baldor will command this raid."

Baldor looked aghast, lost for words.

"With midwinter upon us and the Romans in disarray, the chance of another major battle before springtime is remote. Therefore, I can afford you some men and time to complete this task; it's time to show the army why I made you Hypolokhagos."

Chapter Twenty one

"Open the gate! … Open the damned gate!" A Centurion balled up to the watchtower from between cupped hands. His booming voice lost in the darkness shrouding the tower high above the massive bronze gate.

Torches flared into life along the wall, their flames flickering wildly from the gusting wind. Heads peered cautiously over the parapet then disappeared again the torches moving off quickly along the wall. A gruff voice called from the watchtower.

"State your business! The gate of Placentia doesn't open after dark by order of …"

"You'll open this gate now… by order of Tiberius Sempronius Longus, Consul of Rome!"

A brief silence followed by anxious, hurried talk drifting down from the wall. A torch thrust from between the stone battlements followed by another head that disappeared again. Others appeared, thrusting torches far out into the night attempting to cast the light to see who was below. The gruff voice from the wall shouted again.

"The Consul's in camp with his Legions near the Trebbia, what would he do here?"

There was a moment's silence. When the reply came, it had lost some of the previous sharpness and surety of command.

"The Consul is here … and what remains of the army."

There was silence again then the voice from above called out.

"We're throwing down torches … show yourselves! I warn you! We have archers up here and if you are not who you say, you'll die where you stand."

Moments later, half a dozen torches flew over the parapet, their flames whooshing and flaring in golden arcs as they somersaulted through the air before bouncing onto the ground in a shower of sparks. The vocal Centurion picked up the first one, the rest quickly taken up by others. By the flickering, yellow glow, the men on the wall saw the first of the survivors from the battle of the Trebbia.

"Open the gate; open the gate for the Consul!"

This time the command was directed from the watchtower into the arched gateway inside the wall. The banshee screech of dry metal told of huge bolts drawn back followed by the rumble and thump of timber drawbars lifted clear. Creaks and groans sounded as the windlasses took up slack on the gate chains and a hollow clacking of links moving through pulley blocks. The gates swung slowly inward, allowing the Legionnaires to march into the safety of the city walls.

Inside, the city guard was rousted and turned out to support the night watch on the gate. They too brought torches that darted here and there like fireflies as the sleep-fuddled men sorted themselves into order lining the road into the city proper. Despite their dishevelled state the remnants of the Consular army marched in reasonably good order through the gate, the Centurions and Optios still at pains to keep the lines dressed. Their discipline however couldn't hide the savage mauling they'd suffered, their heads bowed from weariness and the horror of an ordeal that had started before dawn that morning. Their faces showing the shame and dejection that accompanies men in defeat. Most were covered in blood, either dried upon their hands, arms and faces or splattered in blotches across mail and shield faces, some still oozed fresh blood from their wounds. The badly injured whom had been carried looked worst of all, white of pallor most were only semi-conscious, their bandages sodden or leaking fresh, plum coloured blood. Under torchlight, it was found many had actually died along the way, the speed and roughness of the retreat having opened wounds and shaken their lifeblood from them. As the dead were lowered to the ground, their comrades who'd carried them for so long and so far groaned in grief. Shouting and cursing they swore vengeance else just squatted and held the dead close. With the Legions full of fathers and sons, brothers, cousins and life-long friends, the agony seemed all the worse, it seemed the Gods of Rome cared not who'd fallen.

The barracks of the city guard was commandeered and hastily turned into a hospital for the injured. The physicians and citizens of Placentia roused from their beds to help with the wounded and the dying, others tasked to prepare hot food for those that could still stomach it. Tiberius and his immediate staff settled themselves in the house of the Governor, leaving Centurions and Optios to sort the chaos, assess, and list casualties.

It was still dark when a long blast from a cornu brought fresh calls from the gatehouse and had Gaius and Cornelius running up the steps to the parapet to see whom else had arrived. Torches were again thrown down, identifying more Legionnaires arrayed outside the walls. This time the torchlight reflected brightly from burnished helmets showing men in perfect rank and file; nearest the gate was the horses of the command group, the leader of which was in diatribe with the night watch.

"It's my father! My father's here with his Legion from the camp."

Cornelius couldn't hide the relief and elation in his voice, Gaius sighed gratefully, muttering quietly that matters would be duly sorted now that Consul Scipio was here. The gates creaked open again and the column marched in, the appearance of these un-bloodied Legionnaires in stark contrast to those whom had come previously. The pair descended the steps two at a time, holding onto their flapping scabbards and harness then pushed through the dense crowd towards the road as the column entered the city. The chaotic throng of city guards, milling citizenry and Legionnaires from the first column prevented Cornelius from reaching his father. Forced to wait until his horse drew closer he raised and waived his arm shouting above the noise of the hooves, the crowd and marching feet.

"Consul! Consul Scipio!"

Publius turned about looking for the source of the call.

"Sir … Consul! Over here, sir!" Cornelius called again.

Publius caught sight of the arm and recognising his son, his grim countenance and heavy heart lightened and he whispered a brief prayer of thanks to Mars for sparing his boy. Squinting though the torch smoke he saw the blood matted hair and dark stains on Cornelius's face and neck, concern flickered across his features and he pushed his mount across towards him. The press of the crowd was too great and the horse stomped nervously then shied, the pair having to make do with a wave and ready smile. This brought comfort that each was at least alive and for the most reasonably well.

"Later lad! Let me see to this …" Publius shouted and gestured at the surrounding chaos his horse skittering again as the crowd jostled it. "Later! You have it?"

Cornelius waved acknowledgement as the crowd surged again, folk shoving and pushing to see what was happening while the city guards tried to instil order as the Consuls men attempted to progress. Publius's horse stamped sideways knocking two people over while tossing its head and neighing loudly, the noise, the flickering torches and stink of blood unsettling it.

"Get back, back damn you!" Publius bellowed at the crowd who pushed in front of and around his horse, finally in frustration he turned to the column behind him.

"Centurion! Line me a road so we can march through! Let's have some damned order in here!"

"Aye sir!"

Barking orders, the Centurion indicated left and right with his vine cane. The first maniple of the column split left and right and using their shields pushed and drove the crowd apart allowing progress of the column. Reaching the grand plaza and some clear space at last, Publius dismounted passing his reins to a Legionnaire then turned to his command group.

"You!" He stabbed a finger at a nearby Centurion. "I want a situation report, who's here and how many? You!" He pointed to the next Centurion in the group. "Find me Consul Longus and his staff or whoever it is that claims to be in charge here.

Gnaeus, take your men and ensure medical care is being given, see the dead are taken care of and organise some victuals. Assemble the able bodied Legionnaires by Maniple; let's see if we can make sense of this chaos."

Commandeering and setting up his headquarters in one of the larger houses just off the plaza he continued to dispatch his men to specific tasks, namely: the status of the cities defences, the number of able troops belonging to the city, the amount of civilians and the amount of food, water and weapons stored within.

With his staff employed in information gathering, he could do little but wait for answers. Alone and frustrated at the delay he paced the floor of the house's dining room like a caged animal. Finding and pouring some wine he quaffed then refilled the cup. Forcing himself to sip the next drink, he held the cup vice like, a slight tremor betraying his angst as he tried to settle his nerves. Until he received the information he couldn't plan his next moves, however, he reasoned he could use the time to consider the larger picture and the most important question of all, what would the Carthaginian do next?

Publius knew Hannibal to be a meticulous planner but also an opportunist should a potentially beneficial situation present itself. At this moment, he had opportunity and capability to range at large over much of northern Italy with nothing anyone could do to stop him in the short term. However, despite his victory and the opportunities it presented, he too would need time to regroup, on top of which he would desperately need supplies for his men. The Carthaginian navy couldn't land supplies in Italy for him as Rome held supremacy of the middle-sea, so his options remained: living off the land, capturing Roman supplies or seeking support of the local tribes. He would also need to recruit new troops to boost his depleted ranks and replace the many that had no doubt perished in the mountains. Therefore, Publius mused, he didn't think he'd have too much trouble from Hannibal until spring as he had much to occupy him. Yes, he'd have roaming cavalry patrols out and they could be large for Hannibal was rich in cavalry, damn good cavalry! These mounted sorties would need to be countered, as Rome must not be seen to be losing her grip in the north of the country, the 'She Wolf' was in trouble but she must still be seen able to bite. As Publius well knew from the battle with the Insurbes and Boii tribes the previous summer, once the Gauls sniffed weakness or opportunity they'd turn on their former masters like rabid dogs. Another such uprising now, combined with the Carthaginians on the loose could spell disaster.

What to do next then? He couldn't leave all of his and Tiberius's men ensconced within Placentia as the burden on the local citizenry would be too great. On the other hand he dare not withdraw all of them either, leaving Hannibal without guard dogs to watch him was inviting trouble, winter or not! He surmised dividing his forces between Placentia and nearby Cremona while considering the old adage of not dividing your force in the face of the enemy, before countering it with the reassurance that the men would be behind city walls. By leaving them here in defensive mode they applied indirect pressure to Hannibal and should give him pause when considering any large scale movement, as he would constantly have to watch the cities for sallies. Conventional strategy dictated 'no advance' while secure enemy strongholds remained in your rear but would Hannibal follow convention? Publius knew the young General was apt to turn convention and strategy on its head and had done in his earlier actions in Spain at the river Tagus. There he'd carried out forced night marches to outflank his opponents, a very risky manoeuvre and a sure swipe at convention. He'd also divided his forces where and when it suited him and it seemed or rather he'd proved, to no ill affect. He'd then brought an army through a hostile mountain range during the onset of winter; again, this was not tactics of a conventional General.

Still, he reasoned, leaving men here was the best he could do, should Hannibal venture south he would have to allow for or contend with the Legionnaires ensconced in his rear. He would return to Rome as the Senate would need to know what happened at the Trebbia and he had his own political skin to think of in that regard. Though Tiberius had engaged the enemy against his express judgement and thus brought about the defeat, he thought it best that he be in Rome in person to answer questions and defend his stance on it. Also, the Consular elections were imminent; something he'd not even had time to consider, though he did wish to stand for office again as he considered his work very much unfinished. Would the Senate grant him another term? He shrugged deciding not to waste time pondering the question, the Senate was ever fickle and bowed to favour and he didn't doubt, bribes. He would stand again however, that was all he was sure of at this moment in time.

With answers to his questions coming back slowly frustration overcame him, being a doer by nature he left his men to document the information and numbers as they arrived and went to look for himself.

The professionalism of the Centurions had seen the city barracks already taking shape as a hospital; the injured assessed and ranked in order for treatment with those less likely to survive placed at the end of the surgeons queue. The lesser wounded were being found beds where they could wait for treatment in some comfort, the more seriously wounded were being treated in the guardroom which had been converted into an operating theatre.

In the adjoining parade ground, the dead lay in neat rows, the bodies covered with a blanket or cloak, their names and rank collected and logged by Optios. Guards stood by to keep away the dogs, rats and any would be looters. Parties of Legionnaires were gathering timber from the cities firewood stocks using it to build funeral pyres in the manicured gardens and lawns behind the temple of Jupiter. The amount of dead required many pyres and much timber, the priests were already complaining of the damage to their property. The complaints fell on deaf ears and anyone venturing persistence was at the least growled at else threatened with violence, priests or not. Ensuring all was in order and being dealt with, Publius continued his inspection, commandeering another barrack block and the guard commander's quarters as additional hospitals as the first buildings filled to capacity with the injured. He had to throw his Consular weight behind the demand for more food for his troops when confronted by a vociferous deputation comprising the city Governor and his council, all talking at once like a flock of stressed, gaggling geese. Wringing their hands they asked how payment was to be made if they were to throw open the granaries, butcheries and wine stores to feed the thousands now residing within the city. Publius held up his hand for silence but with no respite in the hubbub overturned a nearby table, sending dishes and pitchers crashing to floor, the noise finally silencing the men. Making an effort to keep his temper and his voice calm, he gave his orders.

"Give my men what they require, list your costs and you'll be duly compensated for your trouble." He slipped his Consular ring from his finger handing it to the Governor. "As the Consul of Rome you have my word upon it!"

The Governor looked as if he was about to speak further when Publius cut him short, his tone direct and commanding.

"Give my men the supplies they need or by Jupiter they'll take them!"

Not waiting for further diatribe, he pushed past the group to continue his inspection.

As he walked he thought of his son, how he wished he could drop everything to see that he was well and hear how the day had gone for him. His paternal side tore at him, bludgeoning his mind with all the questions any father would have in regard to his son's safety. Selflessly, he steeled himself to see to the needs of his soldiers first placing his own second.

Finally, when he has was sure all was the best it could be, he made his way back to the courtyard where the dead lay; removing his helmet and bowing his head, his fist held across his heart he offered quiet prayers for the fallen. A breathless Centurion jogged up just as he opened his eyes. The Centurion caught his breath while Publius refitted his helmet and offered a final blessing and plea to the Gods for the men's swift passage into Elysium.

"Now, Centurion?"

"We've located Consul Longus sir!" Pre-empting Publius's next question he pointed. "This way sir, if you please?"

Making his way through the crowds and brushing aside the challenges and the sentries at the Governor's house gate, he strode across the gardens into the portico, his small entourage of staff officers and city officials struggling to keep pace. The door guards, having heard no alarm from their comrades at the gate stepped to one side saluting as he stormed past his cloak billowing behind him. Pausing briefly at the grand double-doors he signalled his party to remain outside then pushed the heavy doors open, banging them back on their hinges. The men seated at the table within looked up in alarm at the sudden interruption and then embarrassed surprise as they recognised their Consul. Chairs scraped back as they jumped to their feet and saluted, Tiberius however remained seated glowering hatefully. The wind swept through the open doorway behind Publius, extinguishing some of the oil lamps and scattering the parchment maps and documents from the table onto the floor while the long drapes of the room flapped violently.

"Out! Leave us!" He barked to the men at the table, his tone as cold as the wind that followed him.

As the men exited and closed the door, he approached the table and the scowling Tiberius. Publius leaned forward resting his weight on closed fists on the tabletop, glaring at his fellow Consul.

"So, oo you survived the Carthaginian … or the 'boy' I think you termed him? The Gods are indeed good and we're truly blessed." Publius's voice dripped mockery.

"Spare me your sarcasm Scipio; I've neither time nor the temper for it! What do you want?"

"Want? … I want nothing from you other than to tell you, you're a bloody fool! A pompous vain-glorious, bloody …"

"How dare you?" Tiberius snapped, outraged and sounding imperious. "Damn you! I'm your equal, not some servant or soldier to be chastised! How dare…" His lips curling into a snarl, his voice rising before Publius cut him off.

"Dare! Now there's a word. You! You, who dare sit here, supping with your favourites, the army broken and your men wounded and dying, the rest needing food and aid."

"Who're you to lecture me Scipio? You're not my superior."

"In rank no, but I swear by Jupiter, a better man!" Publius's face twisted with the effort to control his temper and words. "The defeat, I warned you of …"

"Hah! Publius the soothsayer! Hark at you! The fault wasn't mine, t'was the foul weather, it didn't favour us! You saw it! How could we fight and win in that?"

"Ask the Carthaginian! He did both and very successfully judging by the few that have come safe with you into Placentia."

Tiberius flinched beneath the words but recovering quickly he spat.

"The bastard fights like a brigand, all ruses and tricks, he relies on ambushes and …"

"What did you expect?" Publius laughed a little though his tone was bitter. "He knows where our strength lies, knows our tactics, worst of all knows you! He knew he'd but to prod and goad and out you'd come like a raging bull."

"Aye to meet him on the field of battle like men, to fight in plain sight and settle …"

"When he's out numbered? Out classed in heavy infantry. Jupiter in heaven man! Are you blind or just crazed? Why on earth should he fight on our terms?"

The look on Tiberius's face confirmed that he'd expected exactly that, a pure trial of strength.

Again, Publius fought to regulate his temper, pausing he lowered his voice.

"In truth the defeat could have been mine as much as yours for I would have supported you had …"

"Supported!" Tiberius snapped scornfully. "You stood back …"

"Yes I stood back! I warned you that to hazard battle on his terms and ground of his choosing was to court disaster! If you'd but heeded my advice, we could've waited and watched him go hungry! Watched him lose his allies for the need of a battle and a victory! Watched his strength ebbing away."

"Hah! Sitting back's what you do best Publius, go to it man, leave me be."

Publius's temper finally snapped and his arms shot across the table at lightning speed, his fingers hooking viciously into Tiberius's cloak and neck cloth. He pulled back savagely, dragging the shocked man from his chair and over the table towards him, scattering and smashing crockery, and spilling wine. Tightening his grip further, he pulled Tiberius's face close to his own.

"Sitting back eh! What kind of man sits in comfort while his men are dying from their wounds or suffering for the want of food and drink? Let alone despondent for the want of a kind word or encouragement against defeat! Get off your pompous arse man and see to your men!"

Tiberius struggled trying to pull away but Publius gripped him all the tighter, the neckerchief tight on his throat forcing his words into a harsh whisper.

"They're Legionnaires they'll do as they're told."

"They're Roman Citizens! Free men, fighting for their city."

"You come here to tell …?" Tiberius's mouth moved but no sound came out. Struggling against Publius's grip while colouring from the throttling, he managed. "I'm their Consul; they'll show me respect, do as I command. There are plenty more where they came from, Rome is full …"

"Not so full as you are of shit and your own importance! You're not fit to command the digging of a latrine, let alone a Legion."

He pushed Tiberius savagely away his body smashing the chair he'd been sitting on to matchwood. Reddened from the near choking, his eyes bulbous and his face looking as if it was about to burst he gasped for breath. Beside himself with anger and wounded pride, his temper turned murderous. Struggling to his feet while loosening the neckerchief and rubbing his neck, he glanced around the room before dropping his hand to his sword. Publius saw the move and smiled coldly, his words coming out with chilling malice washing over Tiberius like a cold wave.

"Draw it Tiberius, if you dare? Draw it and I'll kill you here and now! Do you think when news of this defeat reaches Rome they'll care what happened to you? ... I don't think so! So go ahead, draw it."

Tiberius's hand hovered over the hilt; it shook a little though Publius sensed it wasn't from fear of him but rather the gravity of the situation he was in. An unpopular General with a broken and disillusioned army having to face a volatile Senate to explain his shortcomings whilst the victorious invader ranged at will over northern Italy. Tiberius moved his hand slowly away, his sureness disappearing along with his temper. Publius however couldn't resist goading him further.

"I thought not! You may not be as stupid as you seem after all."

The two stared at each other, the hatred so hot it almost scorched the air. Sensing victory from both the verbal exchange and Tiberius's decline of a fight, Publius cooled his temper and carried on in a quiet voice.

"I command as from now. We'll rest the men and let them catch their breath. Tomorrow we will address and empathise with them and inform them of our plans, after which we'll move half of them to Cremona to ease the burden on the folk here. We'll see to and if necessary improve the defences of both cities ensuring they're adequate should the Carthaginian decide to come calling. Not that I imagine he will, with winter setting in he'll be seeking winter quarters and a chance for his men to recuperate, I think we have until spring to lick our wounds and prepare."

Tiberius said nothing, finding another chair he sat down heavily looking weary and physically broken, his features had lost their fire and he stared blankly.

"After that's done, you and I'll return to Rome before Hannibal has his cavalry dominate the land round about. We need to report the defeat to the Senate ere it's blown out of all proportion."

He looked at Tiberius who still said nothing and sat with his head in his hands.

"Do you understand? ... Consul!" He snapped the formal naming, bringing Tiberius back into the world and he turned to face Publius. He nodded slowly.

"Yes, yes I understand." He rose, turned and walked away without another word.

Publius poured himself a cup of wine and quaffed it in one dragging his hand over his mouth to wipe the drops away. He felt the liquid settling his nerves and poured another but this time sipped it, savouring and appreciating the touch of warmth it gave his body. Now he thought, now to find my boy.

Chapter Twenty two

Six days after the battle at the Trebbia the two Consuls, their mounted escort of staff officers, Cornelius and eight Turmaes of cavalry trotted out from the gates of Cremona turning south-eastwards towards the coast and the city of Ariminum. Publius had assumed total command with no objection raised from Tiberius, who had in fact become quietly compliant to Publius's orders and actively thrown himself into the work to add and improve the defences of both Placentia and Cremona. He'd driven himself uncharacteristically hard, striving like an errant child seeking atonement for previous misdemeanours. Sparing neither himself nor his men he'd toiled and participated in all tasks while organising the men into shifts thus allowing work to continue day and night without pause.

Both of the frontier towns were relatively new, having grown rapidly out of old Gallic settlements which the Romans had overrun and captured as they pushed north, conquering the area and naming it Cisalpine Gaul. Having encouraged and instituted settlers into the area, they'd expanded both towns encircling them with stonewalls. Publius's field artillery from his camp at the Trebbia was placed on the walls reinforcing the few mangonels' and ballistas' already emplaced. Within javelin range of the parapet and parallel to the outside wall a wide, vee shaped ditch was dug, its bottom embedded with sharpened wooden stakes and sewn with iron caltrops. A timely deluge of rain had part filled the ditch covering both devices with brown, muddy water. The flat ground between the ditch and wall had thousands of spade width, ankle-deep holes to slow any enemy managing to cross the ditch. The city guards, being a collection of retired Legionnaires and local militiamen were taken to task and subjected to the same habitual training regime that the Centurions instituted upon the regular troops.

Keeping to the lower ground east of the Apennines, Ariminum would be their first staging post; from there they would take the Via Flaminia and head southwest for Rome. They left behind two well-ordered and defended towns along with the additional compliment of surviving Legionnaires from the Trebbia.

The mood of the cavalcade was downcast and sour. Men kept their thoughts and counsel to themselves, not that there was much chance for talk as the riding was either at the gallop where they reached the open field else furtive and silent where they passed through woodland or near villages. Unable to light fires to cook a meal lest they attract the attention of Carthaginian patrols they existed on bread and dried rations. They took their rest where and when they could contrive it, the sporadic woodland aiding them where they could lie up under cover of the trees.

They encountered numerous Carthaginian cavalry patrols, the first equal in size to their own and which they let pass while observing them from the tree line of a small wood they'd been about to exit. Seeing the self-assurance with which the patrol rode did nothing to aid the demeanour of the watchers. The next patrols they encountered were much further to the south and considerably smaller being purely scouting or reconnaissance units. One patrol picked up their trail just after dawn and shadowed them for half a day before a small sortie led by Publius drove them off, the action more to hearten his men than to have any affect. The last patrol was smaller again, being only a dozen men mounted on light ponies and which stayed well back from the Romans, seemingly content to follow them at a greater distance. However, it was disconcerting for all when the Carthaginian patrol did not turn back northwards until Rome itself was less than half a day's ride away. This domination and apparent command of the countryside by the invaders was not lost upon the Romans.

Cornelius was particularly affected with the doldrums and the clandestine behaviour they'd been forced to adopt in their own land. With the lack of conversational peer support to bolster his youthful perspective of the situation he slipped further into misery. For though having fought three battles, the last two had been defeats with the calamitous Trebbia all too fresh in his mind. He wondered whether the Carthaginians could be beaten. They appeared unstoppable, having forced the Alps in the dead of winter, rolled up his father's cavalry at the Ticinus then destroyed the might of two consular armies on the banks of the Trebbia. He was still engrossed in his dark thoughts when they reined up outside the Senate steps on Capitoline Hill. Before he could dismount, his father came alongside indicating he should remain mounted.

"Go home son, I've matters to deal with here then I'll be along directly. See to your mother and reassure her that all is well or will be, for I've no doubt she'll have been much troubled this last while. Be strong for her and our people; don't let them see our weakness."

Publius hesitated as he saw Cornelius's empty stare. His face beneath the grime of the road was ashen and suddenly old with the look of someone pushed too far for too long. The wide, saucer like eyes told of horrors seen and hopes dashed, of ideals torn down and washed away on the torrents or war and savagery, the doubt of the ability to carry on. Publius had fought enough campaigns to recognise battle fatigue. He'd seen the same lethargy on Legionnaires who'd served too long without a stand down period and he knew only too well that Cornelius had been on active duty for over half a year. With his heart torn from the state of his son and cursing himself for not seeing it sooner, he waved away the urgent calls that came for him to enter the Senate. Gripping his son's thigh, he shook him firmly while speaking low and calmly.

"Cornelius! Cornelius, look at me."

Cornelius inclined his head and stared at his father, though his eyes appeared not to see.

"Come on lad, tis sore I know but bear with me just a little longer eh? Home I say, I'll follow, I promise. Eat and rest, there'll be another day, a better day, we're down but not out."

With the firm grip on his leg and the gentle words, Cornelius's eyes flickered as if in recognition followed by slight nodding.

"Good lad! All will be well, I promise you, but home and rest now, do you hear? We'll talk in the morning after you've slept."

Publius pushed the horse in the direction of home and slapped its rump hurrying it forward and away. He watched it and Cornelius until they turned from sight at the corner of the street heading in the direction of the family villa, only then did he turn for the Senate steps.

****

Serfina reclined on a luxuriously cushioned settle on the marble-flagged patio outside her bedroom, her arm and hand resting on a padded stool while her maid gave her a manicure. The heavy rain which had fallen during the night and which still pooled in the shallow indents on the irregular flagging glistened and sparkled as the sun light reflected from it. The evaporating dampness gave an earthy freshness to the grass and shrubs, picking out the smells of soil, leaf and flower filling the air with the scent of the garden. Enjoying the morning's warmth she sipped a goblet of cooled wine and decided that life and this early North African spring was indeed good. The oven-like days of high summer were some months away, which meant the bothersome insects were not yet active; however, there was a vibrancy of wildlife in the garden about her. Blackbirds busied themselves defending their territory against all comers whilst singing and managing to collect nesting material at the same time. A peacock and his hen pecked amongst the grass for morsels, the male pausing only to fluff his splendid plumage in arrogant display as two younger males approached following eagerly in the wake of some other hens.

Serfina held up her hand and flexed her long fingers examining the work to her nails, finding the result to her liking she offered it back so the maid could massage cream into the cuticles and skin. The sun slipped from behind the large cypress trees, climbing higher in the clear sky and raising the temperature a little further. The new brightness caused Serfina to squint. Irritated, she snapped her fingers and a slave boy stepped forward with a brightly decorated shade canopy mounted atop a pole. Carefully positioning himself and it, so to offer cover to Serfina's face yet still allowing the heat to warm her body and legs. Comfortable again, she withdrew her massaged hand sniffing appreciatively at the scented cream before holding out the other hand in readiness. She sipped her wine as she waited for the girl to reposition herself and the small table on the other side of the settle to begin work again.

Feeling less irritable and tense than she had for a long time she gave a small sigh of contentment; so she mused, Targa was finally dead. After all her efforts he was gone, though not executed as she would have wished but dead and gone never the less, the God's were indeed good. When the message advising of his death first arrived she'd doubted what she was told, trusting none she'd demanded the courier brought before her and proceeded to question him as to what he'd seen and heard. Seeing neither deceit nor pretence in his eyes and learning that the message came from none other than Hannibal himself, she'd finally conceded that it was the truth. Though she didn't know the young General in order to judge him as a man of truth and honour or not, she knew of his renown within the city and the Senate as an honest and religious man, none it would seem had a slur to cast against him. She remembered also, that despite her father's ardent opposition to the war and the Barca family's expansionist policies in Spain, he'd also admitted a grudging respect for Hannibal as an honest man as well as a good and able soldier. Thus, with these thoughts in mind she'd finally accepted that the man whose death she'd planned and prayed for was finally gone from the world. As a demonstration of heartfelt thanks to the Gods for answered prayers she'd bought a magnificent Cretan bull and paid for it to be sacrificed on her behalf. As the priest mumbled his incantations then opened its throat, emptying its lifeblood over the already dark stained altar, she whispered her gratitude and prayed to Tannith that Targa's passing had been slow and painful and that his hurt twisted and burned him as her grief had done to her. Yes, if there was judgement and justice to be had he would have suffered. She sighed again and nestled deeper into the cushions, her mind finally free of the need for vengeance … yes it was a beautiful day and life was good.

With the sun warming her skin, she closed her eyes enjoying the peace and scent of the garden along with the whistles and songs of the industrious birds. Her mind wandered, perusing various non-essential matters along with the general day-to-day idiosyncrasies of the household and estate before finally, almost reluctantly, collecting her thoughts and procrastinating over her plans for the day. There were some routine business undertakings that required her input and signature and some statues, which she had commissioned that needed her decision as to positioning in the garden. Most importantly was the forthcoming feast she was planning for her younger brother Sakarbaal, a celebration of him attaining majority. She had a guest list to finalise and invitations to dispatch as well as menus to view, after that however time was her own. Perhaps she would accept her friend, Emerita's invitation and accompany her to the gold and gem markets, then to the cloth merchants to see what was newly arrived on the caravans from the east. Finally, finally they would go down to the port and the slave market. She smiled wickedly for Emerita had also said that today was the auction of the mature male slaves, thus they should go and view the merchandise. After all, these were uncertain times owing to the war with Rome and a woman must look to her safety while her men folk were away. Serfina laughed a little as she thought of Emerita's pretended innocence. Yes, she may just go and view the slave market today. She clicked her fingers at a slave girl who stood quietly to one side of the settle, the girl stepped forward and gave a quick bow.

"I'll take some fruit, cheese and bread with my wine, see to it."

The girl mumbled a quiet "Yes, my Lady" Then disappeared across the garden at the run, her bare feet going noiselessly over the lush grass.

Serfina yawned, stretching slowly like a cat waking after a nap then settled back into the soft cushions closing her eyes, enjoying the peace and warmth. Moments later, her solace was disturbed and the peacocks scattered by the distant but loud laughter and hoarse shouts emanating across the garden from the courtyard at the front of the house. The shouting interspersed with dull clanging of metal that came and went in short hectic bursts. She groaned softly in knowing recognition of the disturbance and as the girl returned with the bread and fruit, she was dispatched towards the noise with a message to the Lord Sakarbaal to 'cease the din, if he would be so kind?'

Serfina was enjoying the taste and firm texture of an orange segment as she cut a lump of bread from the loaf and dipped it in her wine. The smell of the cut bread wafted on the air causing her nose to twitch in appreciation and she reached for the butter and olive oil. Her repast was interrupted by the sight of a young man coming across the garden towards her at a steady trot. Naked to the waist, his only attire being a short blue kilt hung to mid-thigh and leather cavalry men's boots reaching the top of his calves. Like his sister, Sakarbaal was raven haired and long limbed, he also shared her smouldering good looks but little of her temper. Aged twenty years, his body was still developing, though it already showed a good physique with light but defined muscles on his arms, chest and belly. His skin, bronzed from exposure to the sun glistened with sweat from his exertions as if rubbed with oil. Calling a joyous 'good morning' while beaming a white toothed smile, he came alongside and bent to kiss his sister on the cheek. Serfina pushed him away brusquely complaining of the sweat left on her skin and the smell of it as the air wafted with his arrival. Undeterred by his cool reception he ushered the manicuring slave from her stool and flopped down on it.

"What ails you sister?" He said with mock concern grinning all the while. "Is the sun too hot? Perhaps the wine's not cool enough?" He laughed and poked her ribs playfully. "Perhaps you've broken a nail?" He laughed again as he sensed a rebuke coming along with the dark frown already clouding her features.

Looking into the warm, dark eyes and seeing mischief and the youthful, carefree light in his face Serfina lost the frown and lightened her tone to a mock haranguing.

"Brother, for the love of Tannith, a little peace and quiet if you will. Your warmongering din's frightening the birds, assaulting my ears and disturbing my accord, I can't hear myself think."

"I need to practice sister." He shrugged haplessly then flashed a wicked grin. "Perhaps you should get yourself hence into the house and do the womanly things!"

He laughed loudly at his jest and his sister's un-amused, black look while dodging the hand that went to hit him.

"Use your bow then, box or wrestle, I care not. But do something quiet, enough of this shouting and swording." Her tone changed abruptly the words coming out hotly as her irritation grew at his argument and good natured but impertinent defence.

"The bow's no true weapon for a cavalryman sister; we're Carthaginians, not heathen tribesmen from the plains of Scythia." He argued again, his tone still playfully flippant.

"For the love of Tannith! Does it matter what you use? Just give me some peace in my own garden."

Recoiling a little from her temper and sharp manner in front of the servants his anger began to rise.

"I'm not some slave to be ordered and told my own mind, sister!" He said firmly though politely as he jumped to his feet.

Serfina sat up quickly while shooing the servants away out of earshot.

"How dare you speak to me so?"

"I dare because you're neither my mother nor father. What gives you the right to speak to me thus? And in front of the servants!"

"I'm the elder, Sakarbaal! And until you attain your majority, under my care and authority as our brother willed it, thus you'll do as I say while under age and under this roof."

Sakarbaal's lip curled back in anger while his chest puffed up like a fighting cock. Feeling belittled and very young he looked to strike back and sought words that he knew would hurt.

"If you kept your poisonous tongue between your teeth you'd have another house to call your own and a husband to go with it! Baal knows that would give us both peace!"

Shocked at his outburst regarding her personal life she slapped him viciously across the cheek. Her heavy dress rings, having been turned inward away from the maid's file work, cut deep gouges across his skin. There was a moment of highly charged, standoff between them as each took stock of the result of their bickering. Angry as Serfina was, she was traumatised by her attack and the amount of blood that ran down Sakarbaal's cheek onto his neck and chest. Covering her mouth in horror at the damage, she saw the anger burning his eyes bright. Surprised at himself for his verbal outburst but taken aback by his sister's attack he was unsure of what to do. He just stared at her with a malevolence that almost withered her soul, sneering and emitting a low bestial growl he turned away. Serfina reached down quickly to take his hand.

"I'm sorry brother! I am so sorry! Forgive …"

Sakarbaal shook her hand savagely loose while fending her off as she tried to wrap herself about him.

"Brother! … Brother, I'm sorry! Please, forgive me, let me …"

"Leave me! Leave me be!"

Twisting from her grasp, he pushed her roughly away as she sought to embrace him. He marched off quickly putting distance between them then stopped turning on his heel to face her, his finger pointing accusingly.

"I'll tell you this, sister!" He spat. "You can have your peace and you can rule your house but you'll not rule me! Within the month I'll have attained my majority and be gone far from here and there's nothing you can do to stop me."

Serfina stared at him her mind in turmoil as to how fast things had spiralled out of control.

"What? … What mean you?"

Sakarbaal looked smug at his sister's distress.

"I'll be away from here, gone I tell you, to Spain and the war."

Serfina looked at him incredulously, as if he was mad or she'd misinterpreted his meaning. Her eyes wide and her mouth forming words but no sound came forth. Her mind raced, eventually she managed a whispered 'no … no!' Sakarbaal however was rising on his verbal victory and sneered his reply.

"Yes sister! Yes! Come my attainment I go where I please and choose, and I choose Spain and war."

****

Cornelius rolled onto his back while throwing the bedsheets down, his chest heaving from the exertions of his lovemaking, his skin damp with sweat. Aemilia, breathless herself gathered the corner of the sheets to cover her breasts then turned to snuggle into him, her head resting on his chest her arm draped over his hip pulling him close. Cornelius wrapped his arm about her shoulders while dipping his head to kiss her tenderly on the crown, his other hand running down her arm, his fingertips enjoying the feel of her smooth skin. Quickly regaining his breath, he continued to inhale deeply, relishing the sweet, heady fragrance of the perfume on her heated skin and scented hair. They lay without a word for some time content to hold one another and enjoy the closeness. Aemilia was the first to move when she kissed his neck but then stifled a sob. She shuddered a little and Cornelius felt the first of her hot tears on his chest. Raising himself slightly he pulled the sheet up over her shoulders then turned her head so he could see her face.

"What, what ails you? Are you …"

"I'm fine, fine; I just don't want you to go." She replied between sobs.

"Come my love, come now, I have to go. Betrothed to you or not, if your father finds me here in your bed I'm a dead man." He laughed softly.

Aemilia hit him sharply on his chest and he grunted in mock pain. "You know what I mean!" she chided between sobs. "I don't want you to go back to the army, back to the war."

The words sobered Cornelius somewhat and seeing Aemilia genuinely upset, hurt him. Losing the flippancy, he gathered her in his arms embracing her tightly, his tone soothing.

"Hush … hush! I'll be home again before you know it."

"Don't treat me like a fool, Cornelius." She snapped, anger mixing with her tears. "I may be just a woman but I still hear and see things! And young as I am, I know when my father's worried." Cornelius tried to shush her again then change the subject while brushing his hands gently over her breasts trying to draw her back to their lovemaking. Becoming forceful, she shrugged him away and continued. "Yourself and your father, all of you men, though you'll not admit it, know this war won't be over quickly and that many will die ere it is done … I don't want you to die, … I …"

Dissolving into full tears, she wept softly into his chest. He held her tightly, feeling her petite frame heave with the sobbing; he stroked her hair while seeking the right words.

"It'll be alright! I promise it will. We're raising new Legions and will be ready to march within the month. This Hannibal … this Hannibal, is a good soldier and an able General but we're good soldiers too, well led and …"

"Do you think we can win?"

"I know we can win." He said with genuine honesty. "It'll not be easy but yes, yes we can, we will win."

"That was not the way you perceived it when first you returned home."

"I was weary; battle worn and disillusioned at our loss. My father said this melancholy is common amongst soldiers, even victorious ones." His voice lowered then. "All the more so when we returned in sore defeat." He paused, then seemed to perk up, his face lightening and his previous good humour returning. "I tell you my love, we'll win and I doubt it not, neither should you. And you, you've made me whole again." He pulled her close kissing her again.

Aemilia seemed to take comfort from his words and calmed a little. As her sobbing subsided, she began again but quietly.

"You said your father's going to Spain to join your uncle and help prosecute the war there? Will you be going with him or remain here?"

Cornelius heard the trepidation in her voice as if she feared the answer to her question.

"I haven't received my orders as yet and …"

Aemilia looked away quickly as if sensing he was hiding something. He saw the agitation and barely controlled fear on her face, slipping his hand across her hips to the small of her back he pulled her closer.

"I haven't received my orders." He repeated more firmly. "And with my father no longer a Consul I'm not privy to my Legions movements before my orders arrive. Look! …" He said, sounding perplexed. "If I was to hazard a guess I think my Legion will remain here in Italy, we cannot afford …" He corrected himself quickly. "I mean, it doesn't make good military sense to leave the countryside and Rome open to Hannibal. Most of the manpower will be left here to contain him."

He leaned across to the bedside table and the silver tray holding a wine jug and cups, topping up both with more wine. Taking a long drink he offered the other cup to Aemilia, she shook her head and snuggled closer. She seemed a little reassured by his forthright words but still firmly refusing his sporadic but amorous advances, continued her questioning as if needing to have all the facts lain before her.

"Do you think these new Consuls will fare any better than your father and Sempronius Longus?"

Cornelius shrugged disinterestedly, he didn't know the answer and what's more, didn't want to waste what little time he had left with his woman discussing it. Like most young men and especially those waiting for war, he wished merely to drink, enjoy himself and sate his carnal desires. However, with her hand still firmly rebuffing his then sharply pushing his head away from her neck he sighed and resigned himself to her question.

"I have to hope that they are better, or at least fare better, for the sake of Rome and the men, however what kind of a son would I be, wanting to see another rise above my father?"

It was Aemilia's turn to look awkward as she realised his predicament. Cornelius however was now committed to the conversation and carried on, his own suppressed thoughts venting.

"I shouldn't say this Aemilia but if Sempronius Longus had heeded my father's council we'd probably not be in crisis at this time."

Aemilia looked confused. "It was the foul weather that undid the attack was it not? That's what Consul Longus offered to the Senate by way of explanation."

Cornelius bit back his answer, no doubt, the truth of the man's intemperance and poor judgment would out soon enough, he need not help it. Remembering also that Aemilia's father was a powerful man in his own right, having been a Consul some years earlier, he elected to say nothing. Not being politically perceptive, he didn't know where his prospective father-in-law's sympathies lay. To cover his negativity and non-committal answer, he changed to a positive note while trying to answer her first question, all the while hoping that if he could clear her mind of worldly matters it may return to matters more carnal.

"Both new Consuls are able men from what I've heard and know. Consul Gaius Flaminius has a solid reputation as a soldier and is popular among the people for his attempts to keep the Senate or rather the Senators honest."

Aemilia looked a little lost at his explanation.

"Perhaps they seek to appease the people with their choice? Show openness?" He offered with a shrug then continued. "Consul Gnaeus Servilius is also an able soldier and I know he has my father's support and confidence for I've seen him at my father's table during the campaign."

"Why not re-elect your father so he could try again? All know that he's the most able and experienced soldier of them all."

"You know the uneasiness with which the Senate broods if they have to vote the same Consul in for a consecutive term? They see it as inciting thoughts of Kingship or Dictatorship within a man, thus I reason they've chosen anew."

Aemilia fell quiet while remaining attentive, Cornelius continued.

"My uncle Gnaeus has had some success in Spain against Hannibal's younger brother Hasdrubal, whom commands there. With my father to aid him it's hoped that this second theatre will become yet more encouraging."

"But why wage war in Spain when the immediate threat is here, at our own door?"

"If we can subdue or better still control Spain we can prevent the possibility of Hannibal receiving reinforcements from over the Alps. It would also cut off his money supply from the silver mines there, thus making payment to his mercenaries difficult and diminishing his ability to wage war."

"So you would bottle him up here in Italy, like a rat in a trap? You know how rats are when they're cornered." Aemilia seemed to grow more agitated and nervous as the situation dawned upon her.

Seeing his chance, Cornelius added confidently. "And what do rat catchers do to the cornered rat?"

"But surely, surely the Carthaginians will send men by ship then? They're able sailors are they not?"

Cornelius shook his head. "Despite our setbacks on land we have supremacy over the seas, the Carthaginians dare not put to sea and venture that way."

Aemilia fell quiet again prompting Cornelius to attempt his amorous advances once more, nuzzling her ears and neck while slipping his hands down her back to frame then stroke her buttocks.

Just as he thought she was about to consent, Aemilia wriggled free though her extraction was not quite so sharp.

"What of this, Baldor?"

"What of him?" He replied dismissively as if the question was unimportant, his frustrations starting to show.

"He's sworn to kill you, you told me so."

"What are the chances of us ever meeting again? There'll be thousands of men on the field when next we take it."

"He's found you twice in two battles!"

"Then I'll kill him." He said with a cold, quiet finality. "I'll kill him."

Aemilia hugged him tightly as she shuddered. "I love you; love you so much, I can't …"

"Don't fear my love, he …"

"I'm cold." She lied, cutting him short while pulling the sheets up over them both.

"I'll warm you up then!"

Rolling her onto her back, he nuzzled her neck with urgent kisses. She squirmed and tried to push him away though the effort this time was truly half-hearted. Running his hands through her hair, he eased her face around so he could kiss her lips. Responding fully now, her own lips urgent and hungry she moaned softly as he pushed his body on top of hers and gently but determinedly eased her legs apart with his foot.

Chapter Twenty three

Baldor coughed then belched, waking him from his wine induced sleep. Stifling a yawn, he pulled his blanket and bearskin cloak tighter about his neck and shoulders to keep out the cold, snuggling deeper under the covers. Hearing a blackbird twittering softly, almost hesitantly, as if it was too early in the day for such, after a short pause the bird chirped and whistled shrilly before singing briefly. He opened a sleepy eye and although still dark, he saw there was a faint wash of light in the east brightening the mildewed tent wall. Dawn was but a short way off and the blackbird singing briefly once more seemed determined to let the world know.

Winter had been long and bitterly cold but to Baldor it had seemed endless, he'd never known days so short and dark or the frosts and snow and freezing temperatures. Now, with nearly three phases of the moon passed since the midwinter solstice and the battle at the Trebbia the days were lengthening. When the sun shone, there was a hint of warmth in it taking the bite from the early spring wind that seemed to blow relentlessly across these plains of Po. In response to this sporadic early warmth the oak, ash and sycamore were sprouting tentative buds from their naked and dead seeming branches. The thick-needled pines and firs had also joined the race for spring brightening their colours from pale ochre and washed-out winter green. The grass still looked wan and dead but clumps of snowdrops and crocuses pushed up bravely from it with their short but very green leaves, the flowers themselves remaining tightly wrapped in their outer petals awaiting assurance of warmer days. The animals too seemed to sense the seasons change and rabbits had been seen venturing from burrows to graze and caper in the early morning sun. Small herds of deer had also been spotted moving between copses and high above all, large vee shaped formations of ducks and geese dotted the skies as they arrived from wintering in the warmer climes of the south.

The lone blackbird heard a distant answering call to his earlier efforts and with all hesitation gone responded with a loud and beautiful song as if he alone was to herald the coming spring.

With a dull ache in his head and a mouth desert dry from the previous evenings over indulgence of cheap, local wine, he cursed himself for not heeding his colleagues' advice to water it. His drinking seemed to ease the pressure he felt from the burden of his task, for a short while anyway, the headaches were the price he paid. He smelt the familiar odours of the damp tent, musty animal skins, polished leather and the stale tang of unwashed men. He heard the sounds of his comrades breathing in the tent around him, Malo slept quietly with his breath coming in shallow regular, even draughts, Harbro on the other hand sucked in air and grunted every so oft like a contented hog.

The tent itself was now more spacious owing to the occupancy of just three men instead of the usual six. The extra space and long term, winter camp allowing for the luxury of crude bed frames instead of the usual rush mats on the ground. Still half-asleep and hungover, his mind wandered loosely from one subject to another as he half-dozed. He ruminated over the last weeks of intense physical training and the hardship and work that was further toughening and moulding his body. The instruction and advice taught him on matters military that was educating and broadening his mind and the wine he was drinking to help him sleep. He'd thrown himself into his task primarily to help forget the pain of lost friends. He estimated Gestix had been dead now for some five moons with Marko following him barely one moon later at the Trebbia. Despite the passage of time, the loss was no easier to bear and still ate at him like some foul, incurable disease. The usual tightness in his throat that always appeared and which he couldn't swallow away accompanied his memories, along with the feeling of abject sadness that drove his spirits low and brought the quiet but copious tears again. He recalled Balaam's rough words of comfort that it was better for men to die in battle rather than at home in their beds, surrounded by wailing women and grasping relatives. They seemed of little help as he remembered Gestix's plans for them to reside in Spain with Baldor's relations, had they done so the Gaul would still be alive. His gut twisted and burned as he remembered, it had been he who'd argued not to go to Spain and a peaceful life and his decision to sign on under Balaam's command and go to war. He thought sombrely at the question supposedly posed to Achilles by his mother before he sailed for Troy:

'Do you choose a dull, ordinary life that will take you to old age and anonymity? Or a short life filled with glory and fame, your name to be spoken down through the ages?'

He knew what his answer to that question would be if he could choose. Tormenting himself further, he pondered the impossible: to turn back time, to have the chance to reconsider, to have his friend alive. He bit his lip as more tears slipped down his cheek onto the cloak that was his pillow, the dull pain of the bite and the taste of blood stifled the sob building to an ache in his throat. Turning his face into the cloak, he sought sleep to hide his pain.

Armaco! The name wrenched him from his doze, all thoughts of sleep gone as his mind moved sharply into the present forcing him to ponder again on the missing warrior.

'Where was he? What had happened to him?'

How often had he asked himself that question? How many times had he gone through it in his head? Only to find he was no nearer an answer. The morning following the battle, Balaam and Harbro had searched the field for their missing men. They'd found Marko's corpse first, his skin pale as new parchment and his body stiff as fallen timber. His corselet covered in brown, black blood and a huge spear buried deep in his chest. One by one they'd found the others on their list of missing, except Armaco, loading all onto an oxcart for transport back to the camp and burial. With heavy hearts they'd continued their grim search until late in the afternoon, finally with the light fading Balaam had called a halt. Harbro, still reluctant to give up turned back for a last look thinking he'd recognised Armaco's horse blanket. Taking a closer look and easing the dead away, he'd pulled the blanket free searching frantically for Armaco's body. All that remained near the horse was Armaco's helmet wedged tightly under the animal's shoulder. Reasoning he had been thrown from his horse or it killed beneath him they searched the immediate area again for signs of his body yet still found nothing.

With darkness upon them and still empty handed, they returned to camp checking dressing stations, the surgeon's tents and consulting the official lists of wounded and dead. Returning the following morning they scoured the surrounding area in case he'd been concussed or knocked senseless but still able to walk and perhaps wandered off with no idea of who or where he was. Finally, they'd spent two days asking or threatening folk at dwellings and smallholdings that dotted the river plain of anyone having seen a one-eyed, badly scarred warrior, all to no avail. They knew that neither the Romans nor their Cenomani allies could have taken prisoners, the tide of battle, retreat and self-preservation having removed any such possibilities, so where in Baal's name was he?

Baldor's thoughts moved to Marko, Gestix's comrade in arms from the first war and strangely enough a Roman citizen by birth from his father though from a Carthaginian mother. Like Baldor, he'd also had a sad tale to tell which gave reason for taking the warriors path but on the Carthaginian side rather than the Roman, leaving Baldor wondering at how cruelly the God's twisted and shaped men's lives.

They'd washed and laid out Marko's body before burning it the day after the battle. Unsure as to which God's he prayed or whether he really cared or believed anymore, they offered prayers of their own for a good man, a brave warrior and true friend. Balaam had stared impassively as the flames licked around the body shaking his head in silent regret as they roared and devoured it, another old friend gone to Elysium. Harbro offered a further short prayer then snarled beneath his breath and swore vengeance for his friend; Baldor had hung his head, hand on heart and shed his quiet tears.

The passage of time had seen Malo's thigh wound heal rendering him well again, though he now walked with a stiffened leg which became a limp. 'It was of no consequence' he said, 'what did it matter for a horseman to limp? He was born to ride not to walk'. Baldor was given money from Marko's affects that, added to the coin willed from Gestix, provided the four remaining comrades with some fine wine, and better food than they'd enjoyed for a long while. While dreading the funerary feast for what he'd expected to be a sad and morbid affair, instead saw him heartened as his comrades' relayed tales and exploits of the two dead men. Tales both brave and humorous in nature, from younger, perhaps better days and happier times. Baldor found himself listening intently, sometimes in awe other times in laughter while marvelling at the fact that his elder comrades had once been as immature, foolish and impetuous as he, and strangest of all, that they had also once been young.

Hannibal had seen to an early start for Baldor's task and within a week of the battle at the Trebbia had aligned him with older, experienced officers who were to accompany and advise him whilst on the mission; ultimately, however, they remained below him in rank. He realised very quickly that Hannibal would not entertain his appeals of being unqualified or too young to accept responsibility for so many men. His concerns being firmly rebuffed and a structured but one-sided argument countered of how he, Baldor possessed ample experience of combat both personal and pitched battle. Further to that, Hannibal argued, he had been much the same age as Baldor was now when he'd first commanded troops. This confidence expressed in his abilities and backed no less by Balaam, saw him slowly coming to accept that this was his task and that he should set his best foot forward and give it his all.

Now, lying in the grey shadow of dawn with his sadness, hopes and fears mulling in his mind, he allowed himself a whimsical smile as he thought of the huge responsibility laid upon him. He thought it ironic that he who wanted no more to worry or care for others was to be given command and responsibility of some eight hundred and fifty men. Now, when he needed his friends the most they were gone, dead and gone to the Gods in the name of Rome. His smile faded, replaced by a grimace and a lip that curled into a snarl, sleep was gone from his mind replaced by grief and fierce hatred. Beneath his breath, he cursed the name Scipio, both father and son and that of Lugobelinos with a vehemence, the volume of which grew gradually louder. He threw off the covers clenching his fists, his head and shoulders half raised from the bed as his temper flared and he swore death to the three men. Lost in his loathing and bitterness it took a shake from Malo to quieten him and for him to realise that he was talking aloud.

Harbro grunted at the disturbance and turned over while Malo settled back down and he was left alone in the eerie half-light with his thoughts again. Snuggling down again for a last few moments of precious warmth before the trumpets announced dawn to the camp, he thought of Gestix. He could see and hear him, there in his mind's eye, standing with heavy arms folded across his chest smiling knowingly while telling him;

Do as you've been taught lad, be the man we raised you to be. You set your feet upon this path, now walk it!'

A long trumpet blast snatched him from his thoughts; his two comrades stirred and rose slowly to meet the day. For the first time in a long time, he left his bed with a will and purpose to see things through.

Having raked the ashes of last night's fire to expose the smouldering red embers beneath, he heaped on a handful of dried fir cones. They flared and crackled growing the flames to which he carefully added more kindling. Filling a pot of water, he set it to boil while taking three horn cups and a small earthenware jar from his pack, spooning honey from it into the cups. Waiting for the water to heat, he un-wrapped a dampened cloth containing a simple flatbread dough, working and kneading it in his hands forming it into round, flattened patties the size of his palm. Using a broken sword as a poker, he dug in the embers uncovering the flat river-rocks, which had been left to heat overnight. Carefully blowing the ash from them he placed the yellowed bread mix on them to bake. Lining a pan with a smear of oil, he cracked six eggs into it resting it over the flames to cook.

Waiting for the water and the eggs, he groped in his pack again. Finding a simple wooden comb he dragged it through his hair teasing out the tangles and cots, taking a leather cord from his purse he bound the hair into a ponytail. He ran the comb through his beard and moustache enjoying the sensation of the hair being un-tussled and leaving it in some semblance of order.

Leaning over the warming pot, he pushed his finger into it checking its temperature and caught a glimpse of his reflection. Waiting till the water settled he peered again, the movement causing his pony tail to fall forward to reach below his shoulders, his beard had thickened and now stood off from his face long enough to curl his finger in it. His moustache was heavy along his top lip and joined with his beard at the corners of his mouth, the only break to the symmetry was from a thin white scar that begun at the base of his chin and ran across his lips finishing on his right cheek leaving a narrow line where the hair couldn't grow. Tracing his fingers over the scar, he remembered having to fight for his life the day he got it. He hardly recognised himself as the boy who'd fled Carthage some two years previously and which all seemed so long ago, he sighed thinking he looked much older than his twenty-one years, Baal knows, he surely felt it.

He scratched at a louse somewhere in his chest hair and thought about a bath, how long had it been? In truth, he'd lost count of first the days, then the weeks and finally the months since he'd enjoyed such a luxury. His clothes hadn't been washed or changed for as long as he could remember either, though he'd repaired them as necessary, learning from his comrades the skills of stitching leather, sewing cloth and darning wool. His armour and weapons however were maintained to the highest standard, his swords and dagger kept sharp and free from rust, the leather scabbards rubbed with dubbing and polished to a lustre.

His Greek style corselet, tunic and garb were now laid to one side along with his crested helmet, replaced by a Gallic mail shirt and simple iron helmet befitting his new adopted persona. The helmet was bowl shaped around the crown and teased upwards into a raised spire at the dome. Devoid of plumage, it finished instead into a small metal knob, the rear of the helmet having a small peak to deflect sword cuts and protect his neck. The wide cheek pieces formed a cloverleaf shape and covered the side of his face and jaw. The quilted sleeves of the leather jerkin protruded from beneath the three-quarter sleeves of his mail shirt, studded with rows of circular bronze discs. The mail hung midway down his thighs, edged around the hem with a broad leather strip. Over his shoulders, a second layer of mail laid like a short cape and held closed across his chest with three bronze clasps. Around his waist, a wide belt of black ox hide combined with interlinking steel rings supported a dagger at his right hip with his purse to the left. His leather trousers and doeskin ankle boots completing his attire. His one abstention to his change of garb and culture was the retention of his two falcatas, these he still carried crossed on his back, their bronzed, horse head hilts sticking above his shoulders in constant readiness.

After breakfast, he made his way to the training area, walking briskly to put warmth into his body. He reached it just as the sun eased its face from beneath the horizon the clouds parting, allowing a soft golden light. In the shadows, the coldness still held, lurking with the dampness where the sunlight didn't yet reach. In the cold morning light, the camp was still coming to life, the chilled and cloak-wrapped night watch parading and passing over responsibility to the arriving sentries for the day's duties. Activity and chatter started up with soldiers busy sorting their kit, preparing for training or allotted duties. Mounted scouting parties departed the camp at the trot, weapons and harness jingling in time to the cadence of the horse's hooves. Shouted orders carried on the frigid air while horn blasts called companies and regiments together. Horses hobbled at the lines whickered as they anticipated their morning feed while herds of goats and sheep bleated and milled about cropping at the sparse and dead looking grass.

As he walked, Baldor ran through the knowledge already given to him from careful and detailed reconnaissance and subtle interrogation of the local tribes. This had produced information as to the location, type and size of fortification the Cenomani inhabited and an approximate number of warriors the raiders could expect to encounter. This township of Victumulae was high in the hills and encompassed by a circular, wooden stockade, the wall height of which was the equivalent of three fighting spears placed butt to point. It had fighting platforms along the walls and two square stone towers rising either side of the main gate. All nearby trees had been felled affording an unrestricted field of vision to the defenders. The stumps remained in situ with the ground further roughened denying any besieging force a level area for manoeuvre. From this information, Hannibal had made careful deliberations as to the troop numbers and type required. He couldn't afford too many men for the mission as the fast approaching spring would see the Romans on the move again, also he could not be seen to entrust Baldor, an untried and very young Hypolokhagos with too large a force. Thus, the size of the contingent was determined at eight hundred and fifty men. Seven hundred of which would be infantry, fifty being a selection of Cretan archers and Rhodian slingers, with the final one hundred being cavalry to act as escorts and scouts.

The infantry would be a mixture of Gauls and Spaniards and a selection of light and heavy troop types. Two hundred would be Gallic heavy infantry along with one hundred light infantry. These to be provided by Gundulas, whom Hannibal had manipulated and cajoled, albeit tactfully, into supplying, citing there was mutual benefit to the destruction of the Cenomani to be had by both parties. The Spaniards would make up the other four hundred with half being Caetratus, high quality light infantry and half being Scutarius, close order or heavy infantry for support and again of high quality. These troops had been picked for their ability to operate in mountainous terrain and their steady discipline which would be a hoped for positive contrast to the normally wild Gauls. Andulas was summoned and informed that he with his one hundred warriors were to provide the cavalry arm.

This mix of troops had trained and drilled throughout the winter being painstakingly moulded into a cohesive and disciplined raiding force. Hannibal himself overseeing much of the training while demonstrating and explaining to Baldor the finer points of deployment and manoeuvre. Baldor's experience of warfare had all been from a cavalry perspective so learning about and combining infantry units alongside cavalry was an education for him. His Gallic heavy infantry were now trained to fight as close order troops, their famous ferocity funnelled into disciplined shield walls. The task had seemed almost too difficult at first as the warriors continued to fight as they always had, wildly and loosely like individual heroes, all keen to impress comrades and allies with their prowess. They cared little for a shield, most putting it to one side wishing to fight purely offensively using their long swords in vicious windmill like strokes, the more bellicose filling their empty shield hand with a spear or another sword. When advice and demonstration from the Carthaginian training officers and finally screamed threats failed to make headway, Hannibal summoned twenty Libyan heavy infantry and picked out twenty of the most potent Gauls. Arming all with wooden practice swords, he arrayed both parties' fifty paces apart. The Libyans placed in line two deep with shields locked, the Gauls upon his command, were to attack the Libyans as they saw fit. Typically, the Gauls raced towards the waiting Libyans like bulls charging a gate, the Libyans only movement was to brace themselves raising their shields against the attack. The Gauls hit the shield wall like a wave slapping a boat's bows, the clack of the wooden weapons banging against shields. The line shook and buckled under the pressure but didn't break. The wooden swords of the men behind the shields struck like serpents tongues, hammering into stomachs, groins and knees beating the Gauls to the ground. A shouted command took the shield wall a pace forward, the men's swords in mock readiness to dispatch the sprawled Gauls; the stunned warriors staring up at what would have been their doom had the attack been real. Picking themselves up their scowls and black looks told of bruised egos and wounded pride. To balance the scenario and restore the tetchy pride of the wild warriors, Hannibal had the Libyans break into loose order and had the Gauls attack again. This time their ferocity prevailed as they flowed over and around the un-cohesive infantry, without light infantry to support them they fell prey to the fast and savage charge. The first lesson however was not lost on the Gauls and with a semblance of salved pride; they finally deigned to listen to the training officers.

Having demonstrated the usefulness of close order and loose order fighting tactics to the heavy infantry, Hannibal took the lessons a step further and introduced light infantry as skirmishers to the scenarios. Baldor, watching and learning, eagerly salting away these lessons of war.

"Like others of the brood, as the cub grows it becomes a killer of men"

Anon

Part 3

Chapter Twenty four

It was still dark when Baldor led the raiding column from the camp. They moved along quietly, all talk forbidden. The horse's hooves wrapped in sacking or rags to reduce the noise, weapon hilts and harness metals receiving the same precautionary treatment. Those with bronze helmets or bright shield facings had left the metal to dull and tarnish else wrapped cloths or covers over them to reduce any chance of glare.

Dawn was still some time off and the moon remained full and bright though dropping lower as she neared the end of her nightly journey. The morning air was sharp and bitterly cold beneath a clear sky that showed stars dotted across the heavens giving promise of a clear, bright spring day to come. Baldor stared to the southeast to the stars forming 'Orion' the hunter, these stars Hannibal said were his omen, as he was marching southeast and hunting, they were surely an indication from the God's that the Cenomani would fall beneath his sword.

He was distracted from his apathy by half a dozen scouts trotting past in a tight knit group, they separated and disappeared into the blued darkness, the soft thump of hooves the only indication of their direction. Baldor looked back along the silhouettes of horses and men that made up his long snaking column. Directly behind him was a squadron of forty of Andulas's cavalry forming the vanguard, the remaining sixty divided into two and placed a stade either side of the column as protective screens. Behind the vanguard came the archers and slingers followed by the light infantry with the rear brought up by the heavies. In the middle of the column, he'd placed half a dozen oxcarts carrying rations of food, watered wine, scaling ladders and additional weapon supplies. On a large four wheeled, covered cart rode two siege engineers with their tools and pots of naphtha.

He was in terrible awe of his situation, barely twenty-one years old and in command of a substantially sized raiding force, he felt a huge responsibility for the men under his command and the enormity of the task given him. Consequently, he felt very young, inexperienced and more than a little afraid. On the night's when sleep wouldn't come, despite his attempts to aid it with copious amounts of wine, he'd analysed his fears and apprehensions, both of which he'd found growing exponentially as the day of the columns departure drew closer. He reasoned he wasn't afraid of death only failure and thus disappointment of his peers for the trust placed in him. He'd begun to understand the action of suicide some commanders took after suffering failure or defeat rather than face comrades with their shortcomings. The thought of men's lives being subject to his will and thus his mistakes worried him greatly. He knew only too well that despite the planning and preparation and even all the luck in the world someone was going to die, battles were not won without casualties.

Following Hannibal's teachings and his own instinct of leading by example he'd trained alongside his men, gone weary, thirsty or hungry as the exercise demanded and then of an evening slept alongside them. He knew some by name and all of his officers by both name and nature. From his own bloody mindedness and self-discipline, he'd earned their respect for what he could do as a man by way of a physical nature, though he and they knew that the real test would come when battle joined. Then, the ability to think calmly and clearly while commanding decisively under the pressure and chaos of combat, would truly decide if he was to be a successful battlefield commander.

Despite Hannibal's schooling and words of encouragement along with his confidence and trust in him, Baldor still held his own doubts. He knew his capabilities to fight and kill but doubted his resolve to command and press home an attack if he was to see his men falling dead and wounded in great numbers, how would he know when to call a halt? Equally, how would he know when to keep pushing men forward and that the outcome would be worth the sacrifice? How would he live with himself if he were to judge it so badly wrong? Yet more lives again to add to his personal reckoning? Hannibal readily admitted that only experience could teach him these things and yes, there would be mistakes and some men would die that perhaps shouldn't but war was an uncertain business, all a man could do was plan well, lead well and pray to the Gods for favour. With his disdain for the almighty still strong, Baldor reasoned that it was wholly down to him, the God's had never helped him before, why should they care or help now? Furthermore, his stubborn pride and principals wouldn't let him fall to his knees and ask.

The night before the column's departure, Hannibal asked him to accompany him in prayer and sacrifice of a young bullock to Baal Hammon, in return for his blessings and bestowing of success upon Baldor's mission. Baldor's polite though very firm refusal had seen a stern lecture delivered from Hannibal, himself deeply religious and observant of ritual. Baldor's continuing repudiation saw Hannibal change tack and appeal on behalf of the men's lives and souls for him to relent and enter his plea to the mercy of Baal Almighty. Though Baldor faltered momentarily at the suggested jeopardy to his men, he stubbornly refused to acquiesce, citing he'd be no more than a hypocrite if he suddenly sought a return to Baal's grace and that Baal himself would judge him so. Hannibal, albeit reluctantly, finally acceded, judging this was perhaps a battle lost and instead prayed and carried out the sacrifice himself but on Baldor's behalf. The whole scenario weighing heavily upon Baldor's conscience.

Despite the new friendships and respect Baldor had forged amongst his command, he still felt very much alone. His deepest fears he felt obliged to keep to himself for as commander he couldn't share them with Andulas or his fellow officers. Balaam as ever was not the man to share your concerns with and Harbro and Malo didn't seem to understand. If only Gestix were here or Armaco, these two would have had a ready ear, advice and reassurance aplenty to give. He chewed his lip and imagined the pair watching and judging him as he went about his tasks. With all these thoughts in his mind, he led his column on knowing that his actions alone would bring success and glory or failure and death.

As the moon sank and the stars faded, the column was safely off the open plain into cover of the trees. They began the steady ascent

In Hannibal's Shadow

up a winding track taking them higher and deeper into the forest and within two days march of the Cenomani fortress. The forest was dark, gloomy and damp with the strong smell of pine gum and leaf mould, the horse's hooves adding the scent of fresh soil as they broke and turned the soft ground into a pot-holed mess. The tree canopy kept most of the sunlight from the forest floor retarding grass growth, however, clumps of bluebells pushed up boldly where light filtered through. Small ferns and tendrils of ivy and vine creeper also sprung from the needle and leaf carpet, adding the hazards of falls and twisted ankles to that of reduced light.

Baldor had divided the mission into separate operations or phases; the first being the night march across the plain followed by the traverse up through the forest to the fortress, the third phase being the discreet deployment of his men before the attack. All three manoeuvres which he hoped to carry out undetected and unseen. 'Surprise, stealth and trickery, was everything.' Hannibal had told him. 'Do what the enemy believes impossible; else make the enemy see what he wants to see as at the Trebbia. There are no rules to war. All that matters is winning with least amount of losses to yourself and the greatest to the enemy.' The fourth phase was the hoped for quick and successful storming of the fortress, the fifth, its destruction and driving off or capture of those who remained alive. Finally, the return to camp with most of his command intact and the majority of his men still able-bodied. So, six phases overall, it sounded simple enough but he knew it easier said than done, however he judged the first part successful at least and mentally ticked it off. He turned to whisper to Andulas who rode alongside him.

"We'll stop and make camp once daylight comes full, let the men rest up and eat. No fires mark you! Cold rations only. We'll move off again once dusk comes."

Andulas nodded and turned to pass the orders quietly back along the column.

Baldor had sounded much more confident than he felt, purposely assertive.

'Directness! Assertiveness! And sure, quiet confidence in yourself and your decision.' Hannibal had counselled him. 'The men will be better for it if they see and hear clear direction from you, let them know you're in command and confident at what you're about. Like students in class, men will seek direction and guidance. However, any

299

fool can command as you saw at the Trebbia with Sempronius, the clever part's to demonstrate leadership with good decision making, then, then you will engender loyalty, steadfastness and confidence in others.'

So much to learn Baldor thought, and so little time, with no room for mistakes or second chances. Now he alone was responsible for eight hundred and fifty men, all of whom had mothers and most likely sisters, brothers, wives, lovers and children who would look for their safe return. His decisions and performance as commander would determine how many would live to march again, else become another mound in the earth or an urn full of dry grey ashes. Feeling his confidence already faltering he moved his thoughts back to the task at hand and looked for a clearing or someplace suitable in which to rest his men.

A scout trotted out of the trees advising of a suitable place some six to seven stades ahead where the column could lie up. A small hillock rose sharply from the forest floor, large enough to hold all the men and give a height advantage should they be attacked. A spring exited from the hilltop forming a tiny stream, the water was good and would save the men using their supplies. Baldor nodded curtly to the scout and turned to pass his orders back, perhaps things would go well after all he thought? A safe crossing of the plain and now a good and secure area for camp, he felt his heart lift a little.

The hillock proved ideal and as the infantrymen settled to rest, the cavalry dismounted running out ropes forming a hitching rail to secure the horses. As decided previously the cavalry would leave their mounts here progressing the rest of the way to the fortress on foot. Hannibal envisaged no necessity for mounted troops after the completion of their escort duties, being of little use in the forest or at a siege. Therefore, when time came for the night's march, cavalrymen would become infantrymen, carrying their equipment with them like their infantry brothers.

Baldor hobbled his horse while nibbling a stick of hard, dried beef. He wasn't hungry but he ate all the same, hoping the morsel would settle his stomach, which had griped and burned since leaving the camp. He paused to pat and stroke his mount, his gift from Mago and smiled to himself, 'look on the bright side' he thought, 'at least I've only one fight to worry about this time.' Holding the meat between his teeth and sucking the salty juices he unfastened blankets, shield and spear from the animals back then smoothed a blanket over its back and rump. The horse stood patiently until sensing that he was finished, turned and nudged him gently with its head whickering softly.

"Alright, alright!" He whispered softly.

Blowing gently into the horse's nostrils as it sniffed his face he rummaged in his kit bag and found an apple. Catching the fruit's scent the horse sniffed then blew hard before rolling back twitching lips, exposing long yellow teeth seeking the fruit. As it crunched and chewed the apple, Baldor stroked its forehead tenderly.

"I've come to love you in such a short time." He whispered, placing his head against the horse's cheek, the horse flicked its ears as if listening. "I fear that if I name you and love you too much I'll lose you. Don't you die on me eh, don't leave me? You hear? You and me, we have much to do together."

The horse snorted and nudged the bag, causing Baldor to laugh softly and fish in it once more.

"Here! … Here, one more then" He said offering another apple. "That's the last I have, after this its grass and oats till we get back." The horse chewed while watching him from long lashed, dark eyes. Using dry cloths he rubbed it's coat where it was sweat damp, then gently combed out cots in the tail and mane before running his hands down to the fetlocks examining knees, hamstrings and tendons, lifting each hoof in turn checking for stones or foreign objects.

Satisfied with his mount's condition he asked for his officers to be summoned before they settled to rest. Waiting for them to catch up with him he walked about the makeshift camp checking sufficient sentries were posted while chatting quietly to his men as he went. He moved around the small groups of resting warriors picking out those he recognised asking how the march had been for them, the men he didn't know or remember he introduced himself to. He received some strange looks; some were in awe of him while others appeared wary of his actions. Despite feeling awkward, presumptuous and self-conscious, he continued his progress. Coming across one group where he recognised most of the faces he invited himself into their company. Seeking a place to sit, he graciously eased men back to the ground as they stood to make a place for him. Instead, he nestled close amongst them as if just another warrior seeking company of friends while gratefully accepting a pull of wine from a skin and a piece of bread torn from a loaf.

Just as the men began to relax in his presence, his officers found him. Excusing himself, he passed his own wineskin to the nearest warrior then saluted the men, bidding them carry on. Breathing deeply he strode purposefully and as confidently as he could to meet his officers.

"Gentlemen, some food while we talk?" He directed them back toward his chosen spot where his kit bag, blanket, shield and spear lay near a large oak tree. Ordering bread, wine and meat to be brought, he settled on the ground with his back against the broad oak gesturing his officers' make themselves comfortable. Taking a discreet deep breath he smiled nonchalantly; 'Directness, assertiveness and confidence.' Hannibal's words reverberated in his head like a bell's clapper; meanwhile he felt his heart speeding in his chest.

"Gentlemen; your situation reports? Andulas, your horses are tethered and handlers appointed for the next few days?"

"Yes sir"

"Good!" He nodded grateful acknowledgment.

Baldor was still uncomfortable with Andulas deferring to him as 'sir'. Being a Chief's son and a seasoned leader of men, as well as senior in age to himself saw him struggling with his given, higher command and suddenly elevated status. He moved on quickly, changing language from Gallic to Spanish. He struggled a little with the unfamiliar words, trying to recall the teachings from his youth and wishing he'd listened more intently to his tutor.

"Tirus, your Spaniards, no injuries on the march? Any issues or problems?"

"No sir. Both heavy and light units report all's well, this march is but a morning stroll for us, the terrain much the same as in our native land." He answered with a smile.

Tirus was at least twice Baldor's age though he carried the years well. However, like all ageing warriors, he bore his share of battle scars along with a limp from an old spear wound to the knee. Despite this, he still marched with his men, stating that if he could march with one injured leg they had no reason to complain with two good ones. He was of medium height and clean-shaven, his eyes dark but warm with a smooth olive skin that spoke of Mediterranean heritage.

His black hair, worn in the Greek fashion of large loose curls and cut to his collar; middle age was adding wisps of grey at his temples with a scattering of silver over his crown. He'd taken to Baldor and the pair held one another in high regard.

Baldor turned to his Gallic infantry officer while gathering his words, ever mindful of the required protocols and differing status of his officers he groaned inwardly at the added complexities. However, the fact remained that Andulas was senior followed by Tirus then Tuireann and finally Clitus with his Greeks and Rhodians. Looking at Tuireann as he spoke he noted the disdain and contempt lingering in his eyes towards Tirus, the Gaul obviously deemed himself above the Spaniard both in status and combat experience, Baldor surmised each subject to be debateable. He knew Tirus to be an educated man and thus, must have come from some standing in his homeland. Hannibal knew him for his bravery and military skills, having fought alongside and for him since he took command of the army from his brother in law, Hasdrubal the Fair, in Spain four years ago. Hannibal had warned Baldor of such difficulties and the importance of adhering to the protocols no matter what. From his own experiences with Gestix, he already knew how status and prestige mattered above all, in this world of proud and class sensitive warriors.

"Tuireann" He said, keeping his voice level but authoritative. "Your heavy infantry …?"

"Good sir!" The Gaul interjected quickly. "We've no issues, though we didn't expect to stop so quickly to rest. However, it seems we must move at the pace of the slowest."

Baldor saw Tuireann cast a scornful look toward the Spaniard. Ignoring the remark and implied insult, he was for once grateful for the language barrier between his men. Thankfully, the look went unnoticed by Tirus who was occupied selecting food from the platter. Andulas however flashed a stern look at Tuireann.

Baldor guessed Tuireann to be about thirty years old. Like most of his race, he was tall and broad of shoulder and chest. He wore his straw-coloured hair loose and cut to his shoulder along with the traditional full beard and moustache of his race; these however closely cropped to his face rather than left bushy or plaited. His eyes, though hooded and narrow were of brightest sea green and darting as they took in all around him. His nose was distinctly crooked and flattened as if it had been broken more than once, perhaps Baldor thought, others had taken greater exception to his acidic remarks. His lips were thin and slightly downturned giving him an unhappy face along with a look of bitterness and cruelty; this combined with his superior air made him a poor colleague. However, Baldor knew, having seen first-hand that he was an able warrior though unnecessarily hard on his men.

"Clitus, your Greeks and Rhodians, how've they fared the march?" He asked in Greek.

The old archer looked up as he was addressed and answered while tearing some tough meat with his teeth.

"Some sore feet and aching legs sir but no problems, no problems. We missile troops make for mediocre infantry compared to these professionals." He graciously indicated Tirus and Tuireann. "But my lads are hardy and willing. Aye, hardy and willing. We're all hill people, sir, we'll endure!"

Clitus smiled, dipping his balding head briefly in respect as he spoke. Hailing from the ancient city of Knossos on the island of Crete, his temperament and manner as warm and bright as the sun that fell on its shores. Baldor surmised Clitus to be in his mid-fifties and despite his advancing years and easy-going, somewhat humble nature, knew him held in high esteem by his men as both an excellent archer and able commander. Further proof he thought that a commander could be modest and compassionate as well as a respected leader, juggling that balance successfully was the trick.

He settled the officers around him as more food and wine was brought.

"Gentlemen, I'm unsure whether this is dinner or breakfast?" He said smiling, pouring wine and inviting them to eat their fill, he purposely watered his own measure further and sipped rather than quaffing it.

"We'll rest till dusk and be on the march tonight; then lie up and sleep during daylight tomorrow. After that, one more night's march should bring us close to Victumulae before the following dawn. We must arrive well before first light, thus allowing time to be safely in position before sun up. We'll have to forgo sleep and go straight to battle as dawn comes, as there's too great a risk of discovery being laid up so close, surprise gentlemen will be our ally."

Reaching into his kitbag, he produced a leather, drawstring bag. Sweeping the ground in front of him clear of leaves and twigs he tipped the contents onto the ground. Small, rectangular blocks of painted wood fell out along with a flat stone and some marbles. He placed the stone in the centre of the cleared area and tapped it.

"Victumulae! … Just before dawn breaks, we'll leave our cover and deploy. However, I have one small change to make which I'll show you all now but which concerns only Tirus and his Caetratus troops, the rest of you deploy exactly as planned."

The men watched closely as he sorted his coloured props, heads leaned in and tired eyes received a quick rub, wine and food forgotten for the moment. Baldor placed a red block of wood opposite and to the right of the stone then added a red marble in front of the block.

"Andulas, this is you and our former cavalry unit, you're red." He managed a wry smile as he spoke; causing Andulas to chuckle softly, both knew the gripes and grumbles that would come from the cavalrymen who'd become enforced infantry.

"I want you here on our right wing as we deploy in front of the fortress gate, no change there."

Andulas nodded ascent.

"Your colours, Andulas." Baldor passed over a bundle of red cloth strips. "Have your men tie these around their helmets so we can identify you against the Cenomani. Tirus, as I said, the plan change is for your command alone. I'm dividing your heavy and light contingents, I've a special task in mind for you and your Caetratus which I'll explain; your colour's still black."

He lifted a black block and a jet coloured marble, placing them to one side while tapping his nose with his forefinger and smiling, all the while hoping they'd believe his show of confidence.

"We still need a demonstration of force to the front of the fortress, so you're Scutarius heavies I want with me at the front gate and on our left wing, they and I remain green."

He lifted a green block and marble placing it to the left facing the stone.

"Tuireann, I want you and all your men, both heavy and light alongside me; this is you …"

Baldor raised a yellow marble with a swirl of blue across it. "Two colours as discussed." He passed two bundles of cloth strips to Tuireann. "Yellow for your light and blue for the heavy, I want you all in the centre and ready for a fast assault."

Placing the two-tone marble, and yellow and blue blocks to the centre of the red and green ones, Baldor noted a brief glimmer of satisfaction on Tuireann's face as he was given what the Gauls deemed the position of honour, centre of the front line.

"Clitus, you, your archers and slingers are white; I want them divided into two groups and placed on the wings affording us missile cover as we advance; keep those heads down on the walls for us." He added two white blocks, one on the outside of the red and the other to the outside of the green. "Each group to be an equal mix of bows and slings mind you; if we have difficulty coming into range for the slingers, at least we'll have cover on both sides from the bows. Yourself Clitus, I want to stay with and lead the group on the left, your presence will give me additional command on that side." He placed a milk coloured marble in front of the left group.

"Now gentlemen, here's the change to the plan. Tirus, instead of forming up on the left with your Caetratus and Scutarius as we discussed, I want you to take your Caetratus here instead, to the fortress rear wall." Baldor placed the black block and marble to the rear of the stone. "They tell me your men are from the hills and mountains and are capable of climbing even in their armour?"

"Aye sir! We're mountain men and used to rock and crag, these timber walls shouldn't present a problem."

"Excellent! Take ropes and grapnels with you; leave us the ladders for the frontal assault where speed will be of the essence. I envisage a quiet climb for you with no resistance as such, only a sentry or two to silence maybe. Clitus, spare five archers and five slingers to serve as missile support for Tirus."

"I'll give him my best marksmen sir!"

Tirus smiled and nodded his thanks.

"Why the change sir?" Andulas asked, looking thoughtfully at the blocks and marbles. "Why not the straightforward frontal assault as planned? The General determined we've enough men to storm the fortress owing to the manpower losses suffered by the Cenomani at the Trebbia."

"I hope to save men's lives, Andulas. I've thought much on this since we left camp; if we gain a quiet foothold on the back wall then signal the assault on the front gate to begin, chaos will ensue in the fort. I'm sure you'll agree that being attacked from both front and rear in a town with only one gate will generate panic."

Baldor's throat tightened and his stomach twisted as he looked for agreement among his officers.

"Agreed sir, but the risk, what if the rear attack fails?"

"Then no signal! We assault from the front as planned. Yes we won't have Tirus and his Caetratus but they will no doubt have done some damage and drawn some of the Cenomani away from the main gate, it'll be a good diversion even if they cannot gain a foothold."

Andulas nodded slowly while pursing his mouth. "Fair enough sir."

"Other objections or suggestions gentlemen?" Baldor asked feeling some relief. "Please, speak freely, I'm all ears."

He looked around his officers' faces one at a time seeking signs of approval or concern; Tirus grinned.

"I'm for it sir, we've much to gain and little to lose from what I can see."

"We could lose you!" Clitus added with a mischievous chuckle. "Then I'll have to play dice on my own! However, I'm sure that if it's possible, you'll do it."

"With your archers and slingers covering us as we climb we've nothing to fear. I'm sure both I and my purse will survive, if only till you clean me out again!"

The two men chuckled and grinned at each other, Baldor spared a smile too, delighting in his men bonding. Eventually Tuireann found voice.

"We're still dividing our forces in the face of our enemy. Why accept that risk when we have surprise, along with fire pots, ladders and sufficient men to attack as planned?" His tone conceited, bordering on arrogance, he shrugged. "My men will take the walls for you."

"I don't doubt it, Tuireann but at what cost? Do you not wish to spare men if you can?"

Tuireann shrugged. "We are Lingones; we fear nothing and no one, least of all Cenomani scum hiding behind their walls."

"I question neither your abilities nor your courage, Tuireann but if I can save lives, I will! The General divided us at the Trebbia and in the face of superior odds; we can do the same here and with much less risk."

"That was the General." Tuireann quipped sarcastically.

"Tuireann!" Andulas snapped angrily. "How dare …"

"I will have my say." Tuireann bridled.

"Enough!" Baldor shouted both men down. "Enough I say!"

Tirus and Clitus didn't understand Gallic but hearing the anger in the three men's words looked on anxiously. Baldor felt the sting to his pride and his temper stirring, swallowing hard he took time to gather his words; men's lives depended upon this discussion and placed his pride a distant second for appeasement.

"Andulas, I thank you for your support." He said levelly. "But Tuireann is right, I'm not the General, I have no victories to my name as yet, I'm both young and untried ..."

All the men tried to talk at once, with all but Tuireann aligning themselves with Baldor's views; he raised his hands for silence.

"I hold with my decision and am firm upon it. It's worth a try and if we should fail ... well, then I and I alone am accountable to the General for it."

"I'm with you, no matter what." Andulas added, placing his finger on his red marble signifying concurrence.

A chorus of agreement came from Tirus and Clitus as they placed forefingers on their marbles, only Tuireann remained unmoving and silent.

"Tuireann ...?" Baldor asked.

Tuireann looked down his crooked nose at the markers then slowly back to Baldor giving a haughty sniff, the pregnant hush lingered as all eyes fell on him. Andulas broke the silence.

"Tuireann! Answer the question!"

"My lord, I but consider carefully for my men, as mentioned we're trying to save lives." His tone oily with sarcasm.

"My father's men, damn you!" Andulas removed his hand from the marble, stabbing a finger accusingly at Tuireann. "My father's!"

"Enough!" Baldor interjected loudly. He looked to Tuireann and lowered his voice. "Tuireann, I've explained my reasons for the change of tactics. I've heard your concerns and believe, countered them? If you're still undecided and thus uncommitted I'd rather you and your men stay with the horses and await our return."

"He will not!" Andulas interrupted forcefully. "He commands these men only by my father's grace, he will ..."

"No! ... No, we're not slaves to do the bidding of others. We're allies, comrades, brothers in arms, we either commit willingly or not at all." Baldor held up his hands for silence, though he did notice

Tuireann no longer looked quite so sure of himself. Whether it was from Andulas's anger or the thought of being left behind he couldn't tell. "We must all be committed and know where we stand."

He looked at Tuireann, the question hanging. He saw a nerve twitch in his cheek followed by a small scowl. Tuireann reached out slowly and placed his finger onto his marble.

"We will take the field ... and the walls ... sir." He added, with poorly disguised bitterness.

"Thank you! ... Now, Tirus!"

"Sir!"

"You'll have the furthest to go so timing and signalling are down to you. As dawn breaks begin your attack, loose a burning arrow over the fort gate the moment you're on the rear wall then we'll begin our assault at the front. We go forward together under cover of Clitus's archers and slingers. The siege ladders go in the third rank from the front, which should see them safely to the wall." He left the rest unsaid, however the meaning that the first two ranks were likely to go down under fire from the defenders wasn't lost on the group. "Once inside we stay in our detachments and drive the defenders towards Tirus. There's to be no delay for looting or rape, is that understood?"

Baldor looked around each man in turn. With no contradiction, he carried on.

"We kill any one armed that will not throw down. We should outnumber the defenders but it could be close, hence the need to be fast and ruthless. However, anyone surrendering is not to be killed, I'll not have murder done. When we have control of the fortress and any captives are secured, then, and only then, do we sack it. All goods, animals, riches, weapons, captives and so forth will be taken back to camp and divided equally amongst us, shares for any that perish being paid to their kin. Finally, we raise Victumulae to the ground, the Cenomani, as a power in these hills will cease to exist. Am I understood?"

Chapter Twenty five

Baldor was awoken by sun on his face, he'd slept with his helmet on and now the midday heat was cooking his head like a lobster in a pot. Groggy with sleep and uncomfortably warm he slipped the helmet off and threw his cloak and blanket to one side, feeling the cool air on his body he began to wake up properly. His brain went into action immediately, what time was it? What news from the scouts?
He called softly to his scribe who was working quietly nearby, making notes on a wax tablet.

"What news from the scouts, Antigonus?"

"Only good sir!" The small man's head bobbed as he spoke. "That's why I didn't wake you; I trust I did aright? They report all's quiet, the only folk they've seen are woodcutters working half a day's ride from here. The second patrol's not back yet, probably …"

"Nearer sundown I think. Err … thank you for that Antigonus, I'm much rested."

Baldor scanned the camp and the still sleeping men; all was quiet, even the horses stood calmly enjoying the peace and spring sunshine. He upended his water skin over his head, gasping as the coldness stole his breath; shaking his head like a wet dog, he ran his fingers through his hair working the coolness into his scalp. He'd slept soundly and felt surprisingly refreshed; it was good to wake without a dry mouth and sore head for once. Judging it was just after midday, he deemed to leave his men longer to sleep as they wouldn't be moving until early evening and the change of light, reasoning that with guards posted and scouts out it was safe enough to do so.

Picking up his falcatas, he slid them in and out of their scabbards before slinging them over his shoulders strapping them in place across his back. He checked his dagger, sliding it in and out checking the smooth action, content that all was as it should be he rotated his shoulders easing the stiffness from them then settled himself comfortably with his back against the oak tree.

His stomach grumbled loudly, reminding him food was necessary and he rummaged in his pack for some bread and dried meat. Despite the damp cloth wrapping, the bread was already stone hard and the meat as tough as new boot leather, he poured a little wine into a horn cup dipping the bread to soften it. The meat shattered like an icicle into bite-sized pieces that he sucked and chewed, extracting the salty juice until soft enough to swallow.

Running through the plan in his head again, he considered the change he'd made. How he would have liked to discuss it with the General, why hadn't he thought of it before, when there were more heads than his, to think it through? The change wasn't complicated, so why shouldn't it work? Surely, it would help save men's lives?

What if it didn't work? ... Stop it! Stop it now, he told himself, it was done, he couldn't change it back now, how would that appear to his officers?

He drank the wine along with the remains of the breadcrumbs from the bottom of the cup, surprised at his hunger he looked for something else to eat. Counting his meat sticks and small bread loaves, he divided them by the number of meals and days he expected to be in the field. Adding an extra day to the tally as a safeguard as he'd been taught, he saw his ration was tight. Still hungry, he sought a small, white jar with a cork stopper. Popping the lid he sniffed the sweet honey, how he wished for hot water for to make a drink. Instead, he made do with dipping his finger into the runny liquid then leaning his head back transferred it quickly into his mouth. Relishing the taste he sucked his finger, he allowed himself one more dip before closing the lid then sat for some time licking and sucking his finger whilst picking the meat and bread from between his teeth with his fingernail.

Enjoying this moment of solitude and quiet as the camp slept on he listened to the sounds of the forest around him. The afternoon breeze gently stirred the treetops rustling leaves and causing some limbs to creak in protest from the movement. From deeper in the trees, he heard the hollow rapping of a woodpecker seeking grubs in the tree bark, the busy bird accompanied by cooing from roosting pigeons and punctuated with the odd shrill call from a peacock. A honeybee droned lazily past alighting on a nearby bluebell, diligently working its way from bloom to bloom in it's never ending search for nectar before disappearing into the trees as quickly as it arrived.

With time to himself, he reached to his neck and undid the leather cord holding the metal cameo, holding it up in front of him. The sunlight caught the silver and it flashed brightly, he quickly lowered it from the glare. Cursing himself for a halfwit, he shielded the metal in a cupped hand while tracing a forefinger gently over Aiticia's profiled image. The pain of her passing still hurt like a knife twisted in his heart. He couldn't imagine the pain ever going away only that he may learn to tolerate and perhaps accept it as time passed. Closing his eyes, he remembered; happier more carefree days, her beauty and laughter and how she lit up the house with her smile and warm demeanour. He thought of the rich chestnut colouring of her hair and dark, almond shaped eyes that he'd lose himself in. He remembered the peach like feel of her skin and her scent. The fragrances she wore, smelling of flowers and fresh sweetness by day and which she'd change to a heady perfume of an evening when the light faded and the house left just to the two of them. The nights then, when she'd tease and lure him to bed, playing the wanton or the innocent as she chose. He swallowed hard when he thought of the lovemaking and the long, hot nights when there were no worries, no cares, other than pleasing one another. His stomach knotted with the power of the memory he conjured. He sniffed, thinking he picked her scent in the air; he could see her, almost touch her. His lips formed her name and his hand reached up to take hers, then she was gone, a noise in the camp broke his daydream and he was left with a lump in his throat and tears in his eyes once more.

Seeing the noise was nothing more than a helmet knocked over he tried frantically to recall his vision or daydream, the same way a sleeper seeks to return to a good dream. Try as he might, the moment was gone and his mind wandered to other things. He raised the cameo and kissed it gently, a sad smile on his lips.

"I love you … I love you so much … why, why did you have to go?" He whispered.

The tears coursed down his cheeks tickling his skin as they ran into his beard; forcing another sad smile he spoke to Aiticia in his head. 'What would you think of the beard my love? …For old men you used to say … I feel old now, for it feels like forever since I saw you.'

"Excuse me sir."

Startled from his reverie and already reaching to his falcata hilt he looked up to see Andulas. His hand fell away from the sword and the other slipped the cameo quickly into his purse. He wiped his face on his sleeve and cleared his throat, "Andulas?"

"I'm sorry sir; I didn't mean to intrude."

"It's of no matter Andulas, really." He said with poor conviction. "And please, Baldor is fine; there's only you and I here." He managed a smile.

Andulas nodded and following Baldor's gesture to sit, settled himself next to his friend and commander.

"I'm here to apologise for Tuireann."

"There's no need Andulas, really, he has the right to speak freely."

"Granted, but he could have done it without the slight to you! And I mislike his insinuations towards Tirus."

Baldor shrugged. "I've more to worry about than my pride, but I'll watch him with Tirus or anyone else for that matter."

"He can be a poisonous bastard."

Baldor was somewhat shocked for he'd never heard Andulas misspeak or malign anyone.

"How's he risen to his Captaincy then? Granted, he's a good warrior but your people, they don't take kindly to insults and jibes." He touched his nose and wiggled it. "That accounts for the nose I guess?"

"His brother did that to him, twice!"

"Twice!" Baldor exclaimed with a half-smile. "How did you know it was his brother?"

"Because it was me that did it!"

"What? …But! You, you are …"

"My father's son, yes! Tuireann is his bastard. My bastard brother or half-brother if you like, whelped on a serving wench. That taint itself matters nothing to me, for bastards are no different to any born the right side of the sheets, I dislike him for the kind of man he is; arrogant, ambitious, self-seeking."

"He's not your favourite person then?" Baldor jested, trying to keep the conversation light.

Andulas however didn't smile he just carried on in a serious tone.

"What I'm saying Baldor is, be careful. You treat us all well and show us great respect. You have it in return from me and I see it from Tirus and Clitus. Tuireann however, needs a firm hand. He'll construe your respect or civility as weakness and will continue to aggravate, undermine and manipulate you if he can, until you put him in his place."

Baldor rested his chin in his hand looking thoughtful. Another precautionary lesson then, respect and fairness misconstrued for weakness, it seemed that leading men held more hazards and traps than a wily enemy.

"Thank you … thank you for the advice Andulas, I'll bear what you say in mind. I'll be careful and I promise you, if Tuireann does overstep the mark he'll feel my wrath. I have obligations to meet and orders to follow and he'll not stand in the way of me fulfilling and carrying these out. Now, did you sleep well?"

"Yes, Thank you, but now I want to be up and moving, this …"

"This waiting!" Baldor finished for him and the pair smiled at one another. "This waiting is worse than the fighting."

"It is the way of it I think? Perhaps that's why we sharpen our weapons and check equipment over and over again?" He shrugged. "It fills the time and ensures good preparation, focusing your mind I suppose."

Baldor nodded. "How many battles, how many fights, Andulas? You must becoming used to it by now?"

"I don't know, is the answer to both of those questions." He said resignedly. "Too many battles probably! Mostly against other tribes but in particular the Cenomani. As for the waiting and the fretting well, sometimes I think I have it under control, other times it's like fighting for the first time, dry mouth, wanting to puke, needing to piss, you know?"

"Yes, I know. Let's hope this is an end to it then or at least to the Cenomani. Perhaps when they're no more a little peace may reign in these hills instead."

"I suspect there'll always be someone to fight or something to fight for, I imagine the General will expect support from us after the Cenomani threat is removed? Nobody does anything for nothing."

"In truth Andulas, I don't know what he expects or plans, but I do believe the world is going to catch fire. We've made war on Rome and bloodied her nose twice, here on her own soil. From what Gestix told me they're a tenacious adversary, they'll be back."

"So, we may go soldiering together yet, you and me?"

"Selfishly, I would like that but I think when this battle's over you should return to your village and hills and enjoy them, love your wife, raise your children and grow fat and wealthy."

"Is that what you would do Baldor, if you had the chance?"

Baldor looked sad. "That's what I should have done, when I had the chance."

Andulas watched Baldor's features and saw a distant look that told of regrets, mistakes and bitterness. He waited a while evaluating Baldor's feelings but eventually the blunt Gaul in him won out and he asked directly.

"You lost your friend, Gestix? And you blame your decisions?"

Baldor was still looking away but he nodded and mumbled. "Yes, I made another decision too … a lifetime ago now it seems. I chose to fight over some insults that were given and I killed a man but …" He cleared his throat pulling himself out of his misery. "It doesn't matter Andulas, mistakes, I made mistakes. I just wish better luck for you."

"Ah! This man you slew, it started a feud with his family?"

"Yes."

"And it continues? As these things do?"

"Yes."

Andulas shrugged. "The man insulted you, you fought and he died, men should consider what they say before they say it, an offence often brings bloodshed."

"Yes, yes it can, Andulas, it cost him his life but it cost me much more."

"You had to leave your city?"

"Yes, but that was no matter really, I had no reason to stay after my wife was slain."

"He slew your wife?"

"He angered me, insulted me, we fought, Aiticia was caught in the middle of it, she died because we fought. I blame us both."

Slipping the cameo from his purse and shielding it from the sun, he passed it to Andulas. Andulas looked at the silver turning it from side to side to better see the image.

"With respect Baldor, she, Aitic … Aiticia is beautiful."

"Thank you Andulas, she was beautiful, my temper killed her."

"So now you fight to ease your pain."

"Yes."

"Does it ease your pain?"

"No." Baldor huffed. "No it doesn't, Gestix told me it wouldn't, the sword makes for a cold companion. But … I've nothing else to do." He smiled, trying to laugh it off.

Andulas placed his hand on Baldor's shoulder.

"When this is over you're welcome in my village, my house, we're still in your debt and haven't forgotten."

"Thank you, but …" Baldor interrupted only for Andulas to carry on.

"But nothing! Find a woman there, we have plenty single women, the high mortality rate amongst us men folk sees to that. There are some beautiful women too! Though perhaps, perhaps not as beautiful as your Aiticia." He looked back at the cameo shaking his head in wonder.

Baldor was deeply moved by the compliment and the sentiment meant much as he knew such invitations were not given lightly, the Gauls were clannish people and strangers did not always go down well.

"Thank you Andulas, from the bottom of my heart I thank you, for the kind words and the offer. Believe me; I will give it some thought but …"

"Hush now!" Andulas laughed softly holding his finger to his lips. "Hold that thought and let the heart decide, not the head." He passed the cameo back to Baldor.

Baldor smiled back. "Fair enough then, we've a battle to fight and win before we do anything anyway."

****

As darkness fell, they began their second night march. Leaving the horses and oxen with a dozen handlers along with the carts, they transferred the equipment sharing it around for everyone to carry. Heavily laden with their kit and supplies from the wagons and with the terrain steepening, the going was difficult but apart from some blistered feet for the archers and cavalrymen and one or two twisted ankles, the march remained uneventful. Lying up again during daylight, most of the men including Baldor didn't sleep so soundly. For just as dawn broke they'd ascended a whale-backed but heavily wooded ridge and seen a cluster of cottages nestled in the valley below. With no smoke rising from the roofs they reasoned the cottages were just shelters for woodcutters when a storm threatened and presently empty, else all within were still asleep. However, they saw and heard no one, nor did any dogs bark at them, but the close proximity to human habitation began to set men's nerves on edge. Though they gave the tiny hamlet a wide berth, all knew the chances of discovery had suddenly heightened.

To add to their discomfort, they weren't fortunate enough to find a good campsite, having to be content with resting in a strung out column in the same order in which they'd marched. Baldor fretted quietly and walked the camp double-checking his sentry's positions. He scattered archers and slingers over the column's length in a bid to give some firepower to all parts of it. He wondered at the wisdom of the Roman practice of entrenching and fortifying their marching camps but without sufficient trenching tools, it was beyond his men's capabilities for the moment. The day however passed peacefully, men dozed in the sun else continued weapon sharpening or checking rituals while some chatted or diced quietly in small groups. As the shadows fell, men took up their weapons and gear preparing for the final march that would take them to within bowshot of the forts walls.

As the column progressed, the vanguard encountered the first of the territory markers of the Cenomani. Skeletal remains of three human bodies, all fixed upright as if still living. They were mostly just bleached bones with tatters of weathered skin, their rusting weapons bent out of shape and stuck in the ground next to them, their shields hung over their shoulders as they would have been in life. None retained their heads, the skulls nowhere to be seen. Baldor knew the heads would be nailed above a hut door as trophies else left in a shrine as gifts to the God's for a victory. Closer inspection of the weapons declared one of the bodies Spanish or Carthaginian, causing the more religious of his men to ask for the bodies to be decently buried. Baldor refused but gave his word that upon their return, all would be respectably interred.

The Gauls marched past the marker unperturbed; the Spaniards too seemed to take it in their stride having seen similar practices from tribes in their homeland. It was the Greeks and Rhodians, the more civilised, who were unnerved by it. It seemed that civilised ways and higher culture were out of place here in the hills of Cisalpine Gaul.

As the moon set, a scout returned, Baldor halting the column as he relayed time and distance remaining to the fort. Calling a break for water and a bite to eat, he summoned his commanders for a final briefing. Once Andulas and the others appeared, Baldor took his blanket gesturing for them and the scout to settle closely together on the ground. He flicked the blanket, spreading it wide in the air then squatted as it settled over them like a shroud. Hidden beneath, he struck flint to tinder and soon had a tiny oil lamp alight; passing a stylus and wax tablet to the scout the man began to reproduce, in primitive sketch form, the area he'd observed. The man whispered information as he drew, Baldor calculating they were slightly ahead of schedule and therefore should be in position before dawn with time to spare. Satisfied, he extinguished the lamp and threw off the blanket, he had to wait a few moments for his eyes to adjust to night vision again before he could move around with surety.

"Andulas, have your men tie the ribbons onto their helmets now, we may not have a chance after this, Tirus, take your Caetratus and climbing ropes and follow this man now." He indicated the scout by clasping him on the shoulder. "He'll lead you to the rear of the fort. Begin your assault the moment dawn breaks and loose that burning arrow over the gate once you have men on the parapet. We'll begin our assault on your signal and meet inside. Do you have it?"

"Aye sir."

"Tuireann! See to the ribbons for your men. Clitus! Tirus will need those ten men from you now."

"Already arranged and done sir."

Baldor felt his heart pounding and blood beginning to race and the excited, nervous tension emanating from his officers as he issued the orders. Being so close to their target and manoeuvring in the dark adding to the apprehension. If they could manage this third phase of the plan undetected, they would be halfway to success.

"Right, Gentlemen! Our time is good. We can afford to go more cautiously from here to reduce the risk of discovery, surprise remains our greatest weapon let's keep it that way. Reiterate to the men, no talking and no noise! As discussed, once inside there's no stopping to plunder until we have full control. Finally, there's to be no rape or murder done. I'll punish any man who disobeys my orders as such dalliance could compromise us all! Now, is everything clear? … Are there any further questions before we depart?"

Baldor looked at the phantom like faces of his officers; he couldn't see their expressions and assumed their silence meant concurrence. He knew now was the time to give an inspiring speech but with silence paramount, the best he could do was offer quiet blessings for a safe return from battle.

"Gentlemen, officers, brothers in arms. I call upon Baal almighty in his mercy to bless and keep you all this day. To bring you safe from the field of battle and grant us victory." He then called upon Rigisamus, the Gallic war God for the same blessings offering his hand to Andulas and Tuireann. Andulas offered a blessing in return; Tuireann merely dipped his head briefly in acknowledgement. Turning to Tirus and Clitus, he invoked a blessing in Spanish then Greek. Hearty handshakes came from both men, their other hand over their heart as they offered prayers and regards in return.

"Victory and honour!" Baldor whispered and the group broke up to return to their troops.

The column moved off again and in the silence, Baldor was left to his thoughts. He felt fraudulent for his call to Baal for mercy and victory as he deemed the Gods loved him not. Why should they heed the prayers of a wayward non-believer? However, he reasoned the prayers were for his men, not for him. He asked only on behalf of others, for their safety and salvation, nothing for himself, he would take his chances as he'd done since Aiticia's death.

Slipping the cameo from his purse as he walked, he kissed it before tying it back about his neck, whispering. "Should I fall on this field today my love, meet me by the Styx, for I'll have no one to announce me and guide my way. … Gestix, brother, guide my thoughts and my arm, keep me strong, help me lead well and bring my men victory."

The moon was fading to the colour of watered milk when the silhouette of the fortress loomed out of the darkness. Watching from the shadows of the trees, they could see no movement on the walls or the two towers. Only a dull glow from the sentries' braziers showed in the gloom, with the night watch ending and dawn arriving, no fresh wood had been added to keep them brightly aflame. At equal distances along the wall and at the corners, torches angled outwards into the darkness, again, the flames burnt low as the pitch soaked, hessian reached the end of its life. With dawn about to break and dew forming chilly and wet, the temperature dropped dramatically. Hopefully keeping cold and weary sentries huddled behind the parapet or preferably, closeted within the towers themselves.

Sounds from inside the fort drifted on the air, becoming louder emanating out over the walls. At first Baldor thought, Tirus and his Spaniards must already be attacking. Had he missed the signal? Straining his ears, he heard neither clash of weapons nor frantic shouts that accompany battle and so without further hesitation he motioned his men forward. Slipping noiselessly from the darkened tree line, they crept forward like spectres stealing forth from a tomb. They spread over the cleared, dead ground like a shadowy, ghost army forming up in units in front of the gates. Baldor was impressed at the stealth and discipline as they advanced in silence, bringing siege ladders with them as they came.

His mouth was desert dry and his heart pounded like a kettledrum, he felt sure that its beating alone was loud enough to give their position away. Continuing to advance, his eyes searched the sky for the first sign of light and the incendiary arrow announcing Tirus's attack. His men were becoming clearer by the moment, changing from black shadows to blue then to grey, shades of colour from tunics appearing as the sky rolled back its dark canopy, surrendering to the light streaking the eastern sky. Moistening his lips with his tongue, he watched the sky growing brighter. Where was the signal and where was Tirus?

Chapter Twenty six

Tirus and his advance party of Caetratus stepped out of the shadows at the base of the wall. Uncoiling his rope and looking upwards, he gauged his throw. Casting the noosed rope up towards the pointed stakes forming the wall top there was a quiet clatter as it landed over the parapet. Tirus waited, paying to the Gods that no one had heard. With all still quiet, he pulled gently on the rope. It tensioned and he gave a tentative tug, hoping it would tighten about the timber. A moment later, it slipped and fell back down, dropping in large, loose coils at his feet.

Holding his breath, he listened. His men looked anxiously up then back to the tree line where Clitus's archers waited with arrows resting on the string, ready for any sentry that may hear the noise and come to investigate. He coiled the rope again readying his next attempt. Seeing the moon fading with the dawn, he mumbled a quiet prayer to Yarkhibol, the God of the moon, invoking blessings for success then cast the rope into the gloom once more. Another quiet clatter and the rope remaining vertical, again told of at least partial success. He slowly fed the line back through his hands, at any moment expecting to hear a cry of alarm or the whoosh of an arrow heading out of the trees towards a curious sentry. However, all remained quiet as the grave, so quiet that he could hear the soft but fast, nervous breathing of his men behind him. He felt the rope going taut as the tension took up. The feel of the slipknot pulling tight as the rope moved slowly through it. Tighter … tighter, his heart pounded in his ears as the rope went taut as a bowstring. Grasping one of the climbing knots above his head, he carefully leaned his weight onto it, gradually increasing it until content to pull his body weight clear of the ground.

"It's good!" He said in a hushed whisper.

One of his men passed another two coils of rope, which he looped over his shoulder then grabbing the next knot up, pulled his body upwards. Stretching his arms while entwining his feet about the rope, he extended his hands higher repeating the action. Little by little, like a caterpillar on its silken thread, he slowly climbed the wall. The rope creaked under the strain and his leather corselet scrubbed and scuffed on the timber as he ascended, his hands wet and slippery with nervous sweat making him appreciative of the knots for grip.

Just below the parapet, he paused and hung on the rope. Breathless from the climb he made an effort to control and quieten his breathing while he listened. He felt very vulnerable just hanging there, the rope continuing to creak in protest to his weight as he swung gently back and forth. He couldn't hear any footsteps but there was noises from somewhere further within the fortress. He could hear sounds of hooves, men moving about, the occasional shout and then the excited yelping of dogs.

His heart raced and despite the need for air, he held his breath to listen again. Dogs yelping and barking usually meant alarm, had they been discovered? However, it wasn't coming closer nor was it gaining in volume or tenseness! Why was there no shouting of alarm or sentries hurrying along the parapet? Locking his feet on the rope, he slipped his hand tentatively over the wooden posts pulling himself up and over the wall. He was thankful of his corselet as his chest and stomach dragged hard over the pointed timber as he swung his legs over onto the walkway. The walkway creaked as his weight came down; he crouched low, keeping beneath wall height and off the brightening skyline. Seeing no one, he un-slung the ropes tying them off around the timber tops, dropping the length down into the shadows and the waiting men. Drawing his falcata, he turned watching for trouble while the creaking, twitching ropes told of warriors climbing after him.

Though he couldn't see anything, there was still too much noise he thought. At this time of morning the most folk should be doing was rising from their beds seeking breakfast before the day's work. A sudden horn blast made him flinch. He cursed as it repeated again and again in quick succession, as if in chorus the dogs yelping and barking increased in volume. He realised the noise and activity was not an alarm but rather preparations for a day's hunt! Cursing the bad timing he pondered the chances of the attack's success for they were still light in numbers, having expected to storm the fortress before the defenders knew what was happening. Now it seemed they'd have to face warriors that, though not dressed for battle, were armed and very much awake.

'What to do? What in Hades name was he to do?' He didn't have time to contact Baldor and with dawn almost upon them, it would be only moments before the men outside the gate were discovered. Despite the change in circumstances, they had a foothold at the rear of the fort and so far undetected, so there was still hope of some surprise. Reasoning he'd no choice, he would press ahead. If they could cause a large enough diversion with their attack, panic may set in amongst the defenders yet. The light pad of sandals on the walkway heralded the arrival of the first of his comrades with others swarming up the ropes close behind. More ropes were tied off and dropped below, increasing the opportunities for more to climb simultaneously. Soon the walkway was filling with men that Tirus split into two groups, sending one left, the other right.

An archer pushed his way through to Tirus. "Now sir?"

Tirus looked around for a moment then nodded decisively. "Aye, let fly!"

****

Baldor scanned the walls but saw no sentries. Had they been lucky enough to coincide their attack with the changing of the night watch? His men were ready and formed up in their units awaiting his order to attack; he watched the sky anxiously for Tirus's signal.

Undulating blasts on a horn caught Baldor's attention, followed by a loud rumble like thunder in distant mountains; he guessed it to be the gate's drawbar being removed. A dull, metallic rattle of chains and a high-pitched, banshee like screech from the hinges followed as the gates slowly opened inwards. His men looked up not quite believing their eyes as the gates continued opening in front of them. Baldor saw heads turn to him waiting and expecting his command to attack.

What in Hades was happening? Had Tirus scaled the wall and somehow reached the gate without trouble? Had he just forgotten to send the signal? As the gates continued to swing open, he procrastinated. Was it the Cenomani coming out to fight? How would they have known the raiders were coming? Was it a trap to lure them forward to slaughter them at the gate? His mind raced, nothing made any sense. As he watched, reasoned and then fretted the precious moments away a handful of dogs padded out from the widening gap in the gates. Some sniffed the ground while others sniffed the air, looking inquisitively as they caught the scent of the men arrayed in front of them. The dogs began to bark and snarl aggressively, shouts rang out within the fort and the gates ceased to open. As if in indecision the gates stayed where they were. Baldor's men looked at him again and still he procrastinated. Then the sounds of fighting along with shouts and screams to the rear of the fort rose above all and the gates began to close again. At that same moment a burning arrow whistled across the sky landing in the dirt, a half stade forward of the gate.

All along the line men edged forward, straining like hounds on the leash, anticipating the command that would set them loose against the fort walls. Suddenly, from the centre of the line the order to attack shouted loud and long, someone had made a decision. A carnyx wailed and war cries and whoops broke from hundreds of throats as the raiders surged forward. Going straight to double pace they crossed the dead ground. At one stade before the gate, they broke into a run and finally a full-blooded charge as they saw the gates drawing closed. Some dogs ran back through the narrowing gap while others stayed to bark and snarl defiantly at the attackers.

From the raiders flanks, arrows and slingshot loosed. Whistling and humming, the missiles sped low over the heads of the charging warriors across the dead ground disappearing into the gateway. Two dogs yelped as low slingshot bowled them over, one died instantly the other thrashing and rolling on the ground in agony. It's whimpering and howling drowned by war cries as the raiders neared the gateway. The ranks were losing cohesion, opening in places as the faster or braver men or those unencumbered with scaling ladders edged ahead of the others. Line officers bellowed to keep the formation tight but with days of furtive skulking and hiding finally over and bloodlust up, men sought to close with their enemy and vent their fury. Arrows flew overhead, aimed at the wall where some sentries had finally made an appearance. Lead bullets from slings cracked and ricocheted from the wall blowing out pieces of timber. Time seemed to go into slow motion as men raced for the gate in hope of preventing it closing. On the parapet more defenders appeared, braving the incoming arrow and slingshot storm to hurl javelins and shoot arrows into the surging ranks of the attackers, moments later the first of the raiders fell.

A defender staggered drunkenly forward out of the narrowing gap in the gates, two raider's arrows protruding from his chest. Falling onto his hands and knees he didn't move quickly enough and the timber gate rode over him, wedging his body tightly beneath jamming its movement. His legs kicked, he screaming as the gate crushed his body between it and the ground as it tried to close. Seeing this, the attackers increased their speed, hurtling over the ground towards the gate like athletes striving for the finish line. However, as they stretched their bodies for speed, shield arms dropped to their sides making them easier targets for the defenders now thickening the wall. Men fell as the defenders missiles tore into them, sending them staggering and rolling headlong over and over in the dirt as momentum continued carrying them forward. Meanwhile, the man trapped under the gate died in a welter of blood and splintering bone as the gearing forced the huge doors closed, grinding his body into bloodied pulp as they did so.

With the attack underway, Baldor was left with no other choice than to go with it, though he'd little idea of what was truly happening. He felt out of control of his men and the situation and began to panic.

'Control it! Control yourself, Command! Baal almighty, take command!' His inner voice screamed.

He knew the Spaniards were in the fort now but what were the defenders doing, ready and awake? He realised the noise and signal from Tirus had alerted the men at the gate, stopping them opening it further, saving precious time and risk. Worst of all, he'd compounded all by delaying the advance overlong.

'Fool! You bloody fool!' He cursed himself. A vicious bang on his shield from a slingshot had him instinctively raise it higher covering his face. The impact jolted his forearm and left a deep imprint of the shot in the shield shocking him back into reality. He had a battle to fight, should he survive there would be more than enough time to examine his failings.

In the brief moments of thought, he and his troops had covered the dead ground to the base of the wall. The men were bunching up as siege ladders pushed through the ranks to be set against the walls. Shields raised aloft as rocks, arrows, javelins and the occasional dead defender hurtled earthward. Raising his shield he dashed from ladder to ladder encouraging and urging his men upward. Arrows and slingshot flew overhead from their flanks as Clitus and his men moved their attention from gate to parapet, this barrage hopefully keeping some heads down. Before the ladders made contact with the wall top, men clambered quickly up, shields' held in front of them. The more dextrous climbed or ran up the ladder with both hands holding shield and sword, the less agile climbed using one hand while sheltering behind their shield. Some fell as they climbed, either missing their footing or hit by a missile. With the attackers' scaling the walls Clitus's archers and slingers had to cease their salvos for fear of hitting their own men, with this respite the parapet thickened with defenders.

The warrior next to Baldor crumpled as a javelin hit him in the neck, bursting his throat open the hot blood splattering Baldor's face forcing him to blink and wipe his eyes. The man tried to scream but all that came out was a wet bubbling noise as he collapsed to his knees. Forked poles pushed out from the wall and the first ladders forced backwards away from the wall, sending the climbing men screaming and crashing into their comrades below. Undaunted, more ladders went up with men eager as ever to climb, risking death on the ladder was better than waiting for its surety on the ground.

The fight at the gateway was savage as the raiders heaved and pushed against the closing gates in a bid to force them. Probing spears thrust through the contested gap while rocks rained from the parapet. A deadly crossfire from the towers wreaked havoc causing the raiders to abandon their push and raise shields in defence.

Having advanced so quickly the warriors charily carrying the naphtha pots had fallen behind. Now, with men packed tightly about the gate they couldn't throw or win through to deposit and ignite them. Bloody chaos ensued, with ladders going up or crashing down, arrows, javelins and slingshot flying, bodies and rocks falling. The whistle and drone of missiles and the clash of weapons mixing with shouts, war cries and howls of agony. The volume and tempo rising as more men engaged, the noise like demented souls breaking loose from the gates of Hades.

****

Tirus led his men down the steps, the second group advancing down a stairway on his left. They quickly overcame the few defenders at the stair foot but not before some fled, raising the alarm as they went. With the need for silence gone, Tirus bellowed, urging the two groups to form up quickly. He was still bullying his men into line as the howling of dogs and clatter of hooves grew louder drowning his words. Before the two groups finished forming a shield wall, a pack of hunting dogs bounded around the corner coming straight for them at full speed.

"Form up! Close the …"

The dogs hit them like a fast, low wave of fur and fangs. Their weight and impetus knocking shield arms down allowing snarling, bared teeth to seek throats, arms and faces. The attackers became defenders, fighting to hold their ground as men staggered and fell as the dog's weight, speed and savagery knocked them off balance. As the ranks opened under the onslaught the dogs laid waste amongst them, like wolves amongst sheep, they ripped and tore. Men and animals died together amidst growls, war cries, howls and screams. Blood spurted and blades flashed as men hacked and stabbed and dogs bit, savaged and shook. Moments later Gallic horsemen arrived driving their mounts into gaps created by the dogs. The raiders, attacked now from the sides and front, dying from bites, trampled by hooves or cut down by the defenders.

Looking to his left, Tirus saw his men driven back up the stairs to the parapet. At the stair foot, bodies lay like a tide line of debris marking the limit of their advance. Men continued backing away up the stairs, limiting the dogs to attacking from the front. Here, the narrowness allowed three men to stand abreast behind their shields offering good defence against the canine terror. Those on the floor still showing signs of life were savaged by the dogs, the horsemen slaughtering any still standing. Tirus looked to his men of whom only a handful remained, his decision made he pointed a reddened falcata towards the parapet.

"Back! Fall back to the parapet! Out ... Out!"

The men needed no more telling. Horrified by the surprise and ferocity of the dogs they moved quickly to disengage. The more experienced backed towards the stairs while still fighting to their front, the less experienced who turned to run were speared by the horsemen or dragged down as dogs leapt onto their backs. Tirus stabbed viciously at a horse as it forced alongside him, he dodging sideways as the rider tried to spear him. The animal whickered horribly as his blade went deep then seemed to cough, cutting off its cry and collapsing onto its front legs as he twisted the blade and pulled it out. He stabbed up at the unbalanced rider, the sword rupturing his kidneys. As the man crumpled, Tirus pushed him towards the dogs coming his way as he edged back to the stairs. Frenzied by the scent and taste of blood the dogs went out of control and savaged the fallen Gaul then began attacking anyone, regardless of who they were. The battle between defender and raider forgotten as men fought to survive as dogs went berserk.

Making use of the added chaos Tirus hurried his men up the stairs, he acting as their rear-guard. On a landing halfway to the parapet, he turned to check his rear and saw a black, deerhound leap clear of the bodies and bound up the steps two at a time towards him. The dog was at full speed and coming straight for him like an arrow. Its lips pulled back showing yellowed fangs, eyes narrowed to slits as it prepared for the impact. Tirus squatted low on the landing, his left leg extended onto the lower step for balance. Bracing himself he angled his shield over his body while pulling his falcata back low ready to stab. The dog seemed to fly up the last few steps then scrabbled up his shield, its weight pushing down, its claws scratching and raking the smooth surface as it strove to reach him. He grunted as the dog's weight came down on his arm, his face a hands breadth from the snacking maw and foul stink of its breath. He thrust hard; stabbing behind its front leg and the animal's snarl diminished into a gasp as the sword burst its lungs and found its heart. Slumping and snacking futilely at the air, it rolled off the shield back down half a dozen steps taking Tirus's blade with it.

Looking past the dying dog to the base of the stairs, he saw the Gauls now engaged defending themselves from their dogs and that no immediate pursuit was forming. Looking up, he saw his men were clear of the stairs and running along the parapet towards the ropes. Two men were on their way back towards him calling frantically.

"Come on sir! Come on!"

Nodding and slinging the shield over his back, he took the last few stairs two at a time, the two warriors helping him up the last step and onto the walkway. At the ropes he urged them over the wall while taking a sword from one of them turning back to cover their retreat. Below, the Gauls had killed, driven off or brought their dogs under control but were in no state to chase him and his men further. With a final look around, he sheathed the sword and climbed over the wall onto the rope.

On the front wall, there was still no sign of a secure foothold and men continued to fall as ladders were pushed over or the men themselves hurled and beaten back from the parapet.

Baldor had fallen from a ladder as it was pushed away and landed badly winded. Shaken and gasping for breath he sought another but found he had to queue at the base amongst the chaos, slaughter and milling warriors. Looking around at the ensuing bedlam he saw the attack was slowing, though men still wished to climb if only to be free of the nerve shattering waiting. Arrows, rocks and javelins rained down incessantly, banging off shields like metal hail, every so often finding a gap and another man fell. There were fewer ladders now, most having broken as they were pushed from the wall. Thus, the defenders were able to commit more men to any point where they saw a ladder going up.

He saw his men's actions changing from belligerently offensive to defensive. The attack was stalling, losing ferocity and impetus as men fought to stay alive and survive. The tide of battle was flowing against them and he quickly considered his options. Blinking to clear the sweat that streamed from under his helmet, he instinctively ducked as the head of the man next to him exploded when a slingshot burst it like a ripe melon. Grimacing and swearing, he wiped the hot blood and grey-jelly substance that splattered his face, neck and corselet. Horrified at the carnage and chaos and for which he felt responsible he realised enough was enough. He knew now what Hannibal meant about experience teaching him and he grabbed his signaller roughly by the shoulder.

"Sound the withdrawal, now!"

The man raised the horn to his lips and blew the first notes of the recall. He stopped abruptly, the sound becoming disjointed and awry as a javelin thumped into his chest, driving the breath from him and dropping him to his knees. Baldor reached out to help him but the man was already dead. Dropping his instrument his head lolled and his body pitched forward. The javelin butt stuck in the ground preventing his collapse propping him upright, dead on his knees. Baldor swore viciously then called out.

"Withdraw! Withdraw!"

The men closest to him took up the call and soon it repeated along the lines. Men, already nearing breaking point began backing away, those on the ladders stopped their ascent and climbed backwards else turned to jump. Blood lust was replaced with hope of survival and living for another day and on both sides men began to disengage. The raiders backed away helping and dragging their injured with them, shields held towards the fort as missiles continued to rain down from the walls. With most ladders down, Clitus and his men again brought their missiles to bear on any defenders visible and still firing at the retreating men. With the chance of killing or injuring their own men gone, they sent heavy showers of arrows and slingshot to rake the wall top. Having divided his men into ranks he was using each in turn giving the others time to reload. The first few salvoes claimed dozens of lives before the defenders realised that to show themselves was to court death. Taking cover below the parapet, they remained there, wisely letting the raiders retreat without further harassment.

With the raiders almost out of range of the walls and no further sign of defenders, Clitus ceased the barrage. With the whoosh of the arrows and whine of slingshot stopped an eerie calm settled over the field. Heads cautiously poked above the parapet again and the defenders broke into ragged cheers as they watched the attackers retreat. As the taunts and jeers subsided, the only sounds were cries of pain or the begging for help that came from the injured and dying at the foot of the walls. Bodies littered the ground like autumn leaves, lying thickly around the ladders else scattered singly or in small groups in others. Dead men draped the parapet, some hanging like broken puppets from the few ladders that still leaned against the wall. The wall resembled a pincushion with a mass of brightly fletched arrows protruding from it, along with dozens of white, pockmarked scars where slingshot had blown the bark away exposing new timber beneath. With the sun barely clear of the hills, the battle had been short but ferocious. What should have been a soft target full of sleeping defenders had instead transpired into a viciously fought action, what had gone wrong?

Baldor had the Carthaginian standard raised near the trees, marking the site as his headquarters and serving as a rallying point for his men. Having travelled fast and light they'd brought no tents or shelters, thus the officers briefing like the men's sleeping arrangements would be in the open air. He sent a runner to find his officers and bring them to him at the standard by midday. Seeing Andulas and his men returning, he directed them back towards the gate, having them form ranks once more in case the defenders dared sally out attempting to turn the retreat into a rout. Sick to the stomach and feeling the strain he turned back to the standard where he saw men drifting towards it in ones, twos or small groups. Some came staggering or limping, using spears as crutches else supporting and carrying their wounded or dying comrades, all looked despondent and beaten. The plight of the injured and the pitiful cries coming from those left on the field tore at Baldor's nerves while he wracked his brains as to what to do next.

'Secure your rear … see to the injured … regroup … screen your retreat.'

The military lessons drummed into him over the winter battered his head. Was this the correct order? Did he have things right? What about the men? What should he do from here? What had gone so badly wrong? His head spun.

His medical orderlies were already at work assessing the injured, seeking those they deemed had a chance of survival, leaving those who were beyond help and for whom Elysium was calling. The orderlies plugged wounds and applied bandages, working quickly to staunch any blood flow. The few surgeons Baldor had were already underway with amputations. As always, there were too many casualties; too much pain and not enough surgeons, orderlies or time, to save those who shook, whimpered and bled.

Fighting to separate his emotions from rational thinking and steeling himself against the screams of the wounded, he took a deep breath trying to retake command. With Andulas watching the gate and their rear, he waited for Clitus, Tirus and Tuireann to appear. He had the line closers form small units from the uninjured, dispatching them back towards the wall as defensive screens while keeping them safely out of bowshot. Very quickly, order began to appear on the field and the defenders made acutely aware that though they'd won or perhaps survived the attack, the raiders were regrouping and still very much a force to be reckoned with. Seeing order coming out of chaos Baldor felt his resolve strengthening and with his rear well secured, he could look to his men. He turned to an adjutant.

"I want a list of the dead, wounded and those likely to survive and those not!"

"Yes sir."

Tuireann and his men arrived. All were battered bloody and looking physically despondent from their defeat and having to abandon most of their wounded as they retreated from the fort.

"Tuireann, it's good to see you!" Baldor called though there was little warmth in his words, the sentiment offered from politeness rather than sincerity. "We'll meet for council at midday, have your men who are still fit for duty aid the orderlies with the injured, they'll tell you what they need in that regard. Detail some to find and fetch more water and prepare food, we all need to eat."

Tuireann's face clouded like a thunderstorm waiting to break. Ignoring Baldor's orders, he approached quickly. His words coming out fiercely as his anger boiled over and he snatched Baldor's arm pulling him around to face him.

"Damn you, Carthaginian! Damn you for changing the plan." He spat.

Baldor was shocked by Tuireann's aggression but with his own nerves still raw and adrenalin still coursing through his veins; his response was just as vehement.

"Enough Tuireann! Do not! … Do not, dare to chastise me in front of the men!"

He shook the restraining arm loose while his outburst saw Tuireann step back and reach for his broadsword. Before the Gaul had pulled his blade a palm's width from its sheath Baldor had drawn both falcatas. One now pointed at Tuireann's throat with the other held low ready to disembowel him.

"Go further, Tuireann and I'll kill you were you stand!"

The Gaul froze, leaving his sword barely drawn. The sunlight glimmered brightly on the two falcatas as Baldor watched him, searching his eyes for intent and his face for any tremor that might betray movement. Tuireann returned the stare for a moment, his eyes burning like fanned coals, his mouth twisted in a hateful sneer. He slowly pushed the sword back in its sheath and moved his hand away from the hilt.

Baldor lowered his falcatas though he never took his eyes from the Gaul. Composing his words, he spoke quietly.

"I'll hear what you have to say once the men are seen to and when Andulas, Tirus and Clitus are here; not before! At that council you can have your say but try to do it here in front of the men and I will kill you … do you understand?"

Tuireann's eyes continued to smoulder, his anger and hatred toward Baldor barely controlled.

"Do you understand?" Baldor hissed.

Tuireann gave a nod and a long contemptuous look then turned on his heel shouting orders as he went.

Chapter Twenty seven

Tirus was already spluttering apologies as he approached Baldor at double pace. Both he and his men gasping for breath having made their escape over the wall and retreating quickly, lest they be hit by archers or slingers who'd made the parapet.

"I'm sorry sir, sorry! We were over the wall and down, we damn near had the bastards …"

"It's alright Tirus! There's no fault on your part, it was …"

"But we were in, down on the fort floor sir." He continued his regret, his tone bitter as bile. "Those bloody hunting dogs! Damn it! … Damn …"

"We picked the wrong day." Baldor said with a sad smile. "That's all, we picked the wrong day, combined with me changing the plan and sending you in there."

"No sir! And with respect, I won't accept that! That was a good idea! A good plan! It would have worked save for the bastards deciding to go hunting and those damned dogs! We were that close to success." He held up forefinger and thumb showing a small gap between them. "I tell you sir that close! There was nothing wrong with the plan."

Baldor offered Tirus a water skin and clasped him warmly on the shoulder. He was deeply touched by the sincerity and loyalty, if all else had failed he still had a good and true man in Tirus.

"Thank you for your brave efforts, Tirus and those of your men. I rejoice to see you alive and uninjured. Now, rest awhile and catch your breath. We've redeployed and are secure, at least for the moment, have your injured attended by the orderlies."

Baldor pointed to where the wounded were being treated then looked quickly at Tirus's men to see how many were hurt, seeing only minor wounds he then noticed how few there were. Tirus saw him look and reading his thoughts gestured him out of earshot of the men.

"In truth sir, there's way too few of us left, they hit us hard! Horses, dogs and men! All very much awake, however it could've been worse! … I'm sorry! We'd no time to bring our wounded out, though in truth I don't think many survived the dogs."

Baldor nodded slowly, not daring to speak his dread thoughts. He fidgeted with the marble at his throat then stopped, trying to remain composed and above all a commander, who though in trouble was still in control. His mind raced as he calculated the losses to Tirus's command and the worsening situation. He cleared his throat to ensure his words came out unfalteringly and certain, though his tone was grave.

"I don't envisage any reprisals from the Cenomani yet. We've shocked and no doubt hurt them badly; they'll be licking their wounds too. Once we've assessed our losses and heard from Andulas, Tuireann and Clitus I'll decide our next move."

Tirus took another gulp of water and nodded wiping his hand across his mouth before passing the skin to his comrades behind him. Both men knew the best chance for success was now gone. They didn't have the time or manpower for a siege but with the element of surprise lost there seemed no other options. Baldor felt physically sick as he realised failure or at best stalemate, seemed the only outcome now. If only he hadn't changed the plan, if only he hadn't hesitated? If only the God's didn't hate him so.

With his confidence shattered he felt very young, inexperienced and frighteningly alone. He was out of his depth with the situation and responsibility of it all and while his men looked to him for orders and guidance, he wished with all his heart that someone would guide him. Realising he was torturing himself; he decided, what was done, was done and nothing could undo it. His energies best employed trying to salvage something from the day and think a way forward.

He made his way to where the injured were being treated. He wasn't sure if he went because it was what a good commander should do or from guilt and compassion for his brothers in arms. He saw the less injured first, those who were already treating themselves and managing to bind and tend their own wounds. Orderlies ministered to the more badly hurt, working quickly to reset broken bones, wash and clean wounds and stitch flesh closed. Some were beyond help and had been made as comfortable as possible as their life slipped and bled away. Others panted trying to ease their pain, some cried like children as if they could bear the pain no more. Those wounded in the belly were the worst, they convulsed as if poisoned their hands trying to stop their guts spilling out. They begged incessantly for water, drinking it as quickly as it was given, despite the orderlies trying to limit them to sips. Some coughed and spat blood, mumbling red-flecked words and tortured cries then mercifully died, while others lingered oblivious to all but their agony. Baldor helped where he could, though he felt awkward, almost a nuisance, as he knew little of wounds and treatments. He did notice that the men he spoke to or helped seemed to draw comfort from it. His presence and concern must mean something? At least it was moral support, from a commander to his soldiers. He sent for more men to help as he made his way across to where the surgeons were busy.

He saw pairs of men carrying limp bodies, which they laid in neat rows alongside others lying still as stone. Most were half-dressed where armour and clothing had been removed to allow treatment or amputation, many had died of shock, else bled to death as the amputations cut main arteries and the surgeon couldn't staunch the flow. Blood was everywhere; over the bodies, the grass and the men who carried the dead, while the surgeons looked as if they'd bathed in it. Their hands and arms red to the armpits as if painted, their faces and hair splattered with crimson spots and spray marks.

Baldor looked at one man, his eyes wide and staring yet seeing nothing, he whimpered and begged the Gods for mercy and to take the pain away. His leg was smashed in numerous places, the splintered bones sharp and yellowish-white where they'd burst through the skin. The surgeon lifted a large knife, placing a bone saw within easy reach then gestured for the man to be held still. Like a carpenter checking timber before making his cut, he eyed the leg then laid the blade on the flesh.

"Hold him steady!"

The man let out a blood-curdling scream as the knife sliced deeply into his leg, the muscle twitched as the blade drowned in a welter of blood. The man thrashed and moaned like a chained demon, the veins in his neck standing out like worms beneath the skin. He strained and heaved against the men struggling to hold him down until mercifully passing out. The surgeon quickly picked up the saw inserting it into the knife cut. It bucked and jumped until the teeth wore into the bone after which he sawed smoothly and evenly as if cutting a log. As limb and body separated, Baldor looked away but forced himself to remain alongside as the surgeon applied a tourniquet to stanch the blood flow.

"Next!" The surgeon called as he hefted the leg onto a growing pile of destroyed limbs.

The man was lifted to one side. The orderlies binding the leg in linen then elevating it on a discarded helmet, his survival in the hands of the Gods.

Baldor noticed two men quietly and methodically working their way amongst the injured as if assessing them, he noticed they picked out the most badly hurt. Nodding to one another in discreet and quiet agreement one approached the selected body from the front while the other came from the rear. They gently raised the wounded to a sitting position while speaking quietly and reassuringly, though most they approached were incoherent, being delirious or unconscious with pain. The man at the front lifted the injured warrior's head up, supporting and placing his own face alongside the man's cheek while whispering a blessing in his ear. His partner carefully positioned a bronze rod as thick as a man's thumb and half the length of a man's forearm, against the base of the injured man's skull where the spinal column connected. Hefting a hammer, he struck the rod hard, driving it against the bone. The dry sound of a breaking branch followed, the injured man pitching forward into the arms of the man in front who laid him gently down. Bowing their heads and mumbling a prayer, they moved on, seeking more whom the surgeons couldn't save.

Baldor stared at the blood, the injured, the dead, and the growing pile of body parts. His nose assailed by the stench of gore, urine and faeces, his ears ringing with cries of the injured and the dying. The place resembled a butcher's yard on market day and he felt sick to the stomach. This was all madness, madness beyond belief and he was the orchestrator of it all. He thought of the women and children anxiously awaiting a husband or father and of the mothers who would weep rivers and tear their hair as their son's body was brought home.

Home? Where was home? He hadn't been home since … since? What was he doing here? Amongst this chaos, slaughter and dying. He couldn't command these men or cope with this pressure, this responsibility, this task given him by his General. His world seemed to close in on him, tightening his chest and stealing his breath. His heart thumped and pulse quickened until he could hear a drum-like pounding in his ears. Sinking to madness like a man drowning, he felt a hand clasping his forearm and looked up to find Andulas. Andulas was speaking but no sound came from his lips. Baldor stared as if in a dream, slowly the words found volume.

"Sir? … Baldor sir! Come … all is as you wish on the field, we're secured and awaiting your next orders."

Baldor didn't seem to comprehend and stared as if in a trance.

"Sir? … Baldor … Tirus, Tuireann and Clitus are waiting for you."

"What? Who?"

Andulas realised the affect the injured were having on Baldor's mind. He'd seen and experienced it when he'd had to go amongst his people and sort the living from the dead. He knew Baldor would be holding himself responsible for all of it and though he'd fought many times, this was his first time in sole command and that burden often rested heavy. Sorting the injured and the dying was traumatic after a victory but coupled to a defeat it was harrowing.

"Andulas?"

"Yes sir! I'm here. We're secure and await your orders."

Baldor didn't reply immediately, he seemed to be trying to understand the words. Andulas offered him a wineskin, which he accepted but remained motionless, appearing lost.

"Drink sir, it'll help." He said, quietly pushing the skin gently towards Baldor's mouth.

Baldor stared blankly as if in another world. He removed his helmet, passing it to Andulas as he massaged his sweat soaked temples. He shuddered as if a sudden chill passed through him; taking a grip of himself, he drained the liquid in huge gulps like a man lost in a baking desert. He stopped and gasped for breath inhaling deeply, eventually the breaths grew smaller and regulated while wine trickled from the corners of his mouth running off his chin. Wiping it with the back of his hand his eyes livened and Andulas saw recognition returning.

"Andulas! Forgive me, I needed a moment."

"There's nothing to forgive sir, we're secure and await your orders is all." Smiling reassuringly, he gestured Baldor back towards the standard and main body of men. As they walked, Baldor began taking control of himself asking for a situation report and casualty numbers.

"The fort's quiet sir, they watch from the towers but do nothing. The injured we managed to carry away are being treated, though we've yet to reclaim our dead and wounded from the field."

Baldor listened in silence, his head bowing in sorrow as he asked the dread question.

"What of our losses?"

Andulas took a breath, his hesitation confirming Baldor's fears; the losses were heavy.

"We've counted those who are here, the able, the injured and the dead. The missing are presumed still on the field and badly wounded or most likely dead, we've added them to that ..."

"I need to ask if we can retrieve my men's bodies." Baldor interrupted quietly.

Andulas said nothing but chewed his lip and looked to the ground.

"Your pardon Andulas ... the numbers of our fallen?"

"The archers and slingers under Clitus are intact with no casualties."

Baldor nodded. "The good Clitus! His support during the attack was excellent and his covering of our ..." Baldor sought the right word. "Our withdrawal, well executed, without which ... the others Andulas, what of the others?"

"Yes sir, the others. Tirus lost forty-nine men in the fortress, those who returned are for the most sound, though some are walking wounded. Tuireann bore the brunt of the casualties with one hundred and sixteen dead and thirty-one badly wounded."

"And yourself and your men Andulas? What have I done to them?"

Andulas looked at Baldor seeing the regret and blame in his eyes and the terrible responsibility that seemed to weigh him down.

"I have twenty-nine dead and six wounded, sir."

Baldor groaned and stared blankly as his mind worked the maths. Calculating he'd lost just over a quarter of his force with one hundred and ninety four dead or missing and thirty-seven wounded.

"Most of the wounded are unlikely to recover sir. I've not counted those with minor wounds and still able to fight. This … this just makes it a little more difficult to take the fortress is all?" He spoke positively as he made the last remark.

Quietly appreciating the support, Baldor motioned Andulas to where Tirus, Tuireann and Clitus waited at the standard. As they approached, Tirus and Clitus stepped forward offering their hands and thanks to the Gods that Baldor and Andulas had survived. Tuireann remained stationary his arms folded and face sullen. The pair stared at one another for a moment, their eyes cold as a winters morn and in stark contrast to the empathy passed among the others moments before. The group fell silent, all feeling the tension and mutual dislike emanating from the two men. With a herculean effort, Baldor swallowed his pride putting his mission and command before his personal feelings and offered his hand in friendship.

"Tuireann, it's good to see you well." He spoke politely but feeling hypocritical struggled to sound sincere.

The Gauls arms remained folded, his eyes smouldering. A nerve in his cheek twitched his disdain for Baldor clear. Baldor's hand remained extended, though his temper began to flare from the insult.

"Tuireann, your hand!" Andulas snapped.

Tuireann ignored him and Baldor lowered his hand. Tirus and Clitus eyed one another then looked back to Tuireann. Baldor moistened his lips to speak.

"We still have a problem between us then, Tuireann?"

"I have no problem! I'm withdrawing my men from this chaos and from your command before you slay us all!"

"You will not!" Andulas interrupted hotly. Stepping in front of Tuireann his finger pointed accusingly. "They're not your men they're our fathers! You but command …"

"Command! There's the essence brother! Command! Thus, I can and will command they withdraw." He retorted angrily.

Andulas's brows furrowed. Biting back the rebuke and making an effort not to lose his temper he lowered his voice attempting to reason with his sibling.

"We're here to finish this feud once and for all. These men …" He gestured to Tirus, Clitus and Baldor. "These men are helping make it possible!"

"Hah! Helping us be slaughtered more like!"

"Enough!" Baldor shouted. Stopping the diatribe, he lowered his voice to a harsh whisper. "Not in front of the men damn it! Their spirits are low enough! They need to see confidence and cohesion not hot tempers and squabbling children! Now, for the love of Baal, enough! I'm in command here. No one's leaving and we're going to take that fortress, one way or another!"

He looked around at his commanders in turn then asked questioningly.

"Andulas! … Agreed?"

"Agreed sir!"

"Tirus! …Agreed?"

"Agreed sir, I owe them bastards for my lads!"

Baldor remembered the protocols and looked at Tuireann.

"Tuireann! Setting our differences apart for now …" He held up his hand sharply, silencing Tuireann trying to interrupt. "Which we can settle later and on that, you have my word!" He emphasised heavily as he was still smarting from the insult in front of his officers. "Are you agreed?"

"He's agreed!" Andulas cut in quickly while glaring threateningly at his half-brother.

Baldor ignored Andulas, staring balefully at Tuireann. When he didn't respond Baldor continued, his tone level but heavy with malice.

"When this is over, seek me out and we'll settle this with blades. We'll let the God's decide who's right and wrong? If I've hastened men to Elysium before their time the Gods will judge it so, if not you'll pay for the insult! Now, I ask you for the final time, are you agreed?"

Surprised by Baldor's sudden assertiveness and the lack of support for himself by his peers, Tuireann grudgingly muttered agreement. Baldor pressed him further.

"You agree to the continuation of the attack?"

"I just said that I did!" He snarled.

"And you agree to the settling of our differences?" Baldor pushed again.

"I agree!" Tuireann's lip curled back as he spoke.

Baldor offered his hand again while looking him straight in the eye. "I agree!" He said with finality.

The command group looked awkward as they watched Baldor's hand hovering in mid-air and open once again. Tuireann stared, his eyes full of fire and his cheek twitching slightly, his arms still folded across his chest.

"I'll not offer my hand again, Tuireann! Take it damn you! The men are watching and they need to see unity amongst us."

Tuireann slowly unfolded his arms, deliberately stretching the tension, leaving Baldor feeling awkward before unhurriedly placing his hand into Baldor's. There was an audible exhaling of breath from the others as the two finally shook hands. Tuireann tried to snatch his away quickly; Baldor however held it vice like, saying politely.

"Thank you for this Tuireann, thank you but I'll see you ere this battle's won, you have my word upon it!"

Tuireann's face twisted as he snatched his hand back, this time Baldor let it go.

"Now gentlemen onto matters military; despite our setback we still have much to our advantage." Baldor spoke positively, trying to instil confidence and enthusiasm into his officers just as he had seen Hannibal do. "We're secure for the moment and have the Cenomani contained. They'll be shocked and wondering about our numbers and if more are coming in support, for all they know we could be the vanguard of the Carthaginian army. I doubt they're able to withstand a long siege, having just come out of winter they'll have little food left in the fortress, so, I envisage they'll be keen to fight to drive us of. Remember also, their numbers are down from their casualties at the Trebbia. Therefore, their ignorance of the situation, a weakness in numbers and shortage of food will help us win. I know it's easier said than done, but this time we plan it better and keep it simple but for now, our most important issue is our casualties."

Andulas, knowing the numbers cradled his chin looking thoughtful while the others became yet more attentive.

"Our casualties' amount to one hundred and ninety four dead and thirty seven wounded, in total just over quarter of our force." Though the men said nothing, Baldor noticed their concern from their body language and continued quickly. "And though a setback, this won't prevent us prosecuting this siege to a successful conclusion. After the men have eaten and rested, we'll spend this afternoon preparing for another assault tomorrow and as I said, we'll be better prepared his time. The men carrying naphtha must have a clear view of the walls so it can be hurled without risk to our own, we'll batter the gates to splinters or burn them down, one way or another we'll take that fortress. Andulas! Collect the naphtha, I want you and your men responsible for that, burn the walls down for me!"

"Yes sir."

"Tirus, tomorrow I want some diversions around the walls, no assaults this time, just movement. Let yourself be seen and keep them guessing as to where and when another assault is coming. They'll have to sacrifice men to watch you and any strength taken away from the gates will help."

"Sir."

"Tuireann, find the siege engineers and supply them with manpower to build a battering ram. Just a simple affair mind! A tree trunk with sufficient handles for men to carry it."

Tuireann nodded but showed neither enthusiasm nor disdain for the order.

"We don't have time to build a Vineae over it for shelter so I'm relying again on you, Clitus to keep the parapet clear of defenders and cover Tuireann's men."

"Consider it done sir." The old Cretan smiled.

"You've sufficient arrows and slingshot? For the gates look to be of stout timber, this battering may take some time?"

"I'll check again sir though I'm sure we've sufficient. I purposefully overestimated the supplies we brought for I believe in too much rather than too little." He smiled again.

"You're a good man Clitus! Gentlemen, questions?"

"Do we attack at dawn again, sir?" Tirus asked.

"Have you considered a night assault sir?" Andulas asked. "They may not expect a second attack in the same day. The reduced visibility would disguise our numbers and perhaps reduce our casualties?"

The question raised some murmurs of support.

Baldor nodded while looking thoughtfully at both men. "Yes, to the dawn assault Tirus and yes Andulas, a night assault's a good idea for all the reasons that you state, but my answer is no, no to a full assault anyway."

The men looked at Baldor sensing a plan forming.

"Settle the men and let them rest ready for the morrow. However, I want four separate groups of ten men to raise a little trouble at different periods throughout the night thus ensuring the fortress doesn't sleep. If we're probing their defences I'd imagine they'll think we're all still up and about."

"And therefore less likely to assault them come the morning?" Tirus added with a grin.

"Hopefully yes! Let's keep them awake while most of us sleep."

"Who's to lead the groups, sir?" Clitus asked.

"I will. I think you have all done enough for one day."

"You'll need some help, sir." Tirus ventured.

"Thank you but no. Rest! All of you, you've earned it. Take this fort for me tomorrow and I'll be eternally grateful."

"When will you sleep, sir?" Andulas asked.

"When this fort is no more. Now! I want our dead back."

****

Shortly after midday, Tirus along with a Gallic interpreter carrying a spear with the shaft whitened by chalk and a Standard-bearer carrying the gold circle and crescent of Carthage made their way across the open ground towards the fortress gate. Baldor had deemed to go in person until Andulas explained that, being the commander of a host he should not be seen to negotiate with a robber Chief. The Cenomani would see it only as elevating the status of Lugobelinos. Furthermore, as blood feud existed between the Lingones and the Cenomani, he or Tuireann would be killed on sight were they to go, regardless of the white spear. Tirus had offered to go, citing that Clitus would be required to organise covering fire should the situation sour, Baldor had reluctantly agreed.

The three men walked slowly, noting their approach being relayed by sentries dashing along the parapet followed by a general 'stand-to' sounding in the fort. Approaching bow range, they slowed their pace then stopped. The interpreter held the whitened spear vertically at arm's length in front of him then turned it point downward. They waited and watched the walls. There was more movement on the parapet but no verbal response. The white spear was rotated slowly through ninety degrees to horizontal then lifted above their heads.

With this symbol for conciliatory talks displayed, Tirus motioned them forward.

"Let's move but keep it slow!"

As they moved off, Tirus felt the hair rising on the nape of his neck and his skin taking on a prickly feeling. His chest muscles tightened as if expecting to be hit by an arrow, his feet feeling as if he walked through clay. Coming within bowshot there was still no challenge from the fort and thankfully no arrows.

"Baal Almighty!" He hissed through gritted teeth. "See me through this, gracious Lord and I'll sacrifice my last drop of wine to you, I swear it! ... They're either prepared to listen else making certain they cannot miss!"

He saw the interpreters eyes were closed as he mumbled his prayers a glance to the Standard-bearer saw the young man stony faced but perspiring heavily, the beads of sweat like dewdrops on his cheeks and chin.

"Steady lads!" He mumbled trying to sound confident. "If they wanted to kill us we'd be dead already."

Coming closer to the fortress he saw the carnage of bodies, limbs and discarded weapons from the morning's assault and the winter grass stained dark with blood. Men lay twisted and broken where ladders had collapsed, some that died near the walls squashed and misshapen were rocks had smashed heads to pulp or crushed bodies. The afternoon sun, which brought a little heat, also brought the stink of death, vomit and excrement from burst bodies and leaking bowels, along with the first black clouds of buzzing flies. High above, red and black kites circled lazily, riding the thermals their wings stretched wide. Below, the crows and ravens were already stalking tentatively about the bodies before hopping up to peck, pull and gulp at entrails and eyes. A sudden whoosh and thump saw an arrow quivering in the ground a few paces ahead, the men stopped and stood motionless.

"Come any closer and we'll feather you!" A voice boomed from the fort.

The interpreter left his prayers and cleared his throat to speak. Despite feeling like a game bird caught in front of the hunters, Tirus stood proudly, gesturing the Standard-bearer to do likewise. The young man having to rest the staff on the ground to disguise his shaking hands.

"What do you want?" Came from the parapet.

The interpreter translated quickly and quietly to Tirus and the Diatribe began.

"We come to ask for our dead? We'll come unarmed if you'll allow us take them for their funerary rites."

"They stay where they lie till they rot and stink to high heaven!" The voice rolled over the sward and the men like approaching thunder. Lugobelinos, resplendent in bronze helmet and mail shirt stood on the parapet, dwarfing his men and seeming out of proportion with all around him. "Who are you anyway, that dare come hammering at my door and setting about my people, then asking meekly for your dead?"

"We're of the army of General Hannibal of Carthage, whom you fought at the Trebbia."

"Carthaginians eh!" Lugobelinos said contemptuously then hawked and spat over the wall. "I see you have your lick-spittle, lap dogs the Lingones with you as well."

"All this is immaterial, we ask only for your leave to collect our dead, nothing more."

There was no immediate response and with both he and his men's nerves fraying Tirus sought to speed a decision. "It would go easier for you if you let us take them, for when we overrun your fortress you may wish to seek our clemency?"

Lugobelinos's face coloured.

"You dare to threaten me?" He roared stepping forward, his hands grasping the top of the wall. "I'm the Lord of these hills and valleys and I say your dead stay where they lie, let the wolves and birds eat! Now, begone! Ere I send you to join them."

Tirus cursed softly as he motioned his party to retire then gasped as two broad head arrows hit him high in the chest, his leather corselet no defence at the short range.

"Mother … al …mighty!"

He staggered with the impact, groaned then fell to his knees his hands clutching at the Standard-bearer for support. The interpreter stepped bravely forward holding the spear up while shouting his objections loudly, Lugobelinos shouted him down.

"No one threatens or speaks to me so in my own land, white spear or not! I'll warn you no more, begone! You're trying my patience!"

Tirus fought for breath and coughed blood as the interpreter and the Standard-bearer lifted him to his feet, helping him back towards their lines. They weren't out of bowshot when Baldor and the others met them, having ran towards them when they saw Tirus fall. Arrows began to fall in front of them as the Cenomani archers sought the range. Shields raised to shelter the group and with the extra hands helping carry Tirus, they were soon out of bowshot once more.

Tirus coughed and gasped, his words gargled and wet. The arrows were in deep, perforating his lungs, drowning him slowly in his own blood. Baldor motioned the men to put him down though they had to sit him up to help him breathe. Baldor grasped his hand and tried to quieten him while calling for an orderly. Tirus beckoned him close mumbling through bloodied bubbles while sucking air like a drowning man.

"Ki ... kill ... the ... bastard ... for ..."

His grip slackened on Baldor's arm and his eyes rolled back. He laid quiet and still, the blood colouring his neck and chest red. Baldor ran his fingers over Tirus's eyes closing them. He lowered his head holding his closed fist to his heart in salute.

"Look after him." He said quietly as he stood and walked back towards the Carthaginian lines a low growl in his throat.

Chapter Twenty eight

Baldor found a quiet place in the sun a little way from his warriors the crying wounded and the madness. Un-slinging his falcatas and dropping them at his feet he pulled at his helmet strap cursing under his breath. Dropping it carelessly next to the swords, he sat heavily, pulling his legs under him crossing them for comfort. Ever mindful of appearances to his men he resisted the temptation to place his head in his hands; instead, resting elbows on his knees cradling his chin in his hands, deep in thought.

His throat ached with anger and stress and he bit his lip hard to stop the tears he felt welling up. Tirus had been a friend and a brave warrior and they had grown close over the winter months but now, like everyone else Baldor befriended he was gone. Despite the lump of skin he'd bitten from his lip and the bitter taste of blood on his tongue, tears filled his eyes stinging them and blurring his vision. The tears pooled then flooded; coursing through the grime and dried blood on his cheeks, feeling hot at first then with the cool breath of the breeze, chilled icy-cold as they trickled through his matted beard. The hate building in his heart seethed like a pot on the boil and he knew that when his temper rose to such levels, destruction and murder was his answer. His lips curled back baring, gritted teeth and he cursed again. The battle was turning to blood feud and he wanted to tear the Cenomani fortress down with his bare hands and slay Lugobelinos to ease his pain.

'Keep your temper Baldor! Do you hear?' The words slipped into his mind like tendrils of smoke, yet he clearly remembered the day they were spoken. That fateful day, a day that seemed so long ago, when Gestix cautioned him before he fought Adharbal Samilcar in the market square at Icosium. He'd won that fight but only after heeding the big Gaul's advice.

What had reminded him of this now? Was it fate prompting him to think rationally? Cautioning him before he committed to action, to make him use his wits and guard against rashness, thus saving men's lives and most likely he reasoned, his own? He didn't know any more, it was difficult to think straight, he was tired physically and mentally, his body ached and his head spun as if from too much wine. It was hard to envisage anything beyond the next few moments. He did know he was weary of battle and the burden of command, weary of the incessant slaughter, burying his friends and grieving for them. He also knew that this was the way of war and that it had been his choice alone to commit to such. He remembered Gestix's words of caution to think carefully about the commitment and connotations involved in soldiering. The deaths of those close to him however had not been in those thoughts, had he been so young and foolish to think that he and all those he knew were going to survive unscathed? Deeming himself both foolish and pig headed he answered his own question, which did nothing to ease his sorrow nor calm his temper until another voice pervaded his thoughts.

'You're an officer now, whether you like it or not … the men will look to you for direction and leadership. Remember! There are more lives than just yours to consider … mind it!'

Those words spoken by Armaco in recrimination and anger at Baldor's reckless breach of orders, which had prompted the fight at the Lingones fishing village and he remembered, the reason for them being here today. He shook his head in remorse; surely, he was the harbinger of his own troubles and most likely his doom. He wondered again at the mystery of Armaco's disappearance but also the significance of his words to the situation he found himself in. He had men's lives to consider! Yes, he was charged with destroying Victumulae but also with bringing as many men back alive as possible;

'So think Baldor! Think! Use your head and reason a way out of this.'

This time the voice came from deep within and he redirected his anger at himself.

'Enough of the self-pity, you have a duty and men to lead, so go to it!'

Undoing his neck cloth he wiped away the tears then dampened it with water from his bottle and cleaned the grime and blood from his face. Using a finger to block one nostril then the other in turn, he blew a stream of thick mucus onto the grass. Taking a deep breath, he refitted his helmet and looped the falcatas over his shoulders just as Andulas came up.

"Your orders sir?"

"Same as before Andulas." He said firmly. "Though I'll have to use another to lead in place of Tirus." He saw the regret on Andulas's face for he too had grown close to Tirus as the units trained together over the winter. "They'll suffer for what they did." He pointed towards the fortress. "Tirus was unarmed and under protection of the white spear, we'll repay the Cenomani for his murder, you have my word on it!"

The afternoon remained mild and bright as Baldor made a tour of his men. He still felt awkward as he pushed among the ranks and the resting groups and it was equally difficult for him to talk encouragingly or optimistically as neither trait was congruent with his character. Some said nothing while others just smiled, some apologised for their failure to take the walls. The apologies he waved away, speaking of the sure to follow success while trying to sound quietly confident.

He found the siege engineers with the assistance of Tuireann's men had already felled and de-limbed a pine tree to build the battering ram as commanded. They swarmed about it like soldier ants, each group intent on their given tasks. Some fed and stoked a fire while monitoring a dozen, spear length iron pokers. Each as thick as a man's wrist and which had been set to heat in the glowing embers. One of the engineers, clad in leather apron and hands covered in thick leather gauntlets used the poker tip to gradually burn holes through the trunk. The timber smoked and hissed as the metal boiled the sap, when the poker cooled he passed it back for re-heating, setting to with another deepening the hole further. Warriors cut and trimmed the straightest limbs before stripping the bark, fitting them through the holes forming a handle on either side of the trunk. The limb was bound with rope affording a handgrip and preventing the handle moving back through the log. The odour of fresh timber, pine resin and greenwood smoke cleared their noses and stung their eyes as they toiled. At the trunk butt and under the supervision of the other engineer, men nailed bronze strips in place giving protection to the timber face to prevent it splitting on impact with the gate. Baldor watched as the men worked, noting a drive and a will to their movements, catching the eye of the engineer overseeing the plating he gestured him over.

"Why leave the front of the ram flat? I imagined it would be fashioned into a point."

"No sir, no. We need the flat shape to batter and smash. A point is only good for stonewalls and prising the joints apart, loosening masonry. If a point bursts through the gate there's a chance it will jam and we'll be unable to withdraw it."

Baldor nodded slowly looking thoughtful.

"The same as a warship ram then? In truth, I hadn't thought on it until you explained. So! We hammer the gates and burst them from their hinges rather than just hole them?"

"That's it sir! Ideally we'd fit a cast bronze head to add more weight but that would make it too heavy for the men to wield. With no time to build a roofed shelter and suspend the ram, it'll have to be the simple and crude method but it's still effective!"

"Crude but effective will do fine! I just need to be into that fort."

"If we can keep heads down on the parapet for a few moments sir, we'll soon have that gate broken. I pray to Baal they don't have any oil or sand on the heat though, for without overhead cover …"

"Never fear! Clitus will ensure you have cover. You're confident you can break the gate?"

"Yes sir, I've broken better with less." He gestured in the direction of the gate and smiled.

Baldor waved acknowledgement and moved on, pleased with the preparations and beginning to feel more confident after seeing the men at work and listening to the engineer.

He toured the units working as covering screens ensuring the men were rostered for rest and to eat. Once again he found men in readiness and somewhat recovered from the first setback and spoiling for another attempt at the fort. Content that his position was secure and the men fed; watered and resupplied for the morrow, he took one last look towards the fort before seeking sustenance for himself.

Other than sentries watching, it had remained quiet with little movement on the walls. Now more heads appeared on the parapet and suddenly a carnyx blew.

In immediate response, a trumpet sounded the 'stand to' in the Carthaginian camp and Baldor set off at the run towards the fort and the front ranks of his men. Officers urged men to their feet amidst the rattle of spear shafts and clatter of shields. Baldor looked to the gate as he ran, expecting to see the Cenomani sallying out but no movement occurred, all activity was on the walls. Arriving at the foremost ranks of his warriors he found Andulas, Tuireann and Clitus already there and watching intently.

"What's to do?"

Another carnyx blast sounded drowning the men's replies, as it quietened Andulas pointed.

"There's something happening on the walls sir. Exactly what, I don't know. There's no sign of an attack, it seems they want our attention."

The carnyx blew again and this time Clitus spoke.

"Look!"

They followed his pointing hand to the wall where a man waved a brass standard high above the parapet to attract attention.

"Do they want to talk?" Baldor asked hopefully.

"There's no white spear sir, so it's not to talk surrender. That, I'll warrant."

Baldor and his officers began walking towards the fort, stopping just out of bowshot. The standard continued to wave and Baldor stepped forward.

"With respect sir, I think we're close enough." Clitus said motioning the group to a halt. "Any further and we risk a feathering."

The wall was full of warriors. Myriad flashes of light from the setting sun reflected from helmets and spear points. Lugobelinos was in the midst of the throng and clearly visible above all by his height. He pushed through his men like an adult passing through small children then leant over the parapet to shout.

"Carthaginians! … Lingones! You murdering scum! … Listen to me." Shading his eyes, he looked to see if the men arrayed outside were ready to listen.

"What does he want, if not surrender? They can't be considering an attack as he can see we're ready and more than a match for him on open ground." Baldor mused aloud; the answer however was but a moment in coming.

"We see you making ready, thinking to attack us in the morning! But know you this; we have some of your people here."

Lugobelinos turned to the side to grasp and pull amongst the tightly packed crowd next to him; he dragged a shaggy haired man forward, pushing him into view alongside him. Seizing him by his hair and lifting him upwards, he forced the man to stand tall so Baldor and his men could clearly see him.

"If you attack us, we'll slaughter any Carthaginian or Lingone in the fortress, man woman or child!"

He turned and gestured to his men who pushed about thirty dishevelled looking folk forward to the front of the wall and clear view. All were unkempt and dressed in rags their heads down like whipped dogs.

"Your choice? Should you attack, this scum will die before you reach my walls."

Baldor turned to his officers to consider the dilemma while his men talked avidly amongst themselves.

"Now what?" Tuireann asked sourly and stared at Baldor.

"He'll kill them alright Baldor, and without a second thought." Andulas added unhelpfully.

Baldor looked at his officers as if seeking suggestions while his mind raced seeking options. Andulas looked on thoughtfully while cursing beneath his breath, Tuireann gazed disinterestedly while Clitus shook his head slowly and shrugged haplessly as Baldor's gaze fell on each man in turn.

"Where's he found these people? Nobody's ventured out of the fort since the attack so it's not our wounded they have. Do you think they seek to trick us? Could they be their own folk, dressed to look ragged?" Baldor agonised.

Andulas answered. "I hazard a guess they'll be some of my people who've disappeared over the years. Often we've searched for a child whom we thought gone astray or a missing woodsman or hunter, sometimes we'd find signs of a scuffle but no body ... Bastard!" He glared at the fort and spat into the dirt.

"I'm going to talk to him." Baldor said and stepped forward.

Andulas put a restraining hand on Baldor's shoulder. "Wait sir, please." He shouted back into the ranks for a whitened spear to be fetched.

"What does it matter for a white spear Andulas? They didn't respect the last one!" Baldor snapped, his tension beginning to show.

"Take a shield at least then sir? Else, you won't live long enough to say what you want! Believe me they've no notion of honour!"

Baldor began un-slinging his falcatas, Andulas taking the chance to call for a shield. As he passed the swords over, Andulas began to protest again, Baldor cut him short.

"The blades will make no difference. If they want to kill me these won't save me. Give me the shield; we're wasting time for it'll be dark soon."

Andulas shouldered the swords and stepped back as a long, elliptical shield was passed to Baldor.

"Andulas! Should I fall, you're in command. As you say, they'll kill those folk anyway. So at dawn, tear this fortress down and slay any male old enough to bear arms. Do you have it?"

"Yes sir."

Baldor hefted the shield across his chest and strode purposefully forward. It was deathly quiet and his soft, padding footsteps seemed strangely loud to his ears. Some Greylag geese flew overhead honking as they travelled, their cries and noise from their wings disturbing the pregnant silence. He'd walked another hundred paces before a 'whoosh' announced an incoming arrow. He tensed as it punched into the shield face, splintering into shards of wood and broken fletching. Flinching from the impact, he stopped and waited for the challenge.

"Any closer and you die!" Shouted down from the walls.

Baldor cleared his throat to speak while keeping low behind the shield.

"I would speak with Lugobelinos!"

"What do you want, Lingone dog? Make it quick, ere we feather you like a rooster."

This drew some laughter from the men on the wall.

"We want our folk back."

"Come and take them then, if you can! Come, if you dare!" Lugobelinos urged, beckoning with his hand while more laughter broke out. "And if I give you your folk, what then? Will you just march away?" He added flippantly.

"No! We'll burn your fortress, kill you and mount your head on a pole but it'll go easier with your people that survive the battle."

"Hah! Here's a rarity, an honest Lingone dog! But a dog nevertheless! Begone! I'm weary of your words, they're hollow."

"Consider what you do Lugobelinos! Consider your people's lives!"

There was no immediate answer and Baldor peered cautiously over the shield rim where he saw Lugobelinos struggling with the man he'd thrust forward. Warriors were knocked to one side as the giant crouched slightly, then straightened, lifting the struggling man, holding him horizontally above his head. The man wriggled and squirmed like a fish on a line but was securely held by the hair and the rope at his waist. Lugobelinos grunted in effort as he hurled him over the parapet. The man screamed as he spiralled towards the ground, his arms and legs clawing and scrabbling the air as if they could find purchase and prevent the fall. He hit the ground heavily like a sack of flour and lay mercifully still.

"Consider that, you Lingone dog! I'm Lord of these hills and valleys and hold sway over pit and gallows! I say who lives and who dies here!"

Baldor cursed. This wasn't working and now another man was dead.

"You can have more of your people back, Lingone! Choose! And I'll send them down to you."

Laughter broke out again. Baldor, deciding he was verbally beaten began backing slowly away.

"You don't want any more of your men back, dog? Perhaps a woman then? Some pox-ridden bitch to warm your bed?"

The laughter grew again as Baldor edged away keeping his shield and face to the front.

"What about this one, dog? He's Carthaginian and half-blind and doesn't walk too well anymore but he must be worth at least two of you Lingones?"

The parapet erupted into laughter and Baldor took a chance to look while the defenders were distracted. Lugobelinos had another man by the hair; he had a dirty brown patch over his left eye and struggled defiantly under the giants grip. Lugobelinos punched him hard in the side of the head to quieten him, the force of the blow knocking him senseless.

"Armaco! … Tanith, Mother of Heaven, it cannot be … cannot be!" Baldor said aloud into the curve of his shield.

"Nothing to say Lingone dog?" Lugobelinos shouted.

Failing to interrupt Baldor's apathy and receiving no response the giant punched the man twice more, breaking his face then dropping him from sight behind the parapet. Baldor was still lost for words and rooted to the spot as Lugobelinos continued to taunt him.

"Are you are still here, dog? Do you want another sent down to keep you company?"

Lugobelinos snatched another prisoner, this time a woman, forcing her forward to the wall. Baldor found his voice.

"Enough! Enough! I have a message for you Lugobelinos …" His voice dried in his throat.

"Here's my message, dog!"

Lugobelinos forced the woman's head quickly forward and down, smashing it into the timber points of the wall. She screamed horribly as blood spurted into the air. Lugobelinos pulled her head back showing a lost eye and a broken face. Only semiconscious she hung limply in his grip.

Baldor thought quickly then wet his lips to speak.

"My … my commander, the Lord Armaco would meet you on the morrow at dawn …" He paused as words failed him, though he noticed a flash of interest from the giant when his head rose at recognition of Armaco's name. Releasing the woman, he stepped forward grabbing the parapet with both hands.

"What? … What did you say, dog?"

Baldor tried to settle his nerves while un-sticking his tongue from the roof of his mouth.

"I'm sure the name will be familiar to you? The Lord Armaco will meet you at dawn; in single combat … you have matters to settle."

Lugobelinos glared as if he didn't believe his ears, Baldor had stopped backing away and asked.

"What message do I carry to my Lord Armaco?"

Lugobelinos raised his hand and pointed at Baldor, his face crimson in anger.

"Take this message to your master, scum! I'll meet him in on the morrow and tear him limb from limb. I'll take his head and nail it to my gate. After the ravens have taken his eyes and his skin's rotted to tatters, I'll use his skull as a pot to piss in!"

"On the morrow then! … You and an escort of ten men and him with the same. The middle ground between our lines and your fortress."

"Agreed!"

"Weapons of your choice and the fight is to be to the death, no quarter asked or given."

"I promise you, he'll beg for death ere I'm finished with him! Moreover, if I see you tomorrow, you too will be food for crows. Now, begone from my sight before I have my men turn you into a pincushion, I'm weary of your stink and woman's drivel."

Lugobelinos turned away and Baldor backed away until out of bowshot, his mind a mixture of emotions from anger and retribution to excitement that he was sure he'd found Armaco. He arrived back at his command group raising his hand to halt their questions and calling for a meeting at sunset.

****

Andulas, Tuireann, Clitus and Tirus's replacement Carro, found Baldor stripped to the waist and staring at his reflection in a small square of polished bronze, scraping the last bristles from his face. His body was pale where it had been hidden from the elements over the winter. His hair cut short to his collar. His long trousers replaced by a Carthaginian tunic belted at his waist and hung to mid-thigh. Carthaginian cavalrymen's boots reaching to mid-calf replaced his doeskin ankle boots. Shaved and groomed, he looked very much a boy again and his officers stared, not recognising him at first glance.

Towelling his face dry, he pulled a padded shirt over his head while smiling at the four, bidding them a cordial good evening. He shook Carro warmly by the hand, the man dipping his head in respect holding his right fist over his heart.

"Gentlemen, the plans for tomorrow have changed a little." He raised his hands quickly as he saw questions forming on their lips. "No doubt you're wondering what I'm about?" He wiped his hand over his clean-shaven chin while gesturing his attire. "I'm going to fight Lugobelinos at dawn, though he thinks its Armaco Salamar he faces, hence the shave and change of garb to Carthaginian."

All but Andulas looked confused and he spoke first.

"Armaco? He was your commanding officer. The one with the eyepatch who slew Magalus during the attack at our fishery?" He said, answering his own question.

"Correct Andulas! Then I lost him on the field at the Trebbia. Until now, I thought him dead and gone. I don't know how he has ended up there but I swear it was him I saw on the wall. Gentlemen, for those who don't know, Lugobelinos is desperate to slay Armaco in atonement for the death of his brother, Magalus. Lugobelinos obviously doesn't realise who Armaco is, else he would've been killed long since. If I slay Lugobelinos tomorrow it'll weaken his peoples resolve and it may give us a chance to break into the fortress, if he takes the bait."

"Hah! Lugobelinos will kill you!" Tuireann said with sour contempt, unable to resist a jibe at Baldor.

"Silence Tuireann!" Andulas snarled turning and pointing towards his half-brother. "Taranis above! Is there no end to your spleen? If you've nothing to say that's good, keep your forked tongue between your teeth!"

Tuireann bridled and coloured at the sharp chastisement and was about to argue, Andulas however was too quick for him.

"Say another wrong word, brother and I swear …"

"For the love of Baal! I say enough!" Baldor hissed though clenched teeth.

Gaining silence once more, he lowered his voice though his eyes remained cold.

"Tuireann, pray to your Gods that Lugobelinos kills me tomorrow, for I swear that if he doesn't, I'll be seeking you out."

Tuireann huffed scornfully while looking in disbelief at the thought of Baldor surviving the duel. However, something in Baldor's quiet words gave him pause and shook his resolve. Baldor appeared unafraid of the coming fight, which made him either confident or a reckless fool and as much as Tuireann hated him, he didn't think him reckless or foolish. With decorum returned, Baldor continued his strategy for the morning.

"I want the men breakfasted and ready for a full assault at dawn, should I fall to the blade of Lugobelinos, attack immediately. Don't wait for him and his escort to withdraw into the fort, no matter what protocols or assurances I promise or agree to."

Andulas, Clitus and Carro looked up in surprise as he spoke.

"Yes, I'm through with honour and protocols. You're right Andulas, Lugobelinos has no notion of either; we saw that today with the murder of Tirus's and the innocents. Tomorrow I'll kill him then we'll burn out his rat's nest and any, any at all, who bear arms against us or resists, will die."

Baldor paused for a moment, looking again at each in turn as if expecting objections. Hearing the bitterness and iron in his words, even Tuireann was silent.

"Now, we'll deploy exactly as before. Andulas, disperse the naphtha pots along the lines. Tuireann, have the ram ready for the gate, if you cannot break it down, then Andulas, burn it down! Clitus, I need you on the flanks again with continuous volleying fire at the gate and towers if you please. Carro, you start work tonight, pick four teams of ten from your Caetratus. Probe the forts defences and cause some trouble, keep our un-friends awake, give them an uneasy night. Don't become too involved though; don't risk lives, just raise a little ruckus! Gentlemen, questions?"

"If we take the walls tomorrow what happens once we're inside? What's your orders from there? Andulas asked.

"When Andulas! Not if! After we've stormed the walls, we kill any male old enough to bear arms who'll not throw down. The women and children are to be taken prisoner or driven away. I'll tolerate neither rape nor slaughter of the young or defenceless, they're not to blame for the doings of their men folk, is that understood?"

"Some will be hard pushed to conform to that order." Tuireann answered disdainfully.

"Then they'll hang for it!" Baldor retorted curtly. "I charge each one of you, make my orders abundantly clear to all, for ignorance of them will not be taken as defence."

The group fell silent looking intently at Baldor. He returned their gaze, looking at each in turn, waiting until he received a nod or a quiet 'yes sir'.

"Good! Gentlemen, we all need to rest so I'll bid you goodnight. Carro, once the moon's up begin your trouble making!"

With all prepared, Baldor checked his harness and weapons, cleaning the leather and re-touching the edges of his blades. He had Tirus's helmet brought to help finish his character deception and as he polished the metal to lustre, he promised the Spaniard the shade of a Gallic giant to serve him in the afterlife.

Distant, sporadic shouts and torches darting along the parapet like fireflies was followed by the occasional scream as a defender fell to an arrow or javelin, for carrying torches at night made for an easy target. Baldor smiled in grim satisfaction at the thought as he looked over the dark huddles of his men wrapped in blankets and sleeping soundly. He sought his own blanket but before bedding down dropped to his knees closing his eyes as if in prayer. Remaining very still, his heart slowed and breathing regulated. Feeling calmer and removed from his surroundings, he mumbled quiet words into the darkness.

"Father, Mother, I ask forgiveness for where and how I find myself. It's a poor son that disobeys his parents and of that, I'm guilty. Against all your advice, I have taken the warriors path believing none other open to me, in truth my temper, rashness and selfishness has brought me to this. Mother, my only consolation is that you're not here to see me break your heart.

Father, I'm sorry for the shame I've brought upon our house. I'll do my best tomorrow and will fight until I can fight no more. I'll try at least to be a good man, if not a good son. I will look to the men in my care and try to lead well."

He paused for a moment as if considering his words and heard the leaves ruffle from the light breeze.

"Gestix, my brother. I mourn you every day and curse myself for your death. You paid the ultimate price for loving me. I ask that you guide and make me strong tomorrow, help me to be the man you raised me to be. I fight knowing I can win, if I keep my temper, I ask you, beg you walk with me."

Fumbling in his shirt, he pulled out the cameo touching it to his lips. Holding the silver in his palm, he traced his thumb over the fine lines as if like a blind man he could picture the image by touch.

"Aiticia, my love! You, I save till last." He allowed himself a sad smile and wiped the back of his hand over his eyes as he felt his tears. "My heart's still broken and I think beyond mending, our time together too short. Should I fall tomorrow and am judged worthy of Elysium all I ask is that I spend eternity with you."

His tears flooded, hot and wet on his shaved skin. His chest heaved as he sobbed then crouched lower to muffle the sound. He cried softly, his pain and loneliness eating at him and breaking his heart. After a while, the tears ceased and he felt the tightness in his chest slacken, his breathing regulated and he felt better. Laying his weapons in readiness and using his cloak as a pillow, he rolled in his blanket his body relishing the needed rest. He gazed at the sky finding it speckled with stars, finding Orion he thought of Hannibal's words, yes tomorrow he would go hunting, within moments, he was asleep.

Chapter Twenty nine

Baldor woke before dawn. Despite the lingering darkness, blackbirds had already begun their shrill chorus and somewhere off in the trees he heard a fox bark. The camp was quiet and the fortress a dark blue shadow with no torches burning from the towers or walls. His blanket was damp and covered in water droplets from the morning dew, he breathed deeply in the cold air enjoying its clearness and the earthy scents of forest and grass. He was about to rise when a thrush joined the blackbirds in mantra, its tune sweet as a love sonnet plucked on a lyre and putting even the blackbirds to shame with its richness. He lay longer enjoying the performance, his heart lightening from the beautiful sound.

As dawn came full, the birds quietened. Throwing off the blanket, he stretched his back and shoulders then eased the night's stiffness from his legs. Walking to the trees, he relieved himself against a trunk, shivering a little with the morning chill and opting to seek an additional shirt to keep warm. The Carthaginian and Spanish garb, which he now wore, was not the best for this cool, highland climate and he missed the comfort of his leather trousers and padded shirt. Smiling to himself, he silently blessed Gestix for his advice on mountain attire all those moons ago.

By the time he'd fastened the shoulder straps of the leather corselet he was feeling warmer and marvelling at how light it felt compared to the mail shirt he'd worn since the beginning of winter. He flexed his arms and twisted his body, feeling secure and well protected but faster and unrestricted in his movements. He slipped on leather bracers covering his wrists and half of each forearm, teasing the lacing tight using his other hand and his teeth. He buckled on the heavy belt of pteruges fashioned of broad, thick leather strips adorned with bronze studs to protect his groin and thighs, fastening his dagger belt over the top, positioning the hilt snugly at his right hip. His neck cloth covered his necklaces, the material soft against his shaved skin though catching and hooking a little on the previous night's bristle growth. Picking up his falcatas, he automatically slipped each in and out of its sheath, content with the smooth action he slung both over his shoulders fastening them in position over his back.

Hearing light footfalls he turned quickly, his hands automatically reaching for the hilts at his shoulders; he relaxed when he saw Andulas approaching with a plate and two steaming cups.

"I hope you're hungry?" The Gaul asked setting the plate and cups down and settling himself alongside. "I was up early, baking!" He chuckled as he gestured the hot bread.

Strangely, Baldor was hungry, in fact ravenous. He couldn't remember his last meal or when he'd last had a hot drink. He beamed at the Gaul while picking a piece of steaming bread, tearing it apart like a half-starved street beggar and pushing it between his teeth. There was meat too, albeit cold and salted but it was good and he washed it down with the hot, honeyed water, muttering his thanks through a full mouth. Andulas watched him while eating more slowly.

"You look strange in that garb; I think you made a better Gaul!"

"Agreed! But as long as I make a better man than the one I face today I'll be content."

Andulas said nothing for a while though he looked thoughtful as if considering his words.

"Lugobelinos is the elder of the two brothers and perhaps the most dangerous. I've seen him fight before and his speed belies his size."

Baldor was still stuffing his mouth. "Tell me all you know Andulas." He said, spraying crumbs.

"For a big man he's fast but he uses raw power as well. He'll use his weight and strength if he can, so watch for the push or backhand from his shield. Whatever you do, don't let him come to grips with you."

Baldor slurped the honey water nodding sagely.

"I remember his brother fighting Armaco; he nearly throttled him before he sliced his innards!"

"He uses a boar spear …" Andulas saw Baldor look questioningly. "A boar spear, it's an outsize spear with a huge head. We use it for hunting wild boar in the forest, it's not a weapon of war as such, being too cumbersome for speedy use but he wields …"

"Marko! … Tanith in heaven! Poor Marko!" Baldor said quietly.

It was Andulas's turn to be confused and he looked at Baldor who shook his head slowly as his face saddened.

"After the battle at the Trebbia when they searched for Armaco they found Marko slain, he had a huge spear such as you describe in his chest." Baldor's sad look changed as his lip curled to a bitter snarl. "So the bastard slew Marko as well! I owe him another death for that!"

"Marko was another friend?"

"Yes, he was with us that day at your fishery."

Andulas dropped his head and mumbled a quiet prayer. "I'm sorry for your friend."

"It's Lugobelinos who'll be sorry, Andulas! Mark my words."

Andulas saw the hatred and heard the iron in Baldor's voice. "You must wear him down Baldor, you're younger, fitter and faster, keep him away and weary him. If he loses the spear he'll use a broadsword but watch for his other fist for he brawls as he fights but that combined with his strength makes it a dangerous combination."

Baldor nodded as he drank. "If it comes to blades I'll be happy, the spear's not my first choice of weapons."

"You will use both?" Andulas gestured towards the twin falcatas.

"Yes."

"You're good?" He asked with a hopeful smile.

"We'll find out soon enough." Baldor replied quietly while pushing the last of the bread into his mouth and draining the cup.

"Will you do something for me, Andulas? Should I fall this morning?"

"You will win Baldor, I …"

"Yes, but if I don't, will you …"

"You know I will! We're friends are we not? … Good friends I like to think?"

"Yes, yes we are and I am much honoured by your friendship." He dipped his head, his fist over his heart.

"What would you have me do?"

"Should I fall, see to my remains." He continued quickly as Andulas was already trying to interrupt. "Burn my body here, when that fort is no more. Burn it near the trees and the green of the meadow, scatter my ashes on the wind."

Andulas tried again to interrupt but Baldor continued.

"Call down my ancestors for me, Andulas for I've no one else to remember me to my people … will you … will you do that for me?" He voice thickened as he asked.

Andulas chewed his lip watching the emotion on his friends face.

"I would be honoured." He said very slowly. "But there'll be no need." He added with quiet confidence. "The Gods will see you victorious. But name your people and I'll learn and remember their names."

Baldor smiled grimly.

"I'm Baldor Targa of the house of Targa of the city of Carthage. I am the only son of my father, Asmilcar Targa and grandson to Hasdrubal Targa and great grandson to Hasdrubal the younger and great, great grandson to Hasdrubal the elder."

Andulas listened carefully then repeated the words slowly; he struggled with the names then with coaching from Baldor could soon repeat the lengthy eulogy word for word.

Baldor smiled as the Gaul mastered the acclamation. "Thank you." He said quietly.

"It's an impressive lineage Baldor, you name five generations of your family but the names there are three the same?"

"We Carthaginians aren't good with names!" He laughed a little trying to lighten the conversation and his mood.

"I've learned the names and won't forget them; you have my word upon it, though I think it'll be many years before I have to call it down."

"I will think no more on it now for the words are safe with you."

The pair shook hands and Baldor reached for Tirus's feathered helmet placing it in the crook of his arm, his other hand took up his shield. Seeing Andulas had recognised the helmet he gestured to it.

"I've promised Tirus."

Andulas smiled understanding and the pair walked towards the fort as the first pale yellow rays cleared the distant mountaintops. Passing through their lines a trumpet blast sounded 'stand-to' and warriors rose to their feet and took up their weapons. Word of the duel had spread like wildfire amongst the men and a cheer rose. In front of the ranks, nine men had already assembled dressed in the full panoply of war and waiting as an escort, their equipment cleaned and polished to lustre. Held above them was the standard of Carthage with the leaping boar of the Lingones alongside. Andulas saw Baldor counting heads and pre-empted his question.

"Ten was the number you said and I'm the tenth man. I'm not letting you go on your own; you've already done enough for us, the Lingone."

Baldor dipped his head and smiled. "It ends today Andulas!"

"It ends today." The Gaul echoed.

They made their way to the open ground in front of the fort while the cheering rose to a deafening roar accompanied by a cadence of weapons clashing on shields. Reaching the agreed place the escort arrayed themselves in line, spears vertical and shields held across their chest. Andulas stood in the middle of the line just behind Baldor. The cheers fell away and the raiders settled to await the Cenomani.

Baldor's stomach heaved and despite Andulas and his escort alongside the loneliness came again. He wondered if he feared death. Was that what made him anxious, tightened his throat; churned his guts and left a hollow feeling in his bowels? He remembered Gestix telling him that a little fear was a good thing, it kept a man focused and near to his God's he'd said. He was certainly focused and knew what to expect in the coming fight having seen the style of Magalus and listened carefully to Andulas. His piety however was as cold and dead as he hoped to make Lugobelinos, so instead he'd made his peace with his parents and offered his heart and soul to his wife. His faith he placed in Gestix, for in life he'd heard and seen the wisdom and truth of his words. Gestix would be his talisman, his shield for battle, if anyone could see him through the fight it was he.

A fanfare of carnyx droned loudly. The sound flowing from the wall drifting across the sward. The brassy noise scattered the carrion from their grisly feast, sending them cawing and flapping in black clouds to the walls and towers. The wall seemed to sprout men as spears and heads appeared above the parapet in a blaze of gleaming helmets and brightly painted shields, their arrival scattering the birds again. As the fanfare fell away, there was a dry rasping as the drawbar slid from the gates followed by the rattle of chains as the heavy doors eased open. The timber creaked in protest and before they'd reached their full travel, the entrance filled with Lugobelinos, his Standard-bearer and escort.

The giant wore a high domed bronze helmet that added to his already imposing height, as he stepped out from the gate shadows it shimmered like polished gold as the morning sun danced upon it. His fire-red beard pulled tight into a short, thick plait and his groomed moustache lying like a small snake across his mouth ending in short plaits below his chin. Trailing from his shoulders was a black bearskin cloak that rose gently behind him on the air of his passage. It was fastened at each shoulder by gold brooches, each holding a piece of amber in their centre as large as a bantam egg. His mail shirt hung mid-way down his thighs, scoured with vinegar and river sand it shone and glimmered in the sunlight like salmon skin. A broad belt of chased silver squares, each as wide as a man's palm, gathered the shirt and held a dagger and broadsword on his hips and like their owner, both seemed un-real by their size. On his left arm was an oval, bronze faced shield, the face decorated in concentric patterns and swirls etched in black; in his right hand he carried a boar spear.

As the party advanced, they passed the corpses littering the gateway from the previous day's battle. They didn't deviate from their path but marched over the bodies in unhurried progress towards Baldor and his men, their disrespect raising an angry roar from the raider's ranks. Lugobelinos's escort were probably his personal guard, consequently their attire was also of the best with high quality weapons and brightly painted shields on display. Their standard, fixed atop a bronze shaft wrought of pure gold and cast in the shape of a rearing stallion. Both men and equipment made an imposing display, looking the very essence of barbaric splendour.

Baldor watched the grand procession while his anger gnawed at him over the disrespect shown to the dead. Realising it was purposeful to unsettle him before combat he turned his attention to how Lugobelinos walked and moved. For a big man he seemed light on his feet with no sign of plodding, heavy footsteps. Could he move all his limbs freely or did he harbour old wounds that left him debilitated in any way? He was right handed but could he use weapons with both hands as Baldor could?

Another group exiting the gate interrupted his study. A warrior led a stumbling line of ragged men and women, each tethered to the other by a hempen rope around their neck. They shuffled along, ankles fettered, heads down and shoulders hunched like whipped dogs, all except one. Having seen the captives and guards, Tuireann sensed treachery and called his men to attention. However, there seemed no urgency or covert reason to the procession and the guards only amounted to three. The captives were led along the front of the wall while Lugobelinos's group continued at the same unhurried pace towards Baldor. Baldor turned to Andulas indicating the captives with a flick of his head, the Gaul could only shrug and shake his head in mute answer before facing front as Lugobelinos and his retinue arrived.

As the two sides stopped opposite each other, the air became charged. Men's eyes locked and breathing shallowed while hands flexed tighter around spear shafts and shield straps. The two protagonists took a moment to study one another; Lugobelinos raised his head in haughty superiority. Disregarding Andulas with sneering contempt, he looked Baldor up and down in seeming disbelief at his tender years, then leaning forward hawked and spat on the ground. Baldor stared unflinchingly back, his look so hot it could burn Lugobelinos's soul.

Lugobelinos held the stare for a moment then pulled himself up even taller pushing his chest out like a fighting cock. His voice boomed as he spoke.

"I'm Lugobelinos! Son of Maponos, son of Teutorigos, Lord of the Cenomani and I seek justice for the murder of my brother and vengeance upon this!"

Stabbing a forefinger towards Baldor, he spat the last words like bitter poison.

Pretending to listen to Andulas translate the giant's words, Baldor watched the hatred form on his face seeing it twisting his mouth and narrowing his eyes. He would feed that hate for it was another weapon, an unseen one but powerful never the less. He smiled mockingly, dipping his head as if he'd rendered a service. It had the desired affect and the giant's face coloured scarlet. Baldor then announced his lineage.

"I am Armaco Salamar of the house of Salamar of the city of Carthage. I am the only son of my father, Asmilcar Salamar and grandson to Hasdrubal Salamar and great grandson to Hasdrubal the younger and great, great grandson to Hasdrubal the elder."

As Andulas translated, Lugobelinos scowled then tilted his head inquisitively, looking at Baldor as if recognising the voice or perhaps suspecting trickery? He hawked and spat again.

"That's for your lineage boy! And for the whore of a mother that brought you into the world. And seeing how you've so many ancestors I'll send you to meet them!"

No longer able to contain his anger Lugobelinos gestured to his cloak, one of his men stepping forward easing the huge skin from his shoulders. Baldor fitted his helmet tying the strap under his chin. Both men hefted their shields and canted spears as the groups backed away a dozen paces to give the combatants room. Activity at the walls foot caught Baldor's eye. He saw each captive was spaced ten paces apart from the other and their neck ropes were being thrown up to men on the wall who took up the slack. Looking quickly from face to face, pausing when he saw the bloodied, one eyed, yet proud face of Armaco, he found his tongue.

"What's that about?" He snapped to Andulas flicking his head towards the captives. "Ask the freak what's afoot?"

"You dare to question me boy? On what I do at my own house?" Lugobelinos snarled back in retort.

Baldor made a poor attempt to hide his anger and Lugobelinos sensing it, delighted in it.

"Do you think I trust you Carthaginian scum? Trust you to be honourable and fight fairly? Do you think us fools or blind? You've an army at your backs! If my men and I aren't dealt with fairly out here or I suspect trickery your people hang. I'm Lord of the Cenomani and of these hills and valleys and my word is law!"

Turning to the fortress, he raised a hand. The first rope pulled tight then slowly upwards hauling the captive in short jerking stages up the front of the wall before stopping half way. The man kicked and wriggled, jerking like a marionette on a string, his heels scrabbling and raking the timber, frantically seeking support as the noose tightened cutting off his air. His eyes bulged while his face reddened turning a ripe plum colour, the gagging, rasping noise of his choking carried over the sward to the watching men. His tongue forced from between his teeth while his trousers darkened as his bladder let go, the piss running down his legs dripping from his feet. Baldor's anger surfaced and threats rose in his throat as to the consequences he'd unfold upon Lugobelinos and the Cenomani for the needless killing. His previous calm and rationality fast diminishing replaced by a terrible savagery that cried out for bloodletting. At that moment there was nothing he desired more than to slay Lugobelinos and raise his head on a spear and to trample his bones. An inner voice interrupted his thoughts cutting through the anger.

'He'll die just as quick and be just as dead once you've finished. Keep your mind on what you're doing; remember what you've been taught!'

Without any signal, the pair began circling, each eyeing the other seeking an opening to attack. The hatred and bloodlust from both raw, overflowing, almost tangible. Baldor held his shield high, peering over the rim watching as the giant rolled the huge spear in his hand, spinning it like a quarterstaff in a display of confident handling. Baldor stepped left then right quickly, shifting his body weight as if to move again. Watching Lugobelinos's reactions to his tentative movements, he judged the speed at which the man adjusted to counter his attack. The pair advanced slowly, gradually closing the gap while feinting and shying. Then, without warning, the giant rushed the last few paces, his spear striking forward like a lightning bolt. Baldor saw him coming but surprised by the speed only just managed to side step as the spearhead whistled past where his head had been a moment before. He quickly adjusted his balance only to find Lugobelinos back swinging the spear, letting the shaft slide through his fingers lengthening its reach. He ducked again as the blade whooshed over his head like a scythe seeking grass. Roars and sighs emanated from both sides as they watched their champions at work.

Baldor speeded his movements and took the offensive attacking Lugobelinos in quick side steps, his spear aimed low under the giants shield. Lugobelinos crouched, lowering his shield to deflect the probing point then smashed down on the shaft with his spear trying to break it. Baldor retracted it quickly. Stepping across Lugobelinos, he drove it forward again and again like a striking snake, aiming low seeking the giant's knees or shins. He was rewarded when a strike deflected off the shield into Lugobelinos's shin. It felt as though he'd thrust the spear into timber but it wrung a grunt from the giant followed by an explosive counter attack. Baldor backed quickly away driving his spear at Lugobelinos's feet trying to trip him. He came on fast yet nimbly. His feet zigzagging as if following the steps of a dance, he avoided the spear then suddenly seemed to stumble, almost fall. Baldor immediately turned back to the attack only to find Lugobelinos not falling but ready for him and an upswept shield smashed him backwards while the stabbing spear glanced off his shoulder strap. The shield blow unbalanced him while the edge of the spear cut his neck cloth nicking skin before he twisted away. Lugobelinos retracted then spun his spear like a parade mace. Unleashing a rain of clubbing blows on Baldor's hastily raised shield he stepped after him smashing the heavy head down onto his helmet. Baldor's senses went awry and he staggered then collapsed onto one knee. Raising his shield roof like over his head, he jabbed blindly with his spear to keep the giant away. Lugobelinos roared in triumph and spun the spear again altering his grip to make a side swipe that splintered Baldor's spear shaft in two. Still giddy from the helmet blow, Baldor swung the broken shaft at the giant's ankles but didn't see his foot come up to kick him backwards, sprawling in the dust. Lugobelinos stepped closer twisting the spear again to stab down as if spearing flat fish. The blows skidded and slipped off Baldor's shield raising awful, Banshee like screeches as metal scraped metal.

Andulas's hand strayed to his sword hilt and the men about him fidgeted, straining like hounds on a leash waiting to be loosed. Lugobelinos's escort displayed the same behaviour, the men of both sides knowing that whatever the outcome of the duel a battle would follow.

Though winded from the kick, Baldor rolled and twisted sharply as the spear stabbed up and down like a scorpion's tail. Lugobelinos roared like a maddened bull, driving the spear harder and faster as Baldor desperately evaded the blows. He stepped closer, stamping down hard trying to break Baldor's legs or at least pin him to the ground so he could skewer him. Suddenly the spear stuck deep in the ground where Baldor's hips had been but a moment before. Lugobelinos snatched at it trying to free it. Seizing the moment, Baldor slammed the edge of his shield down on the giant's foot.

Grunting loudly, Lugobelinos instinctively stepped back from the pain. In the brief respite, Baldor rolled onto his knees then came unsteadily to his feet. Snatching a falcata from its sheath as he rose, he slashed the blade backhanded at Lugobelinos's hands straining on the spear shaft to pry it loose from the ground. The blade missed his hands by a hairsbreadth as he pulled them quickly away abandoning the immovable spear to the earth. However, instead of chopping the shaft in two, the sword blade clanged against what was a solid bronze shaft. The impact shocked the nerves in Baldor's hand, reverberating up his arm to his shoulder. Almost dropping the sword, he also backed away trying to control his fingers and take a better grip.

The moments respite allowed Lugobelinos to draw his sword. Breathless and panting like a dog in the sun he raised it high pulling the shield across his chest then limped forward. Baldor was still suffering from the head blow and his chest heaved like ruptured bellows from the kick and his high-speed evasive moves from the giants spear. Despite this, he felt relief now the spears were gone. He flexed his shocked fingers around the sword's hilt testing their grip. Satisfied, he dropped his shield and drew the second falcata. Fluidly rotating the swords, he moved them in whistling intersecting arcs across his chest. A roar of approval emanated from his men as they saw his tactics change from cautious to confident offensive.

Comfortable at last, he moved forward at speed to meet Lugobelinos's attack. Lugobelinos, seeing the approach swung his sword in a downward arc towards Baldor's left shoulder. Catching it between both blades, Baldor drove it to one side while stepping forward spinning his body completely around Lugobelinos's deflected sword arm. He swung low at the giant's ankles with his right blade. Lugobelinos side stepped the low blade but was almost too slow to turn and face Baldor, who having completed his turn was coming at his back. A hastily backswept shield only just deflected the incoming blade while the swords clashed and screeched again, both men stepped back panting for breath.

The pair circled again each seeking an opening. Frustrated, Lugobelinos shouted his hatred beckoning and taunting Baldor on. Baldor pointed a falcata at him while giving a baleful stare. He carried the fight forward, changing his footing as he came, presenting the blades in shimmering arcs again. The giant raised his shield and crouched slightly, his sword arm out to the side. Remembering Andulas's advice, Baldor engaged Lugobelinos's sword with his left blade while hammering repeatedly with his right against the shield face. Under the determined attack, Lugobelinos increased his efforts, his sword parrying and slashing in response to Baldor's seeking blade. Feeling the tempo of the fight increasing and sensing Lugobelinos's frustration, Baldor stepped closer tempting the giant to use his strength. The giant roared, pushing forward with his shield to batter Baldor backwards but this time Baldor was ready. Going along with the push, he slipped a darting right blade over the rim into Lugobelinos's extending shoulder. The falcata's heavy point burst the mail rings apart driving into flesh while his left blade still battered the giant's sword away.

The shock of the blow stalled Lugobelinos. Breathing raggedly, he pointed his sword at Baldor to keep him away. He glanced in disbelief at the ruined shoulder and the blood leaking profusely down his mail shirt. Baldor faced him with his left blade extended; his right held horizontally over his head, his body slightly crouched.

The giant hawked and spat again then laughed grimly while pointing his sword and mumbling something Baldor didn't understand. Baldor smiled caustically then attacked, the swords flashing and striking like sheet lightening in a summer storm, the Gaul having to give ground under the onslaught. As Baldor closed, Lugobelinos swung clumsily with his shield only to find Baldor no longer there, having already stepped back from reach and waiting, ready. The giant cursed in frustration and shook his head like a dog after a swim. Sucking in a huge breath, he launched at Baldor his sword swinging in huge whistling strokes. Baldor let him come while stepping nimbly backwards, his left blade parrying, the right keeping up the assault on the shield.

After a dozen paces Lugobelinos stopped. His breath coming in short, heavy snorts, his chest heaving, his shield arm sagging. Baldor blinked sweat from his eyes. Raising his swords again, he stepped forward changing his footing as he came. Lugobelinos moved to counter and swung his shield left to right as Baldor's footing changed; the shield however was dropping lower as his arm weakened. Baldor darted in again, trading clanging blows with the giant's broadsword while striking the shield repeatedly, forcing its continuous movement before evading another powerful swipe.

Stepping back again, Lugobelinos shrugged his arm from the shields straps casting it away, his wounded arm no longer able to support it. His shoulder was bleeding heavily yet he tugged his dagger from its sheath and with a weapon in both hands came at Baldor again. Baldor's falcatas and the giant's broadsword and dagger hammered and clanged the metal screeching and raising tiny orange sparks. Baldor suddenly switched both blades to the giant's sword as if ignoring the dagger in the man's left hand. Lugobelinos stepped back under the vicious onslaught and Baldor moved closer as if trying to overpower him, at the same time exposing his side to the dagger. More than one amongst Baldor's escort mumbled an oath as they saw the dagger driving in from the side. Swords started to leave sheaths in expectation of Baldor being gutted. At the last moment, Baldor knocked the giant's broadsword aside and jumped back, the dagger missing his ribs by a hair's breadth. Spinning like a top around the dagger arm, he swung low with his left blade chopping the giant behind the knee. Completing his turn, his right blade drove into the small of Lugobelinos's back and kidneys. Lugobelinos grunted as his leg gave way, his back arching as the second blade drove deep.

An angry roar erupted and the giants escort charged forward towards Baldor, swords drawn to protect their Chief. At the same moment, Andulas and his men attacked them. All along the raider's lines war horns blew, battle cries rang out and hundreds of men surged forward, running towards the still open gate.

Chapter Thirty

The escort parties clashed like heroes from a skald's fireside saga, hacking and slashing like demons. Swords clanged and blood splashed, flesh cut and bones broke as men screamed, died and went down. Baldor found himself forced back from Lugobelinos as two of his personal guard engaged him while another two helped the wounded giant to his feet attempting to steer him back towards the gate. The remaining Cenomani warriors fought savagely, selling their lives in an attempt to hold Andulas and his men back from their Chief.

As the raiders charged the gate a maelstrom of arrows and slingshot whooshed and whined overhead raking the parapet, forcing the defenders below the timber top. Arrows splintered and broke or quivered forcefully as they stuck in the timber wall else disappeared over the parapet falling from sight into the fort. Lead bullets whipped and zipped like passing hornets as they ricocheted from the wall, as hell broke loose.

High on the ecstasy of battle Baldor fought like a God. He slew the first warrior in a moment, deflecting the man's broadsword while the second falcata stabbed under his shield into his groin. With euphoria replacing tiredness, he turned his full attention to the second adversary dispatching him in a blur of flashing blades; whooping in triumph as a slash to the throat saw the warrior fall in a haze of wet, red mist. With grim rapture at the bloodletting overflowing, he shouted loudly.

"Lugobelinos! You murdering whoreson! Fight me! Fight me if you dare!"

The giant stopped his retreat, pushing the two escorting warriors roughly to one side, turning to face Baldor once again while trying to balance on his ruined leg. Like a maddened bull, he stood his ground. His face contorted in pain and feral hatred he bellowed defiance while beckoning Baldor hurry to face his doom. Baldor ran towards him, rationale and restraint long gone. Lesser men cleared to the side of the private battle concentrating on their own salvation. Like rutting stags the pair roared their challenge and as Baldor closed the last few paces both men's weapons rose in readiness. Lugobelinos had discarded the dagger and now used both hands to raise his broadsword to his right and above his shoulder. Baldor ran straight at it, catching the descending sword on his left falcata the blades screeching hideously as they parried then scraped together. Unable to stop the herculean blow, he slowed then deflected it away while trying to stab Lugobelinos's unguarded belly with his right blade. He had to duck as the giant spun around following his deflected blade. Pirouetting with unbelievable speed, he brought his sword around in another attempt to decapitate Baldor. The blade missed Baldor's ducking head, managing only to chop through his helmets crest, breaking it off as it passed. Though shaken from the impact, Baldor powered upwards from the crouch under Lugobelinos's guard, driving both blades at an angle, one aimed at disembowelling him, the other at his groin.

The blades struck home. The higher one bursting the mail links rending the padded shirt beneath to enter the stomach. The lower driving under the mail shirt into the unprotected groin and stalling the giant. Baldor growled with effort as he forced the blades deep, sending blood splattering like warm summer rain over his face and chest. Twisting both blades viciously, he stepped back dragging them free, his hands red to the wrist. The blood emptied from Lugobelinos's stomach and groin as if tipped from a bucket. The giant groaned long and low like a butchered animal at the slaughter yard. He shuddered as if from a winter's chill, dropping his sword, instinctively clutching his groin and belly then staggered drunkenly. He collapsed to his knees then sank back on his haunches, staring at Baldor with a look of disbelief at the ruin wrought on him by one so young.

Baldor was panting heavily from his efforts. His head ringing from the blow on his helmet he watched the dying giant from behind guarded blades. Lugobelinos swayed unsteadily and his eyes seemed to dim. His mouth twisted in anger then agony as he coughed blood and spit. He tried to rise but couldn't, mumbling disjointed curses at Baldor amidst flecks and bubbles of thick blood. At last, his eyes rolled back and he pitched forward into the dirt like a felled oak. Stepping cautiously closer, Baldor kicked savagely at the prone body seeking signs of life but found none. Kneeling to remove the helmet, he seized a handful of wiry hair, lifting the pumpkin sized head to chop at the neck. It took four heavy blows of the falcata to sever the massive spine and part the head from the body. Lifting it by the hair, he held it at arm's length while he studied the sallow face. The demonic eyes were closed and the jaw hung slackly, the bloodied lips parted to show rotted, yellow teeth.

The elation of victory mixed with the primitive instincts of the desperate survivor and raising the head and his sword aloft in triumph, he looked skyward. As the blood and gore ran down his forearm, he roared long and loud like a lion defending its kill, then cried.

"Gestix! ... Father! It is done!"

He maintained the position for a moment then gradually lowered his arms crossing them over his chest and bowing his head. Carrying the head like a milk bucket, he walked towards the walls his trophy leaving a bloodied trail across the grass. His heart lifted further as he saw the fortress gates wide open with the last of his men bunching to funnel through the gateway. The covering showers of arrows and slingshot still whistled and droned overhead raking a now empty parapet. He saw four of the roped captives now hung from the walls, two of which still twitched and shook like fish on a line. Armaco was not among the four. He and the other captives presumably escaping the hanging as the attack started and the defenders forced to let the ropes go. Picking up a discarded spear and dropping the giants head to the ground, he drove the point into the base of the neck as if spearing a turnip. Hefting the gory totem aloft, he walked quickly towards the rear ranks of his men pushing through the gate. Men saw the head and cheered loudly. Passing the prize over he urged them on into the fortress itself where he hoped seeing Lugobelinos's head atop a spear would take the fight from the defenders and thus save lives. He called another warrior across to him.

"Cut those bodies down from the wall and find the remaining prisoners! See they're brought safely to me."

With that, he pushed on through the throng of men and the fortress gates.

Inside, the raiders were spreading down the narrow streets and alleyways driving the defenders before them like sheep, slaughtering them as they ran. With little in the way of cohesive resistance, the defenders battled individually or in small groups but were no match for the disciplined raiders and the streets ran red. Baldor noted that despite the hopelessness of the situation none looked to surrender. The cornered Cenomani fought tooth and nail selling their lives dearly with no thought for quarter. Baldor's officers chivvied their men along, keeping them together in good-sized groups as they systematically captured building after building securing an area at a time.

Fleeing women and children were pushed or knocked out of the way. Some came at the warriors brandishing kitchen knives or skillets. At the very least they were battered to one side at worst they were cut down as the warriors pressed on, determined to prevent any rallying by the defenders. Others sought shelter inside the buildings only to flee once more as doors were smashed in.

Exiting the choked streets into the market square the advancing warriors were assailed by a flurry of arrows as a handful of archers still on the wall fought to stem their advance. Men staggered and fell; shields raised as they ran for cover dragging their wounded with them. Officers barked orders, sending two squadrons of men in block formations to force the parapet walkway and sweep the wall clear of all defenders. Calling time to the cadence of their feet they advanced at double pace, tightening their ranks as they went, shields interlocked over their heads like a roof.

With the archers' attention now on defending themselves from the new threat, the advance on the ground began again. The men rushed from cover shouting war cries, others howling like dogs on the hunt. Within moments, they caught some retreating defenders in the rear, venting their anger for the archers attack the flight dissolved into bloody slaughter. Women and children cried and screamed as their men folk died fighting in front of them and their homes went up in flames. The scent of blood and the mayhem set dogs howling and barking madly, some already running loose others chewed through their leashes to flee or join the fray. Horses that had broken loose from the stables or escaped the corral reared and stomped as the swirling smoke and smell of blood drove them mad with fear.

Baldor looked about the madness seeking his officers. His previous elation fast replaced by a gut wrenching queasiness as he witnessed the horrors of a falling town. People scattered in vain attempt to escape the raiders, running and darting haphazardly like chickens seeking to evade a fox in a henhouse. Mothers and children became separated in their haste to flee. Some fell, being trampled and dying in the crush and pandemonium of the battle as the fight grew desperate. The old and infirm or those too slow to move perished underfoot, crushed or hacked to death as the victorious warriors spread through the streets in search of any still looking to fight.

Baldor shouted himself hoarse trying to instil order in the chaos and summon his officers to him. Having finally caught the attention of some he bawled his orders, delegating separate tasks to prevent further fire raising, stop the slaughter of women and children and ensure a structured cohesive sweep of the streets. Clitus jogged up, bow in hand, the older man breathless after his long run from outside the walls.

"Sir, we're clear outside, what are your orders from here?" He gasped for air as he spoke. Aye sir, your orders from here, if you please?"

"Divide your men Clitus; send them onto the left and right walls. Cover our men on the ground as they drive the Cenomani before them. Kill any that won't throw down!"

"Yes sir." Barking orders to his men, he set off for the parapet steps at an ungainly run.

Baldor detached twenty men to herd the straggling women and children left in the wake of the raiders drive through the town. Roughly shepherded towards the wall and forced into a huddled group they were placed under guard. The children, distraught and horrified at the slaughter clung to their mothers, the women in various stages of distress from quiet shock to horror-struck weeping. Steeling his heart against the pitiful sight, he charged the men with the women's safety then sheathing one sword picked up a discarded shield and headed deeper into the town.

Making way through the streets, he followed the trail of dead and dying warriors, following the direction of the running battle. Stepping over bodies and across stinking gutters carrying the towns waste he saw what he thought to be Lugobelinos's hall. Markedly different from the other buildings with their simple thatched rooves, it was a huge white stone construction with a red pantile roof. Sat high upon a knoll it towered above the other buildings, noting its position he continued onward to find the battle.

Near the rear wall of the fortress, the houses thinned out giving way to cattle sheds and empty animal pens. Inside the pens, lining the corral style fence the remaining Cenomani warriors stood their ground behind a wall of raised shields. Tuireann and Carro were marshalling warriors into shield walls of their own for a unified and final assault against the defenders. Baldor came alongside the two officers, commanding a halt just as they prepared to unleash their men in a charge. Surprised by his sudden appearance and brusque commands, Tuireann bridled and began to protest and to which Baldor curtly silenced him. Tuireann saw the change in Baldor's demeanour, no longer seeing a young, indecisive boy but a much bloodied and confident seeming warrior, very much in command of himself and the situation.

Baldor beckoned the warrior forward who carried Lugobelinos's head and who'd followed him through the town. Pulling him alongside he turned towards the Cenomani shield wall.

"Men of the Cenomani, listen to me!"

Though shouting and addressing them in Gallic his words were lost in the mayhem. Silencing his own men, he shouted again but louder, cutting across the din of rattling weapons and shields and exchanged curses. An eerie silence fell over the courtyards.

"Men of the Cenomani, I say enough! Your Chief is no more!" He pointed towards the spiked head. "Throw down and live! I offer you this chance but once then no more!"

The tense, pregnant silence was interspersed by the hiss of muted voices from behind the shield wall followed by a rasping tone.

"To hell with you, you bastard!"

A hastily flung javelin came over the shield wall aimed directly at him and which he avoided by casually stepping to one side. His calmness and confidence only bolstering his men's bravery and ardour further to fight. The raider's ranks surged and flexed like a wave crest about to break as shields and weapons came up ready to attack. Baldor held up his hand crying 'hold' for up on the left and right parapets, Clitus and his men appeared. Having cleared the walls of defenders they jogged towards the standoff below, some men carrying on to the rear parapet placing themselves above and behind the cornered warriors. Clitus signalled a halt, bows, and slings aimed downwards at the Cenomani. Recognising the dire situation a charged silence fell over the two sides. Baldor could hear the bow staves creaking under tension of the draw and the whine of the spinning slings. Clitus looked to Baldor who waved his arm down sharply in the direction of the defenders.

"Loose!"

The Cenomani began raising shields against the enfilading missiles while watching the raiders to their front. Surrounded, shocked and suddenly disorganised the arrows and slingshot exploited the gaps in the ranks, the short range driving arrows and bullets deep. Groans and cries rent the air as blood sprayed high and men twisted and fell under the torrent of missiles. The whooshing, zipping volleys continued unabated and with nowhere for the warriors to run or hide the ranks quickly thinned, men falling like scythed wheat. Realising their doom but refusing to die like butchered animals some ducked under the fence rails and ran towards the raiders. Most died as they exposed their backs, the rest fell within a dozen paces of the fence as the archers picked them off. Not one reached the waiting ranks of the raiders alive. The numbers dwindled quickly as the relentless fire flayed their ranks bloody. Some stood stupefied as if accepting their fate while others threw down shields and weapons raising their hands. Seeing the capitulation Clitus commanded a halt but as always, once the killing started it wasn't easy to stop. After shouting himself hoarse he looked to Baldor for further instruction.

There was sudden quiet as the archers, the Cenomani and the waiting raiders all turned their gaze towards Baldor. The faces showing differing emotions, the archers poised and eager to complete their destruction, Tuireann and Carro's infantry almost sour as if cheated of their kill. The remaining Cenomani demonstrating a combination of fear or calm resignation of their impending doom. Some daring to look hopeful that the killing would cease and their lives spared. Baldor stared at the battered group of wretched, surrendering men and the carnage of shot and arrow stuck bodies littering the ground of the pens. He heard the pitiful moans and cries of the wounded as they called on their Gods to take their pain away or wept in agony. Some thrashed and rolled trying to escape their misery while others panted and coughed as punctured lungs filled with blood drowning them slowly. Those hit in the stomach frothed at the mouth and coughed blood.

The gentle side of his nature was abhorred at the slaughter. His heart seeking pity, mercy, and an end to the killing; however, the dark side, the angry, malevolent and bloody side remembered the reckoning he'd promised. He thought of Baraan and Marko, the murder of the folk at the fishery, his men left to die in front of the fort and of Lugobelinos's cruelty to his captives and … and finally, Armaco. His face hardened to a scowl, a low, savage growl grew in his throat.

"Finish it! … Loose! … Loose!"

Arrows flew and slingshot blew heads apart like rotten fruit, within moments not a man in the pens remained on his feet. Instead, a mangled heap of bodies, shields and limbs squirmed and twisted on the ground. With all the Cenomani down, he called a halt and dispatched a dozen infantrymen to finish off those that still drew breath. He turned quickly to his officers.

"Tuireann, Carro! I want a full sweep of the township. Herd any captives back towards the gate. Strip this place of anything of value, be it gold, treasures, food or weapons. Round up the horses and oxen and seek out carts, wagons and sleds for we'll need all to carry our spoils. We'll spend the night here then fire the place in the morning, go!"

Leaving Baldor with a handful of warriors as guards the men moved off quickly, eager to begin their looting. He squatted to pull a cloak from a dead Cenomani warrior, using it to wipe his blood-slicked hands and blades clean of the congealing gore. Rubbing hard at the cloying redness, he mumbled heartfelt thanks beneath his breath to Gestix and his father as realisation of victory began to dawn. Andulas appeared with his men, the Gaul supporting a wounded arm but beaming a smile.

"The fortress is yours sir!"

Baldor rose as Andulas's men broke into loud cheers and gathered around, their words of praise filling his ears. Uncomfortable with the honour heaped upon him, he accepted the lauding with awkward grace then quickly made towards the Gaul.

"Andulas! You're hurt! Is it …"

"No sir! Tis nothing and the dog that gave me it didn't live to speak of it! What of yourself?"

Baldor smiled by way of an answer. His concern being the injured Gaul, for despite Andulas's dismissal of the wound, the amount of blood showed it was deep. He turned to a nearby warrior.

"Find a seat for my Lord Andulas and bring it out here." He gestured towards the southern wall of a hut where the sun fell, while ushering Andulas over and calling for a surgeon to be fetched. Settling him, he commanded his men sort the living from the dead and the wounded taken to Lugobelinos's hall or a building sufficiently large for the purpose.

Using his good hand Andulas undid his helmet strap; throwing it down, he ran his good hand through his wet hair and massaged his temples. He sighed contentedly as he accepted a drink from Baldor's water skin.

"You have a victory sir." He said, wiping his mouth. "And if I judge aright I think our casualties light. We were into the fort and amongst them before they'd chance to stop us."

"Aye! And my thanks to you all for making it so." Baldor smiled again.

"It was you sir, whom brought it about." Andulas held up his hand to silence Baldor as he tried to interrupt. "It was you whom slew the giant, a mighty deed and one that'll no doubt secure your reputation in the halls and villages hereabouts."

Baldor shrugged as if it was unimportant and moved to one side allowing the arriving surgeon to examine and treat Andulas's arm. Tipping his head back to take a drink, he saw two warriors and a group of dishevelled folk making their way towards him. Shading his eyes from the sun and looking past the warriors, he studied each haggard face in turn. At the rear and slightly behind the others he saw a figure that limped and dragged his feet in a shuffling, crippled gait. The man swung his arms in an exaggerated motion using their momentum to help move his legs. Baldor's jaw dropped open in shock as he looked past the thin, wasted body and long, shaggy hair recognising the broken face and familiar brown eye patch.

"Armaco? … Armaco!" He shouted, though his words dried in his throat.

The cripple looked up and shouted back though the words were unintelligible.

"Baal almighty, Armaco! … For the love of Tannith, what've they done to you?"

Baldor was already running towards the sorry procession and calling for help from warriors nearby. He stopped two paces from Armaco, his eyes wide in horror as he saw the state of him. His face grossly swollen and misshapen from the previous days beating. His skin a mixture of ingrained filth, black and yellow bruising and caked, brown blood. His lips were swollen and his jaw hung slackly, badly broken. He muttered Baldor's name again though this time the tone was thankful almost a gratuitous pleading. Trying to reach Baldor he stumbled, Baldor stepped forward catching him in his arms.

"I've got you, I've got you!"

Baldor fastened his arms fiercely around him drawing a whimper as his shoulder strap caught Armaco's jaw. He could feel the ribs protruding from beneath the skin of the wasted, thin body. He held him, his chest heaving with sharp, irregular intakes of breath as he fought to control his emotions. Armaco clapped him weakly but tenderly on the back. Baldor stood back from him; his eyes wet, the tears cutting tracks through the dry blood on his cheeks. He cuffed them savagely away trying to compose himself.

"I … I, thought you, what … have …" Again, his words faded, changing from heartfelt pity to burning anger. "What … what, have the bastards done to you?"

He looked down at the awkwardly placed legs then back to the gaunt face and black ringed eye that stared blankly as if the man had seen demons eating his soul. Abandoning his questions and coaxing gently, he led him to where Andulas was already rising from his seat, offering it to the injured man. Baldor turned to the guards.

"Bring more seats! … Water and wine! See to the others, help here! Quickly mark you!" He pointed and snapped.

Helping Armaco into the seat, he gently pushed Andulas into another as more were brought. Removing his neck cloth and wetting it, he gently cleaned some of the filth and blood from Armaco's face while giving him a wineskin to drink from.

"By all that's holy I thought you dead, lost! We all did! We searched for you. The Captain and Harbro looked for you for three days. We found your horse but no trace of you."

Armaco gulped the wine as best he could. Most spilled from his mouth as he couldn't move his jaw to swallow.

"The bast …ds came, the night, I …" His words slurred from the displaced jaw, he coughed as some of the wine entered his windpipe. "The giant slew Marko … they cut my tendons … I went to kill him … they crippled …"

Baldor couldn't follow the threads of the tale and seeing Armaco breaking under the strain, gently hushed him.

"Later, later Armaco, rest now! Let's have you treated and fed first."

Armaco fell silent and his eye took on the vacant stare again, his mind drifting, his fierce warrior spirit badly broken. Baldor crouched and slowly lifted the hem of Armaco's tunic and saw the thick white scars across the back of the knees from the blade that had slashed the tendons to ruin. Growling like an injured animal, he charged the surgeon with treatment of both men. Turning on his heel, he summoned two warriors to accompany him.

He felt madness descending upon him. Strangling him and stealing his breath as if the world about him was closing in, suffocating him. Rational thoughts clouded from an enveloping red haze, which offered only dire retribution and murder as outcome. His heart began to race, his temperature soaring, flushing his skin scarlet as his temper flared. All the pent-up anger and frustration of the last few days bubbled to the surface venting as growls and muttered curses. Drawing both falcatas, he strode briskly towards the forts centre, the two warriors hurrying to keep pace with his long strides. Catching up with a group of prisoners, he singled three captive warriors to one side while pushing the women, children and an old man onwards again. As the departing group turned a corner, Baldor drove a falcata into the first man's belly; decapitated the second and cut the third down as he turned to run. Pointing a bloodied sword at his two accompanying men, he screamed.

"Kill any warrior you find! Any! Spare none that's carried a weapon this day. Kill them! Kill them all, do you hear me!"

The men nodded and departed quickly seeking other groups to relay their orders to, thankful to be away from their commander who now seemed possessed of demons. Baldor strode onwards, passing another group consisting only of wounded warriors, he slew the first ordering his men to dispatch the rest. Moving on again he saw his orders were being followed and the few Cenomani warriors who'd survived were being singled out and killed.

Turning onto another street, he saw Tuireann and his murderous rage deepened further. With blood lust hot and reason teetering on the cusp of insanity, he remembered the put downs and insults and the promise he'd made for retribution. Coming to the side of the Gaul, he cut through the man's conversation to a group of his men while pushing him roughly to one side.

"Tuireann!" The name came out in a feral snarl from between clenched teeth. "I promised you a reckoning should this fortress fall!"

Tuireann, caught off-guard by Baldor's manner stepped back further from the snarled words.

"Now! We settle our dispute here and now!" Baldor ranted.

Tuireann saw the anger and murder in Baldor's eyes and the gore stained falcatas in each hand. Surprised but recovering quickly, he stepped back again drawing his sword and pulling his shield in front of him. The moment the blade brandished in defence, Baldor attacked. The two falcatas a silver blur, striking high then low, the metal whooshing, the blades clanging and ringing as they beat Tuireann's sword down and hammered his shield.

Tuireann fought furiously against the onslaught but was forced to give ground under the pressure as Baldor drove him backwards. Realising he was outclassed he tried a desperate counter attack. As he over extended his arm, Baldor's falcata hooked the broadsword from his grasp sending it spinning away to clang against a house wall. Tuireann lost his balance and stumbled forward falling to the ground. Landing hard, he snatched for his dagger as Baldor stepped across him, the falcatas at his throat.

"Baldor! Baldor!"

The loud, desperate shout somehow permeated Baldor's senses and he stayed his hand.

"Baldor, sir enough! Enough I beg you … enough!" Andulas shouted as he ran to come alongside Baldor. His good hand up in a halting motion as he stepped across and between the pair, shielding his prone half-brother from further destruction. "Please, enough!" His voice dropping to a cautious whisper as he saw Baldor looking at him in bewilderment. "Come sir, please! Your honour is satisfied. Enough killing for one day?"

Baldor stared as if waking from a dream. His eyes looking but not seeing, his pupils dilated as if from too much wine and unable to focus. Andulas continued quickly but calmly.

"We've much to do before tomorrow."

"Yes …yes, we've much to do." Baldor repeated in a hushed whisper though the words were monotone. Lowering his swords, he stepped back, allowing Tuireann to get up. Andulas took Baldor gently by the arm steering him back to where he'd left Armaco on the seat.

Chapter Thirty one

Having sat awhile, taken a drink of watered wine and gathered his senses Baldor stood and fitted his helmet. Andulas made to rise with him but again Baldor gently pushed him back into his seat.

"I'm going to see that all's in order. Nothing else, I promise you. I'll not further the altercation between myself and Tuireann, as far as I'm concerned the matter's done."

Andulas nodded respectfully. "Thank you! I'm sorry about Tuireann he …"

"It's over and done Andulas." He said quietly. "Think no more on it, now rest and look to Armaco for me when he wakens."

Despite having guzzled a pitcher of un-watered wine on an empty stomach before quietly passing out, Armaco slept fitfully, he twitched, moaned, and sometimes cried out in anguish. Baldor grimaced at the marks of savagery and ruin wrought on his friend's body then wondered what tortured nightmares he suffered. Patting Andulas warmly on the shoulder, he stooped to throw a cloak over Armaco, tucking it firmly about his restless body. Armaco's eye flicked suddenly open, alert and showing a momentary fear and lack of recognition as to where he was.

"It's alright Armaco! It's all right; it's me … me, Baldor. Baldor, you remember?"

The wary eye darted left then right seeking familiarity, then peered confusedly at the face in the helmet. Baldor held him down firmly but gently, stopping him getting out of the chair while tucking the cloak back about him, talking quickly but quietly. "You need more rest and your hurts seen to and then you must eat … a little less wine eh?"

It was recognition of Baldor's voice more than physical identification that settled him, mumbling something incoherent his eyelid flickered and slowly closed as exhaustion took over. Seeing Armaco's body still shook as if from a chill, Andulas offered his cloak as well and as Baldor finished wrapping him in it the Gaul offered.

"Go sir, I'll see to him. I promise I won't leave him until you return, go and see to the men."

Baldor clasped Andulas's hand and managed a nod and a smile. "I'll think no more on it, he's safe with you."

Taking four men as escort, he began a tour of the fortress. The fire raising had ceased and the buildings that were still ablaze had been isolated by tearing down the ones next to them, the gaps acting as firebreaks leaving those aflame to burn themselves out. Treasures and spoils were heaped outside ransacked houses, ready for collection by packhorses, carts and sleds that were being hastily assembled. The need for draft animals was huge, so donkeys and small ponies found themselves pressed into service alongside oxen and plough horses. Food supplies were already being loaded, innumerable sacks of grain, oats, dried fruits and baskets of nuts. Haunches of smoked meat and fish both pickled and smoked, pitchers of wine, amphorae's of oil and kegs of heady Gallic beer. The quantity had surprised all and prompted Baldor's thoughts as to the uselessness of a siege had the fortress not fallen to storm. Wool blankets, animal furs, skins and clothing along with weapons, shields and armour formed other loads, while the animal pens were emptied of cattle, goats, pigs and sheep, even chickens and geese were caught and put into baskets ready for transportation.

The prisoners; consisting now only of old men, women and children were under guard, sitting in a large, huddled group in the lee of the east wall. A few still wept, though for the most there was a fearful silence as they cast furtive glances at the raiders, wondering at their fate. A dressing station had been set up in one of the larger houses with additional beds and trestles dragged into place for the wounded. There was already an orderly row of cloak covered bodies off to one side and Baldor noticed the same two men he had seen on the first day of battle, going from bed to bed quietly assessing the casualties. Steeling himself against the horrors of the injured, he made his way to where the head surgeon was directing operations.

"How goes it?" He asked in Greek.

The surgeon continued giving orders while answering Baldor and retying his bloodstained apron.

"We seem to have gotten off lightly sir, the rush of injured has slowed though there are some few still trickling in."

Baldor heaved a quiet sigh of relief. "Bring me the list of casualties both wounded and dead as soon as you have it."

Moving on, he passed Lingone warriors busily removing heads from the fallen Cenomani for trophies, paying them little heed he walked on following the steepening road towards Lugobelinos's hall. He was surprised at the enormous pile of gold plate, coin filled chests, jewellery, silver ingots and gem studded artefacts already deposited on the road outside the hall door. His warriors appearing in procession from within, arms laden with yet more to add to the heap. Stepping through the wide, bronze-sheeted door, he was surprised by the grandeur within. Far from being some primitive, stark hall, hidden away in the hills he found it magnificently appointed. The walls plastered smooth and colourfully decorated after the Roman and Greek fashion. The floor covered in a herringbone pattern of orange and black tiles that continued up to and around the central fire pit. Long trestle tables caparisoned in cloth of gold and black silk and littered atop with dozens of bronze, oil lamps. The lamps hung in pairs or groups of three and four, suspended on delicate chains from finely wrought stands that stood a sword length in height. Next to them and again in huge quantity were silver wine jugs, patterned and encrusted with precious stones of amber, emeralds and garnets. Above, the high set, narrow windows had stout wooden shutters to keep out the weather. Some had been forced open allowing more daylight in, one of which now banged gently against its jamb in the breeze. High above, the massive roof of smoke blackened thatch rested on enormous trusses and purlings of dark oak. The place smelled of wood smoke, ashes and timber with a taint of burnt bread, which still lingered from the forgotten breakfast.

Baldor's reverie was interrupted by a shriek from somewhere deep within the living quarters at the rear of the hall, followed by a loud clatter as though furniture had been overturned in a scuffle. Dispatching his escort with a curt nod to investigate the noise, he motioned to the distracted gold carriers to continue their task. Drawing his sword, he paced quickly across the feasting area in lee of his men towards the gloom of the rearward passageways and rooms. Taking a spluttering, near spent torch from the wall cresset he stepped silently down the dark corridor. Signalling his men into pairs, he sent them into opposite sides of the passage to sweep the rooms.

Holding his torch high he saw a small, dark shape laid on the floor at the corridors end. Advancing warily, he recognised the body of a child and the growing dark stain alongside as blood. It pooled lazily across the floor like spilled lamp oil and showed in blotched, spotted spray up the white plastered wall. Hearing agitated fumbling and a harsh but suppressed voice from within the nearest chamber, he kicked the door open. The door banged back on its hinges and the muttered curses went suddenly loud. Stepping quickly through the doorway his torchlight reflected back from an outstretched sword and he sidestepped. The aggressor drove forward then stumbled as their missed lunge sent their balance askew. Kicking savagely in the direction of the passing sword, he felt his foot connect and heard a grunt as the blow drove the air from the swordsman's lungs. Using the flat of his sword, he dealt a heavy blow to where he thought the man's head would be and heard his shadowy adversary crash to the floor. With his blade extended guardedly in front of him he advanced slowly, his ears straining for the slightest sound that may herald an attack. Twisting and turning quickly he searched the room, his blade darting and probing like a serpents tongue. The torch light revealed another man struggling to his feet from a low bed while trying to disentangle himself from frantically flailing arms and legs beneath him. Baldor's escort, having heard the commotion now followed behind him their swords also outstretched. One covered the prone man on the floor while the others threatened the second who was clear of the bed, hauling at his trousers and frantically seeking his blade.

The man's eyes cast about like a startled fox that had just seen the hounds. Recognising the newcomers as his own kind, he relaxed a little giving a forced, false laugh.

"There's enough for us all here brothers, she's a feisty bitch see!" He wiped at two sets of bloody furrows across his eyes and cheeks then pointed back to the bed. "Help yourselves lads, the trull will be all the sweeter for being ..." Seeing the still un-lowered swords he looked nervous again then visibly paled as he recognised Baldor.

A woman struggled from the bed holding her torn clothing amidst weeping and shouting desperate agitated words that were unintelligible to the watching men. Her balance awry as if drunk, she stumbled and staggered across the darkened chamber pushing past Baldor into the corridor. Letting out a bone-chilling wail she sank down heavily alongside the dead child. Easing the small form up from the floor, she embraced it tightly whilst weeping and nuzzling the shock of curly, copper-red hair. With the light from the additional torches, Baldor saw her hair was in disarray, her lips burst and bloody and an eye swollen, forcing it closed, the bodice of her dress ripped to the waist. Sickened to the stomach he turned back to the man pointing his blade accusingly.

"You heard my orders did you not?" Not waiting for a response, he struck the now edgy man savagely on the side of the head with the torch. Orange sparks and pieces of smoking wadding showered onto the floor as the man fell like a slaughtered beast. "Take them out! Out I say! They'll hang for this!" He signalled their removal to his men.

Semi-conscious and stammering innocence, the pair were dragged from the room and past the weeping woman. Baldor sheathed his sword and taking her by the arm sought the words that were stuck in his throat.

"I'm sorry lady; sorry for your child … for you … this was not intended."

Lowering the child the woman came to her feet. Though much the same age as he, she stood slightly taller. Her long hair, orange as fox fur, hung straight and loose where it had been torn from the binding atop her head. The skin of her face, neck and shoulders was white as fresh milk, her tear filled eyes cold and chillingly blue as sea ice. Shaking his hand loose her features changed from heartbroken sorrow to scowling, venomous hate as she recognised his helmet and harness.

"You! … You." She said accusingly through bloodied lips, her tone like whispered venom. "I saw you from the walls this morning, you slew my father and now you've murdered his grandchild!" She spat forcefully in Baldor's face then tried to batter him with her fists. "I curse you! Curse you with all the hate I can summon! I curse your living and your breathing! I pray you die choking on your own blood!"

Ignoring the blows falling harmlessly on his helmet and corselet, he just stared as she ranted before his one remaining warrior took both of her arms bundling her roughly back along the corridor. Continuing to curse, she struggled and fought and surprising the warrior with her strength broke loose. Standing in the corridor with the torch light behind her and her finger pointing accusingly, her shadow loomed frighteningly large on the wall as she decried him further.

"I curse your lites and your black heart, I curse your loved ones, and any that will love you. May your woman and daughters die poxed and rotten! Your sons fall dying before your eyes and your seed die as cruelly as you have slain mine!"

The warrior took hold of her again this time with his forearm tight about her throat, still struggling but now firmly held she was dragged away.

"Bastard! … Hades is calling for you! Bas …tard!' She managed before she was out of sight.

****

Baldor didn't sleep at all that night, despite the indulgence of wine, beer and good company of his friends. Wrapped in his blanket, alone in the cold and silent darkness his mind conjured up pictures of dead warriors and slain women and children, his head full of curses and blind hate. All of which he told himself was his own doing, if only he'd not interfered that day at the fishery; surely … surely, he was a curse onto himself. Thus at the first glow of dawn he was quick to rouse his men. Before the morning light came full, the vanguard of heavy Gallic and Spanish infantry were leaving the fortress and marching back towards their winter camp. The Cenomani cavalry mounts went next, having being put to use as additional pack horses they were heavily loaded like the donkeys and ponies. These preceded the long line of carts, wagons and sleds all packed high, laden with goods, treasures and the badly injured. Amidst much screaming and weeping, the prisoners were sorted; the old and infirm separated and turned loose, being seen as a hindrance and thus unnecessary. The young women and children tied together and herded behind the carts and in front of the Spanish Scutarius who brought up the columns rear. Some additional joy came for the raiders as former prisoners of the Cenomani were found and released, many long lost friends and family of the Lingones being discovered. Missing women and children, all thought to be long dead were reunited with kinfolk amidst tears and words of disbelief. Baldor took some comfort from this adding it as further justification for the laying waste of the township.

The raiders burned their dead on a mass pyre. The sight of which Baldor endured until the timber structures collapsed into a pile of reddened embers, only then did he give a final salute and readied to leave. He assigned Tuireann and his men to the destruction of the fortress and as the fire raising started up once more the bodies of the dead Cenomani were collected and hurled into the flames.

With smoke thickening and swirling across the fortress like a descending winter's fog, it stung his eyes and burnt his throat. Watching as it blackened the sky, he contemplated his first victory as a commander. Was it a victory? His men deemed it such for they had secured desperately needed provisions for the army and sweetened it with the chink of gold and bodies of slaves. His Gallic allies in particular rejoicing at the demise of the hated Cenomani. For himself, he judged his quest for vengeance fulfilled with the death of Lugobelinos, retribution for Marko and Tirus and the maltreatment of Armaco. From a military perspective he had attained his objective, even his casualties could be deemed acceptable at a final count of two hundred and thirty three dead and forty wounded. 'Light' he was told, 'considering the taking of a fortress'. He'd justified the faith placed in him by his peers, that thought at least brought him some comfort.

He admitted to himself, albeit a little shamefully, that standing there, amidst the burning ruins, dressed in the full panoply of war, his enemy vanquished and he the toast of his small army that it felt obscenely gratifying, intoxicatingly powerful even. Was this what drove men to command and conquer?

However, when the cloying, sickly sweet stench of burning flesh pervaded the smoke, making him cough and gag he thought of the dead. The innocent, the guilty and of his own men and friends who'd died to make it so. The elation of victory suddenly replaced by a strange heartfelt shame for what he'd done. His conscience once again asking the inevitable questions, 'could he have done better? Could he have saved more?' Was this new reckoning to be added to his growing list of atonement?' Walking past the dangling bodies of the two men he'd ordered hanged for the slaying of the child and the attempted rape of Lugobelinos's daughter, he was perversely relieved no others had been caught. There would have been others guilty of such, of that he had no doubt and which he would have had to hang also, had they been caught. Shaking his head, he wondered at the madness of it all.

He had to walk some distance to catch up with the column, it took time to find the cart, in which Andulas, and Armaco rode. Putting his thoughts and conflicting emotions to one side he bade them a hearty good morning as he walked alongside.

"Have you both breakfasted?"

Andulas nodded whilst beaming a smile and returning the salutations. Armaco just nodded and grumbled about having to survive on porridge thinner than piss. His words even more difficult to understand now that the surgeon had reset his jaw and strapped it closed with bandages. Baldor smiled warmly.

"Complaining already old friend? … Good! That tells me you're recovering."

****

With nothing to fear and secrecy no longer required the heavily encumbered column made an almost leisurely journey northwards back to the winter camp. Having paid respects to their dead and sent them onwards to Elysium the bittersweet taste of victory began to dawn on the men and helped overlay the loss of comrades and their own hurts. Also, with an abundance of good food and drink filling empty bellies and the promise of their share of spoils and slaves to come, the men were altogether in good humour.

With the dry weather holding and the sun bright in the clear spring sky, it made for a pleasant few days with the pace easy on all. Allowing for the more relaxed mood, Baldor still maintained discipline of his column placing scouting parties to the front, sides and rear. The work becoming easier when Andulas's cavalrymen reunited with their mounts and took over the duty, escorting and herding all like sheep dogs. Baldor took time to walk his column, checking his men's condition, the state of the wounded and ensuring his prisoners were fed and not mistreated. He fussed over the care of

Andulas and Armaco, seeing to their comfort and wellbeing when and where he could. He appointed a tire woman giving strict instructions to ensure both men ate well, their wounds were dressed and they continued to rest.

As the column would pass within a day's ride of the Lingone's township he tasked Tuireann and fifty of his men with escorting the liberated prisoners home, along with their allotment of captured Cenomani women folk and children, the warriors to follow onto the winter camp the following day.

Chapter Thirty two

The column was escorted into camp by squadrons of racing Numidian cavalry, the dark riders blowing long, droning notes on hunting horns announcing the approach to all. Men emptied from tents or left their work and midday meal, lining the road to watch and cheer as the snaking column made its way in. There was much to see with carts piled high with foodstuffs and spoils, a lengthy train of heavily laden pack animals and the heads of the dead Cenomani atop spears or hanging by the hair from the horse's harness. Herds of cattle, sheep and goats came next, lowing and bleating in protest as they were goaded along by drover's sticks. Then came the huddled, cowering group of prisoners, the women in especial a source of interest and lustful delight.

Baldor, his officers, Standard-bearer and signaller rode out front in a small group. Despite their dishevelled state, they rode regally up the warrior-lined road towards Hannibal's tent. The cheers, whoops and whistles grew in tempo as more men joined the raucous crowd to see who came to camp. The hullabaloo drawing Hannibal and his staff outside to see what caused the stir. Baldor straightened his back when he saw his General while his heart seemed to swell in his chest. He couldn't keep the smile from his face or the pride from his being as Hannibal raised his hand in greeting coming personally to take his mount's bridle.

"Hail Baldor!" He said reverently, dipping his head and saluting then reaching up to stroke and settle the horse as it whickered and stomped nervously from the excitement of the crowd. "The scouts' didn't exaggerate then; you've brought much booty for I see wealth, a mass of victuals and human goods in your train."

"Fortuna favoured us sir!" Baldor said, returning the salute then dismounting to unfasten a darkly stained wicker basket from his horses harness.

"Sir, Generals, Victumulae and the Cenomani will trouble us no more."

He opened the basket lid and hefted Lugobelinos's head out by the hair. Devoid of blood and fluids, the skin was even paler than before; dried and shrivelled, it pulled tight across the face dragging the lips apart in a grimace showing the rotten teeth. The eyes had opened unnaturally wide leaving the red pupils frozen in an empty, hollow stare, the stench of decay already evident in the warm spring air. The officers still pushed forward to gaze at the monstrous head, offering congratulations to the victor. Mago in particular grasping Baldor's hand hard while slapping his shoulder forcefully in rough affection.

"I'm pleased I didn't kill you lad!" He roared with laughter whilst continuing to pump Baldor's hand. "Well done, well done! That's one bastard less in the world!"

"A great victory Baldor and I see your casualties are light for you've brought many safely home." Hannibal added as he ran his practised eye over the column then back to Baldor.

The mention of casualties sobered Baldor somewhat and he nodded.

"I still lost too many Sir! Including the good Tirus, brave men all." He replied sadly while lowering his head. "Without the bravery of the fallen and these people here." He indicated his officers. "Taking the fortress would have been impossible. I'm deeply indebted to all for their support and courage for I but commanded, they it was who fought and won."

From behind him came a chorus of denial, Andulas spoke above all.

"General! General Sir; I say our commander is too modest; it was he who slew the giant, Lugobelinos in single combat! This feat alone brought about the fall of the fortress."

"Aye! Aye, Baldor! … Baldor!" Chanted aloud from the rest of the group.

Hannibal allowed them their head for a moment while smiling at Baldor's embarrassment then gestured for them to enter the tent.

"Come warriors; tell us of the fall of Victumulae and the slaying of this Titan."

The sun was low and the table cluttered with empty wine jars by the time Baldor finished relaying all the details, both good and bad to Hannibal and his staff. He'd began by individually lauding his officers for their bravery and support, adamant that it was from them that the true victory stemmed. He admitted to his indecisiveness before the gate but before he could take further responsibility, was shouted down, albeit politely by his officers. With the greatest of respect, they said; he was mistaken, yes, much mistaken. Hearing and seeing the loyalty, Hannibal smiled raising his goblet to Baldor who looked embarrassed from the touching devotion. Taking a long drink to hide his discomfort and reddened face, he opted to leave out the altercation with Tuireann. Hannibal in turn acknowledged all for their part, announcing that this sacking of Victumulae had been a separate campaign, a war of its own. Thus, by Carthaginian tradition a bracelet would be awarded to each in recognition of their service. As he closed the bright silver around Baldor's wrist and shook his hand, he added 'Captain' to his thanks.

Then, despite Baldor's pleas for peace, he was coerced by both staff officers and his men to relay details of the fight with Lugobelinos; in the end, it took a polite yet firm order from Hannibal to his new Captain to give account. With the tale finally wrung out amidst many toasts and much praise, Hannibal dismissed them to bathe and refresh, requesting their presence the following noon for the division of the spoils, both material and human. As Baldor rose to leave, Hannibal bade him sit longer while pouring another cup of wine.

"If you'll permit me." He began then laughed softly. "Or rather I've taken the liberty of your permission." He smiled when Baldor looked at him clearly not understanding. "Don't return to your tent tonight for I've had your affects removed and placed elsewhere."

Baldor continued to look confused as Hannibal gestured him to his feet and to bring his cup. Picking up the wine pitcher, he led him outside then a half stade northwards to another tent ushering him inside.

The tent was not unlike Hannibal's only more modest in size. Baldor saw his Carthaginian helmet and armour placed on a stand in the corner with his bag and personal belongings beneath it. Rugs and animal skins covered the floor. His bed had been fetched and his blankets washed and made up ready, cushions replaced the rolled cloak he'd used as a pillow. A small table and chairs stood next to an already glowing brazier. Two young women appeared at the door their chatter and giggles interrupting his bemused study. Hannibal gestured them forward and they struggled into the tent bearing a round wooden tub between them. Setting their heavy load down next to the brazier amidst sighs of relief, they disappeared only to return laden with buckets of steaming water, which they tipped into the tub along with sandalwood oil. Baldor was already muttering stumbling words; Hannibal smiled placing his finger to his lips for silence.

"Yours my friend, with my thanks." He said indicating the tent. "These ladies will bathe you and see to your needs; rest and relax, take your ease and I'll have dinner sent to you." He shushed Baldor again as he saw questions and most likely objections forming on his lips. "All else has been seen to; your men, horses, prisoners and the like. So rest while you can for we've a briefing on the morrow, the day after we break camp then march south." That said he was gone.

Baldor gazed dumbstruck about the tent, his weary head struggling to take in all that was happening. Despite Hannibal's instructions, his mind automatically went to the needs of his men and horses and to seeking out Balaam and the others. He was still contemplating when one of the women tied the canvas door closed while the other approached him, bowing low and announcing in invitingly husky tones and smouldering eyes that his bath was ready. Stupefied, he allowed himself led towards the steaming tub; he was further surprised when both women shrugged out of their dresses leaving themselves naked as new-born babes. Between smiles, giggles and sensual pouts they began unbuckling his armour and weapons before attempting to help him out of his tunic. Surprised and embarrassed, he stammered and stumbled weak words of insistence that he could manage and that they could now leave, he received a smiling but determined argument from the prettier of the two.

"The General ordered, my Lord. All's to be taken care of. He was quite clear."

Too weary to argue against the women's dogged insistence and past caring for his modesty he acquiesced to his stripping. Seeing his body properly for the first time in months he noticed the ravages the campaign and its privations had left upon him. Though his muscles were toned and hard he was thinner and underweight, his skin pale and dry, cracked and flaking in places for the need of moisture and care, his body ingrained with filth for want of a wash. His inner thighs rubbed bare of hair and calloused from constant riding, his feet blackened with dirt and stinking. The women however were efficient and quick and as soon as they had him naked, they helped him into the steaming, aroma sweet, water. He couldn't suppress a contented sigh as he settled into the tub and the heat and water caressed his body, nor did he argue as one of the women soaped a sponge, washing his shoulders, neck and upper back. The other washed his hair massaging his scalp with strong fingers, the first helping by tipping clean hot water over him to rinse it. Allowing him time to relax and enjoy the water one sorted his armour and weapons from his dirty clothes, while the second produced an armful of new clothing for him. Seeing he was drifting to sleep, they raised him to his feet washing his chest, back, midriff, and buttocks and to his embarrassment his genitals. Here, eager hands replaced sponges, exchanging efficiency for sensuality as they gently cleaned him. Despite the betrayal by his maleness to their gentle and lusty ministrations, he managed somewhat unsteadily to take over the work himself while declining further offers of promised pleasure. With both looking somewhat downcast and asking anxious questions as to whether they displeased him, he felt obliged to assure them that despite their comeliness and beauty, he was weary … yes tired from battle, weary and hungry. With the women eyeing his still thickening manhood they looked doubtful as to his excuses, all the more so when he asked that they put on their dresses again. The elder of the two asked, albeit delicately, if he would rather a young boy was fetched for him, his sudden dark scowl and snarling decline finally silencing her. Resigned to his objections and it would seem orders, they eased him down in the water once more and lifting his legs began to wash and scrub his feet, efficiency once more to the fore. Reaching for the warming towels, they raised him from the water wrapping his waist then settled him in a seat. The two-pronged attack continued with one drying his hair and the other using a lice comb to tease out his chest and body hair to remove any which may have survived the bath. The treatment continued with a shave followed by nail clipping and a massage with warmed oil that left him dozing off. He was shaken gently awake as a tray of food was placed on the table next to him, the women then bowed and left. The aroma of the hot meat and bread set his mouth watering and his belly growling in anticipation but despite his body's needs, he managed only a few mouthfuls and another cup of wine before abandoning the effort and collapsing onto the bed sound asleep.

****

The news at the council of war the following morning astounded Baldor. During the short time, he'd been away reducing Victumulae; the Romans had completed their Consular elections and raised another four legions replacing those lost at the Trebbia. Now, with the approaching campaigning season they were once again preparing for war. Neither of the previous Consuls had been re-elected, Longus was in relative disgrace after the truth emerged of his failings at the Trebbia. Publius Scipio however, much to Hannibal's discomfort, had been dispatched to Spain to join his brother Gnaeus and the Legions there. The brothers were the most able of Rome's Generals he said and together required especial watching. Hasdrubal, the youngest cub of the Barca brood, who commanded the Carthaginian forces in Spain, was already finding Gnaeus a resourceful and worthy adversary. No doubt, things would only become more difficult with the second Scipio joining him.

With the first signs of spring the new Consuls elect had been despatched northwards, along with the newly raised Legions to block any Carthaginian advance towards Rome. Consul, Gnaeus Servilius Geminus was marching to the city of Ariminum on the east coast protecting the route along the Via Flaminia and southwards to the Umbrian plain. Consul Gaius Flaminius and his Legions held the city of Arretium protecting the western coast, the Via Aurelia and the Etruria plains leading south to Rome. With the Apennine mountains rising in the centre of the country as a natural barrier, it appeared to all that victorious or not, the Carthaginians were securely contained in the north unless they could force a passage past one of the

Consuls. Having explained all and demonstrated on the map, Hannibal offered his plan to his commanders for their thoughts.

"Gentlemen, in hindsight we should have been up and away from these plains of Po long since and onto the Umbrian or Etruria plains along with this first breath of spring. However, rightly or wrongly I opted to tarry here to rest and recuperate the men." The officers about the table nodded sagely, muttering agreement. "The Romans have recovered and reacted quicker than I expected, further to that I hadn't bargained on them splitting their forces. I thought after the Trebbia they'd become cautious and come at us as one. But it matters not, you divide you forces at your risk and I think in this case at their peril." He shrugged and chuckled at the irony for he'd done exactly that on more than one occasion. "Here's my thoughts." He said becoming serious again. "We'll avoid battle with them until on ground of our choosing."

"We still have Placentia and Cremona to consider or deal with sir, you know it'll be dangerous to leave them secure in our rear?" Gisgo grumbled.

"True my friend, but we've no siege train with which to winkle them out, nor can we afford time to starve them into surrender so we'll draw them out. Once we destroy these Romans field armies, their cities become isolated allowing us to pluck them like choice fruit and without having to watch our backs. Therefore, when we reach the plains we'll trail our cloak, so to speak. We'll invite attack by burning and destroying everything in our path and driving the country folk out else killing them if they won't go. We'll turn these central plains into a desert! I venture nothing will force the proud Roman's out from behind their walls to harry our tail quicker than burning their villages, fields and crops, for they're all farmers at heart!"

There was some laughter around the table and excitement at the mention of burning and looting then hesitation as they saw Hannibal gesturing for quiet so to unfold more of the plan.

"So, east or west then brother, which is it to be?" Mago asked, as ever cutting to the chase.

"Neither!" The men looked on, all puzzled. "Neither, we're going directly south, through the Apennines."

There was a moment's taut silence as men looked wide eyed at their General then one another. This highly charged, stretched moment followed quickly by noisy denials and ready arguments against. As usual, Mago was the loudest.

"Baal save and protect us brother, you cannot be serious! More damned mountains?"

"I am serious, General Mago." The formal naming letting all know that the matter was already decided and any objections, though they may be raised would be discounted through sound planning and reason.

"Spring's here, the weather kinder and the snows melting, a safe passage achievable. These Apennine passes compare favourably to the Alps being neither as high nor as difficult to access." Hannibal injected enthusiasm and excitement into his words helping make the venture sound all the more plausible. "The Romans are sure that we've no choice but to venture east or west for they know we don't have the numbers to risk splitting our forces but they don't expect us to come directly south. They could hope, perhaps even pray that we lay siege to Ariminum or Arretium thus allowing their other army to come up behind, trapping us between them and their city walls then beat us like a hammer on an anvil. Methinks however, they know we're not that stupid and will most likely march past their cities, which still allows them chance to sally out and pin us against the mountains where we've little room for manoeuvre."

"Why would they leave their fortifications at all sir?" Maharabal asked. "They could shut themselves up almost indefinitely and refuse to fight, just leaving us out here. Yes, we can loot and burn but then what? Without battles to fight, it becomes stalemate. Our allies would eventually drift away to their homes; not so much these early months but you know what boredom does to soldiers."

"True, General! However, remember these Romans are a field army by nature. Fighting from behind walls doesn't suit their notions of war nor does it allow them to bring their heavy infantry might to bear. I wager their Latin pride, arrogance and imagined superiority over us will ensure they fight us in the open and in the traditional, dare I say unimaginative, Roman way."

"I agree with your thoughts sir, but what if when we emerge in their centre they attack us from east and west together, a pincer movement no less!" Maharabal asked.

"A good question General; and if it was role reversal I'd do exactly that. I am gambling on us being through the mountains and onto the plain before they even know we're there. I'll also gamble that Flaminius won't wait for Geminus to help box us in and you all know I only gamble when I know I can win!" He grinned broadly while his officers laughed. "From what I hear we've another Sempronius in this Gaius Flaminius, with the same inflated ego and over confidence and worst of all I think; a disrespect of his Gods." He glanced briefly at Baldor. "He's already out of favour with the Senate and his men for not observing the correct rituals before marching; I say that bodes ill for him! So all things considered, I say we do exactly what they don't expect and cross the mountains onto the plain. Then we burn, destroy and lay waste, inviting them to come and catch us, either one army at a time or both together, it matters not."

"One at a time would be better odds, for with these new Legions they'll outnumber us no doubt?" Gisgo grumbled into his wine cup.

Hannibal shrugged then smiled. "With you good Gisgo, and all here at my back and on ground of our choosing their numbers matter not, for I tell you the outcome will be the same; Roman defeat!"

Aye's, cheers and banging wine cups announced agreement.

It was late afternoon before Baldor returned to his tent, having gone straight from the council to seeking out Balaam and the others. However, the visit to his former tent found all but Armaco out on patrol and most likely he thought, not expected back before dark. Armaco lay cocooned in blankets like a caterpillar chrysalis, sound asleep, his dressings changed, hair cropped in his old style, his face washed with a new eye patch completing the look. Though he appeared cared for and cleaner, the bruising on his face had coloured to shades of a storm-racked sky with the swelling of his jaw still evident. As Baldor stepped closer, a young serving woman appeared with an armful of wood for the small brazier burning near his bed. Startled by his presence but recovering quickly she berated him angrily in sharp, coarse whispers for his intrusion. Baldor didn't understand all her words but took the meaning. Satisfied that the injured warrior remained undisturbed she put the wood carefully on the fire while scowling at the intruder. With her finger on her lips, she ushered him unceremoniously out of the tent like a hen chasing a threat to her chick. Put out at his treatment but complying with her instructions he stepped outside then turned to question her.

"How is he?" He indicated back to the tent. "And who're you?" His tone sharp and his manner abrupt.

Realising he was no threat to her charge and that he appeared to genuinely care for the injured warrior she moderated her tone.

"He's recovering and eating well sir, considering his injuries. Though he needs to rest, undisturbed!" She emphasised the last word.

"What of his legs?"

Her face fell to sadness. "The surgeon says he'll never walk properly again sir, the damage done was deliberate and precise to make it so."

Baldor nodded bitterly, his thoughts confirmed. "His face then? His jaw?"

"His jaw's mending though he won't be able to eat solids for some time yet, the swelling will be gone in a few days."

Baldor nodded. "And you are?"

"Breda." Seeing her name meant nothing to him, she continued. "The Captain paid me to see to Ar …ma, Armco."

"Ar … ma ... co!" He corrected sharply. "Armaco!"

"Armaco." She repeated mastering the name. "I'm to feed him, bathe him and sit with him till the Captain and his men return from patrol."

Accepting her explanation, he nodded. "Very well then Breda, when he wakes tell him Baldor called. His friend, Baldor! Do you have it?"

"Yes sir." This time she bowed her head.

Returning to his tent, he settled himself in a chair thinking to enjoy the peace and some time alone. However, still trying to come to terms with his further elevated status and his change of fortune his mind refused to relax. Frustrated at not finding Balaam and the others and deeply concerned for Armaco despite the care he was receiving, he poured a drink. The cup was no longer his simple horn beaker but a chased silver goblet set with tiny garnets, no doubt the former property of the Cenomani or some wealthy Roman. The wine was the colour of ripe plums, potent and heady though he quaffed it readily, pouring another which he forced himself to sip. Thinking of the two women, he argued with himself whether or not he should have bedded them, was that need adding to his irritation? How long was it now since he'd lain with a woman? Remembering all too clearly that Aiticia was the last woman he'd enjoyed, his embarrassment surfaced at what he construed an insult to her memory and he calmed his frustration. Pulling the cameo from his shirt, he kissed it then gazed at it thumbing it lovingly. With the wine settling his mind and relaxing his body, he sighed, stretching his legs resting them on the table for comfort. Before the wine was finished, he felt his eyelids growing heavy and he drifted off to sleep. He came to with a start as the crumpling noise of the canvas door lifting woke him, jumping clumsily to his feet his wine spilled onto the floor as Hannibal stepped into the tent. Outside he saw the daylight was fading into blue shadows of twilight and realised he'd slept most of the afternoon and early evening.

"Hail Captain."

"Hail … hail General." He said straightening his back and coming to attention.

Hannibal motioned him to relax. "I didn't see you for the distribution of the spoils?"

"Err, no sir, no. I have all that I need and more. You've been most kind."

"Hah, you're too modest Baldor! It's no more than you deserve for you've done the army a great service by sacking this Victumulae. Most importantly though, you boosted the men's morale and filled their bellies as well as their purses. So once again I've taken liberties on your behalf." He smiled widely, dropping a bladder sized, leather drawstring bag onto the table. "Gold coin for your purse, also …"

Baldor began his objections but was waved down by Hannibal, who was looking back out of the door and beckoning, while continuing his conversation. "Also, someone to keep house, as well as warm your bed."

He stepped back as a tall, shapely redheaded woman was pushed stumbling through the door. A smaller, middle-aged, portly woman, wielding a stout stick and holding a leather leash fastened to the metal collar about the redhead's neck, followed her.

"I'll let you choose which you bed?" He said roaring with laughter.

Baldor paled as he recognised Lugobelinos's daughter.

"Sir … sir, your pardon, but do you know who this is?" His tone anxious, incredulous.

"Lugobelinos's daughter I believe, Baldor? Though somewhat chastened and tamed from when you saw her last methinks, thanks to Sulis here."

The older woman smiled and hefted her stick.

"The ladies …" He laughed softly. "The ladies I left you with last night said you were too weary to enjoy them? So perhaps she'll make amends?" He pointed to the redhead.

Baldor ignored the joke regarding the two whores. "General, I … I slew her father but a few days since and she knows it, I …"

"You slew the old dog, so enjoy his whelp!" Hannibal answered matter of factly. "Or 'hell cat!' … Yes, I think that's the term Sulis used? Though my Gallic's not good, perhaps 'bitch' is the better term for her?" He nodded towards the redhead. "She's proved a handful."

Seeing Baldor perplexed and somewhat embarrassed he continued.

"She's yours Baldor; bed her or whip her if she displeases you. Better still, save your strength and have Sulis whip her, else sell her or strangle her if you so choose." He shrugged casually. "She's yours by right of conquest, do what you will, the spoils of war Baldor, the spoils of war!" He repeated to Baldor's now shaking head.

"Baal almighty sir! Baldor exclaimed somewhat louder and sterner than he intended. "I don't need a woman and certainly not this one. She … she's a problem I can do without."

"You forget yourself Baldor! And to whom you speak!" Hannibal snapped as his face clouded and temper took hold. "A gift normally renders gratitude not curses! Give her to your men then! Do what you will it matters not to me! I but looked to your needs and comfort was all."

Scowling, Hannibal turned and strode to the door. "I bid you goodnight!"

Baldor was left with the two women and a rising temper, though it was aimed at himself for his rudeness and lack of manners. Gods above! Would he never learn to guard his tongue? Pouring a drink, he gulped it down; fortified from the intake he poured another and downed it as he studied the women. The elder was black haired, big breasted and strong looking with a broad face that showed wear lines of her advancing years but with sharp, cat like eyes that hinted at a stern, cruel nature. What she lacked in height she made up for in width, a true matron figure, she smiled weakly at him.

"Do you wish her stripped, beaten and sent to your bed sir?" She asked nervously while nodding towards the redhead, her anxious tone at odds with her persona.

"No damn you, I do not! Get her away from me, you get away …
leave me be!"

"But sir … sir, we're part of your household, your servant and
slave to do your bidding!" She implored. "The General commanded
so."

"Baal's breath!" He smashed the cup to the floor in temper.

The elder woman flinched while the redhead stood motionless her
head down, resigned it seemed to her fate.

"Sir, we're here to take care of you and your needs, the tent, your
meals, your affects, your, your male needs." She entreated, nodding
again towards the redhead.

Baldor gripped the table edge tightly with both hands, leaning
heavily as he calmed himself. His breathing gradually slowed and his
temper eased as he gathered his wits and rationale returned. Cursing
beneath his breath at his behaviour he silently promised to apologise
to Hannibal at the first opportunity then took stock of the situation.

"Very well then, you!" He pointed to the elder. "You are?"

"Sulis, sir."

"See to my dinner Sulis, then and fetch me some more wine."

He strode across to the dirty armour and harness that was still on
the floor from the previous night, picking it up he threw it at the
redhead's feet.

"Clean it!" He snapped while fishing in his belongings for a block
of leather soap, cloths and oil throwing them on top of the armour.
When the redhead didn't move, Sulis slapped her viciously across the
shoulders with the stick, the force pitching her forward onto the
floor. Baldor caught the stick as she raised it for another blow.

"That's enough!" He barked.

"It's alright sir, the stick won't tear her flesh and spoil your
pleasure, its broad made see, to give chastisement without damage."
Sulis pulled the redhead's dress off her shoulders to show redness but
no broken skin.

"That's enough." He repeated quietly. "If she'll do as she's bidden
that's enough. Now, her name?"

"Lasairiona, sir. Lasairiona of the Cenomani, the Chiefs …"

"I know where she's from, I asked only her name." His sharp
words cut Sulis short. He turned to the redhead. "Lasairiona, I'll tell
you this but once, do as you're bidden!" He lifted the armour with his

foot. "Clean it and clean it well, else I'll let Sulis and her stick loose on you."

Lasairiona gathered the armour, soap and oil, settling herself cross-legged on the floor she began her work. Sulis tugged the leash, forcing her to move towards the main tent pole where she tied it securely, Baldor made no objection.

With his dinner brought, he settled to eat but as palatable as the food was he took little enjoyment from the repast, his mind and nerves strangely on edge. Lasairiona worked quietly but diligently on the armour and Sulis settled herself next to the oil lamps with needle, thread, and some of his freshly laundered clothes, carefully mending.

Having wolfed the last of his food and wiped up the juice with bread, he swilled it down with copious amounts of wine. Despite his best endeavours, he seemed incapable of getting drunk, looking from woman to woman, shaking his head in consternation.

"Sulis!"

The woman looked up dutifully.

"Yes sir?"

"When did you last eat? Both of you?"

"At breakfast, sir."

"Go! Fetch food for you both, if this is to be a household then it'll be run like my old one."

Sulis looked at him not understanding.

"When I eat we all eat, for I have to fight and you've to work, now go! See to it."

The older woman bowed and scurried away, keen to be about her task and no doubt hungry.

Baldor lounged back in his chair while draining his cup, the wine it seemed finally calming and relaxing him, he noticed Lasairiona had not stopped work nor looked up during the exchange. Resting his chin on his hand, he cast his eyes over the woman who sat so quiet, meekly doing as she was bidden. It was hard to comprehend that a few days ago she had been so vigorous, angry and full of hate.

He remembered then, being very young and sitting much as he was now but watching a leopard lounging in its cage. As with this woman the hunters had fought hard to capture it, now it lay quiet and seemingly subdued, accepting its fate. Mesmerised by its lithe physique, colouring and feline beauty he'd sat for a long time admiring until an old hunter came alongside him, the man saying much that he'd been thinking; such a beautiful animal, so formidable, so fierce, yet now so placid and tame seeming. The hunter smiled, motioning him to watch as he slowly pushed a stick into the cage toward the leopard. It cast a lethargic eye at the stick before sighing, flicking its ears, seeming to settle further as if disregarding the intrusion. However, when the stick probed just too close the beast exploded into action. Ripping, tearing and savaging the stick, claws and teeth slashing and biting, shredding it to ruin. As the hunter pulled it away, the leopard carried the fight up to the cage bars, the leg, paw and claws coming through the bars seeking to rend anything in reach.

Baldor had jumped back in alarm as the hunter laughed and gave up the stick.

"A lesson for you lad." He'd said. "A leopard never changes its spots! Vicious bastards, vicious! Purring and eating out of your hand one day, take it off the next. Leopards and women lad, no difference, mind it!"

With this in mind, he considered the woman before him; she was beautiful, her hair thick, lustrous and layered to her shoulders and coloured vixen orange. Her skin, though strangely pale, was unblemished by disease, seeming flawless and marble smooth over high cheekbones and sharp but shapely nose. He couldn't see her eyes or lips but noted a narrow but shapely chin and elegant neck. Her shoulders were broad but not unfeminine, her breasts full and swaying gently as she worked soap into the leather. Her waist narrow, her belly flat and her legs long in both thigh and calf, ending in surprisingly small feet for one so tall.

Nodding appreciatively of her beauty while sighing as if faced with a troublesome dilemma, his wine soaked mind spoke his thoughts aloud.

"What am I going to do with you? … What in Hade's name am I going to do with you?"

Historical Note

The battle at the river Trebbia in December 218 BC was the first tactical and set piece battle fought by Hannibal and his allies in Italy against the Romans. It was fought at the time of the midwinter solstice and during atrocious weather conditions as described in the book.

Having successfully exploited the intemperate character of Consul Tiberius Sempronius Longus, Hannibal lured the Roman Legions into battle to suit his time and onto ground of his choosing. With his men already breakfasted and prepared for battle and his ambush carefully laid, the odds for victory were again stacked in his favour. The battle however still held a risk in that the outnumbered Carthaginians were required to hold their center against the heavily armed Legionnaires, while the Numidian and Carthaginian horse brigades stripped the Roman flanks of their cavalry and until Mago's ambush force arrived to attack their rear.

Despite their catastrophic defeat, the Romans deserve credit for their endurance, bravery and tenacity. Having being surprised and attacked in their camp at dawn they force-marched to the river without breakfast and forded the rain swollen, icy Trebbia. Emerging onto the plain, they committed to battle without pause and attacked at double step, possibly believing in their own supremacy or driven on by a commander who held no doubt of it.

The Cenomani Gauls fought as Roman allies but were also driven from the field along with the retreating Roman cavalry, who fled leaving their infantry unprotected and to their fate. The casualties suffered by the Romans were as high as described in this book but would have been much worse had the deteriorating winter weather not prevented the Carthaginians from completing the rout, by contrast the Carthaginian casualties were inversely light. Hannibal did however lose all of his war elephants except one, some to their battle injuries but most to malnutrition and the harsh northern winter.

Publius Scipio was left in camp, taking no part in the battle and later made his way to Placentia where he and the survivors from the battle regrouped. The towns of Placentia and Cremona were additionally fortified and remained as bastions against the Carthaginians who had no siege train with which to take them by storm.

The Consuls then returned to Rome to explain the armies defeat to the Senate and to take part in the Consular elections and at which neither were re-elected. Tiberius Sempronius Longus was deemed culpable for the defeat at the Trebbia and never held a significant public position again. Publius Scipio was exonerated and dispatched to Spain to help prosecute the war there alongside his brother Gnaeus. Meanwhile Rome quickly raised and trained another four Legions ready for the coming campaign season.

Cornelius Scipio fought at the Trebbia and is said to have attained the rank of Junior Tribune around this time. (I have chosen to raise him through the ranks much slower) The hard learned lessons of a weak Roman cavalry arm at the Ticinus and the benefits of sound preparation, chosen ground and ambush as at the Trebbia, accruing him first-hand knowledge of Hannibal's strengths and tactics. Also, watching and suffering from an over confident commander no doubt teaching him 'how not' to go to war against the Carthaginian! These lessons to be salted away and used when he himself stepped up to Generalship in 211 BC.

It is known that he was betrothed to Aemilia Paulla at this time and perhaps the society wedding saw him remaining in Rome in the short term.

Hannibal now had a second but this time substantial victory to his credit and he and his allies could roam at will in northern Italy (Cisalpine Gaul). It is said that he wished to push on immediately for the south and press his current victory to further advantage but the worsening weather and poor condition of his army forced him to remain in camp on the plains until the spring.

The Carthaginians thus wintered at a camp on the plains of Po or in the Padus valley but laid plans to march south to central Italy and Rome via the Apennines with the coming spring. They did however attack and destroy the township of Victumulae and slaughtered the inhabitants as an example to other tribes not to resist or ally themselves with Rome. It is recorded that it yielded up booty and a large supply of victuals, a huge boost to the Carthaginians and their allies. Victumulae is described as a Gallic settlement but whether or not it was the home of the Cenomani tribe is not clear.

In the coming summer of 217 BC, Hannibal would continue his success with the massacre of the Consular army of Gaius Flaminius at Lake Trasimene.

Thus, Baldor and his comrades must take up their weapons and march again while Cornelius continues to suffer more Consular ineptitude.

Printed in Great Britain
by Amazon